About the author

Secrets, Lies and Butterflies is Susi Osborne's third novel, following *The Ripples of Life* (2008) and *Grace and Disgrace* (2010). The books form a trilogy, although each book can be enjoyed individually. Susi admits that being published has been life-changing, bringing her a busy schedule of book signings and personal appearances and leading to her organising the first Northwich LitFest, which is now set to become an annual event. For updated information about Susi and her books, follow her on facebook: Susi Osborne – Author Page, or Twitter: @susiosborne.

By the same author

The Ripples of Life (Book Guild, 2008)

Grace and Disgrace (Book Guild, 2010)

SECRETS, LIES AND BUTTERFLIES

Susi Osborne

Book Guild Publishing
Sussex, England

First published in Great Britain in 2013 by
The Book Guild Ltd
Pavilion View
19 New Road
Brighton, BN1 1UF

Typesetting in Baskerville by
Norman Tilley Graphics Ltd, Northampton

Printed in Great Britain by
CPI Group (UK) Ltd, Croydon, CR0 4YY

A catalogue record for this book is available from
The British Library

ISBN 978 1 84624 891 7

Dedication

At the heart of *Secrets, Lies and Butterflies* lies frendship, so how could I not dedicate this book to my very best friend – artist, Diana Bernice Tackley? She's inspired, advised, dragged me from moments of despair, listened to my rants, and cheered me on at all times … in fact I'm amazed she's still my friend, now I stop to think about it! I jest (mostly); we are like a mutual support team, encouraging each other to go from strength to strength through laughter (a lot of this) and tears … had we met in our teenage years we could have been on top of the world by now!

Thanks to:

Robert, Nik, Sophie and Naomi – my family, my life. Our house is sometimes referred to (affectionately I hope!) as the madhouse. This explains a lot.

Will, John and Rob – my pink-tinted posse with whom life is never dull.

John Tackley – a truly amazing gentleman of the finest degree, and one whose praises I cannot sing highly enough (and actually maybe I shouldn't, for he is not totally enamoured with my singing!).

Laura – for her guidance and friendship ... and her multitudinous snippets of invaluable advice during the past however many years.

All of my wonderfully supportive friends – you know who you are, hugs all round!

Damian Barr – for being the hugely inspirational man that he is. In fact I was so inspired that I named a character in *Secrets, Lies and Butterflies* after one of his chickens – Gertie lives on!

Everyone at Book Guild – for publishing my three novels, obviously ... but also for being so friendly, approachable, and just lovely to work with. Carol Biss especially – thank you.

All the lovely people – who have read my books, given me such fantastic feedback ... and clamoured for more!

1

So could you? Could you ever trust your husband and your best friend again when they'd slept together behind your back? Would you rush to the aid of that so called best friend when you heard that something really bad had happened to her? And would you – could you – ever face your husband again, knowing what he'd done? But knowing also, despite everything, despite absolutely everything, that the very thought of him made your insides squish to a pulp.

'Mummy?'

Kate shuffled in her seat and brought herself back to the here and now.

'Sorry, Jess, what did you say?'

Two big blue eyes stared up at her, so like Tom's it almost took her breath away.

'Are we nearly there yet?'

'We won't be very much longer now.'

The sound and movement of the train made it hard for Kate to keep her own eyes open. She hadn't been able to sleep properly for what seemed like forever, the stress of all that had happened over the past couple of years preying permanently on her mind. The warmth and the rocking motion soothed her as Tom tip-toed back temptingly through the dark tunnels of her soul, the longing for him returning surreptitiously, the dream of him next to her once more.

A small hand shook her own.

'Mummy! Wake up!'

Startled back to reality, Kate gave a rapid intake of breath. 'Sorry, darling, I wasn't really asleep, just daydreaming,' she said, stretching and yawning reassurance to this amazing little daughter of hers.

'But you were snoring,' accused Jessica, a smile on her face.

'Hey cheeky!' said Kate, grinning as she tweaked Jess's nose. 'Okay, I might have fallen asleep for a minute or two but I promise I'll stay awake now.'

Kate settled back in her seat, staring out of the window, every passing scene reminding her that she was being transported closer and closer to Tom, closer to the world that had once been hers.

'I wish we were going to stay with Daddy.' The words came from Jessica's mouth but they echoed Kate's sentiment exactly.

'Me t… Um, you know we can't stay there Jess, Daddy and I don't live together any more.' Saying those words out loud still hurt even after more than a year of being apart. 'You'll see Daddy the day after tomorrow, you're going to spend the day with him while I go and visit Auntie Chloe.'

How had she got herself into this? How would she feel coming face to face with Chloe again? Why couldn't she just have said 'no?' Because underneath it all despite what her head told her, her heart pitter-pattered with a nervous excitement at the thought that maybe, just maybe …

Was it really only a year ago that this nightmare had come to her notice? She'd gone over it all a million times in her head, looking for clues, signs she must have missed. Because really, it had started well before then. It had started with the tragic death of Jake, Kate and Tom's baby son, when Kate had been inconsolable and had gone away to Cornwall to spend some time with her parents. But why hadn't she realised that Tom would need consoling too? What had she been thinking, throwing them together like that? Inviting Chloe to move in and help Tom with Jessica while she was away. Help Tom full stop, more like. How naïve had she been? Almost like giving them carte blanche. Carry on. Fait accompli. What did she expect?

But everything had seemed normal when she'd got back. The fact that Chloe announced her pregnancy shortly afterwards, despite being in the midst of an exceedingly non-amicable split with her excessively aggressive husband, John, amazingly didn't raise a row of question marks with Kate.

Well, maybe one, or maybe half an eyebrow. Chloe's daughter, Olivia, had been somewhat more suspicious and prompted the one question mark. But Kate had soon dismissed the idea. Tom cheat on her? Never. Never say never.

Chloe had been adamant that John was the father of her baby – who else? Who else indeed. She must have been squirming inside with guilt, as well as with baby movements, and must have heaved a sigh of relief when the baby, J-J, made his entrance to the world sporting a shock of red hair to match that of his siblings and of John, his paternity no longer in question.

Kate had never really doubted it in the first place. Why should she? Tom loved her – he did! Okay, so she was naïve.

'So why can't we stay at Auntie Chloe's?'

'What?' Kate had almost forgotten where she was.

'If we can't stay with Daddy, why can't we stay with Auntie Chloe?'

'Because we can't, that's why not,' snapped Kate, uncharacteristically.

Jessica's eyes rounded and welled as she turned to look up at her, face pale and strained. She'd gone through a lot of changes herself for one so young and Kate sometimes forgot that.

'Sorry, darling, Mummy didn't mean to sound cross, I'm just a bit tired, that's all. We can't stay at Auntie Chloe's because she's having a bad time at the moment and is feeling sad.'

'But we could cheer her up, I make her laugh, she said so.'

A little stab of something resembling jealousy pricked at Kate. Possessiveness of her child, understandably. Chloe had had her husband, no way would she get the daughter too.

'Even so, Jess, we can't stay there and that's that. Anyway, I thought you were looking forward to meeting Auntie Grace and having Izzy to play with.'

'She's not my real auntie though, is she?'

'Neither is Auntie Chloe, they're both just good friends of mine.' Or were, in the case of Chloe.

'Tell me about Auntie Grace again.'

'I think you'll really like her, Jessica, she's kind and smiley – just like a mummy should be.'

'What about Izzy?'

'I've never met Izzy. All I know is that she's four years old – a bit younger than you. I would imagine she'll be quite a sweet little thing who'll want to copy everything you do and follow you around all the time.'

Kate smiled to herself as she thought of her friendship with Grace. Despite not having known each other for all that long, the two of them had become very close. They had originally met in London when Grace had been visiting her sister, and had hit it off straight away, almost as though they'd known each other all of their lives. Because of the miles between them and their other commitments, it had been difficult to meet up often, but they were regularly in contact and had been a constant source of support to each other through the good times and the bad since they'd met.

Kate lived in St Ives in Cornwall with Jessica now, but it had been an amazing coincidence to discover that Grace lived in Cheshire, only about fifteen miles away from Tom –

from where she used to live herself. It had seemed the obvious thing to do when the phone call came from Chloe, that she should ask Grace if she could come and stay for a while. And Grace had seemed pleased, she'd had problems of her own and said she would appreciate some company.

As the train pulled into the platform at Crewe, Kate struggled with their luggage, Jessica clinging on to her like some kind of clip-on doll. For such a beautiful, angelic and intelligent child, she was certainly lacking in the confidence department. Kate put it down to the fact that she was an only child and she felt an interminable sense of guilt about this, even though it was totally unfounded.

'Let go of me, Jess, or I can't get out of the door.'

'But Mummy …'

'I'm not going to leave you behind.'

Kate's eyes scanned the platform but to no avail. Grace had said they'd be here to meet them, proud that she'd passed her driving test only relatively recently. Kate hoped they were okay.

'They're not here,' said Jessica, stating the obvious, as other passengers from their train went on their way, leaving them alone, abandoned.

They sat on a nearby seat, their suitcases next to them, and waited. This was odd. Kate tried ringing Grace's mobile. No reply.

'I'm scared.' Jessica's confidence, already at nought, was sliding down the minus scale.

'Don't be silly, they've probably just been delayed somewhere.'

Delayed was right. Grace sighed with frustration outside a closed cubicle door in the ladies' toilet block.

'Izzy, could you please hurry up.'

'But I'm doing a poo.'

'I know you are, but could you hurry?'

'I am.'

'Let me in. I told you not to lock the door.'

'You lock the door.'

'That's different. Let me in.'

'Can't.'

'Why not?'

''Cos I'm doing a poo.'

Ogghh! Grace was the most patient of people but some-times...

Finally, finally, finally – the sound of a sliding bolt: clunk!

'At last!' said Grace, going in to flush the toilet, Izzy heading towards the sinks.

'Where are you going now?'

'To wash my hands.' Izzy was not one to be rushed.

'Well, quickly! Leave that now, let's just go. They'll think we've got lost,' said Grace, dragging a reluctant and obstinately rooted child towards the exit.

'But you always say ... Ow!'

Grace transposed a smile upon her frustrated countenance. It wasn't difficult. She was overjoyed to see Kate and as she came into her line of vision, the two of them rushed excitedly towards each other, arms outstretched, leaving their daughters standing by somewhat shyly, eyeing each other up and down. Not known for interminable patience, and becoming somewhat bored by the incessant chatter of huggy mothers, to say nothing of not liking to be ignored, Izzy made the first move.

'Hello, I'm Izzy,' she said beamingly, and as if butter-wouldn't-melt.

'Hello.'

'What's your name?' She already knew, obviously, but thought she should ask – it could have been anybody.

'Jessica.'

'What?'

'Jessica.'

'You've got a very little voice,' said Izzy, whose direct stare caused Jessica to blush to the very roots of her curly blonde hair.

'Oh good, I see you two have already met,' said Kate, turning at a sudden sense of her daughter's discomfort. 'Hello, you must be Izzy.'

'Sometimes people call me poppet,' said Izzy.

'Oh, would you like me to call you poppet then?'

'No,' said Izzy, decisively.

Kate looked somewhat bemused at this unexpectedly feisty little character and smiled at her warmly. 'It's very nice to meet you Izzy. Jessica has been looking forward to it, haven't you, Jess?'

Jessica's hand slid into Kate's in response. Her mummy had said Izzy would probably be a sweet little thing who would want to copy what she did and follow her around all the time. Didn't seem like that to her.

'Hello, Jessica,' said Grace, 'What beautiful blonde hair you've got and those gorgeous big blue eyes.'

'Everybody says I've got eyes like my daddy's.' Quite a sizeable introductory speech from Jessica, confidence growing at the mention of her father.

'Where is your daddy?' asked Izzy, a picture of wide-eyed innocence.

'He's … he's …'

'… at his house,' said Kate, coming to the rescue. 'Jessica's going to see him the day after tomorrow – aren't you, darling?'

'Doesn't he live with you?' asked Izzy, not one to be fobbed off lightly.

'Izzy,' scolded Grace, 'don't ask so many questions.'

'My daddy lives at our house,' said Izzy, quite smugly. 'His name is Charlie.'

7

'Anyway,' said Grace, taking control of the situation and attempting to silence her daughter, who always seemed to have an overly large mouth for one so small, 'let's go to the car. You must be tired after your journey.'

It didn't take them long to get back to Grace's house. Charlie came out to greet them as the car pulled into the drive, an ecstatic and affectionate Alfie, the dog, bouncing excitedly at his side.

'Daddy!' shouted Izzy, loud enough for the whole world to hear.

'Hey up, poppet,' he said, swinging her up into his arms as she ran towards him.

'This is Jessica, my new friend,' said Izzy, proudly.

'Hello Jessica,' said Charlie, to the angelic looking child who seemed to be attached to her mother with Superglue. 'And I take it this is your mum, Kate. Pleased to meet you both. Here, let me give you a hand with your luggage,' he said, putting Izzy back down so he could carry their suit-cases. 'Get down, Alfie.'

But, amazingly enough for one so timid, Jessica seemed to have made a friend of Alfie already. She giggled as he lavished her with licks, even though they were somewhat dribbly. 'Think he's giving me a wash,' she laughed. Alfie's tongue seemed to have prompted her to find her own.

'Come and meet my Gran,' said Izzy, taking her by the hand.

'Have you got a Gran? I've got one too.'

'Bet she's not like mine,' said Izzy, as the two of them disappeared into the house together, their four-legged friend waggling along behind them.

'Phew,' said Kate, heaving a sigh of relief, 'thank good-ness for that, I thought the cat had got her tongue. She can be really shy sometimes.'

'Well at least the dog found it for her again! Don't worry, I have the opposite problem with Izzy. I don't know which is worse. Come on in anyway, welcome to the madhouse!'

The aforementioned Gran was sitting expectantly at the kitchen table. Oops, Grace had inadvertently forgotten to explain about Gran – in any depth anyway.

'Oh, Mother. I thought you'd be in your room.'

'Now why would you think that?'

'Because, erm …'

'Because that's where you like me to be, isn't it? A poor defenceless old lady like me and you have me locked away in my room – out of sight, out of mind. You'll be old your-self one day and then maybe you'll understand what it's like when nobody wants you. Heartless you are, heartless …' she said, stopping mid-sentence as her eyes came to rest on Kate. 'Who are you?'

Kate stepped forward, holding out her hand, about to introduce herself, but Grace interrupted. 'Mother! That's no way to speak to visitors. This is my friend Kate and her daughter, Jessica. Remember? I told you they'd be coming today to stay with us for a while.'

'Hello, pleased to meet you.' said Kate.

'Well I'm not sure I can say the same about you. Aren't you the one she met in London when she went down to stay with that trollop of …?'

'Mother!'

Nothing wrong with her memory sometimes, although for anyone who wasn't used to seeing people who had dementia, it could obviously be quite difficult to deal with.

'I know who you are,' said Gran, undeterred. 'Your husband slept with your best friend.'

'Mother! Stop it right now!'

'Well, you've come to the right place then. Go off with other people's husbands all the time round here.'

'Mother!'

Sometimes Grace wondered whether her mother even had dementia at all. She seemed to just use it, along with her age, as an excuse to be downright rude.

'If you can't be nice to people, just go to your room and leave us in peace. These two poor souls have travelled all the way up from Cornwall on the train today, all they want is a nice cup of tea, not you being nasty.'

'Tea? Alright I'll stay and have a cup with you then, somebody needs to talk some sense into you.'

Grace turned and rolled her eyes at Kate, who was looking somewhat bewildered, understandably. Jessica's eyes, already large, seemed to have doubled in size.

'Sorry, I should have explained before. Mother has dementia and does some strange things at times. Nevertheless, that doesn't excuse the way she speaks to people sometimes.'

'I'm not deaf, you know.'

'I know you're not, Mother, I wanted you to hear. Just think before you speak, is what I'm saying.'

'But I can't think, I've got dementia – or have you forgotten?'

Aaagghh! Grace sometimes had to scream inwardly, with the frustration of it all.

'Is that tea ready yet? A poor old lady like me could waste away.'

Charlie looked slightly bewildered. The whole situation seemed somewhat déjà vu, reminiscent of having Grace's sister coming to stay with them last year. Even worse in fact – there'd only been one of her and he'd had Zak then, Grace's son, who was now away at university. The only male in a house filled with five of the female species was not a good place to be. Decidedly not.

'Charlie, has the dog been for a walk?'

Well obviously not, unless he'd been by himself. But at least Alfie was a male dog, a furry sort of ally. Charlie was glad to escape with him, to be honest. A little male bonding. They walked around the field together exchanging

10

pleasantries, although to be fair, the conversation was a little one-sided, Alfie being selfishly sidetracked by sensory stimuli, smelling at grass clumps and tree trunks and ... was that a lamp post over there? Eureka!

By the time they got back it was getting quite late and Charlie was surprised to find Izzy and Jessica still up. He peered around the living room door to find Grace and Kate chattering away, completely impervious to the needs of their daughters.

'Haven't forgotten about these two, have you?'

'What?' snapped Grace, resenting the interruption.

'Think it's past their bedtime.' Charlie nodded his head, indicatively, towards the hallway.

'Couldn't you just ...?'

'No way, Grace, no way. I don't mind getting my own daughter ready for bed but not someone else's – your mother would have a field day with that.'

He turned on the television, settled himself down and took charge of the remote. Hmm, maybe being the only man in the house wasn't so bad after all. Alfie sank down to the floor at Charlie's feet with a groan. Of agreement, obviously.

2

Izzy was loath to go to nursery the next morning.

'Not fair,' she huffed into her cereal. 'Jessica's not going to school.'

'Izzy, I've explained that to you. You're going to nursery and that's final.'

'Ow! My tummy hurts and I 'spect I'll be sick in a minute,' she said, scraping around the bowl for any missed morsels.

She suddenly looked up expectantly, tummy-ache forgotten. 'More please.'

'Hurry up then,' smiled Grace, tipping more into the bowl and adding milk, hurriedly. 'We don't want to be late.'

Late? When were they anything but? Mrs Clarke, Izzy's teacher, and a frosty-faced one at that, glared at Grace as she opened the nursery door. The other children were sitting on the mat, eyes raised expectantly, anticipating a story. Izzy scuttled across to join them.

'Sorry,' mouthed Grace.

A reply was not forthcoming. Just a cold glare.

''Bye,' squeaked Grace, feeling more like a child than a responsible mother. The hurried baby steps she suddenly found herself doing along the pathway towards the gate as she left didn't help. What was she doing? Ogghh! She wasn't really insane – it was just the effect Mrs Clarke seemed to have on her!

*

Dogs are the most loyal and loving creatures in the world, and Alfie was no exception. His sixth sense made him rush to the front door and sit behind it patiently waiting for Grace's return for at least five minutes before she actually arrived. He shuffled about on his bottom, tail moving gingerly from side to side as he sensed her approaching. As the door opened, he could contain his excitement no longer and shot up to greet her like a cork popping from a champagne bottle.

Despite pushing him firmly aside after hastily ruffling his soft and familiarly pungent fur with her hands, Grace loved the ecstatic welcome she always received from him. Nevertheless, today she was impatient to hear other tales, and didn't want to waste any more time on waggly doggy ones. She was looking forward to this catch-up with Kate, and there would be fewer interruptions whilst Izzy was at nursery.

It was remarkably quiet in the kitchen. Jessica seemed to have found a new friend – in the form of Gran. They were colouring in pictures together at the table. Kate was clearing away the breakfast dishes.

'Hi. It's looking very organised in here. You didn't have to do all of this,' said Grace, her eyes scanning the ultra-spotless kitchen in amazement. Sudden inadequacies surfaced. How come it was always chaos in here normally? Even Gran seemed quiet and affable.

'Sorry, I didn't mean to take over. It's just that … well, I haven't come here to be waited on. I bet you'll never be able to find anything now though,' said Kate, suddenly realising. 'Think I can be a bit OCD at times. Sorry.'

'Hey, stop apologising, it's great – really. Are you okay, Mother?' asked Grace, turning her attention momentarily to the grey-headed one.

'Mm,' replied Gran, deep in concentration.

'Mm?' Unbelievable.

'… except …'

Here we go.

'You've hidden my teeth again, Grace.'

Two pairs of eyes rounded in disbelief.

Grace winked at them in a vain attempt at reassurance. 'I haven't seen your teeth, Mother,' she said, glancing furtively towards the sugar bowl. Please don't let them be in there. 'I'm sure they'll turn up.'

Amazingly, all three seemed reassured. Perhaps she should have explained. Oh well, time enough. But what Grace knew she really must do this morning, above all else, was to get some time alone to talk to Kate. For, despite the smile she was painting on her face, Grace could see that something was troubling her deeply.

The lives of Grace and Kate were like an open book to each other most of the time, but about some things, the most important ones in fact, Kate remained closed. She found it hard to open up to anyone, even Grace. The full story about her leaving Tom and going away to start a new life in Cornwall had still not been told. Odd, but that's the way it was. Kate had revealed that she'd left Tom after the discovery that he'd slept with her best friend, but she had never felt able to discuss it with anyone. Her feelings had remained bottled up inside, agonisingly churning around. She felt as though if she didn't talk to someone about it soon, she would go crazy.

It wasn't as though Kate had been to blame in any way at all, but in her head she felt ashamed, inadequate, as if in some way she had been responsible. Ashamed, also, that she hadn't been enough for her man, hadn't looked after Jake, hadn't been there when … It was all in her head. However, she needed to talk to someone now, the time was right and Grace was the only person she felt she could share her troubles with. In all probability she would have done so before had they not, geographically, been so far apart. For

14

how could you discuss something like that on the phone? And similarly, how could you pour your heart out to someone, even your best friend, when you're only seeing them for a short time? Those all too brief meetings were joyous reunions meant for happy chatter, not blubbing friends pouring out their soul.

The time had come though. This latest crisis had brought things to a head. Kate needed to be able to talk about it before her own head exploded. She knew that facing up to them over the next few days was going to be horrendous and as to what the future held she had absolutely no idea, but one thing she was so grateful for was this special friendship she had with Grace. She knew she would stand by her no matter what, and felt cocooned by the fact that Grace had told her she could stay here for as long as she liked.

Kate walked over to Grace, eyes welling, arms outstretched. 'Give me a hug. I'm so glad we became friends.'

'You soppy thing,' smiled Grace, hugging her back. 'Me too, though. I can't tell you how much I value our friendship.'

'Hey up, what's going on here then,' asked Charlie, as he walked in through the back door.

'Charlie! I wasn't expecting you back.'

'Evidently not.'

'Idiot,' she laughed, giving him a peck on the cheek. 'I meant, how come you're not at work?'

'Just been to do a couple of estimates.' Charlie ran his own painting and decorating business. 'One of them was just round the corner so thought I'd call in for a quick brew.'

'Brew? Brew? Does that mean tea?' asked Gran. 'Yes I'll have one, an old lady could die of thirst around here.'

'Nothing wrong with your ears, is there Mother?' said Grace, filling the kettle. 'A "please" would be quite nice though,' she said, a trifle sarcastically.

'Eh?'

'Hmm.'

'Anyway,' said Charlie, sensing tension brewing, as well as tea, 'I've got another three jobs to look at then I was thinking I might leave the lads to it – take the rest of the day off.'

Grace turned tentatively from the teapot. 'Oh?'

'It's okay, it's okay, I'm not meaning to invade your space, far from it. I know you want some time with Kate so I thought maybe I could take Izzy out somewhere for a bit this afternoon. What do you think?'

Jessica glanced up, crayon poised in her hand. Grace's eyes flicked from one to another, questioningly. Kate nodded her approval.

'Would you like to go too, Jessica?' asked Grace.

'Um …?' Jessica responded nervously.

'We could take Alfie, if you like,' said Charlie, persuasively.

A flicker of a smile flitted across Jessica's face. 'Okay,' she agreed, a little more confidently.

'What do you say to Charlie, Jess?' asked Kate, thinking shyness was no excuse for bad manners.

'Thank you.'

'Good girl.'

'This tea's taking a long time,' grumbled Gran. 'It would have been quicker to get up and make it myself. But then, I have to do everything round here already, I haven't got time to be taking on any more jobs. Grace! Get a move on for goodness sake!'

'Mother! Stop being …'

Charlie silenced her with his eyes. It really wasn't worth the hassle.

Grrr! Grace felt so cross with her mother sometimes. The anger just seemed to bubble up inside. She could be so frustrating, almost as if she was trying to be awkward on purpose simply to wind her up. But Charlie was right. She counted to ten under her breath and put the teapot on the table – with somewhat of a bang.

'Ooh, temper, temper, Grace, you'll be breaking it in a minute if you carry on like that. Pass the sugar could you?'

Jessica leapt to her feet, anxious to please, not liking hostile situations and sensing the tension. It is however, truly unfortunate that in moments like this, filled with nervous anxiety, we have a tendency to become clumsy. Jessica was no exception.

'Oops!' she exclaimed, as the bowl slipped through her fingers, depositing its gleaming white contents onto the kitchen table.

Gleaming white? Well, not all of it. For there in the middle, and now fully exposed for all to see, lay something gleaming and pink, as well as white.

'Mother!' Grace was mortified.

'I knew you'd hidden them!' retorted Gran.

'How many times have I told you not to put your teeth in the sugar bowl?'

Jessica's face said it all.

Grace thought it best to take Kate and Jessica with her when she walked down to nursery school to collect Izzy. After the false teeth episode it maybe was not a good idea to leave them alone with Gran – at least until they'd had time to get a bit more familiar with her little foibles. Not surprisingly, they'd looked horrified, as would any outsider. It was amazing really, when Grace came to think about it, how you just grew to accept all the random, obscure and often totally disgusting incidents that occurred when you live with someone who has dementia. It could be almost unbearably frustrating sometimes, but your shockability threshold became practically non-existent. It was only when, like today, someone from outside the household saw something which made them register shock-horror, that it made you stop and realise that other people didn't live like this.

'Sorry about Mother.'

'What?' asked Kate.

'The teeth. You know. Well, everything really. I'm sure there'll be lots more of her little "moments" while you're staying with us. I feel as though I should apologise in advance.'

'I don't know how you cope, Grace, you must have the patience of a saint.'

'Huh, I wouldn't say that! I feel really cross with her sometimes, she can be so frustrating, but most of the time, well you just get on with it don't you?'

'Don't think I could – I'm full of admiration.'

'Oh it's not that bad – just routine when you're living with it day to day. And she has the back room converted into a granny flat that she's in some of the time, so it's not like I'm with her constantly. That really *would* drive me mad.'

'Did you never think about putting her in a home?'

'Well yes, of course, we've talked about it, and as she gets worse I'll probably end up having to. But for now, well, I just think the guilt would be harder to live with than the mother.'

'Well hats off to you, is all I can say. Don't think I could do it. Well, I know I couldn't.'

Jessica looked up at Kate inquisitively. 'Hats off – what does that mean? You haven't got hats on.'

Kate smiled. 'It's just an expression, Jess. It means that I admire Grace for taking care of her mum even though it must be so difficult sometimes.'

'Talking about difficult, I meant to explain to you a bit about Mrs Clarke, Izzy's teacher, before we got here. Bit late now, but I've just got time to say she's "difficult" personified and does not like me one iota.'

'Good morning, Mrs Clarke,' said Grace opening the

nursery door and ushering the two of them in.

Jessica's eyes grew wide as the imposing figure loomed before them, beaming hostility from a face with features so frozen that Birds Eye itself couldn't have done a better job.

'You're late – *again*, and it is *not* morning. It happens, by now, to be afternoon.'

Did she spit as she was speaking or were they snowflakes falling? Certainly frost seemed to have formed on her eyebrows. Oh no, pardon the mistake, they'd just gone a bit white and bristly, must be her age.

'Oh', said Grace, nonplussed, 'has everyone gone?'

'Well of course they've "gone", as you so nicely put it. It may surprise you to hear that other parents actually turn up on time to collect their children. And, incidentally, this is meant to be my lunch break but I could hardly go off and leave this poor unfortunate child to wait on her own, could I?'

The 'poor unfortunate child' sidled up to Mrs Clarke and played out her role to perfection. 'Drama queen' was an understatement when it came to Izzy.

'I thought my mummy had forgotten me,' she said, clutching on to Mrs Clarke's hand, tears in her eyes, the full works.

'Well she's here now, darling,' said Mrs Clarke, visibly taken in.

'Izzy!' said Grace sternly, and only adding fuel to the fire as far as Mrs Clarke was concerned. 'You're really not the sort of person anybody could forget. Now go and get your coat and stop being silly.'

'Poor child,' muttered Mrs Clarke, under her breath.

'Oh, I'd like to introduce you to my friend Kate,' said Grace, as they waited. 'She's come to stay with us for a while.'

'Friend is it? I thought, for a moment, you had another sister that had crawled out of the woodwork.'

19

The comment hit Grace like a bullet. She found herself incapable of speech, as tears welled in her eyes.

'Pleased to meet you,' said Kate, shaking her by the hand, her words never further from the truth. She understood what Grace had meant now.

'And this is my friend Jessica,' said Izzy, turning and looking at her with pride.

Whether it was the boost to her confidence by Izzy calling her friend, or her sensitivity in noticing how deeply Grace had been hurt by the comment, or the original remark about what a difficult person she was, it's hard to say. But Jessica, normally such a shy and retiring child, marched up to Mrs Clarke and said boldly, 'I don't like you. My teacher is much nicer.'

Even Izzy was shocked.

After lunch, true to his word, Charlie took the girls out, and Alfie too. Where they were actually going was a subject of much debate.

'To the cinema,' said Jessica.

'Not with a dog,' said Charlie.

'Swimming,' said Izzy.

'Not with a dog,' said Charlie. 'Why don't we leave him behind?'

'No-o-o-o!' chorused the girls.

Grace and Kate left them to their discussion. Gran had gone to her room for a nap.

'Let's go through to the lounge and make ourselves comfortable while we've got the chance. Cuppa?'

'Cuppa? Think I'm in need of something stronger than tea, lunchtime or not. I feel a bit of unburdening coming on.'

'At last! You're gonna tell me everything, right?'

'Everything.'

3

Everything? Where to begin, that was the thing. Probably at the wedding – the wedding of Ben, her friend Chloe's son, to Caroline, Tom's secretary. It had seemed such a perfect day for everyone. Ben and Caroline were so obviously besotted with each other and made such a lovely couple that you couldn't help but be happy for them. Ben was such a clown anyway that he always made everyone smile.

Chloe was mum not only to her roguish son Ben, but also to Olivia, who now lived in Manchester with her partner Stelios, and to two-year-old J-J, the most mischievous one of all. In some ways Chloe's offspring were like three peas in a pod, so obviously siblings, their red hair proclaiming their paternity and matching, almost exactly, that of their father John. But it hadn't always been so obvious, for John and Chloe had separated, in a split that was the extreme antithesis to amicable, well before J-J was conceived.

John, a very volatile character, had left Chloe to live with Jackie, but had returned to the house one day and raped Chloe, an incident that Chloe had tried to keep secret for the sake of Ben and Olivia. Obviously, when Chloe discovered she was pregnant, chaos had ensued, and eyebrows were raised; but when J-J was born, his shock of red hair put paid to any doubts that anyone may have had. J-J was, without question, John's son. Not that it made much difference as to his upbringing, of course, he was Chloe's son, and Chloe's son alone; John had never shown any interest or tried to have any involvement whatsoever. Fortunately.

But the other man who *had* become important, suddenly, to Chloe – had slept with her, more to the point – was Tom. Yes, Tom. The very same Tom that was married to Kate. The very same man that loved Kate, her best friend Kate. What a mess. He could so easily have been J-J's father, had thought he was in fact, until the red hair had proved otherwise and had let him off the hook.

Chloe should have been relieved. Had been – sort of. But a part of Chloe had cried out for Tom, had wanted him to be the father, had wanted the whole world to know. For the truth of the matter was she had committed the biggest crime of all – she had fallen in love with her best friend's husband.

And Tom had loved her too, in his own way. Was it possible to be in love with two women at the same time? Because much as he tried not to admit it, he was. Kate had to be his one and only love now, and he *did* love her, but he had a lot of making up to do. He'd been revered by all as Mr Perfect, but his halo had slipped somewhat – certainly when it came to being a husband anyway.

Poor Kate, however, had still been completely in the dark about all of this on the day of Caroline and Ben's wedding. To her he was her man and hers alone, and she loved him to the moon and back. Why should she not? He was kind, he was loving, he was fun to be with, what more could any woman want from a man? Faithfulness, actually. But how was she to know? And how was she to know about a certain little dalliance that had taken place with Caroline too? Yes Caroline, the very same.

Poor Kate indeed. And yet on that glorious day of the wedding no one could have been happier – other than the bride and groom, of course. For, after the tragic death of their baby son more than two years earlier, and month after disappointing month of unsuccessfully trying, she finally had some exciting news for Tom.

She'd hardly dared to tell him, feeling that the secret was safe if she hugged it to herself, feeling that she'd lose control if she told someone else – even Tom. Such a fragile thing and yet so momentous. It could be there one minute and gone the next. But it felt right this time, and she'd been to see the doctor and it had been confirmed. She had to start believing.

It was such a joyous occasion, the time to tell him was now. For with such love and happiness abounding how could it not work out perfectly this time?

Tom was also lost in his own thoughts. He stood watching Caroline as she posed for the camera. How beautiful she looked and how she'd changed over the past couple of years. Kate sneaked up behind him and put her arms around his waist.

'Hey you, you're only supposed to have eyes for me!'

Tom turned round to look at her. 'Remember our wedding day?'

'How could I forget?' Her eyes twinkled at him in the sunlight. 'Tom?'

'Mm,' he felt helpless in her gaze.

'I'm pregnant!'

'Pregnant?'

Kate's head nodded excitely in affirmation, her utter joy having, for the moment, taken away the power of speech. Unexpectedly, tears of happiness squirted forth, threatening her non-waterproof eye make-up with disaster, but what the heck, even panda-eyes couldn't spoil this moment.

'Are you sure?' asked Tom, still in shock.

'Quite sure, I saw the doctor yesterday. I was going to wait until tonight to tell you but I just couldn't keep it secret any longer. Isn't it amazing after all this time?' Kate was clasping her hands together, almost jumping up and down with excitement.

Tom took her hands in his own. 'That's fantastic! Oh

Kate, I love you so much,' he said, as they fell into each others' arms, lost in their own little world.

The bridal party made its way to the reception, Kate anxiously rushing off in search of the Ladies to adjust her make-up before this decidedly unflattering tear-smeared look was captured on camera for future generations to see. Another person on the same mission was Chloe, mother of the groom, and already depicted in several of the family wedding photos looking decidedly red-eyed. Maybe they'd just put it down to losing a son, and it so wasn't that – she loved Caroline like a daughter and was absolutely overjoyed that she had now become a Russell. For her family to expand and grow was all that Chloe had ever wanted. She couldn't wait for Ben and Caroline to start having babies. Babies ...

Kate noticed Chloe's red eyes straight away. For some people seem capable of crying bucket-loads and yet have the type of eyes that revert back to their original sparkling beauty at the bat of an eyelid, but Chloe was not one of those people. Red-rimmed and bloodshot, together with a nose not dissimilar to Rudolph's, was most definitely not a look to be desired on this important day.

'Chloe! Are you alright?'

'Fine thanks.'

Strange, isn't it, the things people say to each other some-times?

'You?'

'Yeah.'

But then the red eyes saw the reflection of panda-eyes in the mirror and the barriers came down. They were best friends, how could they not?

'Just feeling a bit emotional, that's all. You?'

'Me too,' said panda-eyes. Actually, I wasn't going to tell you yet, but I can't hold it in any longer. The secret I mean, not the ... I'm pregnant Chloe! Only found out yesterday.'

'I know ... so pleased for you! exclaimed Chloe, turning from the mirror to give her a hug.

'You know? But ...'

'I was outside the church with J-J, and I overheard you telling Tom the good news. You were both so excited and happy that I didn't like to intrude. You must be absolutely over the moon after all this time. Congratulations!'

Is it possible to tense your eyeballs? Chloe made a serious attempt to do so, in order to arrest the formation of a waterfall which threatened to burst forth and cascade unmitigatingly down her cheeks. She buried her face in Kate's shoulder for a moment, the hug hiding all.

'Can't tell you how excited I am,' said Kate, tears of happiness welling in her own eyes. 'Oghh, why does that always happen? I'm trying to get rid of the panda-look, not make it even worse,' she said, turning back to the mirror in a sudden fluster.

'I know what you mean,' said Chloe, doing likewise. 'I don't know what you've got to worry about though, just look at the state of me – and I'm the bridegroom's mother!'

This feeble attempt at light-hearted banter was definitely what was called for. They were friends, the very best of friends supposedly. Chloe couldn't let this come between them, Kate getting pregnant at some point had sort of been expected anyway. Just a shock when the news actually came, that was all. As for what had gone before, as Tom had said, Kate must never ever find out. And that, in fact, was that hurt Chloe most of all. She had been rejected. Tom loved her, she knew he did, but he had made his choice and his choice was Kate. She was his wife, what else could she possibly have expected? And even more so now there was a baby. A baby would cement them together for ever. Although sometimes babies can cause ... Chloe! Don't even go there!

She had J-J and she loved him, even though he could be a little monster at times. J-J, who could so easily have turned out to be Tom's baby. What a difference that would have made. He would have stood by her. He would have, wouldn't he?

Having patched up their make-up, the two re-joined the wedding party. J-J toddled across at speed, if a little unsteadily, to greet them, a stream of indecipherable baby babble issuing forth from his mouth.

'J-J!' called Jessica, chasing after him. 'Come back, I'm meant to be looking after you.'

Kate looked proudly at her daughter, who was growing up so fast. How good she was with J-J, how excited she'd be at the prospect of having a new baby brother or sister. A sudden flashback though, a little shiver ran down her spine in remembrance of the baby son they'd lost two and a half years ago. Jake. Gone but not forgotten. So much had happened since that tragic day. So many ripples in their lives.

'Why are your eyes all red, Auntie Chloe? Have you been crying?' asked Jessica, looking up from her charge, and a sensitive soul if ever there was one.

And there was Chloe thinking she'd done a great job with the wet wipes and mascara! 'Crying? Me? No, whatever gave you that idea?' she lied convincingly. 'I'm probably just allergic to my eye make-up or something. It happens some-times – makes me look like some kind of red-eyed monster.'

She actually managed a smile, mouth turning up at the corners and everything. Face hadn't cracked – she could do it! Amazing!

'What does allergic mean, Auntie Chloe?'

It's like how your dad's allergic to me, or seems to be now, even though I know he loves me. Jeepers! Did those words just come out of my mouth? Did I say them? Chloe's eyes darted around for signs …

Phew! What a disaster that could have been. It was such a

26

nightmare when that happened, not knowing whether things were just random thoughts in your head or whether you'd actually spoken them. Did that only happen to her or did it happen to other people too? Only to her, probably. And probably because she lived on her own – well, with J-J of course, but spent far too much time on her own, without the company of another adult, without the company of … Stop it! She was going mad, she was sure of it.

'Auntie Chloe?' a small hand slipped into her own.

'Sorry darling, I was miles away then. What did you say?'

'What does allergic mean?'

'Erm, well, it means when you use something and it does funny things to you then you have to stop using it because you know that it's bad for you, even though you may really like it.'

Hmm …

'Auntie Chloe?'

'Yes darling?'

'I think you should stop using your eye make-up then. Your eyes have gone all watery now so you *must* be allergic to it like you said.'

Both thoughts and words failed Chloe this time. She simply squeezed the soft little hand more tightly, within the grasp of her own.

Never still for long, off J-J toddled again. He seemed to be on a mission to complete five thousand laps of the room before he was cut short and taken home to bed. The bulkiness of his nappy made his little legs look even shorter as he bumbled along, hands up to balance himself, somewhat reminiscent of a puppet on a string. No one could fail to smile when he was around.

'Hey lil' bro',' said Ben, ruffling his hair, as J-J whizzed past on his mission.

'Okay, Ma?' asked Ben, concerned that she was looking anything but. 'Not been blubbing have you?'

'Just a bit emotional, that's all. Don't know why, it's not like I'm losing you exactly, is it? You're already living together and it hasn't stopped you coming round to torment me all the time so far, has it? Don't suppose a wedding service'll change that.'

'Ha-ha! You know you love it really, he said stooping slightly, chin jutting forwards as he squinted at his reflection in the glass of the window and gently patted at his hair.

'Ben, what are you doing?' as if she didn't know.

'My hair – it was perfect this morning and look at it now.' He was extremely fond of his red spikes, they were his trademark.

'For goodness sake! It's meant to be the bride who fusses about her hair, not the groom. Just look at Caroline and take your eyes off yourself for a minute – doesn't she look beautiful?'

'Did I hear my name mentioned?' asked Caroline, coming across to join them.

'Mmm. Good enough to … mmm,' he said, sliding an arm around her waist and nuzzling her neck. 'Um, d'you think we could just slip away for a … I've got this … ohhh, you look so hot, babe.'

'Ben!' she responded, embarrassed, and in front of her new mother-in-law too. 'Ben!' she repeated, slapping him down to size, quite literally. 'Sorry, Chloe,' she said, feeling she should apologise on his behalf.

'Don't apologise to me for him, Caroline,' she laughed, 'I think I know him well enough by now! I was just saying you look absolutely beautiful – radiant in fact. Even better though is the fact that you're such a beautiful person on the inside as well. Really glad to have you as my daughter-in-law, I couldn't love you more if I'd given birth to you myself.'

'Oh Chloe, what a lovely thing to say! Love you too!' she said tearfully, giving her a hug.

'Strewth!' said Ben, still a bit concerned about his appearance. 'I'm going to the Gents. Can't cope with all this blubbing.'

4

Back home Tom suddenly had an overwhelming urge to carry Kate over the threshold.

'Tom! What are you doing?' she shrieked in delight, as she was suddenly whisked off her feet.

'Call it a mad moment if you like but I just want you to know how happy you've made me, Mrs Darrington. It feels like a whole new start for us. We can put all the past behind us now and start again.'

You wish, Tom.

She glanced up anxiously at him, as he gently put her back down on her feet.

'Everything? I'm excited about the baby, of course I am, but this new baby will never replace Jake.'

'Of course not.'

'So what did you mean?'

'Just all the bad times we've gone through, and ...'

'And what?'

'And I love you Mrs Darrington,' he said, sealing her lips with a kiss.

Nice way to wriggle out of it Tom.

A little voice soon gave him a reality check, preventing any further development of passion.

'Daddy, will you take me to bed and read me a story please?'

He looked down into her big blue eyes, so innocent and appealing. She never failed to melt his heart – his angel. To think that he could so easily have lost her too, had the truth ever come out, or if his heart had led him down a different path, a path with Chloe.

It didn't bear thinking about. He could only thank his lucky stars that he'd taken the right decision, and that J-J had turned out to be John's son. He knew he had to put Chloe right out of his mind now – well, as far as he could anyway, it was difficult to avoid her altogether of course because of her friendship with Kate. But yes, he was sure Chloe would be feeling the same way too now, moving on with her life. They'd been lucky to escape unscathed. The past was gone. His future lay with his beautiful pregnant wife and his daughter, Kate and Jessica – and their new baby when it came along. He was a very lucky man indeed.

'Yep, okay angel. Let's leave this mummy to slip into something more comfortable and I'll race you up the stairs!'

Kate watched them go, her eyes filled with love for both of them. She felt blessed, and undeserving of such happiness. Tom. He was such a good daddy to Jess. The perfect man all round, in fact. Just thinking of him gave her butterflies, even after all this time.

She wandered into the kitchen and pottered around for a while, then, thinking Tom wouldn't be much longer with the storytelling, she made them both a cup of tea and carried it up to the bedroom. This had been such a perfect day she didn't want it to end.

She must have drifted off for a while as she lay in their big feather-soft bed to wait for him, but suddenly she was aware of his presence next to her, his manliness, the heat of his body.

'Hey,' he whispered, as she opened her eyes.

'Hey, you. Is she asleep?'

'Out like a light,' he said, his hand moving up the inside of her thigh.

'Tom, I'm tired,' she said.

'No you're not. I can feel you want it just as much as I do,' he said, his fingers gently probing.

She could hardly deny that her juices were flowing. It was just that …

'Tom, I …'

'I know what you're thinking. I'll be gentle, I promise.'

'No Tom,' she said, fighting the urgency with all the strength she could muster. 'No,' she said, pushing his hand away. 'Remember the last time? I thought I was pregnant then, and we made love and …'

Tom sighed, and rolled on to his back.

'Look, it's a medically proven fact – making love does not harm the baby.'

'Yeah, right. How do you explain it then?'

'Coincidence, that's all.'

'That's all, huh! You know how much I want a baby Tom, and we've been trying for so long. I just don't want to take risks.'

'But it's further on this time, the pregnancy's confirmed, you said so.'

'Only just. We're only a few days further on than the last time. Anything's possible at this stage.'

Tom sighed again. Tension hovered in the air.

'You can't expect me to abstain for nine whole months. I can't and I won't and that's all there is to it.' He rolled on to his other side, his back to Kate, his frustration all-consuming.

Kate was saddened by his action. 'That's so mean, Tom,' she said.

His head turned swiftly back towards her on the pillow. 'Mean? I think you're the one who's mean. Honestly, I think you've just been using me as a baby-making machine lately. Use now over.'

'Tom! How can you say that?! You know I love you.'

'Huh! You have a funny way of showing it sometimes.'

They turned their backs on each other, each feigning sleep. Each hurt and cross and feeling wronged. Silence pervaded. Tension not only hovered, but flapped its black wings in anger.

Thoughts whirled around inside Kate's head, a silent tear slid sideways onto the pillow and formed a damp patch beneath her face.

'Tom?'

'Mm?'

'I hate this. I hate it when we fall out.'

He turned his head slightly. 'Me too,' he said before turning properly towards her. 'That's probably because we don't very often. Fall out, I mean' he said, grinning sheepishly.

Kate turned towards him also, and snuggled into him. 'I'm sorry.'

'Me too.'

They lay like that in silence for what seemed like an eternity, cocooned in their love for each other, relaxed and warm, happy once more. Arousal lay dormant for a while, but in those circumstances, in the warmth, in the cosiness, in their love, it soon tippy-toed back in. Well, galloped actually. Tom shuffled about, not wanting to upset her again, not wanting. Wanting! Jeeez – wanting!

'Tom?'

'Mm?' His mind elsewhere. Lower down in fact.

'You okay?'

'Mmm ...' he didn't mean it to come out as a groan.

Her hand reached for him, turning his groan into a gasp and then a sigh, as the hand started to move – rhythmically. His sigh, his face, whatever it was, Kate's willpower flew straight out of the window – gone. A tingle, a squish, her nether regions turned to a pulp, and then, well, it could almost be described as a tsunami. OMG! She had to, she had to ... how could she not?

'Tom?'

A grunt.

'Tom?'

'What? He couldn't really think straight, not at this moment.

'Okay then, if you think it'll be okay.'

'U-uh?' Spell it out woman, how can you expect a man to concentrate.

'Put it in if you like.'

What a lovely turn of phrase you have there Kate. Tom opened one eye. 'What?'

For goodness sake! How plain do you want it?! 'In!' she commanded, legs up and splayed in readiness. Really Tom. It could not be made more clear.

'But you said …' he said, hovering above her in a one sided he said/she said conversation.

'Tom! Could you please just do it.'

'Are you sure?'

'No, I always lie like this,' she groaned, sarcasm to the fore. 'Of course I'm sure – you said … you're right. I was just being silly. Go for it.'

Um, very romantic. 'But if …'

'Tom! I cannot wait another minute, another second even, or I shall spontaneously combust, I promise you.'

'That hot, eh?' he smiled, still hovering, but hovering with intent now, as well as just a little bit of torment, it has to be said.

'Tom ple-ease!'

He was enjoying this now, the power, but she even more so, as she threw her arms around him and drew him into her. He too, it was what he had been wanting all along.

The next day started off as normal – well, better than normal actually. The first Kate knew of it was when Jess came bouncing round the bedroom door accompanied by Tom. They were both up, washed and dressed and had brought her breakfast in bed. Kate yawned, stretched, and opened her eyes wide in surprise.

'Thought you deserved a lie-in,' said Tom, placing the breakfast tray before her as she sat up and adjusted her pillows.

Although Kate remained in a state of blissful ignorance about his wrong-doings, in his own head Tom had a lot of making up to do for his misdemeanours. Gazing at his radiant and beautiful wife sitting there, looking like the queen of all that surrounded her, he found it impossible to imagine what could ever have led him to stray. She was kind, she was thoughtful, there was no one in the world that he'd rather spend time with and yet what had he done as soon as her back was turned? Committed the biggest crime ever, and slept with her best friend. And, even although a lesser crime, had also a quick fumble with his secretary out of sheer desperation.

That was no excuse, no excuse at all. He'd been an absolute toe-rag, there was no getting away from it. He'd let Kate down badly and he had to make up for it. And, what was more, she must never find out.

As for Kate herself, she hadn't been this happy for a long time – not since Jake, in fact. She had a truly scrumptious husband, the sweetest little daughter ever and now there was a new baby to look forward to, too. She really did consider herself to be, at this moment, one of the luckiest people in the world, in fact in the entire universe. Kate hugged her arms around herself, feeling a warm glow of contentment. She was truly blessed.

As opposed to Chloe. Kate stopped to think about her friend for a moment. Kate loved Chloe with all her heart and so fervently wished for her to find this much happiness too. Chloe had been there for her through all, and vice versa, they'd supported each other through the good times and the bad. Now that Kate was up there on a high she wanted her best friend to be up there with her too. Some-how, however, she didn't think that was going to happen. Something was troubling Chloe, and Kate had yet to get to the bottom of it. Strange, really, because the two of them usually shared everything, but on this occasion Chloe was holding back.

Kate had half believed her at first when she'd put it down to Ben getting married: Kate knew how close Chloe was to Ben. But then she realised that couldn't possibly be it – Chloe loved Caroline and had been genuinely excited about the wedding. Maybe it was just loneliness; the acrimonious split with John and her eldest two children having flown the nest. It must be hard for Chloe to see her so blissfully happy with Tom and a growing family to look forward to, when she herself was left as a single mum with the mischievous J-J to bring up alone. She should really try to be a bit more understanding of Chloe's situation and to put extra effort into cheering her up instead of being so wrapped up in herself all the time. That's what friendship was all about after all, wasn't it?

'Tom?' she said, devouring her bacon and eggs with a sudden burst of gusto.

'Mm?' he asked, feeling a bit sleepy again now, as he lay next to her, on top of the bedcovers, as she ate. In a man's world he'd done a day's work already.

'What can we do to cheer Chloe up?'

'What d'you mean?' he asked, suddenly wide awake again.

'She seems a bit down recently, have you not noticed?'

'Can't say that I have, no,' he said, clearing his throat apprehensively.

'I was talking to her at the reception yesterday – in the Ladies. She seemed really upset. I was telling her about the baby but she already knew.'

'Already knew?'

'She'd overheard me telling you outside the church.'

'Overheard you telling me?'

'Tom! Could you stop repeating everything I say? It drives me nuts!'

'And she was upset about the baby?' he said, not really hearing what she said, a sudden little frisson of anxiety creeping into his voice.

'Don't be silly! Why would she be upset about the baby, she's pleased for us, she knows how much we wanted it.'

But Tom had other thoughts.

'Anyway,' said Kate, not wishing to get sidetracked 'Why don't we have her over this afternoon with J-J? She'll be feeling really down after all the excitement of yesterday. She could have a meal with us.'

'No!' said Tom, maybe a little too quickly.

'Why not? We're not doing anything and Jess loves J-J.'

'She'll still have Olivia and Stelios there.'

'No she won't, they're going back at lunchtime, she told me. Give her a quick ring now while I jump in the shower then I'll go and get some food in, the fridge is almost empty.'

'No Kate, you can ring her if you want to, but don't invite her round. Wait until tomorrow when I'm at work.'

'Anybody would think you didn't like her,' she teased.

Hmmm. He turned towards her, avoiding her eye and traced the outline of her body with his forefinger, bringing it to rest half way down.

'I just want to spend the entire day with you that's all,' he said. 'What's wrong with that?'

'Nothing,' said Kate, kissing the tip of his nose. 'But I think you should move your hand ASAP, Jessica is likely to walk back in at any moment and the way I'm feeling I could quite easily succumb to temptation.'

They had such a lovely lazy day that even Kate had to admit

she was glad they had decided not to invite Chloe.

'It would only have dragged us down too if she's still feeling sad. I just want to wallow in my happiness for the moment and I don't want anyone to spoil it.'

'Poor Chloe – that's a bit mean,' said Tom, a little quickly maybe.

'Poor Chloe? I thought it was you who didn't want her here.'

'I didn't. I didn't, it's just … well at least we've got each other, she's all on her own.'

Kate looked at him with just a little smidgen of curiosity. Compassion wouldn't, in general, be expected to register on a man's radar. But then, Tom wasn't like every other man.

'You do have a habit of leaping to her defence sometimes, Tom. Should I be worried?' she joked, looking at him, her eyes full of … she'd thought it was trust. Many a true word is spoken in jest. There'd definitely been a slight movement of his eyes then, as he'd looked back at her with what only can be described as guilt.

Okay, so maybe she was paranoid. She admitted it actually, she was. But she'd been down this route before, ages ago, when Chloe had got pregnant with J-J, when she thought, just maybe, that Tom could be the father. But she'd been reassured, it had been a nonsensical thought, and obviously without any basis of truth whatsoever when J-J had arrived looking like a carbon copy of John.

A flicker in his eyes. Was that really enough to make her have these gut-wrenching suspicions all over again? Madness. She must be insane. Tom loved her, why would he even want to look at another woman? Especially when the other woman was her friend. Not a chance.

Okay, so she'd admit it all now. Little things had kept happening that occasionally had aroused her suspicions, for a quite a while now. Like the way he always sprang to

Chloe's defence, like the way he tried to avoid being at home when she came around, like the odd glance she'd seen pass between them, like … OMG!

Paranoia x 1,000 it could be, but had she been blind? Could this really have been happening right under her nose for all this time? Her heart was racing, so much so that she was finding it difficult to breathe.

Tom sensed her discomfort. 'You okay?'

'Mm. Could you get me a glass of water please? I'm feeling a bit funny,' she said, her voice sounding as if it came from miles away.

'Go and play upstairs for a while, Jess, there's a good girl,' said Tom, worriedly doing as he was bade.

'But I thought feeling funny was when you felt like making people laugh. Like the clowns we saw at the circus.' Her mummy's face was certainly as white as one of theirs had been.

'Upstairs, Jess,' he said, much more crossly than usual.

She thought it best just to go.

By the time Tom came back with the glass of water, Kate had managed to calm herself down a little by taking some deep breaths. She'd had to learn to live with these panic attacks since Jake's death, but although they were few and far between, they always managed to take her by surprise and the more she panicked, the worse she got. She continued to breathe deeply and slowly for a while, then took a sip of the water.

'What brought that on?' asked Tom, perturbed.

Should she tell him? Confront him now? Get it over with? But if the answer was 'no' would she believe him. Could she believe him? And if 'yes', what then? Would she throw him out? Send him to Chloe? Be left with two children to bring up on her own?

Sadly, or not, that decision was taken out of her hands – for the moment at least. For that feeling she'd had, that indigestion that she'd put down to the bacon and eggs, was most certainly not caused by the fry-up at all. And that gut-wrenching feeling caused by the shock of her suspicions led to something ... well, let's just say an old familiar pain. It couldn't be, surely, not again. Oh, but it could. And it was.

5

It was several days later as she lay in bed in the cold dawn of a new day. Five a.m. and sleep totally eluded her. Tom lay next to her asleep, breathing heavily. She watched the rise and fall of his chest as he slept and had never felt so alone. In the past she would have reached out for him, cuddled into him, but now she just felt dead inside.

Her baby was no more. Her pregnancy was fleetingly brief and now gone. She'd been consoled by Tom, and by Chloe, each of them individually and even, just once, together. And she'd been watching, always. Watching for a sign. Something that might confirm her suspicions. Anything.

They looked at her with love, both of them. They looked at each other with … no, wait, that was the thing: they did not look at each other at all. And she should know, for her eyes never left them for a moment.

They put it down to the loss of her baby, the fact that she was behaving so strangely with both of them. After all, look how she'd been after the death of Jake – she'd had a breakdown then. But that had been a real baby as opposed to being only a few days into pregnancy, surely there was a difference. Selfishly, Tom thought he couldn't cope with having to go through all of that again. And, selfishly, Chloe thought she most definitely could.

Kate couldn't lie in bed any longer, these thoughts racing around in her head. Sometimes misery and anger can puff you up inside like a balloon being blown up and up and up until you just know it's going to go pop. That is exactly how

Kate felt as she lay there next to Tom, trying not to move, trying to stay still and not wake him. She would explode in a minute, just like the balloon, getting bigger and bigger until – *bang*!

She jumped out of bed, almost amazed to find herself still in one piece, and even more amazed to find that Tom didn't appear to have even noticed. She glanced at him, not wanting to feel that little flippety somersault of her heart that she often had when she looked at him. And finding that she didn't anyway, was disappointed, depressed by the fact. She reached for her dressing gown and slippers, and padded softly down the stairs.

But one of Tom's eyes opened as the bedroom door closed behind her, and then the other. He'd been awake all along, just not wanting her to know that. For how could he sleep, knowing how she was? He loved her, she was his wife, was his world in fact, but sometimes he just could not understand her. She wasn't pregnant any more, okay, but it wasn't the end of the world. It wasn't as though one of them was terminally ill or something, people have much worse things to deal with. And anyway, weren't they meant to be in this together, supporting each other? He couldn't cope with her going all weird on him again like she had done before.

Nothing else for it, he'd have to go downstairs, talk to her, make her see sense. It was the only way. He really couldn't let everything slide down into that black hole like it had the last time. He loved her, he didn't want her disappearing off to Cornwall again and leaving him here, coping with Jess and everything else on his own. No, it had been a nightmare, and he wasn't about to let it happen again. No way. Reaching for his dressing gown too, he followed her down the stairs.

She looked up as he entered the room, not lovingly as she normally would have done, but coolly, indifferently almost, like he was a complete stranger.

'I thought you were asleep,' she said, as if she really wished he was.

'Nah. Just dozing. Heard you come down. You okay?'

'Not really, no.'

'What's wrong' he asked, filling the kettle, putting tea in the pot. Tea in a crisis – does it help?

Well, she supposed, it was now or never. She wanted to know, and there was only one way to find out. Ask him. Would he tell her the truth, that was the thing? How could she believe what he said? But surely, knowing him as well as she did, his face would give him away. He couldn't keep secrets from her, never had been able to … or so she'd thought. Now, though? Now, she'd look him straight in the eye, take him by surprise, a direct question. There'd be nowhere to hide, nowhere, and especially from her.

'Sit down, Tom, I want to talk to you.'

'Hang on, the kettle's almost boiled.'

'Forget the bloody tea! Sit down!'

Well, that did take him by surprise. She rarely swore, for one thing.

'What's the matter?' he asked, pulling out a chair and sitting opposite her at the kitchen table.

Her forearms were resting on the table top, her hands wringing together in nervous anticipation of what the outcome of this conversation might be. He, a picture of apparent innocence, remained totally oblivious to the bombshell that was about to hit him.

'Tom,' she started, her voice calmer and more in control than she felt.

'What? You're starting to freak me out now. What?' he repeated, looking straight into her eyes and seeing a stranger there, not the Kate he knew and loved.

'Okay. I'm going to ask you this question only once, and I want the truth. Whatever it is we'll deal with it, but you have to be honest with me.'

'Jeez, Kate, what is it? Tell me.'

Did he really want to know. Could she have found out? Nah – it wasn't possible. Chloe certainly wouldn't have said anything and he knew that he hadn't himself. Unless he talked in his sleep. He didn't, did he? Surely not, she would have mentioned it before. He shuffled forward to the edge of his seat, elbows on the table, cupping his chin in his hands. He tried to hold her stare, but his eyes kept darting about nervously. He felt as though he was facing the firing squad.

'Bloody hell, could you look at me? Simple request!'

She took a deep breath to regain her composure, it changed the tone of her voice. The six words that she uttered changed the path of her life.

'Have you ever slept with Chloe?'

The firing squad it was. The words shot at Tom like bullets, straight to the heart.

He tried to keep his cool. 'What? Me? Slept with Chloe? What kind of question is that?'

Innocent until proven guilty? I don't think so. Never answer a question with a question. Tom's face said it all.

Kate felt amazingly calm. In control of the situation. 'Please *do not* evade my question. I'm not going to repeat it, but I would like you to do me the courtesy of telling me the truth. And I want to hear it now, no lies.'

Maybe the bullets had been real, he certainly felt as though he had been shot. Nowhere to run, nowhere to hide. And, what's more, he knew he deserved absolutely everything that was coming to him.

He crumpled visibly as he spoke. Hung his head in shame and covered it with his hands. 'Yes,' he mumbled. 'Yes, I slept with Chloe.'

This time it was Kate who felt she'd been shot. For, although she'd suspected it and then built it up to something bigger inside her head, she never really, in her heart

44

of hearts, believed that Tom would ever cheat on her. He was the love of her life and she of his. Was.

'You bastard,' was all she could say. 'You absolute bastard.'

They sat in total silence for several seconds. Seconds? It seemed like hours. They were both in total opposition now, but with the same thought in their heads. How could he? Whizzing and pounding around inside. How could he?

The words burst forth from Kate's mouth, sprayed like venom. 'How *could* you, Tom? How could you do that to me? I thought you loved me, thought we were soulmates, together for ever. And not only that, but with Chloe too? Of all people! My best friend? The classic scenario! I …'

'Kate, I'm so, so sorry,' he interrupted, clasping his head in his hands, eyes screwed up in horror of what he had done to her. 'I don't know what happened.'

'Don't know what happened? You slept with my best friend, that's what happened,' she spat.

'I mean, I didn't mean it to happen.'

'Huh! So what you're trying to tell me is that by mistake your penis went off on its own and jumped into her all by itself – nothing to do with you. A bit like when a child misbehaves and runs off and jumps into a muddy puddle without its wellies. That sort of thing. And, incidentally, I hope that you *did* have your wellies on … only I don't think that you did, did you? Because I'll tell you what I think now: I think this has been going on for a long time, since before J-J was born, in fact,' she said pointedly.

Trying hard to regain her composure, she fanned her face with her hand and took a few deep breaths. She couldn't break down now, she needed to hear this. She brushed the welling tears from her eyes with her other hand and tried to stay calm. There was no turning back now.

An anguished groan escaped from his mouth. 'Okay, I'm sorry', he said, rubbing his fingers through his hair as he

45

collected his thoughts, looking up, and straight at her, ravaged to see the pain etched on her face and to know that he was the cause of it.

He sat back in his chair, arms folded across the front of himself in self-preservation. Head back, eyes closed, he had never felt so bad in his entire life. Not ever.

'I love you, you know that,' he said, looking at her again.

'Well you have a very funny way of showing it,' she snarled.

'I have been a complete and utter low-life. Call me any name you like, I deserve all of them. How could I have been so stupid when I had you?'

'Had, Tom. I'm glad you said "had". So has it?'

'Has it what?'

'Been going on since before J-J was born? For God's sake, are you thick as well as stupid?'

The force of her venom almost knocked him sideways. He had never felt the sting of her tongue before. But their marriage was in crisis, he had put it there, what more could he expect?

'Hang on. Let me tell you how it was, how it happened.'

'I'm waiting,' she spat, arms folded, like him.

'It really all started when Jake died ...'

Kate shot to her feet 'For God's sake!'

'Wait a minute. Let me speak.'

Tom held up both his hands, asking her to sit back down and listen. Amazingly, she complied.

'You took it badly ...'

'Hardly going to be delighted, was I?' she sneered.

'... had a bit of a breakdown, and went off to Cornwall to stay with your parents, leaving me here with Jess to look after on my own.'

'With the help of my very trustworthy best friend.'

Tom lowered his eyes with guilt. 'It only happened once, Kate.'

'And that's meant to make me feel better about it, is it?'

'I just want you to know, that's all. Anyway, you'd gone away and I was missing you. You were gone for ever, or so it seemed. You wouldn't even speak to me on the phone, you ...'

'Bastard!' Kate leapt to her feet and whacked him squarely across the face. 'I knew you'd turn this round on me, make out it was my fault!'

Tom grabbed her firmly by the wrists and lowered her, without any resistance, back down onto the chair. She was openly sobbing now, although still with some semblance of trying not to lose control.

'I'm not doing that,' he said firmly. 'No one is to blame except me.'

'And Chloe goody-two-shoes, don't forget her. Unless you raped her of course,' she said, thinking back to how Chloe had told her she'd been raped by John in anger after their separation, and that was the moment when J-J had been conceived.

'Of course I didn't rape her! What do you think I am?'

'I'm beginning to wonder,' she remarked, sarcastically.

'I don't think you realised how much I missed you, how much I needed you. I'd lost a baby too, I was grieving just like you were, but I was having to try to carry on as normal – hold down a job, take care of Jess, keep the house running smoothly. It was so hard, Kate, I was a mess. All I wanted was you and you'd just shut yourself off from me completely. But I knew I had to keep going, keep things as normal as possible for Jess, she'd had a lot to deal with too.'

Kate was sobbing openly now, her emotions all over the place. Memories of that dark time she'd gone through all flooding back on top of everything else.

Tom carried on. 'Chloe was just there for us, quietly, in the background, helping us get through each day. She was brilliant with Jess, we couldn't have managed without her.'

'Evidently not,' Kate tried to gather herself together.

'It wasn't like that. She was just there, there when I needed … when I needed you actually. It happened one night, Jess had gone for the first time ever to have a sleep-over at her friend Lily's house. Chloe had been sleeping at ours on weeknights like you'd asked her to, so she could be there for Jessica while I was working. But with Jess being out for the night, Chloe said she'd go home.

'Now I know what you're going to think here, you'll think it was all pre-planned, like I'd just arranged it so I could get her into bed with me. But, I can assure you, it wasn't like that at all. When I persuaded her to stay over, nothing was further from my mind.'

'Yeah right.'

'Believe me, all I wanted was you.'

'So what changed?'

'Desperation? I don't know. All I know is, she stayed, we had a drink, we talked, we were both feeling depressed and lonely, and before we knew it …'

'Stop!' yelled Kate, rising to her feet again, clutching the table for support, 'I don't want to hear any more, I can't bear it! The thought of you and her, in our bed. I bet it was in our bed, wasn't it?'

Tom hung his head in shame. She sank back down onto the chair, drained for the moment.

'I'm sorry, Kate! It only happened that one time, I swear it.'

Silence. A long silence. Tension mounting from one side.

'Tell me you're not J-J's father.'

'What?'

'You heard me.'

'I'm not J-J's father.'

'How do you know for sure? The timing was spot on, it must have been.'

'I know because … have you looked at him? He's a minia-ture version of John, red hair, everything.'

'But you were worried for a while, he could have been yours?'

'He could have, yes.'

An almost animal-like groan escaped Kate's lips as she leant forward in her seat, elbows on the table, head in her hands. Those suspicions she'd had, Olivia's words all that time ago, had all been true.

'Oh God, Tom. I don't know where we go from here, I can't bear it.'

He reached forward to take her hands in his, to reassure her it would never happen again. He loved her, he'd do everything in his power to make it right again.

But she shrank back and knocked his hands away.

'Don't touch me!' she screamed.

'But Kate, I …'

A timely interruption. It came in the form of a small figure wearing a candy pink nightdress, who stood in the kitchen doorway sucking her thumb, eyes as wide as saucers.

'Why is everyone shouting?' she asked, in a scared little voice.

'We're not shouting, angel, it's okay,' said Tom, reaching out for Jessica and helping her up onto his lap as she came over to him.

'You were. It woke me up. And Mummy's been crying,' she mumbled, timidly.

'I'm okay now, darling,' Kate said, standing to move round the table towards her, stroking her tousled blonde curls, reassuringly. 'You stay here and have a cuddle with Daddy while I go upstairs and get dressed, then I've got to go out for a little while.'

Tom looked at her questioningly, 'But it's six o'clock in the morning! Where are you going?'

'I think you know the answer to that one, Tom. I'm going

49

to see Chloe. And if you dare to ring and warn her I'm coming, well "do not" is what I'm saying. And you owe me that much at least.'

'You're going to see Auntie Chloe? Can I come?' asked Jess, suddenly perked up by the thought.

'No. Sorry, darling, but this is something I've got to do on my own.'

6

Was that the doorbell? Chloe tried to rouse herself and reached for her bedside clock. She couldn't have overslept, surely. Maybe she was hearing things, nobody could possibly be calling at this hour. She was about to drift off again when she heard it once more. Definitely this time, and whoever it was just kept their finger on the bell push. Oh, for goodness sake, some people had no consideration. They'd wake J-J as well in a minute and that was the last thing she needed, she already had a headache.

She stumbled out of bed and into her slippers, dragging on her dressing gown as she hurried down the stairs. 'Okay, okay, I'm coming,' she muttered crossly, under her breath. 'Saints preserve us, it's enough to wake the living dead!'

She slid back the bolts and chain and unlocked the front door to be confronted by what indeed did look like one of the living dead. Enraged version.

'What the …?' exclaimed Chloe, in total shock, as Kate stormed past her into the lounge.

Chloe closed the front door and followed her, in trepidation overdrive. It was obvious what this was about. She'd known all along that the truth would come out one day. And this was the day.

Kate stood in the lounge, back to the fireplace, arms folded, eyes blazing. Looking somewhat deranged. Not surprisingly.

She registered the panic on Chloe's face. If there had been even the remotest smidgen of a shadow of doubt before, it had now gone up in a puff of smoke, all flames extinguished.

'You know what this is about, I take it?'

'Have you …? Is it …?' stuttered Chloe.

'Don't insult me now by pretending you don't know why I'm here!'

'You've spoken to Tom, haven't you?'

'I speak to Tom all the time. He's my husband, in case you hadn't noticed.'

'I'm so sorry, Kate.'

'Sorry for what? You haven't told me what you've done yet.'

'I'm sorry for … what I did,' the words tiptoed from Chloe's mouth.

'And what is that exactly, my friend?' spat Kate. 'What exactly was it that you did?'

Chloe hung her head as she whispered, 'I slept with Tom.'

The words were barely audible, even to herself. In contrast, her shame echoed around the room almost deafening her with its intensity. She stared at the pile of the carpet, willing it to suck her in, like a vacuum cleaner in reverse.

'I can't hear you!' stormed Kate.

Chloe dragged her eyes up from the ground and forced them to look directly into those of her friend; although the blaze from Kate's eyes which met her own was like a wall of fire, the intensity repelling her action in an instant.

'I know it's about the worst and most incredibly dreadful thing I could ever have done to you but, yes, I am utterly ashamed to say … I slept with Tom.' The last four words caught in her throat and then fell out suddenly, with a splat.

'And, remind me again, who is Tom?'

'Don't, Kate. Don't.'

'Say it!'

'Tom is your husband. I know. I couldn't feel any worse if I tried,' she sobbed.

Kate felt her legs were about to give way and moved unsteadily towards the sofa, her breath coming in rapid little bursts, her heart racing, the sound whirring in her ears as she sank down upon it.

Chloe moved towards her, somewhat hesitantly, but concerned. 'Are you okay?'

'As if you care,' she responded, trying desperately to hold herself together.

'Of course I care, you're my friend.'

'Huh.'

'I'll go and make us a drink, you look as though you could do with one.'

'If you think drinking bloody tea is going to solve this you're mistaken,' gasped Kate.

'Nevertheless …'

Kate actually welcomed the moment – not only to be able to calm herself a little, but also to gather her thoughts. She sat bolt upright, rigid, trying to take deep breaths, breathe slowly. This would be such an inopportune moment for a full-blown panic attack. Gradually, very gradually, the panic subsided and she began to regain control of her body.

Stay calm. Stay calm. She had to stay calm to work out what she was going to do, where she was going to go from here. For how could she possibly stay with Tom now, knowing what she did? And how could she remain friends with Chloe? It was impossible.

This time last week she'd had a baby growing inside her, a husband and a best friend. Now she had nothing. There was only one thing she could do.

She considered just doing a runner while Chloe was in the kitchen. The truth was out now and it would prevent her running the risk of another panic attack. But there was so much anger burning up inside her, anger that had to be vented or she'd explode. Washing over the surface with a cup of bloody tea was out of the question. What was Chloe thinking of? Anyway, even tea makes stains that don't wash out. In Kate's mind, Chloe's character was stained forever.

Chloe glanced up from her task, startled, although unjustifiably so, to see the hatred on Kate's face as she loomed, threateningly, in the kitchen doorway.

'Nearly ready,' twittered Chloe.

'Forget it! Tea's the last thing on my mind. My life's in crisis, thanks to you, and all you can think of is making tea!'

'But you'll feel better for …'

'For God's sake!'

'Okay.' Maybe it was best she gave up.

'Why did you do it?' asked Kate, relatively calmly.

'We only did it once, Kate.'

'Oh, so you think that's okay, then? Why did you do it?'

It was Chloe's turn to crumple now. 'We had a drink,' she sobbed. 'We were both lonely, he made me feel good about myself, and …'

'And what? Tell me!' Kate insisted, becoming increasingly frustrated and angry.

'And I … I fell in love with him,' Chloe blurted out, in a sudden outpouring of emotion.

The statement hit Kate like a boxer punching below the belt. The air shot from her lungs in a whoosh of disbelief, leaving her mouth agape.

'You *what*?'

'I know what you must be thinking. I know. I'm disgusted with myself. I should never have let it happen. I am a total bitch. *Nobody* does that to their best friend. But we never let it go any further, Kate. It never happened again. Tom loves you,' she sobbed, still desperate, despite what she'd just admitted, to hang on to the last remnant of their friend-ship.

'Oh my God!' Kate felt, for a moment, that she'd been hit

right between the eyes with a stun gun. 'Oh my God!' she repeated. 'I thought you were going to say you fell into bed with him, but you fell in *love* with him!' her eyes and mouth rounded in shock. 'But how could that … how did that … Jesus! But you've known him for ages, how could you possibly just decide that? Or maybe it wasn't suddenly, maybe this has been going on for ages, the wife the last to know – that's the way it happens.'

'Stop Kate! Stop that!'

'Don't *you* have the audacity to tell me to stop *anything*!'

'Nothing was going on, you've got to believe me. It was just that one time. You were away, we were both lonely, no excuse I know, but yes, and I'm ashamed to say it, we ended up in bed together.'

'And?'

'And I really thought I loved him. He was kind, I was vulnerable, he made me feel good about myself. But he loves you, Kate, you've got to believe that.'

'So you thought you loved him. And do you still? Truth, Chloe,' she growled, 'you owe me that much.'

Chloe looked up, anguish pouring from her eyes. She knew this would cost her their friendship, but knew also that she could not lie. 'Yes,' she said softly. 'I do.'

Thwack-k-k! Straight across the face.

Chloe clutched at the stinging point of impact with both hands, afraid to utter even the tiniest 'ouch'. It hurt like hell, but she deserved it. The chasm between them had just got irretrievably deeper, their friendship falling into it with a resounding plop. Drowning.

'Chloe Russell, I never, ever want to lay eyes on you again. I trusted you, you were my friend, it turns out you're just a home-wrecking, husband-stealing low-life. Get out of my life and stay out!'

Kate stormed back into her own house like a bat out of hell.

Anger was growing bigger and bigger inside her, expanding, pushing against the boundary of her small frame, wanting to escape. Her face burned with the horror of it all, she felt quite literally as though she would explode.

Tom, now fully dressed, looked up anxiously as she entered.

'Kate, I …'

'Where's Jess?' she barked

'At school. It's half-past nine almost, I thought I should take her. I'm meant to be at work.'

'Work? How can you sit there and talk about work with all this going on?'

'Life goes on, Kate. I rang and said I'd be in late. We have to talk about this, that's why I waited.'

'Oh, very good of you,' she said sarcastically.

Steam actually appeared to pour from her ears. Did he seriously expect them to be able to sit down together and sort this out? Her husband and her best friend? Was he expecting forgiveness? A reconciliation? She bounded up the stairs intent on her course of action, for as far as she could see, it was the only option left to her.

'Where are you going?' Tom yelled after the retreating figure.

'Cornwall.'

'*What?*' his stunned response reverberated throughout the house as he leapt up the stairs two at a time, to find her dragging her suitcase out from beneath the bed.

'What are you doing?'

'What does it look like? I'm leaving you.'

'But you can't go, I love you, I …'

'What a pity you didn't think of that before you started sweet-talking my best friend into bed with you,' she retorted, throwing random items haphazardly into the suitcase, her mind totally unfocused on the job in hand.

'I love you. Please …'

'Too late, Tom Darrington. I'm going to Cornwall to stay with my mum. Just let me think, please. I need to sort out train times, everything.' She was trying to stay calm, her head was in a whirl.

He tried to step back. Maybe if he just gave her some space. But he was unable to contain his anxiety. 'How long are you going for?'

'For ever Tom. This is it. Finito.'

'But you can't, you can't. I love you. What about Jess? We're a family.'

'Were, Tom, were. Jess is coming with me.'

The train journey to Cornwall was the most harrowing of Kate's life. It felt almost as though she was having an out-of-body experience, looking down from above on another life. It couldn't possibly be hers – could it? It all seemed totally surreal. Was it the voice of an angel she could hear in the distance? A hand on her arm, tugging at her sleeve, pulling her towards …

'Mummy!' It was Jess. 'Wake up!'

'Sorry darling, I wasn't asleep – not really.'

'I wish Daddy was here.'

'I know you do, angel, but you're going to love being at the seaside, playing on the beach, staying with Grandma and Grandad, you'll have a great time,' Kate said, fake smile plastered on so thickly that it was already starting to crumble.

'Will Daddy come to stay with us?'

'I'm sure you'll see him very soon, Jess,' responded Kate, eyes welling at the thought of the sadness they'd heaped up on their beautiful little daughter, the distress Tom and Chloe had heaped upon her.

Oh my God, how could she put their names together in the same sentence, as if they were some kind of couple? She choked back a sob, absorbing its attempts to escape from her throat. Couple? They probably were by now. She'd given them carte blanche – again. Chloe would be round there sympathising, doing everything in her power to make him feel better, a seductive temptress reeling him in. The sob regurgitated and burst forth in half-strangled form. Jessica, who was snuggled into her, glanced up questioningly.

'Sorry darling. I've got a bit of a tickle in my throat. Let's cuddle up and try and have a nap, we've still got a long journey ahead of us.'

Reassured, Jessica lay back down, safely cocooned in the warmth of her mother's love. Kate stroked her blonde curls, trying to draw a modicum of comfort from the action for herself, but feeling utterly miserable. For seeing the innocence of her sleeping child only served to reinforce the magnitude of the situation. Not only had she lost her marriage, the love of her life, and her best friend, but she'd become a single-parent family. This sweetest little daughter that anyone could possibly ever have wished for had suddenly been plunged into the status of being the product of a broken home. Broken indeed, as was Kate's heart, but that final thought had just made it shatter into a million pieces more.

As the train tore along the track, it quite literally tore Kate and Tom apart too, the distance between them, in every sense, growing greater and greater by the minute. It had been the last thing in the world Kate had ever wanted to happen – but what choice did she have? A one-way ticket to take her away from the love of her life. Destination unknown, with a broken heart and a child.

Tom, meanwhile, was a broken man with no one to blame but himself. He'd battled with temptation and lost. Battled? Maybe not. But he was a man, brain in his pants. Starved of sex for so long, needs unfulfilled. No excuse at all, he realised that, but Chloe had been there, so soft and warm and gentle, and as much in need of love as he had been.

The problem was, though, that this was meant to have been a one-off occasion, a moment of sexual relief for both of them, callous as that may sound ... but things never work out to plan. For, despite their intention, feelings had slithered in, feelings of love as well as lust and desire. They'd kept it under wraps, struggled to keep their feelings to themselves and never gave way to temptation ever again. But it was hard, very hard. And Tom was disgusted with himself for ever having crossed the line.

How could he possibly have thought he was in love with two women? Chloe was sweet, she was kind and she was caring, the ideal woman in many ways. But Kate? She was his life-blood, the air that he breathed, the frame that held him together. Without her he was nothing, a speck of dust on the ground. He curled himself up into a ball of self-loathing on the bed where he lay. The bed, their bed – or had been. A black cloud of depression hovered over him, then descended, blocking out all sound with its gloom.

Blocking out all sound of the phone. And Chloe. For what else could she do? She'd resisted the impulse for what seemed like hours and she needed to know what was happening. They couldn't just abandon her, both of them, despite what she'd done. Her only crime had been to fall in love. Wrong. Okay, worse than that: to fall in love with her best friend's husband. Not an 'only' crime that one.

But, despite ringing repeatedly, no one ever answered. What was happening? She was desperate to know. Had Tom gone to work as if it was a normal day? Had they had a reconciliation and laid all the blame on her? Had Kate gone off and left him like she had before?

Chloe, Chloe, Chloe, you really should not be thinking those thoughts. Yes, but if she had, then Tom would need … No! Don't even go there. The demons in her head persisted however, as did the ringing of Tom's phone, the sounds of which finally penetrated the black cloud of gloom. It could be Kate … Wrong.

'Tom! I was worried. What's happening?'

He found it hard to form the words, so painful were they. 'She's gone.'

Despite herself, Chloe couldn't help the little frisson of excitement that momentarily tingled right to the very roots of her hair. 'Gone where?'

'Cornwall. Taken Jess.'

'Oh Tom, I'm so sorry, it's all my fault.'

'Both to blame.' Stringing words together was an almost impossible task.

'Would you like me to come over? I could get someone to look after J-J.'

'No!' A most definite 'no', in fact the most enthusiasm he'd injected into anything all day.

Chloe put down her phone. Dejected. Rejected. What more could she expect? Time to face facts. Kate was the love of Tom's life and now, thanks to her, their marriage had been blown apart. Tom would never want her again, he'd just live in hope that Kate would come back to him and wouldn't want anything to stand in the way – especially her.

So what was left for Chloe now?

A little man toddled round the door, runny-nosed, his face enough to melt a thousand hearts.

'Okay, enough,' said Chloe, scooping him up into her arms. 'Let's go and sort you out, it smells as though you need it.'

'Poo,' said J-J, holding his nose and smiling at his mum with adoration.

'Yes, poo!' she said, kissing the top of his head.

For, as distraught as she felt, Chloe was the kind of person who needed to be needed, and nobody needed her right now more than her precious little boy.

7

Amazing though it seems to anyone in the middle of a crisis, life does go on. It has to. To the person, or people, in the midst of the crisis it can often seem heartless, or even cruel, that others are getting on with their lives, enjoying themselves, and the world is still turning. But eventually, astonishingly, feelings become less raw, and we get sucked back onto the bandwagon of life. We return to where we got off, maybe heading in a slightly different direction because of the experience, but returning nevertheless.

And that's exactly what happened to Tom and Kate, and to Chloe too.

It was Kate, of course, who experienced the biggest change of all. For not only had she lost her husband and her best friend, but she'd also forfeited her home and the stability her marriage had brought to her, albeit ringed with a flimsiness she hadn't known existed. But now she was a single mum who had to support herself and her child. To the casual observer, it's fair to say that she was luckier than most. However, had anyone actually had the audacity to say that directly to Kate's face it is probably very unlikely that they would have walked away still in possession of their front teeth. Kate had been wronged, and was smarting from that knowledge, her sensitivity laid bare.

Kate's parents, despite their sadness at her distress, were obviously delighted to have her back within the bosom of their family, Jessica too. Because of the miles between them, hitherto they felt they'd missed out on a big chunk of grandparenthood and now was an opportune time to make up for it. They were not short of money and absolutely refused to let Kate pay any kind of rent for staying with them. It was their pleasure to have her and Jess, their home was big enough and there was plenty of room for everyone. The rambling old house was where they'd lived for all of their married lives. Jessica was fascinated by the coal fire and the cooking range, by the loud echoing tick of the grandfather clock, and even more so by the attic up the stairs where she was allowed to go and play sometimes.

Kate felt guilty nevertheless. She didn't want them to think she was taking advantage, despite their reassurance that she was not. She busied herself around the house and garden and contributed to household expenses as much as she possibly could. Tom was more than generous when it came to sending money to her. 'Guilt money!' she would exclaim. Their house in Cheshire would have to be sold and the proceeds divided at some point, although neither seemed in any hurry to do so. Somehow it would have 'end of an era' stamped all over it. Somehow, strangely, they clung on.

What worried Kate's mum most of all was the dead look she saw in her daughter's eyes. She could be playing with Jessica, laughing and joking, but always her eyes were dead, the sparkle gone. It worried her because of the last time Kate had stayed here after Jake's death, the time when Kate had tried to take her own life. Kate tried to reassure her that she would never, ever do anything like that again, but she wasn't wholly convinced. And so her mother came to the rescue, as mothers often do.

'Why don't you rent a studio?'

'What?'

'Go back to your artwork. We're here to help with Jess, there's nothing to stop you.'

'Um, money?' queried Kate, the first glimmer of hope

and excitement to be seen flickering across her face in weeks.

'Oh, stop that! You know we'll help, Tom as well. Anything to put a smile back on your face.'

'But I'm not very good.'

'Kate! You know you are – don't put yourself down. You'll be raking it in shortly.'

'Ha ha!' But at least she was smiling.

And so life progressed for Kate. Jess started at her new school and Kate found herself a studio. It was small, but it was light, it was bright, and if she stood on absolute tiptoe and craned her neck at an angle of 45 degrees she could even see the sea! Life took on a whole new meaning. She enjoyed immersing herself in her art again and even, on the odd occasion, managed to sell something. It never ceased to amaze her that someone would actually want to pay money for one of her paintings, although admittedly, her confidence did creep cautiously up a notch each time that happened.

There was quite a community of artists in the area and, despite her lack of confidence, Kate succeeded in integrating herself well. She needed their feedback, needed them to bounce her ideas off when she was unsure. But most of all she needed friendship to replace that which she'd lost.

But then, as if by fate almost, she was guided to Grace. The saving grace; she really was. They'd been drawn together almost like two sides of a coin, their only regret being that they hadn't met earlier. What a strange coincidence it had been to discover that Grace lived in Cheshire, only a short distance from where she herself had lived, with … with … Anyway, despite the miles between them, their friendship had blossomed and they were in touch constantly; it was almost as though they'd been brought together for a reason. They enriched each others' lives and now neither could imagine their life without the other in it. A rare friendship indeed and one that was paramount to Kate's happiness and stability at this point in her life, where she had been so filled with anxiety and insecurity, uprooted from all she'd known.

But Tom had no one. Like many men, he didn't really have friends as such. His life had simply revolved around Kate and Jess; any social life they'd had consisted of things organised by Kate, and he'd just gone along with it. He'd not really been interested in other people invading their little world, he'd been happiest when it had just been the three of them.

Uh-h-h! So what went wrong? Just how stupid had he been? Shame washed over him in bucket-loads. What an idiot!

Chloe had rung lots of times to check he was okay. One word from him and she would have been there, on the doorstep. Temptation was there but, whatever happened, whatever the future held, he knew he could never, ever go back down that route again. It had caused so much pain.

And so all he had left was work. He sank himself into it in an attempt to block out all else. He had never been so grateful for his job and nor had the company ever been so appreciative of him. Without the distractions of family life, or any life at all in fact, he worked solidly, all hours, his greatest sense of achievement coming from the amount of money he was able to send to support his beloved Kate and Jessica. She called it 'guilt money', and indeed it was.

Immersed in his job, it was amazing how quickly the year had actually passed for Tom. In a way it seemed like only yesterday that he'd held Kate in his arms and yet it had been a whole year ago. She was still the absolute focus of his being and he lived in constant hope, fragile though it was, that one day she would come back to him. And so he went through the daily motions of life, stepping on the treadmill of work each morning, afraid to get off in case his emotions overwhelmed him, and finally falling into a drug-induced sleep late at night. It was no way to live, but he felt he deserved his punishment.

His only glimmer of light relief in all of this gloomy cycle came on alternate weekends, when he would drive on that long journey south to spend precious time with his beloved Jessica. She was his angel, the light of his life. He would book into a hotel on the Friday night and Kate's mum or dad would bring Jess over on the Saturday morning to spend two days with him. He so desperately hoped that one of these Saturdays it would be Kate who brought her. But Kate was adamant, she did not want to see him at all and, if he had a problem with that, then he wouldn't get to see Jessica either. Okay, so he had rights, but he didn't want to antagonise her. After all, he lived in cloud-cuckoo-land. He still had hopes, vague though they may be. Desires too, obviously a little bit more pressing.

For Chloe also, life carried on. Not as she would have wished, of course; Tom made that perfectly clear. There was only one woman for him, and that woman was Kate despite her absence. So Chloe did what she did best, devoted her-self to her family. J-J, of course, took up most of her time. He was a cheeky little chappy, a mischievous bundle of fun – a real handful, so reminiscent of his big brother, Ben, when he'd been that age. They all absolutely doted on him and Chloe now had all the time in the world to lavish him with her love and attention.

Olivia, Chloe's daughter, lived in Manchester with her partner Stelios, but they often came to stay at the weekends or Chloe would drive up with J-J to visit them. Ben and Caroline, on the other hand, only lived down the road and popped in and out to see Chloe all the time. Sandra, Caroline's mum, would also call round sometimes and had become a bit of a Kate replacement in a way. Chloe never felt as close to her as she had to Kate, but it was good to have someone to talk to.

Chloe of course had had to explain to them all initially about Kate's hasty departure, a daunting task which she had dreaded, unsure of their reaction. Kate had been like a second mum almost to Ben and Olivia; she knew that what she'd done was absolutely despicable, but she couldn't bear it if her children were to despise her for it. However, how could they despise her? She was their mum. They reassured her instead. In fact they'd had their suspicions before, both of them, so the news didn't come as a total shock. Nevertheless, suspicions and reality are far apart, and hearing the truth did take them aback, albeit briefly.

'God, you're a dark horse, Mother. You're even worse than I used to be,' said Ben, in a light-hearted attempt to fill the chasm of silence created by the confession.

'Ben, you dork! Can't you see Mum feels bad enough?' retorted Olivia, reaching out for her mum's hand and grasping it sympathetically within her own.

'Sorr-eee! Keep your hair on sis, only a joke.'

'Well not funny, Ben, not everyone's like you.'

'Like I was you mean, I'm a married man now,' he said, gazing adoringly at Caroline, like some sort of love-sick puppy which didn't realise it was digging an even deeper hole with its two front paws.

'Ben!'

'Oh stop it, you two! I know I've done wrong, no need to pussyfoot around me. I've wrecked my best friend's marriage, I couldn't feel any worse if I tried.'

Olivia threw her arms around her mum and gave her a hug. 'We all make mistakes, Mum, we wouldn't be human if we didn't. You know I'll always love you, no matter what,' she said, whilst simultaneously indicating to Ben, with her eyes, that he should say something and give his mum a hug too.

To no avail. Boys, they can be so thick.

'Ben!'

'What? Why are you twitching your head like that? Is there something wrong with your neck?'

'Mum!' Olivia hissed back at him, eyes bulging with frustration. However had she managed to live with him for all those years? 'Speak to her,' she muttered under her breath.

'Well I know it's, Mum, stupid! What d'you want me to say?'

Grrrr … brothers!

'Only messin'',' grinned Ben, roguishly. 'You know we love ya really, Ma,' he said coming over to give her a hug. 'Don't start blubbing on my T-shirt, though, I only got it yesterday and it cost me a fortune!'

Where does time go? It really doesn't make a difference whether we're happy or sad, time has a habit of marching on at speed. With the blink of an eye, it's gone. And that's how it was for all three of them – Kate, Tom and Chloe. A whole year passed by, it hardly seemed possible.

J-J was nearly two now, a lot more adventurous, and getting chattier by the minute. His mum was the centre of his universe, understandably. There was no one else, and he sought her approval for his every move. Most of the time, anyway; although sometimes he could be a little bit too adventurous for his own good.

Chloe absolutely doted on him. J-J was her world, she was with him constantly. Most of the time that suited her perfectly – she wanted to be the one who was there when he took his first steps, spoke his first words and reached all his other milestones, she wanted to be there to teach him and watch him grow as he achieved new things. It was the most important job in the world and she did not want to miss one little bit of it. She wanted him to be able to look back when he was older and remember how she'd always been there for him, there to care for him and teach him, and ensure that he grew up to be a good person who knew right from wrong. That was how she'd brought up Ben and Olivia and, although she said it herself, she'd done a pretty good job. And now she was doing the same all over again with J-J, and with the added ingredients of maturity and experience, she'd hopefully be able to do an even better job this time around. And most of the time she enjoyed it.

But today, well, she'd just had one of those days. J-J had woken up far too early for one thing and, try as she might, she could not get him to go back to sleep. Finally she'd given in; with a longer day ahead she might actually manage to get some jobs done. So down the stairs they came, dirty washing in tow, J-J excited as always at the prospect of being able to put it into the washing machine – it was his favourite job.

'Dat?' he pointed excitedly.

'Washing machine. Just a minute,' she said gathering the laundry together.

'Dat?'

'Yes, it's the washing machine.'

'Dat?'

'Washing machine. Put it all in for me now then please.'

His butter-wouldn't-melt face was wreathed in smiles as he tottered over on his little chubby legs and painstakingly stuffed all the laundry in through the machine's open door before closing it firmly with a bang, laughing as Chloe pretended to jump with fright at the sound it made.

'Thank you,' she said laughing too. 'You are a good boy. Now let Mummy switch it on and then we'll have breakfast.'

However that became the second thing to go wrong that day, for try as she might, it would not work

'Dat?' pointed J-J, worriedly.

'Washing machine, yes, and I think it's broken. Never

mind, we'll get breakfast and then I'll ring the repair man.'

'Man!'

'Man, yes! Clever boy,' she said, hugging him as she lifted him into his high chair, and got his Weetabix.

But then as always at an inappropriate moment the phone rang. Mid-Weetabix actually. As Chloe got up to answer it, J-J produced an overly enthusiastic 'Dat?' and the contents of the bowl somehow landed on both himself and the floor.

'Oh J-J!' she uttered, maybe a little too brusquely, resulting in not only a missed phone call and a splattered child and floor, but in a sobbing J-J too. For not only had he lost his breakfast and got soaking wet, but his mummy had shouted at him.

Consoled somewhat as she lifted him out of his chair and hugged him to her, transferring some of the Weetabix onto her clean T-shirt in the process, his tear-stained faced peered over her shoulder and with admittedly less enthusiasm than usual he uttered that immortal word. 'Dat?'

'Oh J-J, yes, it's the washing machine.' Keep calm, Chloe.

Tranquility restored, and child, floor and self wiped up to adequacy if not to perfection, she continued with the day – hoping for peace, preferably: she already had the first twinges of a headache. J-J, however, had other ideas, He'd been up early and was starting to get grumpy, as he was tired. It seemed a bit soon to take him up for a nap just yet so she decided to take him out for a bit of fresh air, have a play in the garden while the sun was still out.

It was a bad move. Things seemed to go from bad to worse and Chloe's patience was starting to wear thin. Every grizzle from J-J made her head pound a little more. She had to get away from him just for a minute, even a second, give herself some breathing space. Miraculously, J-J was suddenly distracted by the daisies; there were lots of them, the grass hadn't been cut for ages.

'Dat?' he asked, wide-eyed.

'Daisy.'

'Dat?' he asked, pointing to another.

'Daisy. Why don't you pick some for Mummy?'

He bent down and plucked one, holding it towards her, triumphantly.

'Good boy! Pick some more. Look,' she said, picking up his toy truck and putting it next to him, 'you could put them in there as you pick them.'

J-J carried on with his task, engrossed. Chloe, however, still felt an urgent need for sixty seconds of solitude.

'J-J, pick lots of nice daisies for Mummy and put them in the truck then, that's a good boy. I'm just going into the house, I'll only be a minute.'

Phew! Sometimes just one moment of solitude was bliss. She absolutely loved J-J to bits, but sometimes he could be exhausting. She supposed it was harder being a single parent, no one to talk to, no one to share things with. In fact, sometimes she could go for several days without an adult conversation – 'This little Piggy,' 'Incey Wincey Spider' and 'Dat?' conversations seemed to fill her days. Not only that, but her TV viewing consisted of *In the Night Garden* and *Waybuloo*. No wonder she felt as though her brain was about to explode.

But J-J was worth it, she wouldn't have it any other way. She glanced out through the kitchen window to where she could see him, bottom in the air, concentrating on the daisies that were growing in the grass around his feet. A wave of love for him washed over her and her heart melted. How could she ever feel cross or bored when she had the most beautiful little boy in the world? He was so scrumptious she could eat him. She vowed never to complain again.

Ouch! The headache hadn't gone though. Perhaps she should take a couple of paracetamols before going back out to join him. She checked through the window, J-J was fine, she ran quickly upstairs to get them from the medicine cabinet. She always kept all tablets locked safely away, never wanting to put J-J at risk. There was a glass of water still by the side of her bed from last night, so she drank from that to swallow them and then locked the remaining ones in the packet safely away again. She was feeling remarkably better already, actually, those few luxurious minutes of peace and quiet had done her the world of good.

She sauntered back down the stairs, trying to hang on to this freshly acquired relaxed mode. The sun was streaming in through the stairs window now, highlighting her lack of efficiency in the domestic goddess department. But what the heck, having fun in the sun with the best little boy in the world was much more important.

She ran out of the back door, a new-found spring in her step. They could play in the sandpit, bring out some water, mix it with his toy cement mixer and spread it on the path. He'd love that. Messy play, nothing like it.

'J-J?' Her eyes scanned the garden, disbelieving at first.

'J-J?' Her voice was raised, more panicky now.

The toy truck lay up-ended, the daisies scattered around it on the ground. Chloe rushed out through the garden gate which swung open on its hinges, fear crawling through her body, clawing at her throat, distorted images of cars and people flashed by but not the tiny little person she wanted to see. Not … The drumming of her heart blocked out every other sound, bar that of her own voice which she barely recognised as her scream echoed down the road.

'J-J!'

But J-J was gone.

8

To Chloe the next twenty-four hours were a complete blur. Police, questions. They were out there now searching, searching for her boy, her precious little boy. This felt like someone else's life, not hers. As if she was watching a play, almost, about somebody's missing child. But the truth was, as she watched the drama unfold, the story was about J-J. The missing child was her own.

But how could that be possible? She didn't understand. He'd been there, she'd seen him through the window. How could he have disappeared? The image of the upturned truck and the open gate haunted her. How could she just have left him? And just to get some paracetamol for a headache! A headache? A headache was nothing. In fact she'd have another right now, a million of them, if she could just get her J-J back.

She leaned forward in her chair, her head in her hands.

'Okay, love?' asked Sandra, Caroline's mum, moving across to sit on the chair arm next to her, and putting her arm comfortingly around Chloe's shoulders.

'Don't think I'll ever be okay again. How could I have done it, Sandra? How could I have left him – even for a minute?' sobbed Chloe.

'Oh, love, don't keep blaming yourself.'

'But it was my fault.'

'We all do what we do, do what seems the right thing at the time. No point in recriminations, love. You know you'd never have done anything but your very best for J-J, you're a great mum to him.'

'Not great enough, obviously.'

'Don't be daft, love. Even then you were doing your best for him, trying to get rid of your headache so you could look after him properly. It's hard bringing up a child on your own, nobody knows that better than me, and I think you're doing a brilliant job.'

But Chloe was not convinced. 'Why did I feel so frustrated though? Why did I feel I had to get away from him? I am such a bad mother, and now I might never see him again and that … that'll be the last memory he has of me, going into the house, leaving him out on his own.'

'Chloe, love, stop thinking like that, you're a wonderful mother! You've brought up a great little boy, and you've done it all by yourself, no help from anyone – and that's the hardest, and sometimes can be the most frustrating job in the world. As for J-J, they're all out there looking for him and he'll be back here saying "Dat?" before you know it.'

It was the 'Dat?' that did it. Sandra was in tears too. 'Gawd! I'm no help to you at all am I?' she said, blowing her nose loudly.

'You've been great, Sandra. Thanks for being here for me. I don't know what I'd have done without you.'

'Times like this I bet you really miss Kate, don't you? You two were so close.'

'I know. I do. Sorry, that sounds horrible when you've been so good to me.'

'No, I know how it was with you two. Good friends like that don't come along very often.'

'And I blew it.'

'Why don't you ring her? Tell her what's happened?'

'No. I couldn't.'

'Well at least you've got us, love. Not heard anything from Olivia, have you?'

'No. Didn't like to bother her. They're only on holiday for two weeks and I don't want to spoil it for her. I keep hoping ... well, you know ... that they'll find him, he'll come back.'

'I know, love. I know.'

'Ben's been great, Caroline too, but I really had to insist they both went to work today. You know what Ben's like, and I really felt I needed a bit of time on my own.'

'Oh sorry, I never thought! Would you like me to go?'

'No, no, sorry, that's not what I meant. It's just that, whatever the situation, Ben always thinks he has to be a comedian. I love him to bits, but he drives me nuts some-times!'

'He's a lovely lad,' smiled Sandra, 'and he makes my Caroline happy, so he's okay by me.'

'Besotted with each other, aren't they?' replied Chloe. 'Quite sickening really,' she said, her face breaking into the first smile it had registered in more than twenty-four hours.

'We're just jealous, love, that's what it is. Neither of us have done great in that department, have we! Anyway, while you're smiling, would you like me to leave you for a bit. Give you a bit of breathing space before Ben and Caroline get back?'

'At the risk of sounding anti-social, that would be great, if you wouldn't mind. They're threatening to stay over again tonight so it would be really good to have just a little bit of time on my own before they arrive.'

'That's fine by me. Let me know the minute you hear something. Hopefully, you'll soon have him back safe and sound.'

Even to Sandra herself, as she left, the words she spoke sounded empty. Chloe's heart did a double somersault. J-J was dead, she knew it. For how could he have survived all this time on his own? Was he on his own? Had he been snatched by a disgusting paedophile? Was his innocent little body being used by some monstrous sexual deviant? Bile rose up into her throat at the thought and, hand covering her mouth, she ran to the bathroom where the entire contents of her stomach landed in the toilet.

Oh my God! Is that what had happened? Or was he dead? Murdered? Suffering? Or drowning in the river?

They were all out there looking now. Looking for a body. She tried to calm herself. Maybe he'd just wandered off. He couldn't have been run over or they'd have heard. He could have just walked into someone's garden shed, been locked in, unknowingly. Or he could be hiding, too scared without his mummy. Without her. The mummy who'd abandoned him, who had not kept him safe like she'd always promised she would.

An eerie cry escaped her throat, as she clutched at it with her hands and threw back her head. 'Oh God, help me!' She couldn't do this alone. Her precious child had been snatched away and she needed to hold him in her arms. She hugged her arms around herself, rocking back and forth.

Sandra had been right, the one person she wished was here right now was Kate. Kate, more than anyone, would have some idea of what she was going through. Kate had lost a child herself, in different circumstances obviously, but she had lost a child nevertheless. She would understand what it felt like to have that precious little being you were responsible for snatched away, out of your grasp, taking your heart and soul with it.

Okay, what had she got to lose? She'd phone Kate. A bit of a random thing to do maybe, after all this time had lapsed, but apprehensive though she was, the desire to speak to and gain support from her long-lost friend suddenly became overwhelming.

'Kate?' said Chloe, her voice timid, her hand shaking as she held the phone to her ear.

'Who is this?'

She doesn't even recognise me! Chloe's miniscule amount of courage hot-footed it right out of the door. 'It's me, Chloe.'

'Oh my God! I thought I'd made it perfectly clear to you. I don't want to see you or hear from you ever again. You're out of my life – gone.'

'Kate, please listen …'

'Listen to *you* – huh! I don't think so, madam. Goodbye.'

Bang. The phone went dead.

But Chloe, amazingly, was not to be deterred.

'Didn't you just hear what I said?' said Kate, picking up the phone for the second time.

'Please hear me out, Kate. Something terrible has happened.'

'Well something terrible happened last year but it didn't seem to bother you then,' stormed Kate.

'Please listen to me, Kate,' said Chloe, her voice breaking now. 'J-J's missing.'

There was silence for a second or two.

'Missing? What do you mean missing?'

'Just that. He disappeared from the garden yesterday. The police are out looking for him now.' Chloe fought hard to hold back the tears.

Silence once more.

'Who's with you?'

'No one. Well, Ben and Caroline when they're not at work. Sandra sometimes. Olivia's away.'

'And Tom?' asked Kate, his name catching in her throat.

'Tom? I haven't seen him since you left.'

Chloe started to cry more openly now, she could hold back the tears no longer.

'Oh, Kate. It's been so awful.'

However, Kate's barriers were firmly in place. They'd had to be for her own self-preservation and it was hard to contemplate letting them down, even just one centimetre.

'I've got to think. I'll ring you back,' she said, her own head in a whirl too now.

Five days of gloom and utter despondency passed by in slow motion. Chloe felt as though she was sleepwalking almost … sleepwalking through a nightmare but afraid to come out the other side for what she might find. He was dead, she knew it, he had to be, for how could he have survived this long without her?

The only glimmer of light had finally come in the form of a phone call from Kate. Yes. Chloe had cried out with relief. Jess had just broken up from school for the summer and they had come up to stay with a friend nearby. The words were spoken frostily, but spoken nevertheless. Kate would come and see her. Tomorrow in fact.

9

They say that tomorrow is the first day of the rest of your life. The new day dawned. It was tomorrow. After a restless night Kate awoke, a feeling of dread in the pit of her stomach. Jessica, on the other hand, bounced around in the bedroom they were sharing, with excitement. She could hardly contain herself.

'Yippity, yippity, yip! I'm going to see Daddy today!'

'I know you are, darling,' said Kate, stretching, trying to motivate herself into some form of action, but loath to do so. Getting out of bed would mean she was taking a step forward, a step towards facing the day ahead, when she would much rather bury her head beneath the duvet and pretend that she didn't even exist. Why had she agreed to this?

Jess, meanwhile, was dancing around, looking as though she should be wearing a tutu rather than pyjamas, performing pirouettes in front of the wardrobe door.

'Are you excited?' Silly question, and one she didn't really want to ask. She didn't want her child excited at the prospect of seeing her father, she only wanted Jess to be happy when she was with her. But she was trying to be a good mother. Never slag off the absent parent in front of your child. All the childcare books were insistent on that.

'Yes!' panted Jess, her blonde curls corkscrewing like the rest of her.

'You'll make yourself dizzy,' warned Kate.

'Get up then, I can't wait any longer.'

A gentle tap on the bedroom door revealed Grace and Izzy, and Alfie the dog.

'Everyone alright in here?'

'We were,' mumbled Kate, as she was smothered with doggy licks and almost flattened by both Alfie and Izzy. 'I was just going for a shower, if that's okay?' she said, forcing her way out from beneath them.

'Come down for breakfast first, if you like,' said Grace. 'Kettle's on and Charlie's gone to work already. Shoo, you two,' she said to her offspring and pet, 'You come down with us too, Jessica, let's leave your mummy to get up in peace.'

It all seemed relatively normal, considering she was facing the day ahead with so much dread.

Oh well, she might as well get on with it. Kate reluctantly forced herself out of bed, dragged on her dressing gown and made her way downstairs.

'Sleep well?' asked Grace, maybe a little too cheerfully, as Kate came into the kitchen looking somewhat glum.

'No,' yawned Kate, as she sat down at the breakfast table.

'Mummy's going to see my Auntie Chloe today,' announced Jess to all and sundry.

'Who's your Auntie Chloe?' asked Izzy.

'She used to be my mummy's best friend but they fell out.'

'Thank you, Jess, that's quite enough,' said Kate, flashing her a silencing glance.

'Why did they fall out?' asked Izzy, in typical fashion.

'Izzy!' warned Grace. 'Get on with your breakfast.'

'But ...'

'No "buts".'

'Because your daddy', started Gran, who'd amazingly entered the kitchen without anyone even noticing, 'slept w...'

'Mother!'

Indeed! All eyes were upon her, transfixed in fact, as she stood in the doorway with her Zimmer frame. Upon her head was a large pink hairnet, slightly askew, which attempted to cover curlers of varying kinds. The gummy cave of her toothless mouth, still open, mid-speech, was outlined, or sort of, in the reddest lipstick known to womankind. Her captive audience remained spellbound as their eyes travelled down the entirety of this imposing, and yet sadly tragic figure. A force to be reckoned with and yet slipping into the unknown. A figure of fun, yet not really. But Grace had to laugh sometimes, it was the only thing that kept her sane.

And laugh she did, just a little bit, and the others tittered a bit too: who could not? For as their eyes moved downwards in disbelief, what did they see? The bra on the outside of her jumper was the least of it. Lower down she was completely starkers, naked as the day she was born, although somewhat more wrinkly of course. Somehow swags and tails sprang to mind. Well, not 'sprang' exactly, more like 'drooped'. Antique lady bits. Not a pretty sight.

'Yuk!' exclaimed Izzy.

'Mother!' exclaimed Grace.

'What?' asked Gran, who could not understand what they were staring at. It wasn't as though she'd forgotten to put on her bra, she remembered doing that distinctly, it had been a nightmare. She's had to bend right over and juggle them into the cups. You'd think they'd make it easier in this day and age, wouldn't you?

But no, she'd jiggled and jiggled until she was cross-eyed, almost. In fact she'd jiggled so much that one of her curlers had fallen in by mistake and she'd had to stop and retrieve it and start all over again. It reminded her a bit of going to the fairground, trying to throw a ping-pong ball into a goldfish bowl to win a fish. Perhaps she'd won one, she could smell something.

Anyway, all of that jiggling had set something else off. Jiggle-wiggle, jiggle-wiggle, she'd already been desperate before she'd started to get dressed, but one job at a time. She couldn't understand why her knickers had suddenly got so wet though. Maybe Alfie had sneaked in and cocked his leg up on them as she was otherwise engaged, bent over doing all of that jiggling. They'd certainly suddenly felt very warm, but that'd be the sun shining in on them, her bottom had been facing the window while she bent over. That'd explain the yellow stain on the carpet too: the sun's yellow isn't it? Hah! She was much cleverer than anyone gave her credit for.

'Lets wrap this around you,' said Grace, having quickly found a large towel to cover up her mother's nether regions.

'Get off!' said Gran, hitting out at her with her Zimmer frame. 'I'm not wearing a mini skirt! I don't want men chasing after me, looking at my legs!'

'Well it's better than what they could see before, Mother,' said Grace, holding the Zimmer frame down firmly, waiting patiently for her mother to cooperate.

'What could they see? Where are they?' said Gran, getting increasingly agitated.

'Nowhere, Mother. There aren't any men. Now let's go back to your room and sort you out and then we can all have a nice cup of tea,' said Grace, taking her mother firmly by the arm and guiding her in the right direction, towel thankfully in place.

Kate steeled herself as she reached Chloe's front door. It loomed in front of her like a barrier to her past life. By going through it she'd be lowering the barrier herself, letting feelings flood back in. But was that such a bad thing? For, despite putting distance between them, those feeling had never gone away. It was just the pain of facing up to

82

them that she couldn't cope with. Her hand hovered above the bell push. Butterflies flapped frantically inside her stomach. What was she doing here? Her finger tried to press the bell push but remained an inch away. Like an invisible force was trying to stop it. Like magnetism. But isn't that meant to draw you together? Poles apart. Obviously.

'Hi.'

The decision was taken out of her hands as the door swung open before her.

'Saw you coming down the path. Oh, Kate, thank you so much for coming. I can't tell you how much …' Chloe choked back her tears, wanting to give Kate a hug, sensing she shouldn't, remembering how they'd parted.

'It wasn't easy,' responded Kate, stepping in, feeling hesitant, unsure. Part of her wanted to hug too, give comfort, she above all knew what it was like to lose a child. But part of her, also, remembered the last time she was in this house, remembered Tom, remembered how they'd wrecked her life.

'Tea?' asked Chloe, feeling a bit pathetic but needing something to do to lighten the tension.

'Okay,' said Kate. She needed something to fill this chasm of uncertainty that was between them.

Kate sat down at the kitchen table. Quite like old times and yet most definitely not. 'Have you heard anything?'

'No.' Chloe was finding it hard to speak.

'Has it been seven days now?'

'Mm. A whole week.' Chloe brought the tea over to the table and sat down opposite. The strain on her face was heart-wrenching to see, even for Kate, who had declared animosity forever.

'He's dead, I know he is,' said Chloe.

'Don't give up hope,' said Kate, reaching out to cover Chloe's hand with her own, but hesitating, drawing back.

Chloe flinched. Would they ever be close again?

'But how could he have possibly survived? Seven whole days on his own?' Chloe's lips quivered as she fought to keep control.

'Perhaps he's not on his own,' said Kate, her voice soft and low as she clasped the hot mug between her hands to warm the chill which suddenly ran through her body.

'I know,' said Chloe, choking back the sob which threatened to engulf her. 'And that's possibly the worst thought of all.'

Kate put down her mug to wipe the tears from her own eyes, thinking of J-J, how he'd been when she'd last seen him, thinking of Jake, her own baby, who she'd lost three long years ago. And yet it only seemed like yesterday. Chloe glanced up at her, the awkwardness between them still tenable, but the tears resultant from this tragedy, hopefully diluting some of the hatred that simmered within.

'I knew you were the only one person who would understand,' said Chloe, looking directly at Kate.

But Kate lowered her eyes, stared down at the table, and held her head in her hands. As she did so her soggy balled-up tissue rolled from her sleeve and fell under the table with a silent plop.

'I've missed you,' ventured Chloe.

Sometimes silence can be almost deafening.

'I can't tell you how sorry I am for what happened, Kate.'

'Well, try,' came the muffled response.

'Okay, I know what I did was absolutely despicable. If I could turn back the clock and pretend it never happened, then obviously I would. I behaved like a total idiot and am utterly ashamed of myself, devastated by what I did to you. In my heart of hearts I think that's why I'm being punished now, that's why J-J has been taken away from me.' Chloe could hold back her tears no longer. 'What goes around comes around. Oh Kate, I'm so, so sorry.'

A timely interruption came in the form of the doorbell. Chloe tensed visibly. Her face blanched as she hurriedly brushed the tears from her eyes.

'They've found something! It's bad! I know it is!'

'I'll get it,' said Kate, the colour draining from her face also, as she almost tripped over the leg of her chair in her haste to answer the door, afraid of what may be revealed.

'Oh!' exclaimed Kate, somewhat taken aback.

'Who is it?' asked Chloe, hovering in the lounge, unable to move any further, fear paralysing her limbs. 'What's happening?' she shouted, heart attack imminent.

'It's okay, it's … it's Jackie.'

Chloe's brain was blank for a moment, unresponsive when trying to process this unexpected piece of infor-mation. It suddenly went into overdrive. 'Jackie as in …?'

'Apparently so,' said Kate, ushering her into the room.

'Oh my God!' said Chloe, a hundred and one thoughts now leaping through her head simultaneously.

'I'm sorry,' said Jackie, 'But I had to come, even though I'm probably the last person in the world you'd ever want to see.'

Jackie, the 'slapper', with whom Chloe's ex-husband John had been having an affair during their marriage. Jackie the 'slapper' with whom John now lived.

'You know something, don't you? You know something obviously or you wouldn't have come here!' Chloe sank onto the sofa, weak with fear, her legs no longer able to support her.

Uninvited, Jackie sat herself down in the empty armchair opposite Chloe. The tension was unbearable.

Kate sat down next to Chloe, whose need for a friend now surpassed all that had gone before. Kate squeezed Chloe's hand within her own and continued to hold on to it tightly, pledging her support.

'Tell me!' shrieked Chloe.

'As far as I know, J-J is quite safe. He's with John.'

'*John*!' interrupted Chloe. 'What the hell is John doing with my son?'

'Well, I'll tell you. But first I want you to know this is none of my doing. I knew absolutely nothing about it until today. John had no right at all to do what he did. I don't approve of it in the least and, I promise you, I will help you get J-J back. You're his mum, he belongs with you.'

'My baby! My baby!' Chloe leapt to her feet. 'You know where he is! Take me to him, I need my baby!' Tears of relief, frustration, everything simply poured down her face.

Gently Kate took her hand again and encouraged her to sit back down. 'Hear her out, Chloe, she's here to help you, just listen to what she's got to say.'

Consumed by emotion, Chloe grasped onto Kate's hand like a lifeline, and sank back down again.

'Oh my God,' she breathed, 'I just don't understand. Why would he want J-J now, suddenly? He's known of his existence for the two years of his life and he's never wanted to have anything to do with him before, shown no interest at all. Why now?'

'That's what I've come to explain. Just listen to me first and then I'll tell you how we can get him back.'

Chloe's tears dried up for the moment and, still clinging to Kate's hand, she sat forward on her seat, rigid with suspense, her whole being focused totally on the woman sat opposite, the woman she'd hitherto viewed with contempt, the woman who now brought her hope.

'The fact is, Chloe, and remember this is none of my doing, the fact is that I've never had children, never wanted them either until John came into my life. But then, I don't know whether it was the biological clock ticking away or what, but suddenly I developed this burning desire to have a baby.

'John, as you will know, can be a cantankerous old sod at

times but there's another side to him, and sometimes he can be a real softie. Once the idea had been sown, he became quite keen at the prospect himself. To be honest, I think in his head he thought it would show you that he was getting on with his life and couldn't give a damn about you. He's definitely got a chip on his shoulder, always got to make out to others that he's top dog, nobody's doing better than he is.

'Anyway we tried and tried for a baby but without success. Went to a fertility clinic, everything. To be honest, I've become much more relaxed about the whole thing now – if it happens, it happens but there's no point in making our lives a misery over it. But with John it was a different story. He can't be seen to be a failure – not ever. Not that he is, it's not his fault or mine, just one of those things. But that chip on his shoulder is a force to be reckoned with. Nobody is going to point a finger at him and say he can't father a child, say he is a failure, say he's not top dog: nobody! If we want a child, then a child we shall have!'

A groan of realisation escaped Chloe's lips. 'Oh God – J-J!'

'You see where I'm coming from? Our relationship became like a pressure cooker that had reached boiling point and was about to blow. I found it unbearable. What was the point? If two people love each other and want a baby then fair enough. But all this constant frenzied sexual behaviour, just to prove he was a man and could still father a child, was not what I'd wanted. In fact it was exhausting, it was painful, and it was … well, frightening, if I'm honest. Terrifying sometimes, in fact. There's a side to John that I didn't know existed. I don't know whether you do?'

'I do actually,' said Chloe, her voice lowered to almost a whisper, her eyes half-closed in remembrance. 'We were separated at the time J-J was conceived. John came back to the house and raped me. That's how I got pregnant.'

'Oh you poor thing, I'd no idea.'

'No, why should you?'

'Anyway, I need to finish telling you so we can do something about it. I know you're desperate to get your son but, believe me, he's quite safe with John for the moment. John's waiting to hear from me. In his own deluded way he thinks he's done a good job. He thinks we're going to be a family.

'To get back to what I was saying though, it was all getting too much for me. It couldn't go on, and last week I told him so. Well, I've seen him angry before but never like this, he went absolutely ballistic. That chip again of course. How could anybody ever doubt anything he did? He is the great "I am" and nobody, nobody tells him what to do, or what not to do … except me, on this occasion.

'He'd turned into someone I didn't know, someone I didn't want to know, and someone I definitely did not want to be with. I told him I was leaving, I'd had enough, I just couldn't take any more and he … he turned into some sort of thing possessed, like a wild animal almost, trapped in a corner, fighting with all that it has.'

Reliving the horror of it all became too much for Jackie, and she hung her head in silence for a moment or two, gathering her thoughts.

'Can I get you anything? A drink maybe?' asked Kate.

'No, ta. I'll be fine in a minute. It's just … Anyway, he hit me. More than that – punched. Several times. Clever though, not on my face. I always vowed I would never stay with a man who lay a finger on me, and I didn't. I left. There and then. Went to stay with a mate in Liverpool who's been through a similar thing, knows what it's like.'

Jackie was silent again, the magnitude of it all only just seeming to sink in. 'Actually, I will have that drink if it's not too much trouble.'

'But J-J!' burst forth Chloe, as Kate went to put the kettle on. 'We've no time for tea! We need to get him back now – anything could be happening!'

'Honestly,' said Jackie, 'John won't harm a hair on his head. He's taking good care of him. He thinks J-J is the answer to all his problems.'

'But we should tell the police,' said Kate, returning with the tea. 'They need to know.'

Jackie looked uncomfortable. 'I suppose you're right. It's just … it's just that despite what he's done, I really don't want John to get into serious trouble. He needs help, more than anything, for all this anger inside him.'

'He stole my son!'

'I know. I know he's done wrong. You see, I didn't know about any of this until today. I went off to Liverpool, like I said, never answered his calls, he didn't know where I was. But then today, well I was worried what was happening to him. My mate reckons I'm too soft, but there it is, can't help what I am, can I? But it's a good job I did answer his call today, wasn't it? Who knows what might have happened.'

'I'm going to phone the police,' said Kate. 'They …'

'No! Please don't! I worry about John, despite everything, despite what he's done.'

'They need to be told. We're withholding information otherwise. We'd be in trouble ourselves on top of everything else,' persisted Kate.

'No! I've got a plan. This way we know J-J will be brought back safely. If I ring John and tell him I'm back and I want us to be together, then he'll bring J-J to me, or arrange to meet me somewhere at least. That's what he's waiting for. He knows I'm coming back today, I told him so on the phone. He was excited, he thinks his plan's all coming together. I even told him I love him and can't wait for the three of us to be a family. Don't spoil it now. If you get the police involved at this stage, you know what John can be like – anything could happen.'

'She's got a point,' said Chloe, her voice strained, yet resolute.

Her son, so close and yet not quite within her grasp. It could so easily all go wrong. John was so unpredictable, if he had any suspicion that something underhand was going on, that the police were involved, that he'd been set up, there was absolutely no accounting for what he might do. He'd already proved himself capable of violence – what might he do to her poor innocent baby?

'J-J ...' she choked back a sob. 'We can't let anything go wrong now. I've come this close to getting him back when I thought I'd already lost him. Jackie's right, if John sees any suspicion of police he'd flip, he'd do something to J-J, I know he would.'

'What? So you think we should do this just by ourselves – you're mad, insane! The police have methods for dealing with situations like this. They know what they're doing, they'd make sure J-J was safe. We're just ... Well, we've no idea what we're getting ourselves into. Three women against a violent man with a baby in a hostage situation? Come on!'

'But Kate, he's my baby and I ...'

The loud ring of the phone interrupted proceedings. Whether it was to be a welcome interruption or otherwise, they were almost too afraid to find out. Kate obviously had to be the one to draw the short straw.

'Hello?'

'Hi. Um ... who is this?'

'Kate.'

'Kate! Oh yes, of course. Is Mum there? It's Ben.'

'Ben. Hi. Actually, can it wait? It's just that we're in the middle of something pretty important at the moment. Shall I tell her you'll see her later?'

'Erm, no. This *is* important. I need to speak to her now. Right now.'

Chloe took the receiver. 'Ben, I hope this isn't going to be another of your silly jokes to try and cheer me up again because I really am not in the mood right now.'

'Chill, Mum, I ...'

'Chill? Chill? Is that all you can say? How do you expect me to chill when my baby's missing and I might never see him again?'

'Shut up, Mum, you will see him again.'

'Don't tell me to shut up, Ben. Like I said, I'm really not in the mood. Go and torment someone else for a change!'

'Mum ...'

'Ben!'

'Will you listen to me? I've got J-J!'

'Wha-a-at?' Chloe's heart did a double somersault, but then hovered in mid-flight.

This had to be the most amazing phone call Chloe had ever taken in her life.

'Ben – you'd better not be joking, this is serious. How can you have J-J?'

'I am serious, Mum, I wouldn't joke about something like that. J-J's here at my house, sitting on Caroline's knee drinking a smoothie as we speak, a strawberry and banana one, his favourite!'

'Oh Ben,' cried Chloe, tears of relief flowing down her cheeks unchecked, 'I can hardly believe it! He's got J-J,' she said, turning to tell the others. 'But how?' she asked, still finding it hard to take in, the news almost rendering her incapable of speech. She wanted her baby back in her arms so desperately.

'There was a ring on the doorbell, I went to answer it, and there on the doorstep was J-J! Simple as.'

'On his own?'

'Yep. Nobody to be seen. J-J just said "Daddy gone", but then he toddled into the house like nothing was

91

any different and went straight to the fridge for a drink. Unbelievable!'

'Oh my God – I can hardly believe it!'

'Don't keep saying that, Mum! You better had believe it 'cos we'll be round there with him in no more than fifteen minutes!'

It was the most joyous, tear-jerking, mind-blowingly ecstatic reunion in the history of mankind. Chloe cuddled and squeezed and cuddled and squeezed, and hugged and hugged and hugged, thinking she could never bear to be parted from him again – not even by going into the next room. But J-J had other ideas, as he toddled off to the kitchen to familiarise himself again.

'Dat?' he asked innocently, guaranteeing not a dry eye in the house.

'Washing machine. Good boy,' said Ben, brushing back a tear.

Caroline put an arm around her man. 'I love you,' she whispered.

'What, even though I'm a wuss?' asked Ben, trying hard to stave off an unexpected sudden flow now.

'Especially because, Ben Russell,' she said.

'We should ring the police, let them know he's safe,' said Chloe, hardly able to take her eyes off her precious little boy.

'I've done it,' said Kate.

Jackie flinched, 'Did you mention John? What did they say?'

'Sorry, but I had to. They'll not do anything tonight now, but they're going to come over in the morning to talk to Chloe. Sorry, Jackie.'

'It's okay, I know. I can't protect him, and I shouldn't even want to after what he did to me.'

'You could press charges yourself, you know.'

'I know. But I won't. I could never go back to him though, I could never trust him again.'

Chloe felt a sudden rush of protectiveness towards this woman, for all she'd gone through and for how she'd tried to help her to get her son back.

'What will you do?'

'Go back to Liverpool, I guess. Start a new life there.'

'Not tonight, surely, it'll be late by the time you get a train back to Liverpool.'

'I could stay at the house tonight, I suppose.'

'No!' butted in Chloe. 'It's not safe. We don't know where John is, or what he's capable of. Stay here tonight, there's plenty of room, and the police will probably want to talk to you tomorrow anyway.'

'We're staying too,' said Ben, amazingly masterful for once in his life. 'You'll need someone to protect you if Dad decides to make a return visit.'

'Oh my God,' said Kate, suddenly realising the time. 'I need to call a taxi. Grace will think I've abandoned her completely ... abandoned Jessica, more to the point.'

10

'I'm so, so sorry!' apologised Kate, as Grace opened the front door to let her in. 'You wouldn't believe what a day I've had!' she said, hugging her tightly, relieved to be back in a house that seemed so tranquil after the one she'd just left.

'Are you okay? We were worried about you. We tried your mobile but there was no answer.'

'Oh Grace, I really am so sorry. I ran out of battery and it had gone completely out of my head, I should have phoned you from Chloe's. Is Jess okay? Is she in bed? I'll go up and see her,' she said, heading towards the staircase, overflowing with 'bad mother' guilt.

'Hang on,' intercepted Grace. 'She …'

'Oh my God!' panicked Kate, head thrown into turmoil – anything was possible after the scenario she'd just witnessed. 'Has something happened to Jess? Where is she? What's …?'

'Calm down! Nothing's happened to her. She's stayed overnight with her dad at his house, that's all. I hope that's okay. I tried to ring you but …'

'My phone didn't have any battery. Grrr, I'm such an idiot! Trust *him* to make the most of the situation.'

'Kettle's on. Cuppa?'

'Would love one. Where's Charlie?'

'Bed. He went up ages ago. Think it was just an excuse to go up and watch the football on the other telly, actually.'

'Don't knock it, you've got a good man there.'

'I know. And, incidentally, I'm liking the look of Tom,'

said Grace, her face lighting up mischievously.

'Hmm. Women do, that's the problem.'

'Stop it – you know I'm only teasing.'

'I know. It's been a long day. I take it you saw him when you took Jess over?'

'Well of course I did, I couldn't just leave her on the doorstep, could I?'

Kate gave a sudden involuntary shiver, as though someone had walked over her grave. Déjà vu. She hoped they'd all be okay in Chloe's house tonight. Surely John wouldn't … would he?

Would he or wouldn't he? At Chloe's house they were wondering that too, and with good reason. They'd been fine, happy to have J-J home, unable to take their eyes off him almost, for fear that he might disappear again. J-J was loving it, loving all the attention, playing up to his audience. Even Jackie seemed smitten with him, and remarkably, J-J seemed to have been left totally unscathed by the incident.

'Well at least your dad seems to have taken good care of him,' said Caroline. 'But then, I suppose he is his dad, and he has brought up kids before.'

Understandably overly sensitive on the subject, Chloe leapt in with both feet. 'I think you'll find, if you talk to Ben, that his dad had absolutely no experience of bringing up children, that was down to me, and me alone. As for being J-J's dad – where has he been for the last two years?'

'Sorry,' said Caroline, smarting from the sting of her mother-in-law's tongue, 'I just meant that …'

'It's okay, babe,' said Ben, 'we know what you meant. But it's true, Dad was never around for Olivia and me, it was always Mum who had to do everything.'

'Well she did a pretty good job,' said Caroline, looking at him with adoration. 'I only hope I'll be as good a mum as your mum is to both of you.'

Harmony was restored, but all eyes rounded on the speaker, Ben's wider than most.

'You're not up the duff are you?'

'Oh, no,' she said, flustered. 'I just meant one day ... one day, that's all.'

'Phew!' said Ben, feeling he'd had a lucky escape. Sprogs were okay in small doses, kept you entertained and that, gave you a laugh. But having your own? No way! Just imagine having one throwing up on your Armani T-shirt, getting its sticky fingers all over your stuff ... nappies, snotty noses, no more going out, no sleep ... Ugghh, it didn't bear thinking about.

'You okay, babe?' asked Caroline.

'Sure am,' he said, with a sigh of relief.

Chloe made a move to take J-J up to bed. It was way past his bedtime but routines were of no importance whatsoever today, as long as he was home and safe that was all that mattered.

'Kiss everyone night-night then,' she instructed.

Loving all the attention, J-J kissed each one in turn, lingering the longest with his big brother and rubbing noses, it was his favourite trick.

'Eww, J-J!' Ben exclaimed, 'You've rubbed snot all over me! That's disgusting!'

'Ben! He's only a baby,' remonstrated Caroline. 'You have to expect things like that from babies.'

Point proved exactly, thought Ben.

It was only when Chloe was putting J-J's dirty clothes into the washing basket after she'd put him to bed that she found the note. It fell out of his sweatshirt pocket and landed on the floor. She didn't think anything of it at first, nearly didn't look at it in fact, just presumed it was some scrunched up bit of paper he'd been drawing on and almost threw it in the bin. But then she realised it had writing on it. Very small writing though – she couldn't read

96

it and her reading glasses were downstairs. It had been all screwed up in a ball as though someone had intended to throw it away. Probably just an old bit of rubbish that J-J had picked up off the floor somewhere. He did tend to have magpie tendencies, she smiled to herself.

'Can you read this, Ben? I don't know where I've put my glasses,' she said, passing the piece of paper to him as she came back into the living room.

'That's Dad's handwriting,' said Ben, eyes alighting on the writing thereon. 'Where did you get that?'

'Just fell out of J-J's pocket when I was putting his clothes away. What does it say?'

'Oh my God,' said Ben, as he started to read:

Traitors, every one of them! I thought Jackie was different, but she's the same as the rest. Sneaking around, telling lies, plotting with my ex. I saw where she went, followed her from the station. We were meant to be a family, that was the whole point of it, I can't look after a kid on my own. Never trust a woman, Ben, and take care of your brother, he's a good kid. Dad

Jackie was visibly shaken. 'Jesus!' she exclaimed. 'What's he gonna do? Following me? That's crazy!'

'He's a madman,' said Chloe, 'but I'm just so relieved he brought J-J back – he could do anything in the mood he's in now.'

'I'm glad we're staying here with you tonight,' said Ben. 'I certainly wouldn't have been happy to leave you on your own knowing he was out there somewhere. We should ring the police and give them an update – he could be dangerous.'

But morning heralded an end to their fear. News came: a body had been found in an exhaust fume-filled car, in the car park of a beauty spot nearby. John was dead.

Jackie went with Ben to identify the body. She was the only one really to feel sadness at his passing, although even she knew that her life would be safer with him gone. It was sad to think that one man could have evoked such fear in the lives of those closest to him. Sad also, in a way, to think that anyone could have lived in this world for more than forty years and yet grief at their passing was non-existent, or miniscule at most.

Chloe rang to tell Olivia the whole sorry saga. She was due home from Greece in a couple of days anyway and although she offered to try and get an earlier return flight, Chloe told her it wasn't worth it. There was nothing she could do when she got back anyway, apart from give her mum a hug, of course, and Chloe assured her she could wait another couple of days for that – J-J was home and safe now, and that was all that had mattered.

She rang Kate also, to tell her what had happened. They both agreed that if one good thing had come about as a result of this trauma, it was the fact that it had brought the two of them back together. Understandably, Kate still treated Chloe with a certain amount of wariness; their friendship was not what it used to be, but given time, hopefully, things between them would improve.

But, back at Grace's house, Kate was faced with another dilemma. Jessica was still at her daddy's and needed collecting. Grace was quite willing to drive over there on her own to get Jess but, in her opinion, now was the perfect time for Kate to face her demons. Or to face Tom, in other words.

'But how can I, after what he did to me?'

'Chloe was equally to blame, and you're speaking to her,' said Grace.

'Only just, and only out of necessity.'

'I know but Tom was a much more important part of your

life than Chloe, and if you can force yourself to see her, then …'

'No, Grace – it doesn't work like that!'

'I know, but think of Jess. Think how happy she'd be if she thought her mummy and daddy were at least speaking to each other again.'

'That's emotional blackmail.'

'Sorry, but it's true.'

'I need the loo,' said Kate, beating a hasty retreat.

'Wimp!' said Grace.

'I do, I need …'

'Tom,' insisted Grace, testing the water.

'Don't be ridiculous, you don't know what you're talking about.'

Relief washed over Kate as she bolted the bathroom door. Relief at the solitude. No one to see inside her head as she tried to gather her thoughts. She glanced at her reflection in the mirror. A panic-stricken face looked back at her, red and flustered, tortured eyes. It resembled her face but it lacked its usual sparkle; something special was missing. The total happiness she'd seen there before was gone.

No matter how hard she'd tried to erase him from her thoughts, he was there, popping up in her mind's eye every day, often when she least expected it, and always, always as she lay alone in her big empty bed at night longing for his body next to hers. For, much as she'd tried, she could not get rid of the need she felt for him, the desire that made her tingle at the thought of his touch. There had been no other man since Tom – how could there be? He was the love of her life, always would be. What they'd had together had been so very special, she could not understand how he could simply have let it all slip away by betraying her trust. As far as she'd been concerned, it had been the end of their marriage. Ashes to ashes, dust to dust.

But ashes can smoulder, and hers did – big time. Sometimes her burning desire for him was so great that absolutely nothing would extinguish the flames, try as she might. Sometimes, just thinking about him, she would be consumed by a need so overwhelming that … 'Ohhh,' Kate groaned inwardly as she leant her forehead against the cool glass of the mirror and tried to focus her thoughts elsewhere. For how could she possibly still want him so much knowing that he had slept with her best friend? Because she still loved him, that's why. It was true. The truth was out. Kate faced herself in the mirror.

'I love you, Tom Darrington,' she said.

As she gazed at her reflection, some of the pain she saw in the eyes before her tentatively attempted to trickle away, although it was interrupted in its passage by a tapping at the bathroom door.

'Are you okay in there?' asked Grace, concerned that her friend had been gone for rather a long time.

A sinking feeling suddenly powered through Kate. Was she doing the right thing?

'I'm okay. I'll be down in a minute, just need to use the loo first.'

'Hah! You came up for that ages ago. What have you been doing in there? On second thoughts, I won't ask! Didn't know you talked to yourself though – especially in the bathroom.'

'Eek! Didn't hear what I said, did you?'

'No,' Grace lied. 'See you downstairs.'

Eventually Kate emerged, somewhat sheepishly, and came down to join Grace in the kitchen. Gran and Izzy were there too and, from a purely selfish point of view, Kate really wished that they were not. For how could she hope to have a private sort of conversation now? Three … no, four pairs of eyes rounded upon her. It felt as though the whole world and its dog were staring, and indeed, Alfie was surveying the scene from the safety of his basket.

'Okay?' asked Grace.

'Yeah, fine,' lied Kate, her mind in turmoil.

'Auntie Ka-a-ate,' wheedled Izzy, 'please can I come with you to get Jessica, and can I see her daddy?'

'Izzy!' reprimanded Grace, 'I told you! We don't know what's happening yet. And anyway, you wait to be asked.'

Gran's beady eyes whizzed around the kitchen, alight with curiosity and with a feeling that something not quite right was afoot. For a person with dementia she could be quite astute at times.

'What do you mean you don't know what's happening yet? Of course you know. You've got to go and get that poor child, anything could happen to her. She's been left alone all night with a man. I think it's disgusting,' she said, dunking her biscuit firmly into Grace's tea and losing half of it in the cup.

'Mother! Don't say things like that! And for goodness sake! If you *must* dunk your biscuits, dunk them in your own tea, not someone else's,' said Grace, leaving the table to pour the soggy mass from her cup into the sink.

'What did you say, Gran?' asked Izzy, equally curious now.

'Mother!' warned Grace.

'Men are dirty,' blurted out Gran, before anyone could stop her.

'My daddy isn't dirty,' said Izzy, smugly. 'He has a shower every day.'

Grace heaved a sigh of relief and continued with her task.

'Is Jessica's daddy dirty?' asked Izzy, a picture of innocence.

'No, he's not,' answered Kate, feeling somewhat bewildered.

'Does he have a shower every day?' the voice of innocence continued.

'Izzy!' warned Grace.

Kate smiled. 'Yes he does,' she said, picturing the water

running down his long lean body, the steam, the …

'Kate. Are you okay?' interrupted Grace, seeing the faraway look in her eye and wondering at the cause of it.

Kate dragged herself back from her brief trip to fantasy land with some reluctance. This was getting ridiculous, she was like a dog on heat. Talking about dogs on heat, she was suddenly aware of a warm furry body clung to her leg in a vice-like grip and pounding away like a mad thing. Alfie, going at it like the clappers.

'Alfie! Stop it! Get down and go into your basket – now! Sorry Kate,' said Grace as the doleful dog slunk, somewhat uncomfortably, into his corner.

'Think there must have been some thought transference going on there between him and me,' smiled Kate.

'Uh?' rounded Grace.

'That's his trick,' said Izzy, explaining his behaviour like he was the cleverest dog in the world.

'All men do that trick,' muttered Gran, 'they do it all the time.'

'Mother!'

'Well I've never seen my daddy doing that,' said Izzy, disbelievingly.

'Look, can we just change the subject, please?'

'But why would Daddy …?'

'Izzy!'

'… hold onto somebody's leg …'

'Izzy!'

'… and jump up and down?'

'That's a good question, Grace,' said Gran, triumphantly.

'It's just a trick, I told you,' answered Grace, a trifle flustered. 'Now, go into your room and watch your TV for a while, Mother. And Izzy, go to the bathroom and wash your hands, we're going out in a minute to get Jessica.'

'I'll wait here, then, until you get back.' 'Chicken' could sometimes be Kate's middle name.

'No, you're coming too.'

Kate was somewhat taken aback for a moment. 'You can be very bossy sometimes, can't you?'

'That's what friends are for – to sort each other out when necessary.'

'But …'

'No "buts".'

'Oy! My name's not Izzy, you know.'

'I know. Sorry if I'm sounding a bit controlling but somebody needs to do something. You still love him, don't you?'

'No,' contradicted Kate, a little too quickly to sound even remotely convincing.

'Don't lie.'

Kate's face coloured with embarrassment. 'Transparent as hell, aren't I?'

'Not just that.'

'What then?'

'I lied too. I heard what you said when you were in the bathroom.'

Kate grimaced, the truth was out. 'You mean …?'

'Say it again.'

'I love Tom Darrington,' whispered Kate, tears of emotion rolling down her face as Grace hugged her. She'd known it all along inside, but by admitting it to someone else at last, then it had to be true.

11

'Okay,' said Grace, firmly taking control of the situation yet again. Or trying to at least. 'All you have to do is get out of the car, walk up the drive and ring the doorbell.'

'Simple as,' said Kate, somewhat sarcastically, her heart racing as she stared towards the aforementioned door which, at one time, used to be hers. It had been a bad idea to come, she could have just stayed behind; Grace would have collected Jessica for her. 'Why did I let you talk me into this?' she asked.

'Go on, you know you want to,' persisted Grace.

'Well it doesn't feel that way.'

'I've only got one word to say to you,' said Grace, looking directly into the eyes of her dithering friend.

Kate stared back at her, wishing she was anywhere but here.

'And what might that be?' she asked, holding her gaze.

'Tom.'

Kate's eyes flinched.

'As I said before,' said Grace, her smile full of hidden meaning. 'You know you want to.'

'Want to what?' piped up Izzy from the back seat of the car. For one who was usually such a motormouth she'd been remarkably quiet, in fact they'd almost forgotten she was there.

Grace, however, soon remembered and was, in fact, not overjoyed. 'What on earth are you doing?'

'Plucking,' announced Izzy, steadfastly matter-of-fact.

'What? Kate's head whizzed around astounded, but she'd misheard, inner thoughts playing tricks, not dissimilar to the doggy kind.

'I should go,' she said. Before she cracked up altogether, was what she meant.

'You should,' said Grace. 'Izzy! Why on earth do you deem it necessary to desecrate my cushion?'

'What?' asked Izzy, her tongue protruding from the side of her mouth as she gave the task in hand her complete and utter concentration.

'What are you doing? Why are you plucking all the wool from my cushion?'

'I'm making a fluffball,' said Izzy, scathingly. It was obvious, surely.

'Well could you stop please, my cushion will be bald in a minute.'

'But I need a b-i-i-ig fluffball.'

'Oh Izzy, you do not need a fluffball, now put the cushion down.'

'But I do, I do,' wailed Izzy.

'Okay, now tell me, why do you need a fluffball?'

'It's a present for Jessica's daddy.'

'A fluffball?'

'Yes. Gran said that all men like a bit of fluff so I thought I'd give him some.'

What more could possibly be said?

The slam of the car door announced her departure. Kate had exited without saying a word, which had probably been the best thing for her to do. Grace watched as she walked hurriedly up to the front door and rang the bell. If she felt this nervous herself, how on earth must Kate be feeling?

Yes, how must Kate be feeling? She felt nervous, admittedly, but not paralysingly so. Her limbs could still move – fact. She was breathing, always a bonus, but it was her heart which was giving the most cause for concern. Cartwheels,

105

triple somersaults – it could probably win a gold medal in gymnastics for Britain at the next Olympic Games. That's only if it held out until then, of course. Meanwhile she was left carrying a torch, the heat from its flame burning right through her.

The door opened. He was there.

She'd pictured this moment so often in her mind, but nothing had prepared her for the way she was feeling right now.

'Hi,' he said.

Only one word, but butterflies' wings seemed to be flapping everywhere, the sound of his voice bringing on her squishing sensation tenfold. She was putty in his hands, or wished she was, right at this minute. But no, she mustn't. She was angry with him, he'd slept with her best friend – remember?

His piercing blue eyes twinkled at hers, his face wrinkled into a smile at her confusion. Wrinkling, yes. There were indeed a few wrinkles that hadn't been there before, but they added character, his face was … Ohhh! She just wanted to rip off his clothes and take him right there on the doorstep! No, she did not, what was she thinking? She was angry with him, he'd slept with her best friend – remember?

'Are you going to stand there all day in silence?' he asked, still smiling a welcome.

He might as well have poured warm melted chocolate onto her tongue – is that why her mouth was open? She closed it, hurriedly, and attempted to regain composure.

'Mmm,' she said. Couldn't help it, still enjoying the taste.

'What?' he asked, confused, obviously.

'Oh! Sorry. Sorry. That's what I meant to say – sorry.' Call this composure?

'Sorry for what?'

'Standing here, silent, not speaking.'

'Oh that,' he said, smiling even more at her confusion.

His Kate. She was here, actually here on the doorstep. A whole year had passed by and his love for her had never wavered. He'd never expected her to come here today, had thought she would just have asked Grace to collect Jessica on her own. Was it a sign? Did it mean she still loved him? Did she want to come back? One thing he did know for sure was that he had an opportunity, he couldn't just let her slip through his fingers. A tantalising image if ever there was one.

'Would you like to come in?'

She almost felt that she should be the one asking that question, the sexual chemistry sparking between them was so great. People have paid good money to see worse displays on bonfire night. She was saved from answering, however, by a shriek of 'Mummy!' as Jessica rushed up the hallway to the front door like a rocket.

'Hey, you!' said Kate, hugging her daughter tightly, relieved at having something to do with her hands other than what they wanted to do. 'Have you had a good time with Daddy?' Hmmm, there was nothing she'd like better herself at this moment.

'Yes, we've done lots of things together. Guess what we did this morning?' said Jessica, hopping around with excitement.

'You tell me. What did you do this morning?'

'We made some cakes!'

'You made cakes? You and Daddy? I don't believe it!'

'Come and see,' said Jessica, grabbing Kate by the hand and pulling her towards the kitchen.

Tom smiled. It had been worth getting himself splattered with egg and flour if it meant his beloved Kate was coming in through the door.

To Kate, though, it seemed somewhat surreal stepping into the kitchen where she'd reigned supreme. She forced herself to look straight at the cakes, almost afraid to look elsewhere.

'They're brilliant, Jess, I'm very impressed!'

'Would you like to try one!'

Tom interrupted. 'Maybe I should put the kettle on and we can have a cup of tea with our cakes. How about that?'

'Um, hang on a minute,' said Kate, suddenly feeling a bit cornered, holding up a hand to signal to him to slow down, reminding herself she was meant to be angry with him, he'd slept with her best friend.

'But that would be good, Mummy, like a party,' said Jess, excited at having her mummy and daddy both together in the same room.

Kate was clutching at straws. 'We can't stay, darling,' she said to Jessica, 'I only popped in to get you; Auntie Grace and Izzy are sitting in the car outside, waiting for us.'

'Well they can come too,' said Jessica, her excitement increasing by the minute. 'That will be an even better party then!'

'Sorry, Jess, but no. We could take a cake for them to try later though, if you like.'

'Not fair,' said Jessica, stamping her foot and folding her arms across the front of herself protectively. Her disappointment was palpable.

'Jessica …' coaxed Kate, but the little girl refused to look her in the eye.

Kate looked towards Tom for support, but all she saw in his face was … longing. Longing for her. Who cared about the bloody cakes? He loved her, he needed her, he wanted her. Even if he had put it into words he could not have expressed it more clearly.

Jesus, Kate. Dilemma, what dilemma? She knew how she felt, she'd admitted it. What had she said to her reflection in the bathroom mirror? 'I love you Tom Darrington.' Okay, but that was different. Locked in the bathroom alone, fantasising, not face to face with reality like she was now. She glanced around the kitchen, embarrassed by the silence.

'I know, I don't keep it as clean and tidy as you used to,' he said, apologetically. 'There never seems to be time. I'm working all hours and by the time I get home all I want to do is grab something to eat quickly and then just crash out.'

'I know, I wasn't looking at that, just remembering.'

'Remembering?' he looked at her with an outpouring of love.

'Mm.' But remembering also her anger, why she'd left, how he'd cheated on her with Chloe, Chloe! Of all people. 'Jessica, I think we should go,' said Kate, firmly, resolute.

'But Mummy, it's not fair! I want us to stay here with Daddy,' cried Jessica, emotional blackmail at its best. 'And we haven't had a cake, and Izzy hasn't seen my daddy, and …'

'Jess, do as you're told. Go upstairs and get your things now. If you're ready before I can count to fifty, then Daddy will come out to the car to wave us off so he can say hello to Izzy, won't you, Daddy?'

Kate forced herself to look into Tom's pain-ravaged face. He'd been expecting more, she knew he had.

Tom looked from mother to daughter with tenderness and sorrow. 'Of course I will,' he forced himself to say.

Amazingly, Jessica gave in and ran quickly up the stairs, racing against the countdown. Embarrassingly, Kate and Tom were left alone, each battling their own desires.

Tom wanted Kate, nothing more, but he knew that if he came on too strong he'd frighten her away and she'd disappear and refuse to see him all over again. She'd made a step forwards – come to the house, spoken to him. Any ground that he'd gained would be lost if he tried to make a move now.

As for Kate, she wanted him too. But how could she ever trust him now? He'd betrayed her trust once, how could she be sure it would never happen in the future? And did she really want to put herself through all of that worry?

And so they stood there in silence, waiting for the one precious little person who linked them together and whom they both loved with all of their hearts. The chemistry between them sparked like crazy, sizzled and crackled and …

'Kate …'

'Don't, Tom.'

Each wanted to throw themselves upon the other, tear off their clothes, make love with all the intensity and passion they were feeling inside, scream out with pleasure as their bodies entwined. But they remained standing. Out of touching distance. In silence. Apart.

'Fifty,' shouted Kate.

'I'm coming,' shouted Jessica.

'Hmm,' said Tom. He looked at her with tortured eyes.

'Are you coming out to the car with us?' she asked.

'I suppose.'

'You should. Izzy's dying to meet you. Jessica made you out to be some sort of superstud, er … star.'

He smiled at her faux pas, and the flush that had crept into her cheeks. She was so beautiful. He couldn't let her go again, he just couldn't.

Jessica ran on ahead, up the drive towards the waiting car.

'Kate, please let me see you again while you're here. I can't stand the thought of you disappearing back down to Cornwall without us getting a chance to talk.'

'But Tom, I …'

'Look me in the eye and tell me you don't have any feelings left for me,' he said, holding her by the shoulders and turning her to face him.

Her face flushed with desire at his touch. 'You know I can't do that,' she answered. 'You know I've still got feelings for you, of course I have. What we had together was special.' Why was her voice so high pitched, her breathing so rapid?

Why was she filled with such overpowering burning and throbbing desire for him to take her in his arms, to stick his tongue down her throat, to stick his … Oh my God, Kate, stop it! But she did, that's how it was, no denying. She wanted him to ravage her right here, right now, on the drive, everyone looking. She thought she might faint.

'Kate?'

'What?' she asked, stunned, back to reality. Had it been a dream? A pleasurable one at that.

'Are you okay?'

'Mm. Why?'

'You looked a bit funny, that's all.'

'Thanks!'

'So can I?'

'Mmm. Please,' she giggled.

'What?' he asked. What was wrong with her? She was acting very strangely.

'Can I see you tomorrow?'

That brought her back down to earth with a bang. Hmm. 'Tomorrow? Can you see me tomorrow?'

'That's what I asked, yes. I really need to see you, need to talk to you, need not to lose you again.'

'I don't know, Tom,' she was back on her guard.

'Mummy!' shouted Jessica from the car. 'Hurry up, we're waiting.'

Kate turned and started to move away.

'Ple-e-ease, Kate,' he begged, all manliness deserted.

'Ring me tomorrow,' she said, a woman in control.

As quickly as Kate got into the car, Jessica got out to give her daddy a hug. 'This is Izzy, Daddy,' she said, beckoning her friend to follow, 'She's been waiting for ages to meet you.'

'Pleased to meet you, Izzy,' said Tom, shaking her by the hand – a very formal introduction indeed.

Proud of her achievement and the formality of the

occasion, Izzy held out her other hand towards him, her fist tightly closed.

'I made you a present,' she said. 'Hold out your hand and close your eyes.'

'It's not alive is it – it won't bite?' asked Tom, fascinated by the confidence of this child for one so small.

'No. Won't bite. Might tickle a bit though.'

In the car, Grace cringed with embarrassment. But how could she stop her now? It would cause even greater embarrassment if she did.

Tom did as he was bade.

'You can open your eyes now,' said Izzy.

Tom did. Widely. What was it?

'It's a fluffball,' said Izzy, frustratedly stating the obvious. Grown-ups could be really thick sometimes.

'Oh, a fluffball. Of course.'

'You don't know why I made it for you, do you?'

'Erm …'

'Izzy,' called Grace, 'we should be going now.'

But Izzy was not one to be interrupted, or indeed stopped, not in any way, shape or form. 'My Gran says that all men like a bit of fluff on the side, so I thought I'd give you some. You can keep it on your kitchen side for when you need it.'

'Well thank you, Izzy, I don't know what to say.'

Neither did anyone else.

12

'So,' said Grace, in the car on the way home, 'spill.'

Kate was being frustratingly quiet, lost in thought, but Grace was dying of curiosity and simply could not wait another minute.

'What?' Kate asked, a slightly cross edge to her voice. She felt confused, not ready for someone to intrude into her thoughts, not even Grace.

Grace spoke quietly, chose her words carefully: the two chattering children in the back seat appeared not to be listening but obviously that did not come with a guarantee.

'What was it you said when you were in the bathroom earlier?'

'I know,' she said.

'I know,' piped up Izzy.

Never trust a child not to listen in to your conversations – nothing is sacred.

'What?' asked Grace.

'Aaah! You say you should always say "pardon" not "what",' said Izzy, quite smugly, still feeling pleased with herself after the fluffball saga.

'You asked what did Auntie Kate say when she was in the bathroom and I said "I know", 'cos that was what she said to me when I said there wasn't any toilet roll left.'

Agghh!

'Izzy, please could you not interrupt when grown-ups are talking? How many times do I have to tell you?' reprimanded Grace.

'But you asked.'

'I wasn't asking you though, was I? Now talk to Jessica, make another fluffball or something. Let me talk to Auntie Kate without any more interruptions please – okay?'

'Ooh – I could make a fluffball for Daddy. Do you think he'd like a bit of fluff on the side too?'

'Hmm,' Grace gave up. Why couldn't she just have a nice quiet child like Jessica?

Kate remained silent all the way home and Grace thought it best not to try and intrude on her thoughts any more; there'd be time for that later, when they got back to the house. Much as she was longing to know what had happened, she knew Kate well enough to know how much she valued her privacy at times and, consequently, didn't want to overstep the mark. It would be easier to talk at home anyway, easier to escape from the flapping ears and overly large mouth that called itself Izzy.

But Grace's plans were thwarted once again when they got back to the house, for sitting at the kitchen table comfortably sipping tea with Gran, was none other than Richard. Not so comfortable actually, he looked decidedly depressed.

'Richard!' said Grace, hugging him as he stood to greet them. 'How lovely to see you,' she lied.

She simply wasn't in the mood for his sadness today, he really needed to try and move on. Actually, she felt incredibly mean for thinking that way, but sometimes … just sometimes …

'Uncle Richard!' shouted Izzy, her enthusiasm infectious, as she ran in through the door and flew into his arms.

'Hey, poppet!' he said, with obvious delight at seeing her.

'I like *you* calling me poppet, but nobody else though,' declared Izzy, her statement full of hidden meaning.

He gave her a kiss, looking somewhat emotional, and put her back down.

'How are you?' asked Grace.

'I've had better days,' he said, sadly. 'You didn't mind me coming round, did you?'

'Of course not. Stay and eat with us later, if you like. You remember Kate, don't you?'

'Yes, we met before at ...'

'Anna's funeral,' said Kate, helping him out, understanding the torture he was still suffering.

Although it was a long time since they'd parted, the split had been on amicable terms and Grace and Richard had remained good friends. This was much to the chagrin of Charlie at times, Grace was *his* wife now, and he resented Richard's intrusion into their lives.

However Grace, as one of the homemakers and peace-keepers of this world, felt a certain amount of responsibility towards Richard, for it was she who had introduced him to her sister, Anna. Her sudden death had come as a most dreadful shock to all of them, but to Richard it was an overwhelming tragedy, from which he was finding it hard to move on.

'Disgrace,' said Gran. She slurped her tea noisily, as if to emphasise the point

'Mother!' warned Grace.

Kate and Richard sat down at the table, both staring into space, glumly. Izzy and Jessica chased each other around the table, playing a game, noisily. Alfie sat under the table, looking at Grace, pleadingly.

Grace? She'd had enough. As she busied herself around the kitchen trying to create happiness for all, peace on earth, goodwill to men, women and children, she was overcome by a sudden streak of rebelliousness and the urge to take control. And besides, she wanted to know what had happened with Kate and Tom.

'Right!' she said, vocal volume turned to maximum as she turned to face five startled faces, including one furry one.

'Richard, I'm leaving you in charge. Izzy and Jess, go and

play outside in the garden, you can run around as much as you like out there without creating quite so much havoc. Mother, you go to your room for a little while, your favourite programme will be on in a minute and Richard will bring a cup of tea through for you. And Richard, if you would like to eat with us later, peel these vegetables for me for when I get back, please. As for Kate, you and I are going for a walk and taking Alfie with us.

'We are?' questioned Kate, in a somewhat surprised tone.

'We are,' confirmed Grace. 'Someone has to talk sense into you.'

Kate gave a weak smile of surrender. 'Do you know, sometimes you can be incredibly bossy.'

But happiest of all was Alfie. Walk. Walkies? Alfie? He whirled around with glee. Could someone get my lead quickly please. That means me!

'You didn't mind did you? Coming out I mean. I thought you might want to talk and I knew there wouldn't be much chance back there. I don't know why my house always seems like a madhouse,' said Grace, simultaneously trying to take control of Alfie who, excited at the prospect of a walk with his very favourite person in the world, was pulling her along like a husky with a sledge.

'Heel!' she commanded, but to no avail. They really should train this dog, could do with that lady from *Me and My Dog* right now in fact – what was her name?

Kate smiled and gave Grace's arm a squeeze. 'You just want to find out what happened, don't you?' she teased. She really was appreciative nevertheless. It was incredibly good to have such a close friendship, to have someone who would listen and care and be there, no matter what.

'Well of course I do. Spill the beans, I can't wait any longer!'

A shadow passed over Kate's face.

'Hey,' said Grace, 'You don't have to tell me anything, not if you don't want to.'

'I do, I do, it's just that my head's all over the place.'

'Well, understandably. How did you feel when you came face to face? That moment on the doorstep.'

'Like ripping his clothes off and making mad passionate love, if I'm honest.'

Grace glanced sideways at her friend, a faint smile on her face. 'Mm, I have to admit, he is a bit of a Mr Sex-On-Legs isn't he? I thought that myself when I saw him yesterday.'

'Grace! That wasn't even funny!' spluttered Kate, somewhat taken aback by the comment.

'Sorry, I know, that was a stupid thing to say.'

'The point is that's half the problem. He is a hunk, an attractive man, and he can be quite the charmer at times.'

'Well, he wasn't so with me, just so you know.'

'The thing is though that it all comes down to trust now, as well as forgiveness. How do I know it would never happen again?'

'You don't, love. That's the thing. But if you want him back enough, then you're just going to have to work at it. He's going to have to earn your trust and you have to learn to trust him again.'

'Hmm. Easier said than done.'

'I know. How did it feel, though, the bit of time you spent in the house with him?'

'Like my heart was in constant battle with my head! In my heart and in every part of me, I'm almost screaming out with love for him. He's the love of my life, really and truly, no one else could come close. But my head tells a different story – it senses danger, wraps me up in a shell of self-preservation. I've always been like that. If someone hurts me, or something bad happens to me, I plaster on another layer to protect myself. People have to work hard to break through.'

'I've noticed!' said Grace. 'You don't give a lot away easily do you – I had to chip away for ages to find the real you!'

'Sorry,' said Kate. 'I'm glad you persisted though, it feels really good to have someone I can be so honest and open with.'

'See! Gotta learn to trust! Anyway, back to Tom. How did he seem?'

'Desperate – in a word.'

'Well I'm not surprised! He hasn't had sex for a year!'

'Grace!' Kate exclaimed. 'As for trust, it took flight straight away. How do I know he hasn't been sleeping around all over the place? How do I know he hasn't been with Chloe?'

'Did you ask her?'

'Yes.'

'And what did she say?'

'That she hadn't even seen him.'

'And did you believe her?'

'Yes.'

'There you go then. You've got to learn to trust him again, love, and only you can do that.'

Kate walked along in silence, lost in thought.

'What are you thinking?' asked Grace, after a while.

'I'm thinking about what we had, how good it used to be.'

'And if you can only get past this, you could have it all back again. Your man, your home, be a family again.'

Kate brushed away a tear. 'You make it all sound so simple.'

'I don't mean to, I know it's not, but I'm just saying how it could be. It's not as though he was a serial womaniser, was it, off with a different woman all the time?'

'How do I know?'

'Kate!'

'Sorry, but I don't, do I?'

'Actually, I think you do. From what you've told me

about your sex life together, he wouldn't have had time for another woman!' Grace smiled.

'But he did, though, didn't he? And my best friend at that.'

'I know. I know he did wrong, and so does he. And please don't think I'm saying this because I condone his behaviour – far from it. But it was one time, Kate. You were away, he didn't know whether you were ever coming back and he sought consolation elsewhere. One time, Kate, that's all. You do believe him on that, don't you?'

'I think so.'

'You think so?'

'Okay, yes, I believe him.'

'So do you really think it's worth passing up this second chance of happiness with the man you love, for that one time?'

Silence.

'Kate?'

'Oh, I don't know.'

'Well talk to him at least. Don't just wrap yourself back up in your protective layers and rush off down to Cornwall again. You need to talk to him and see how you feel. Otherwise I could end up with a lonely, bitter, twisted, man-hating friend forever … and that's just me looking at it purely from a selfish point of view!'

Kate ventured a smile, at last. 'Okay, I'll talk to him. He's ringing me tomorrow anyway.'

When they got back to the house they were actually surprised to find far too much testosterone around the kitchen table. So much, in fact, that it had almost spilled out of the kitchen and run out through the door to greet them. The Three Wise Men.

'Tom! What on earth are you doing here? How did you know where to find me?' Kate didn't know whether to feel overjoyed at the effort he'd made, or annoyed by the intrusion into her privacy. That was her head anyway. Her body, on the other hand, overflowed with love. This proved how far he'd go to win her back, how much he loved her and regretted what he'd done.

'It wasn't that difficult, to be honest. Grace told me yesterday the name of the village where she lived, so I thought I'd take a chance on finding you. It's not that far away anyway. When I got here I asked around and just about everybody I spoke to knew Grace and Charlie, so they pointed me in the right direction.'

'And Izzy,' interrupted Izzy, transferring her weight alternately from one foot to the other in a sort of little Izzy dance.

'Oh, sorry, how could I forget? Of course, everyone knew Izzy too,' smiled Tom, obviously captivated by her beguiling charm already.

'And me,' said Jessica, sliding onto Tom's knee, putting an arm around his neck and looking adoringly into his face. This was *her* daddy, she was his number one girl, and he wasn't going to be allowed to forget that in a hurry. 'Did they know me as well?'

'Well no, Jess, how could they know you? You've only been here a few days. But I know you, angel, and I love you more than anyone else in the whole world.'

'More than Mummy?'

Tough question in front of such an audience, and one which filled the auditorium with expectant silence as it waited for an answer.

'Okay, you got me. I love Mummy too, and we both love you right up to the stars in the sky.'

'In heaven where Jake is?'

'Yes, angel, where Jake is.'

'But I told you to ring me tomorrow,' Kate said lamely, tears in her eyes as she tried to battle the wealth of emotion which threatened to engulf her.

'I know you did,' said Tom, 'but I had this fear that you'd answer your phone and say you were already in Cornwall, so I decided to do something about it. No point in always living with regret.'

'No, I know that feeling, mate, and it's not a good one,' chipped in Richard.

Charlie studied these two men who had invaded his kitchen – handsome buggers, both of them, but he wished they'd bugger off, right now actually, and leave him in peace with his Gracie. He'd had a busy day at work and all he'd wanted was a nice quiet house to come home to. He may be shorter, balding somewhat, and have a little bit of a paunch, but at least he had the love of a good woman. Or thought he had, although he didn't like the way Grace kept looking at the other two, and never at him. Tom was here for Kate and as for Richard, he was her ex. Grace would do well to remember that.

Charlie got up from the table and moved across to put an arm around his Gracie, staking his claim. 'What's for dinner tonight? I'm starving.'

'Charlie!' she admonished, at his interruption to the proceedings. 'Anyway, you don't look as though you need anything to eat for the next six months with that belly you're getting on you lately. Look at that!'

Poor Charlie – how to bring a man down to size.

'I have to keep my strength up, I've been at work all day.'

'Yes, and it looks like it – you're covered in paint! You could have a least had a wash before you sat at the table – you don't see the other two looking like that, do you?'

Even Richard sprang to his defence. 'To be fair, Grace, the poor man's not had a minute to himself. He came back from doing a hard day's work to find his house full of uninvited guests.'

'Can fight my own battles thanks, mate,' glowered Charlie.

'*His* house? To be fair, Richard, as you so nicely put it,' said Grace, sarcastically, 'this is actually *my* house, not his!'

Below the belt that one, Grace. Where had this argument come from? Too much testosterone of course. But for two people in that room, the argument was a good thing. Prior to it, they had been centre stage, with an audience captivated, tentatively waiting for their love scene to develop. Now the audience was in the middle of its own kitchen-sink drama, and had eyes for no one but itself.

Tom and Kate's eyes met across the chaos that surrounded them. A frisson of a smile played on Kate's lips. It was now or never.

'I love you,' mouthed Tom, his soul bared through his eyes. His heart pounded in his chest, fearful of her reaction.

She lowered her eyes shyly for a moment. Nervous. Feeling almost like a teenager asked out on a first date. So much rested on her response. So much trauma and turmoil had been worked through to reach this point. Was it the right thing to say? She hoped so, and now seemed like the right time to say it.

'I love you too,' she mouthed in return.

For them it felt as though the world stood still at that moment. Tom wanted to rush across the room to where she stood, to take her in his arms, and for the whole world to know. But she put her finger to her lips to signal silence. For the moment this was their secret and she wanted it to stay that way. They smiled across at each other in the knowledge of their love, the joy of it shining from their eyes.

In complete contrast to this silent happiness which radiated across that one part of the room, raised voices continued heatedly in another.

'I'm sick of this constant jealousy,' yelled Grace. 'I thought you'd begun to get over it but …'

'Stop!' screamed a voice louder than any other. The

banging of a stick helped. 'Does an old lady have to die around here before anyone realises she's not had anything to eat? For goodness sake Grace! You have guests – stop all this bickering and get some food or they won't ever come here again. Do you want me to do it? Is that what you're waiting for? Because I saw some of those big round pizza things in the fridge – they'd boil up nicely in a pan. Oh, and I took the ice-cream out of the freezer while you were out so that should be nicely defrosted by now – shall I put it in the oven?' she asked, making a feeble attempt to get to her feet.

'Mother! For God's sake, sit back down!' exploded Grace, rounding on her. 'You surely know that …'

'Leave her, Grace, it's not worth it. She's right, though, let's get some food on. I'll give you a hand.' At least it stopped their argument.

'Okay,' sighed Grace, feeling deflated and somewhat annoyed to be stopped whilst at full throttle, but also somewhat embarrassed and feeling guilty towards this man who was her rock, and for whom most women would give their right arm.

'Sorry, Charlie, you know I don't mean it, I just can't help myself sometimes and I always seem to take it out on you.'

'It's okay, I've got broad shoulders – they go with my paunch,' he said, smiling. He hated it when they argued.

'I'm sorry,' she said, giving him a hug, 'You know I love you, I don't understand myself sometimes.'

'Not much hope for me then, is there?' he joked. 'Now, what do you want me to do?'

'When you've finished over there, Grace, could you help me find my teeth? I don't know where you've put them this time.'

All eyes, with the exception of those belonging to the unsuspecting Tom, rounded on the sugar bowl. Several faces turned a shade of green.

Kate cut in quickly before another situation developed. And besides, did she really want to eat around that table tonight? 'Actually, Grace, Tom and I are going to go out for a meal tonight if that's okay,' she said, trying to convey her secret to Grace with just the use of her eyes.

Message received loud and clear, despite the silence. 'Are you?' asked Grace, with obvious delight.

As for Tom, he stayed silent too, looking simply like the cat who'd got the cream.

'Is it okay to leave Jess with you?'

'Of course it is.' Grace smiled.

'I'd better go too,' said Richard, feeling he'd outstayed his welcome, after such a fracas.

'No, stay Richard, honestly. We'd feel bad if you left now.'

Would we? Personally, Charlie thought he would feel quite glad.

But Richard stayed, the three of them playing happy families once more.

13

It felt strange for Kate and Tom – like a first date almost. Neither of them wanted to take charge of the situation, each afraid of saying or doing the wrong thing. Today had been a big step forward in trying to get their relationship back on track again, and both were wary of being the cause of it slipping back to square one. Even the choice of restaurant seemed like a big deal.

'Seafood,' said Tom.

'Seafood?' queried Kate.

'Well yes. Do you not remember? We went to a seafood restaurant on our very first date.'

'But that was in St Ives,' she pointed out. 'There's an abundance of them there.'

'Okay, Italian then, that's similar.'

'Huh?'

'Well okay, maybe not similar, but you can probably get shellfish.'

'And I like Italian anyway.'

'I know you do.'

They tried not to tread on eggshells, that really was not the point. For if they were to stand a chance of getting back to how things were, the idyll of how things had been, then the air had to be cleared, the slate wiped clean.

Which is why Tom felt, at this point, in just a li-i-ttle bit of a turmoil. Caroline. Should he tell her, get it over with, off his conscience once and for all? Or are some secrets best kept? It had taken him a whole year to win her back after she'd found out he'd slept with Chloe. Now here he was balanced on the cusp, about to get his life back together. Telling her now could ruin everything all over again, and maybe for ever this time. For being forgiven for a wrong-doing once was surely gratifying enough … but twice?

It wasn't as though he'd actually slept with Caroline, not in the full sense, it had just been a little dalliance, that was all. And instigated by her, not by himself: he'd been the one to put a stop to it. But Kate? Somehow he didn't think she'd see it that way. Hmm. Maybe some secrets are best kept.

'What are you thinking?'

'Me?'

'Well I can't see anyone else, can you?' she smiled. Her face glowed in the candlelight as they gazed into each others' eyes across the table. He had never seen her look more beautiful. 'And remember, no more lies. We have to be truthful with each other now, no matter what.'

Dilemma, thy name is Tom. Decision made. In an instant. Right or wrong.

'So …?'

'So what?' he teased.

'What are you thinking? Grrr – you're starting to frustrate me already, and we've only been together for five minutes!'

'I'm thinking I'm the luckiest man on earth to be given a second chance like this.'

'Well just keep that thought in mind, Tom, because if you ever, *ever* did anything like that again there would be absolutely no way that we could ever be together. I haven't forgiven you for what you've done and I don't know that I ever can. All I do know is that I love you despite what happened and I want us to try to draw a line under it and move forward – give our marriage another chance. A final chance, actually, last chance saloon. Because like I say, nothing like this can ever happen again – I would be gone, out of your life for ever.'

Right decision then, Tom? Maybe, maybe not.

'You know I wouldn't. Not ever. I've learned my lesson.'

Hmm.

He reached across the table and took her hands within his own. 'I remember the very first day that I saw you. You were sitting on the beach, lost in your own little world, your sketch pad on your knee as you worked away. Your hair was blowing in the wind, and you were wearing patchwork trousers and the craziest purple jumper I'd ever seen. Even though I didn't know you, you looked so vulnerable sitting there I just wanted to scoop you up in my arms and protect you.'

'Oh Tom, you say the sweetest things. I just remember you coming up to me and watching, I could feel you staring. When I turned to look up at you I was transfixed by your eyes, so blue … the intensity of their colour …'

'That's because you're an artist,' he teased.

She smiled. 'You know what I mean. I just felt as though I was being drawn into them.'

'Love the pun,' he joked.

'Tom! I'm trying to be serious!'

'Sorry. I know what you mean.'

'Is that love at first sight? That's how it felt.'

'For me too. I couldn't stop looking at you,' said Tom reliving the moment in his mind. 'I remember asking lots of questions about your work, not that I wasn't interested, but it was you that I wanted to know more about, not your artwork.'

Kate smiled, and squeezed his hand. 'I know, it took me a while to realise that, though. I thought you were someone with a passion for art, even dared to hope you might be going to commission me.'

'Well, someone with a passion is right – but the passion was for you.'

'Oh, Tom. I just remember thinking you were such a handsome guy, why on earth would you be interested in someone like me? I was a real hippy in those days, I thought you'd be thinking I looked like something that had been washed in with the tide.'

'You're joking! I'd never seen anyone look more beautiful. I was in awe, actually, I thought you'd think I was really staid and stuffy in comparison. I'd always longed, you see, to feel free like that, to fly in the face of tradition and dress to please me, but I never had the confidence to carry it off.'

'Until you met me.'

'That's true, you did change me, you turned me into a hippy too for a while,' he laughed.

'We changed each other, I think,' said Kate, 'until we met somewhere in the middle. We were good for each other. My confidence soared when I was with you, I felt I could do anything, achieve anything.'

'Me too. And we did, didn't we? We had it all ... until I blew it.' Tom's eyes clouded over, he looked down at the table, remembering how he had so stupidly been the cause of it all going wrong.

Kate gave his hand a little shake. 'And we can have it all again. Look at me, Tom. We'll have to work at it to get things back on track, it's not going to be easy, but I'm willing to give it another go. That's if you'll still have me back.'

'Still have you back? It's all I've ever wanted since the day you left,' he said, a huge smile spreading across his face.

It had actually been immaterial which restaurant they'd chosen, food had been merely secondary to their conversation, in fact they barely remembered eating at all – were quite surprised, in fact, when the waiter came over to the table to ask whether they would like dessert.

'I know what I'd like for dessert,' smiled Tom pointedly.

'Tom!' reprimanded Kate, embarrassed, especially in front of the waiter. 'Could we see the menu, please? Thank you,' she said as he passed one to each of them and left them to decide.

'And I bet it's not even on the menu,' said Tom.

'Tom!' Kate warned again, despite the sudden flush in her nether regions which made her want to throw both caution and her knickers into the air and dive upon him, there and then.

'What?' he asked, the picture of all innocence.

Ohh! She really could ... 'You know what I'm talking about.'

'Well I'm talking about panna cotta, I don't know what you're talking about,' he said with a cheeky grin, stringing her along.

Kate's flush had spread to her face.

'Gotcha!' he winked.

In fact they ordered ice-cream, Kate hoped it might cool her down a bit ... in all areas. They fed it to each other, spoon by spoon, a romantic end to a romantic evening.

But *was* it the end of the evening? Tom rather hoped it was not.

'Are you coming back to my place? Ohh! I mean our ... I mean home? Oh, this is so awkward. Sorry, you know what I mean.'

'For coffee?'

'Or whatever,' he said longingly. He'd waited so-o-o-o long.

His eyes almost tunnelled into hers, seeking out her approval, hoping against hope that the wait was over, his sexual drought at an end. He needed her in his bed tonight, their bed, needed her.

'No Tom. Not tonight.'

Did she really just say that? Her need was as great as his. This was no longer merely a case of tingling and hot, this was now a case of pounding and on fire.

'Do they have fire extinguishers?' she asked, in a faraway kind of voice.

'What?' asked Tom, studying her breasts, which pointed

perkily towards him, seeming to want him back with a vengeance, holding him at gunpoint in fact.

'If you could pop it in there please, sir'

'What?' The world had gone mad.

'The pin number for your card, sir,' explained the waiter, patiently holding the payment machine out towards him. How much had this customer had to drink this evening, for goodness sake? If he didn't stop ogling the lady's breasts she'd surely slap him in the face in a minute, if she had any sense.

'Thank you, sir,' said the waiter, as Tom took the machine from him and started to enter his number.

'Does this include a tit? Er ... tip?' asked Tom, mind still elsewhere, obviously.

Jesus. 'Yes, sir, the service charge is included in that. Thank you.'

'I'm not going to sleep with you tonight, Tom. No sex tonight. Not on our first date.'

'But ...'

'Ahem!' the waiter cleared his throat nervously, as he tore off the receipt and handed it to Tom. 'Thank you, sir. Enjoy the rest of your evening.' Oh my God! He so wished he hadn't had to say that last sentence, but that's what he'd been told to say. Jesus. His first evening in his new job. He didn't know whether he could cope with a second.

Their discussion continued as they got into Tom's car.

'But you don't have to stay all night – not if you don't want to. You could just come back and have a ...'

'Coffee. Yeah, you said,' smiled Kate.

'I could drive you back to Grace's afterwards, it's not that far.'

'Seems like a long way for a coffee to me,' she teased.

'Okay, so it's not just for coffee. God, I've missed you Kate. You don't know how much,' he said, the proximity of her leg next to his in the car almost more than he could bear.

His hand caressed the gear stick, only inches away from her leg. Her perfume, still the same one, lingering, enticing.

'I can see how much,' she said, her eyes alighting briefly on the obvious. The very obvious.

She battled with herself, her own needs somewhat pressing. Pulping … squishing actually. She'd been transformed into a harvest of grapes, was going through the machine, producing wine, she was sure of it.

No. It could not be. She had to say no. Was she sure? No … but she had to say no.

'No, Tom. I'm sorry, but it's a no. Believe me, I want it as much as you do.'

'Maybe not quite so desperately,' he said, trying, with some difficulty, to keep his mind focused on driving them safely.

'Oh, Tom,' she said, unable to resist putting her hand on him briefly, removing it again swiftly as he pulsated at her touch.

'Don't – please! Not unless …'

'Sorry. No, Tom, I don't think we should. I want us to work at this properly. Do things a step at a time to get us back on track, not leap into bed together at the first opportunity. I want this to be like a first date, build up a relationship like the one we had before. I've got to learn to trust you and it's going to take time. I don't want to feel rushed.'

'First date, huh?'

'Yep.'

'But people have sex on a first date.'

'Not on this one they don't.'

'I'm gonna have to pull over.'

'For a cigarette? But you don't smoke.'

'I know,' he said, pulling into a lay-by.

He stopped the car, slid his hands around the top of the steering wheel and leant forward, his forehead resting on them. He was silent, his jaw taut. A nerve twitched in his temple.

'I'm sorry,' she said. It sounded pitiful, even to her own ears.

'I don't understand,' he said, overwhelmed by frustration. 'Where would be the harm?'

'I just think it's too soon.'

'Too soon? We've been married for years and I've been suffering from enforced abstinence for the past one of them.'

'Brought on by yourself, remember.'

'Okay, yes, of course I remember – but has that not been punishment enough?' he asked, sitting back up again, turning to face her.

'Tom, this is a big deal for me – trying to move forward, trust again, rescue our marriage. It's not going to be done overnight, I need to take it slowly. Spending time with you this evening has been a big step forward and I've really enjoyed myself but …'

He couldn't help himself. He was listening to the words she spoke, couldn't fail to, but as for taking in what she was saying, there was no way at all. For he was studying the beauty of her face, so animated when she spoke, her eyes like misty pools of sincerity as she tried to make her point, her skin almost translucent in the glow of the street light, her mouth … her mouth so soft and …

Bang! He did it. Completely without intention. Like a reflex action almost. His lips locked onto hers and took even him by surprise.

'Mm!' she exclaimed, tensing.

That was a 'Mm!' of warning, not a 'Mmmm' of pleasure, easy to confuse.

But Tom persisted. How could he not?

Her repelling of his lips was all too brief. It was a kiss. Kisses were allowed on a first date. She relaxed into his arms, her lips parted to signal her welcome, her love for him intensifying, the hairs on the back of her neck standing on end. Their kiss was long and lingering, electrifying, their year apart making them so appreciative of each other, wanting to savour the moment, each wanting to drink the other in.

For Kate, that kiss could have lasted forever, it really felt like they'd pressed rewind and were starting at the beginning of their relationship all over again. Exploring new ground, trying to familiarise, arms enfolding, tongues probing. This was so perfect, just how she had wanted it to be, no pressure, just gradually trying to put the broken pieces of their marriage back together again. She wanted him desperately, of course she did, but for the moment she needed to try to keep that feeling on the back burner. She felt pure and virginal – like a teenager in love, she thought to herself, as she snuggled in closer to Tom's arms … arm.

For where was the other one? Tom could wait no longer. His hand moved slowly down, following the contour of her body, until it came to rest on her thigh. Her skirt was short, he moved his hand round slowly but another 'Mm!' pushed it away.

The kissing continued, in passion overdrive. His hand returned to the point of no entry, speeding before it was stopped. His fingers slid stealthily inside the lace.

'No, Tom!' her lips parted from his with a 'schmwack'. 'I said no, you know I did,' she said, pushing him away.

But he was under starter's orders, fumbling with his trousers, shaking with need as he pushed her back down and tugged at her knickers.

'Come on Kate – please! We've got to,' he panted, desperation over-riding everything she'd said, a pounding need so urgent he was almost seeing flashing lights.

'No!' she said firmly, holding on to her undies with a grip of steel, battling to push him away.

She'd wanted him too, but not like this, not being forced into having sex just to relieve his frustration. She'd been angry with him – did he not understand? He had to play by her rules now, win back her respect, and this was no way to go about it. She'd said no, and she meant no, all the throbbing need she'd felt for him earlier just shrivelled up and died. 'No!' she repeated, not an element of doubt in her voice.

But Tom was beyond reason. 'But you're my wife,' he stated misguidedly, releasing his throbbing member from the restraining clutches of his undergarments and prodding purposefully at her panties. 'I love you, I need you. Please Kate,' he begged, almost forcing his way in.

'I'm warning you Tom – stop!' the former welcome sign was now transforming itself into an octagonal stop sign, red with anger as well as danger. '*Stop it now!*' she yelled, with every breath in her body,

Tom, however, was beyond the point of comprehending. He'd reached the oasis in his desert, the journey had been long. He was banging away trying to gain entry, couldn't seem to understand the door was firmly locked, padlock in place.

Banging, yes. Kate struggled to push him away from her. 'Tom. The door!'

'What?' he gasped, still intent on mission impossible, hot and panting and frustrated as hell.

'Somebody's banging on the car door – you need to see what they want.'

'Jesus,' he muttered, through his purple haze, drawing back, reaching across to lift the handle, fumbling. On another planet, anywhere but here. In this state of utter fluster, the door handle escaped his grasp, the car door swung open – unintentionally wide in fact, revealing all …

Two police officers.

'Good evening sir,' said one, his eyes alighting on Tom's protruding member which was pointing towards him like a pistol. 'You may wish to cover yourself up a little, sir.' A little? Phwoar! For this was the pink-tinted policeman who'd had some dealings with Grace's family in the past.

The sudden rush of cold night air brought Tom down to size somewhat as, flustered, he dragged his trousers back up from around his knees squashing in his now softening appendage and, with some difficulty, fastening his zip.

'Sorry, officer,' he said.

Although, if anything, the addressee looked grateful rather than in need of an apology. A bit of titillation like that could last him all week. Well, in this case, somewhat more than a bit.

'Sorry to disturb you, sir, but we drove into the lay-by behind you for our break and when my colleague here opened the door, we couldn't help but hear shouting coming from your car. Sounded like someone was in difficulties and we just wanted to check that everything's alright.

'Well it is, officer. Thank you for your concern, but my wife and I are fine. And now I bid you goodnight because, as you can see, we were just, erm ...' Frustration had knocked any embarrassment Tom might have had, clean off the planet. Grrr! What a moment to pick! Tom reached across to close the door, but a hand held it firm.

'And you, madam? Are you alright?' continued the officer. 'Because it was most definitely a woman's voice that we heard.'

'Oh,' laughed Tom weakly, a sudden frisson of uncertainty creeping into proceedings. 'That's my wife. She can get a bit over-zealous at times.'

Kate glowered at him. He'd dug himself a hole so deep he may never get out again.

'Could you let the lady speak for herself please, sir?'

'Sorry, officer. Of course. Kate?'

Tom looked at her pleadingly. Surely she wouldn't say he'd gone too far? He loved her, he'd wanted her, that's all. She knew that surely, knew he'd never hurt her.

She eyed him with some reproach. 'I'm fine, thank you,' she said, turning back to face the policeman. 'Thank you for your concern. A bit too much alcohol maybe.' It was the first excuse that came into her head.

'Who was driving the vehicle? Was it you, sir?'

Tom nodded his head in affirmation.

'Have you been drinking this evening, sir?'

'Well, only a …'

'Could you step out of the car please, sir. I need you to do a breathalyser for me.' He was determined this fiend wasn't getting away that lightly – he'd interrupted his break after all.

14

Grace was waiting up for her when she got back. Fortunately everyone else had gone to bed.

'What a night!' exclaimed Kate, as she came in through the door, deposited her handbag on the floor, kicked off her shoes, and flopped onto the sofa with a sigh.

'Good as that, eh?' winked Grace, knowingly.

'Don't even go there, my friend. You couldn't be further from the truth.' Kate lay back and closed her eyes. 'Got anything white with fizz in it?' she asked, eyes still closed.

'Lemonade?'

'Ha-ha!'

'G and T do?'

'Couldn't be better.'

Kate mulled over the evening's events while she was gone. She didn't know whether to laugh or cry. What had started off as such a perfect evening had ended up like a scene from a farce. Brian Rix could not have done a better job. Hmm, although maybe theirs had been a little more risqué. OMG! When she thought about it ...!

'That okay?' asked Grace, returning, a drink in each hand. 'Now, tell me what happened, from the beginning if you don't mind. Judging by the state of you, it's been an eventful night.'

'Do you think I led him on?' asked Kate, suddenly feeling a slight element of guilt creeping in as she related the scenario to her friend.

'No, Kate, I would never condone what Tom did, not at all. When a woman says "no" a man has to respect that choice. You made it clear to him that you didn't want to have sex, told him repeatedly, and yet he still persisted. That's called rape in my book.'

'He didn't actually manage it though.'

'Only because of police intervention. Goodness knows what would have happened otherwise.'

'He would never have hurt me, Grace. I think I know him well enough to know that. He loves me. He's been bottled up for so long it must have been like … well, like needing to pop the cork on a champagne bottle.'

'Nice analogy there, love!' smiled Grace.

'Hah – you know what I mean,' Kate sipped at her drink, thinking out loud. 'Why didn't I just submit? Throw off my knickers in wild abandon? It's what I've been wanting to do all year. What stopped me?'

'Because you were trying to keep hold of your sensible head and you were right. He let you down so badly before, that you know you've got to learn to have respect for him again. If you'd just thrown caution to the wind and sub-mitted instantaneously, it wouldn't have been like taking steps towards building your relationship again and getting your lives back on track, it would have been more like instant gratification by jumping into the sack.'

'So you do get me, then?'

'I do, yes. I have to admire your willpower nevertheless, I don't think I could have been so … so strong minded.'

'I'm just a fool to myself sometimes though. If you knew how much I wanted to …'

'Like a virgin on a first date?' teased Grace.

'Exactly. Well, trying to be. More like a sex-starved nymphomaniac trying to keep her cool, actually.

They sat in silence for a while, the only sound being the clinking of Kate's ring as she tapped her finger on the rim of her glass.

'What are you doing?' questioned Grace.

'Nothing. What?' Kate asked, looking down at her left hand.

'That's your wedding ring – is it trying to tell you something?'

'I do love him, you know.'

'I know you do. Just as long as he knows it too.'

'I did lead him on, really. A bit anyway. When I think about it.'

'No excuse though.'

'I know. Poor Tom – he's paid for his crime this past year.'

'So have you, and you hadn't even done anything wrong.'

'Until tonight. That was cruel what I did to him tonight. I did nothing but send out mixed messages all evening, he knew I was as desperate as he was. And then that long snog, a come-on if ever there was one.'

'Hey, don't turn this round to it all being your fault.'

'I'm not but … Oohh, I so wish I'd let him now, I've been in a state of squish for days!'

'You have such a lovely turn of phrase, Kate,' smirked Grace, 'Such a genteel way of putting things.'

'Sorry, but you know when you're desperate and you …'

'Too much information!'

Whether it was the gin or just simply the ease of their friendship was debatable, but both Kate and Grace were soon in hysterics. Their laughter and general chatter, however, were soon interrupted by a morose-looking figure wearing a pink hairnet and very little else.

'What on earth is going on here?' demanded Gran, her teeth chattering in the cold – or they would have been had she been wearing her dentures. 'It smells like a brewery. Have you been drinking, Grace? I don't know what your father will say when he comes home!'

Kate looked confused. Surely …? Grace winked at her in response.

'My father won't be coming home, Mother, he died a long time ago,' said Grace, getting up from the sofa to take her mother back to bed.

'Your father's dead? Well, why didn't anybody tell me? I've got a funeral to organise, I need something to wear.'

'You certainly do, Mother,' Grace replied, leading her safely back to her bed.

Kate's eyes followed them sorrowfully. What had she got to complain about in comparison to that? Old age could be so cruel, dementia such a terrible illness, it paid you to make the most of each day.

Her mobile bleeped from her handbag. A text message. Right on cue.

'I'm sorry. I love you. xx'

'Love you too,' she typed back. 'I'm sorry too. xx'

'See you tomorrow?'

'Ring me.'

'Will do.'

'Night night. xx'

'Night night. xx'

After a somewhat restless night, Kate's slumbers were disturbed the next morning by her sudden awareness that she was being observed. She opened her eyes with huge effort, to find a pair of large blue ones staring directly into her own.

'Are you awake?' asked Jessica, in all innocence.

'Well I am now.'

'I thought Daddy would be here when I woke up today, I thought you were going to be together again.'

'What made you think that?'

'Izzy told me.'

'Izzy doesn't know everything, darling.'

A look of disappointment clouded Jessica's blue eyes. 'But ...'

'Don't look so sad, Jess, you never know what might happen.'

Kate's phone bleeped from her handbag

'I'll get it for you,' said Jess excitedly. 'That might be Daddy now.'

And indeed it was. Another text.

'Morning beautiful,' it read.

Jessica read it over her shoulder.

'Nosy!' admonished Kate.

'Beautiful? Does he mean you?' asked Jessica, wrinkling her brow.

'You ask far too many questions, lady! Now go downstairs to Auntie Grace and tell her I'll be down soon. She'll think we're never getting up today.'

Glancing at her bedside clock, Kate was astonished – 9.45 already! Hurriedly, she went to get a shower. She'd text Tom later.

In his office, Tom's mind was definitely not on the workload in hand. Why hadn't Kate responded to his text? Ten o'clock, surely she couldn't still be asleep. Maybe she was still angry with him about last night after all, now she'd had a chance to sleep on it. Things sometimes looked different in the cold light of day. What he should have done was to ring her instead of text. With a text you never knew whether the other person had picked it up or not. Maybe she was just letting him sweat. Well, it was working.

It wouldn't have been so bad if he could have taken the rest of the week off to try and sort things out, but he'd already taken Monday and Tuesday to spend time with Jess, and now he was a bit snowed under, to say the least.

Things had never been quite the same in the office since Caroline had left. He'd understood why she'd felt she had to go, of course, Chloe being her mother-in-law and all of that. But she'd been such a good worker, always so organised. With the series of temps they'd had since then it was just impossible. And, apart from anything else, Tom really missed having her around, she'd always been good at handing out advice, and a bit of tea and sympathy never went amiss.

'Tom, have you got a minute?' Tom's boss came round the door. 'I just want to run through a few things with you, ready for tomorrow.'

'Tomorrow?' Tom looked blank.

'Yes, those meetings in London. Oh, did she not say? I asked her to book accommodation for you for a couple of nights – that temp we had in yesterday. I can't believe she didn't mention it, I told her specifically. Not a problem, is it?'

Tom's heart sank. But what could he say? His job could be at stake, he knew the company was floundering at the moment. 'Leaving in the morning, is that?' he asked.

'Ah! Here are the details,' said Arthur Jepson, scrabbling through the papers in the file. 'Drive down tomorrow, and back after the second meeting on Friday. Just in time for the weekend, eh?'

Well, great. That was just great.

Someone else's mind was also dwelling on Kate, and that someone was Chloe. Would their friendship ever get back to how it was? She'd heard nothing more from her at all, although Chloe did have to keep reminding herself that only two days had passed. With so much happening it seemed a lot longer, that's all. It's just that at one time she would never have been off the phone, but that was before ... It wasn't only that, though. Kate had a new friend now – Grace.

Grace – Kate spoke of her in glowing terms. Grace – she'd never sleep with her best friend's husband. Grace – an angel in disguise by all accounts. Whereas she herself, well, she was just a cow.

But life wasn't all bad, she had J-J back home safe and sound and that brought her the greatest joy of all. In addition she had a houseful of people at the moment and there was nothing she liked better. She needed to be needed – always. Although Jackie had returned to her house after John's death, Ben and Caroline continued to stay. She hinted to them that maybe they could return to their flat, it was only down the road anyway, but Ben insisted.

'No Ma,' he said, in his usual jovial way. 'We'll stay a bit longer, just to keep an eye on you like.'

'I'm fine, Ben, honestly.'

'I think you just want to get rid of us so you can move your secret lover in.'

'If that's meant to be a joke, Ben, it's not even funny!'

'Oops – sorry Ma, I just love winding you up, that's all.'

'So I've noticed.'

Olivia and Stelios would be arriving tomorrow too. Back from their holiday, coming to stay here until after the funeral next week. After Jackie, Olivia was the one person who was most upset by John's death. He was her father, after all, however bad he'd turned out to be. Ben found it hard to feel any grief at all, although Chloe and Caroline between them had managed to persuade him that he should go to the funeral. As they said, he may live to regret it in the future if he did not. Despite his original protests, he did finally agree. He would attend the funeral.

Chloe, however, would not. Despite protests from others, in her own mind it had not been a difficult decision to reach. In the latter years of their marriage his behaviour toward her had made her love for him turn to hatred.

The rape, the kidnapping of J-J, all added to her feelings of loathing towards him. It seemed like a sad and very horrible thing to say about anyone, let alone about someone to whom you'd been married, but the truth was, she was glad he was dead. How could she go to his funeral and show sorrow? It would be hypocrisy at its best. No. Absolutely not. No way would she be at his funeral.

Supporting Chloe in her decision was Sandra. She'd had a bit of a run-in with John herself once, and knew what an ogre he could be. Husbands were not always what they seemed, it was a fact, and she should know better than most. In fact hers had turned out to be gay – but that was a whole other story. The ripples of life they come and go, but that had been one ripple too many in Sandra's life – one that had hit her like a tidal wave.

To have been together for so many years, married, and having a six-year-old daughter, Caroline, the last thing you expect to discover is that your husband is gay. However, it had all turned out alright in the end. Sandra had struggled through and brought up Caroline on her own. As for her husband, David, he'd followed his heart after years of living a lie. But now, many years later, David was back in their midst, living close to them. It worked well. Although Sandra and David realised they could not go back to being man and wife as they had been before, they continued to be the very best of friends, and not many days passed by when they didn't see each other at some point. Funny how life works out sometimes.

Should he ring or should he text? Tom battled with himself over what to say to Kate. He was dreading the conversation, by whatever means. Suddenly saying that he had to go away, after the situation last night, it really did sound like he'd slept on it and was angry – like he was making an excuse and didn't want to see her today. Texting would be so much easier, but it was the wimp's way out; he knew he had to speak to her. She probably hadn't even got the text he'd sent to her earlier, as she hadn't sent one back.

He pressed the button. She picked up straight away, and

with a voice so sexy it coiled around his heart and tied a bow.

'Hey, it's me.' Well of course it was him, his name would be showing up on her screen – doh! 'Listen, something's come up.' Please choose your words a little more carefully, Tom, and think about what you're saying. 'I've got to go away.' Okay, brief and to the point.

'What? But I thought I was seeing you today.'

She'd been too much of a tease last night, she knew it.

'Until Friday night. Sorry.' Sorrier than she'd ever know, in fact. He wanted her so, so much. Had been hoping that tonight maybe … But even just to have seen her again …

'Until Friday? But how come you never said?'

'Because I didn't know myself until a few minutes ago.'

Disappointment flowed along the phone line, from one end to the other and back again.

'Hmmm.'

Was that a 'hmmm' as in 'I really wish you weren't going, or a 'hmmm' as in 'I don't believe you, you're just angry with me about last night?'

'I really wish you weren't going, Tom.'

Question answered. And on a positive note too.

'Darling, I really, really wish I wasn't going, I just want to spend time with you.'

Darling. He'd called her darling. He really wasn't mad at her at all.

'I love you, Tom Darrington,' she said, the words sounding almost as though they should be accompanied by a fanfare.

'You don't know how much it means to me to hear you say that, Kate,' he said, eyes moist. 'I love you too.'

'So can I see you on Friday?'

'It might be late when I get back.'

'It doesn't matter, I can stay over.'

'You mean …?'

'I think we've waited long enough.'

145

15

'Not fair!' scowled Jessica, petulantly. 'I want to see Daddy *today*!'

Her reaction was somewhat out of character, she was usually such a placid child. It was understandable, however: she'd been so excited at the prospect of coming for a long holiday to Cheshire and she had mistakenly thought that they would be spending most of their time with Tom. Hopefully, that's the way it would turn out eventually – they'd be moving back up here permanently, in fact. But Kate didn't want to say that to Jess, not for the moment anyway, just in case anything was to go wrong.

'You'll see him at the weekend, darling, he can't help it that he's had to go to London, he still has his job to do.'

'But you always say that, "you'll see him at the weekend", always. This is meant to be special.'

'Well it is, Jess, and this weekend *will* be special, I'll make sure of it. We'll do something together, just the three of us. You'd like that wouldn't you?'

Jessica glanced up at Kate from beneath her furrowed brow, showing definite signs of interest now.

'What? Me, Daddy and you as well? All three of us?'

'Yes, Jess – all three of us,' Kate promised, giving her a hug.

Deep-seated feelings of guilt came to the fore. Poor Jess, the innocent face of childhood in the midst of parental feud, Kate had seen so many other children scarred by adult behaviour and had vowed nothing like that would ever touch her child. Jess had been such a much-wanted baby, born into a loving home with two parents who doted upon her and upon each other. Raised by the book, determined on a course of parental perfection, nothing could ever damage their beautiful blue-eyed daughter, she was their little angel – Tom called her so, in fact. But it had all gone horribly wrong.

Jess had lost a lot of her confidence, had become so much more shy and clingy, almost afraid to let Kate out of her sight sometimes in case she left her too. Try as she might to make a happy and stable life for just the two of them, Kate knew how much Jess had been affected by the break-up, how much she missed having Tom around. But hopefully now they would be able to work things out and build their little family again for Jessica's sake, as well as their own. She was, without a shadow of doubt, the most important person in the world to both of them.

Happy at the prospect of an exciting weekend ahead, Jessica went off into the garden to play with Alfie. It was a bit boring at Auntie Grace's when Izzy was at nursery, although it was going to be her very last day there tomorrow so she'd have someone to play with after that. In the meantime, at least, she had Alfie, and in some ways he was even better than Izzy because he always did what you told him, whereas Izzy never did.

'Sit!' commanded Jessica.

Alfie sat.

'Fetch!' said Jessica, throwing a ball across the garden.

Alfie fetched, overjoyed by the attention from this new little miss. He dropped the ball at her feet, eager and wagging his tail, wondering what his next trick was to be.

In the house, Grace cornered Kate. She had been desperate to get her on her own. 'So?' she questioned, eager to know.

'So what?' teased Kate, relaxed in the knowledge of the

way things were hopefully turning out.

'Come on, I'm dying to know! Have you heard from him? What's happening?'

'D'you know, the phrase "sticky beak" springs to mind sometimes.' Kate was enjoying this.

'Oy! Tell me!'

'Okay, okay!' she laughed. 'I'm seeing him on Friday.'

'Friday? Whatever happened to the state of squish? I thought you'd be seeing him today.'

'I thought so too, but he's got to go to London for a couple of days for work sooo …' said Kate, wrinkling her face with disappointment.

'Bummer.'

'I know. Got a favour to ask, though.'

'Really? I wonder what that could be?' Grace asked, with a grin. 'Anything to do with Friday, by any chance?'

'Um, Friday night? Could I possibly leave Jessica with you if I decide to stay over?'

'If?'

'Okay, I give in, it's pretty much a definite.'

'That's more like it,' said Grace, her face wreathed in smiles. And just think, if this leads to you moving back up here permanently we'll be able to see each other *loads*!'

'*Yesss*!' exclaimed Kate, hugging her friend tightly, thinking life couldn't get much better.

Still on a high, Kate somehow found her thoughts drifting to Chloe and, weirdly enough, they were impregnated with just a little tiny bit of guilt. She had been so close to Chloe at one time, but now a big wedge had been formed between them and it was doubtful whether their friendship could ever be the same again. That was strange, in a way, because Chloe's crime had been no greater than Tom's, and yet Tom was being forgiven. Well, not forgiven exactly, but he was being given another chance. Somehow with Chloe it was different. Was it something to do with female rivalry?

Or maybe it had moved on from that, maybe it was because Kate had now formed such a strong bond with Grace that she no longer felt the need for Chloe's friendship. And that was where the guilt lay. For Grace and Kate had formed one of those once-in-a-lifetime friendships that many aspire to have but never achieve. Kate's friendship with Chloe, although it had been close, had paled by comparison.

Okay, the guilt was growing. Chloe had been through a lot. If she was giving Tom a second chance then maybe she should be a little bit more considerate of Chloe too. Apart from anything else, Jess had really missed her, still talked about her in fact, her memory kept alive by the cards and little gifts she received from her occasionally.

'Jessica!' Kate shouted from the doorway. 'Come and get ready: we're going out.'

Jessica ran in from the garden, Alfie in tow.

'Out where?' she asked, unsure.

'To visit Auntie Chloe,' said Kate, closing the back door, all safely gathered in.

'Auntie Chloe?' shrieked Jess, her eyes wide with excitement. 'Really?'

Jessica's reaction proved it to her – she was doing the right thing.

Grace had offered to drive them there, but it would have meant waiting until Izzy came out of nursery which would have taken up too much of the day.

'You don't trust my driving, that's what it is,' teased Grace, when told they would be catching the bus. Two buses actually, there wasn't one which went direct.

Jessica was overjoyed to see her Auntie Chloe again, a little bit shy at first, but that was soon overcome. As for J-J, he followed her around like a wide-eyed lapdog and she adored him. Eventually the two of them went off to the playroom, leaving the adults in peace.

In silence, actually. After the clatter of children, there was a sudden awkward silence.

'So,' said Kate, breaking through it, 'how've you been?'

'I don't know really – like I'm living in a parallel universe is probably the best way to describe it. Nothing seems quite real.'

'Well that's understandable,' replied Kate, 'your child being kidnapped – missing for days, the death of your husband …'

'Ex-husband. Don't forget the ex,' interrupted Chloe.

'How do you feel about that? He's the father of your children, I suppose you must feel *some* grief at his passing.'

'None, actually, not one iota. In fact I've already said there's no way I'm going to the funeral. It would be too hypocritical. I feel absolute hatred for him after all that he put me through. I couldn't possibly go there and pretend to be sorry that he's gone. I just feel relief that he's not around any more, happy that he's dead. Does that make me a terrible person?'

'No, not at all, I can sympathise with that. I know how badly he's treated you in the past, as well. No wonder you feel as you do.'

Buoyed by such understanding, Chloe decided to take a risk.

'I've missed you, Kate. Missed not having you around to talk to.'

Kate's lack of response spoke volumes, she stared down at the floor, biting her lower lip, unsure what to say.

'It's been a tough year,' said Chloe, her words tip-toeing onto dangerous ground.

'For me too!' snapped Kate, her eyes flashing like neon signs. 'Don't think it hasn't – I had to give up my whole life, change everything.'

'I'm sorry, Kate.'

'So you said.'

Sometimes silence can be deafening, and this one was. Chloe broke it with a million-dollar question.

'D'you think we'll ever be able to be good friends again?'

'One step at a time, that's all I can promise.' The anger, though less intense, still registered on her face.

'Have you had contact with …?' Chloe's voice faded out, afraid to finish the sentence even by whispering the last word.

'Tom. It's okay, you can say his name. Have you, more to the point?'

'Me? No, like I told you, I've had no contact at all with him all year.'

'Well, I have.'

'Have you?' Chloe looked up, startled.

'Does that bother you?' Kate was ever-suspicious now, trust not being top of her list.

'Well no, of course not. I was just surprised that you had, that's all.'

'You said that you loved him, so there's no "of course not" about it. Do you still?'

'No Kate, I don't.' How could she say any other? 'I was just being stupid, I realise that now. He was your man and I committed an unforgivable sin. I've hardly been able to live with myself this past year knowing what I did to you and to our friendship. I destroyed everything on a whim, I don't know how I could have done that.'

'Well, you certainly destroyed me,' said Kate, sadly.

'I know, and I'm interminably sorry. I'd give anything if I could only turn back the clock as if it never happened. When J-J went missing I thought that was it, I thought I was being punished for what I'd done.'

'But then you got him back.'

'Thank God! It did give me a reality check, though, made me realise what's important in life.'

Kate looked at her with some understanding. 'It gave me

a bit of a reality check too. I've actually seen Tom.'

'You've seen him?' Chloe's reaction, although surprised, seemed one of genuine delight.

'We had a meal. I'm seeing him again on Friday.'

'Oh, I really am so pleased for you Kate!'

'We-ell,' said Kate, not quite wanting to run into congratulations mode just yet. 'It's early days, but hopefully we can start to try and get back on track.'

Chloe clasped her hands together with joy. 'Wow! That would be fantastic! You mean you'd move back up here and everything?'

'Hold on, Chloe,' said Kate, a bit taken aback by her reaction. 'One step at a time, remember, one step at a time.'

The bus was quite crowded on the way back. Rush hour. She should have thought, they could have come back earlier – or maybe not, as there'd been too much to discuss.

'I love Auntie Chloe,' sighed Jessica, leaning back against her, tired after her day out.

'I know you do, darling, and she loves you too, very much.'

Kate was so glad they'd made the effort and gone over to see her today. At least the 'Tom' subject had been broached and the situation made clear. Chloe had said that she was no longer in love with Tom and Kate was inclined to believe her. She'd said that she'd not had any contact with him all year, and again Kate thought she was telling the truth. In the same way that Tom would have to earn her trust, so would Chloe. But for her own part, Kate felt she'd taken another step forward today, and she was glad.

'Mummy?'

'Yes, darling?'

'Why did you fall out with Auntie Chloe?'

'Oh, just some silly little thing,' answered Kate, aware of

the other bus passengers surrounding them, making it feel almost like theatre-in-the-round.

'Izzy said it was because she slept with Daddy.'

The acoustics in here were deceptively good. Ears tuned in from all sides. The passengers had simply paid their fare to be transported home from work; entertainment which transported them to someone else's world was an added bonus.

'Jessica! Whatever gave her that idea?' Kate's face suddenly became reminiscent of a sun-blushed tomato.

'Her gran told her,' she said, still unaware of her audience – an unusual occurrence for her, she was usually so shy and quietly spoken.

'I've told you before, Jess, her gran has an illness called dementia. That means she gets into a lot of muddles and often says things that are not true.'

'But I've slept with Daddy sometimes and you haven't fallen out with me,' said Jess, in all innocence. 'Were you jealous of Auntie Chloe?'

'Jessica, I really think we should talk about this later.' Kate looked inside her handbag in search of something distracting. Chocolate. Perfect. The best antidote in the world. 'Would you like a piece?' she asked, offering it to her suddenly somewhat problematic daughter.

'Yum!'

It worked.

'How did it go with Chloe?' asked Grace, when they finally made it back to the house.

'Hmm. Better, I suppose. A bit anyway. I am trying to make an effort because, after all, her crime was no greater than Tom's.'

'Erm, except she was meant to be your friend,' said Grace, quite bitterly, in fact, for one who'd never met her.

'So was Tom, as well as being my husband, I mean.'

'Even so …'

'Anyway, she reckons she doesn't have any feeling for Tom any more.'

'And you believe her?' asked Grace, eyes wide with incredulity.

'Well she hasn't seen him all year, for one thing.'

'Hmm.'

'Grace, you don't know her. She's been going through a really tough time.'

'Sorry.'

'She seemed pleased at the possibility of Tom and me getting back together. She wouldn't be if she still wanted him for herself.'

'I suppose.'

'She's really excited at the thought of me moving back to live near to her again. Although, like I told her, it's still only one step at a time.'

Grace was quiet, sorting out food from the fridge in preparation for their evening meal.

'What's wrong?'

'Nothing,' mumbled Grace.

'There so obviously is something,' said Kate, though the thought of what it could possibly be never entered her head.

'Um, think I'm feeling just a tiny bit jealous actually,' said Grace, feeling somewhat foolish, also, for her admission. She deposited ingredients for a salad on the kitchen work-top, trying to cover her embarrassment.

Kate's eyes widened in disbelief. 'Of Chloe?'

'Well …' A cucumber slid from under Grace's arm and rolled onto the floor.

Kate bent down to pick it up. 'You daft bat,' she said, grinning all over her face and bopping her friend on the head with it. 'You know you have absolutely no need to be.'

The two hugged, their closeness unbreakable.

154

16

The level of excitement felt the next day could best be depicted, randomly, by an image of Mr Happy bouncing on a trampoline.

'Izzy Wizzy let's get busy!' shouted Izzy, dashing through to the kitchen at breakneck speed.

'You really are an Izzy Wizzy, the way you're whizzing about today.'

'Would you like me to take her to nursery this morning, Gracie, if you want to stay here with Kate? I've got plenty of time,' offered the ever-obliging Charlie. 'I'm only working on Kingsmead today and the lady won't be there to let me in until after nine-thirty.'

Grace poured some cereal into a bowl for Izzy as she smiled up at him. 'Oh, thanks Charlie, any other day I would have been really grateful, but today … well …' she chuckled.

'I get it,' he smiled back at her. 'The last day of seeing the wonderful Mrs Clarke. No wonder you can't wait.'

'I'm going to big school after the holidays,' said Izzy proudly, shovelling her cereal into her mouth with gusto. She needed to eat lots if she wanted to be big: Mrs Clarke said so and Mrs Clarke knew everything, or thought she did. For Izzy really was teacher's pet – Mrs Clarke doted on her, and Izzy played up to it for all she was worth. When it came to Grace, however, Mrs Clarke was under the misapprehension that she was the worst mother in the world, and the two were permanently at loggerheads.

'D'you know something, Gracie?' I really think you're going to miss seeing Mrs Clarke, despite all your complaining about her.'

'You might have something there,' Grace grinned mischievously, 'I quite enjoy our little spats.'

'Well I'm going to miss Mrs Clarke 'cos I love her. She's the best teacher in the whole world.'

'I'm sure you'll get to love your new teacher just as much, Izzy. Big school – just imagine.'

'That's 'cos I'm a big girl.'

'I know you are. Hurry up then now, if you've finished your breakfast. Go and brush your teeth, we don't want to be late on your last day.'

As Izzy left the table and dashed upstairs to the bathroom, Charlie got up from his seat and came over to stand behind Grace, putting his arms around her as she put the dirty breakfast dishes into the sink. He nuzzled the back of her neck.

'You okay?' he asked, lovingly, caring as ever.

She turned to face him, looking deep into his eyes. It had taken her a long time to realise what a good man she had in Charlie. In the beginning, much as she hated to admit it, she'd never been head-over-heels, heart-flippingly in love with Charlie. She'd seen him, in fact, more as a kind, big, teddy-bear of a man who'd entered her life just when she needed him most – like some kind of guardian angel sent to rescue her, almost. She'd been amazed when he'd proposed to her, for who in their right mind would want to take her on, plus all the baggage that came with her? Well, Charlie had – and indeed, Charlie did.

'I love you,' she said, kissing him gently on the lips.

'I know you do,' he replied, secure at last in her love for him.

For Charlie's insecurities were somewhat deep-seated, feelings of his self-worth dismally low. Consequently during the first few years of their marriage, the green-eyed monster would often pay him a visit, always bearing a calling card in the name of Richard, Grace's ex. However, Grace in particular had been through some tough times this past couple of years and Charlie's unwavering support had been invaluable to her. She had shown her appreciation and this had made him grow in stature, making him so much more of a man in her eyes. Prior to this she had sometimes thought that maybe the grass could be greener elsewhere but now, well, he was no longer just a cuddly teddy-bear, he was all man and, what's more, he was *her* man.

It would have been nice if they could have got to nursery on time just this once, it being Izzy's last day. Indeed, Grace had really and truly intended that would be the case, but somehow things never seemed to go to plan.

'Mummy!' scolded Izzy, as she walked carefully along the pavement, 'Don't tread on the cracks!'

'I'm not,' retorted Grace, dragging her attention back to the game they always played on their way to nursery school.

'You are,' reprimanded Izzy. 'I just saw you.'

'Sorry. I'm concentrating now.'

No wonder they were always late, it took twice as long to walk anywhere when you were avoiding treading on the cracks. It wasn't going to happen today, though, she'd allowed extra time – they couldn't be late on the very last day. Apart from anything else, Grace wanted to see Mrs Clarke's face when they got there on time. Or early, even better.

'Mummy!' The word flew from Izzy's mouth as if her life depended on it.

'What?' Grace turned, somewhat panicked by her tone.

'We forgot the present for Mrs Clarke, and it's the last day and *everybody* will take a present – you said so.'

Me and my big mouth, thought Grace. 'Okay, we'll call at

the shop,' she said grudgingly. Did Mrs Clarke really deserve a present?

'But they only sell sweets at the shop,' complained Izzy, sulkily. 'I wanted to buy something much better than sweets 'cos I love Mrs Clarke.'

'Well sweets will have to do,' said Grace firmly.

Izzy, of course, was not one to be rushed. By the time they had actually reached the shop, chosen the chocolates and finally arrived at the nursery school door, the big hand on the clock, as Izzy so nicely put it, was no longer pointing straight up, in fact it was pointing straight down.

'Oh dear,' exclaimed Izzy, 'You'll be in big trouble now.'

'Me?'

Grace peered around the door. Why did she always feel about three years old herself when confronted by a teacher?

'Sorry,' she mumbled.

'I bought you a present,' exclaimed Izzy, rushing up to Mrs Clarke clutching the gift.

'Oh Izzy, you're such a sweet child,' said Mrs Clarke. 'Thank you, my favourites too. I'm really going to miss you.' Indeed her eyes were quite moist, much to Grace's amazement.

'Will you miss my mummy too? 'Cos my daddy says she's going to miss you.'

'Izzy!' Children – they can be so embarrassing at times.

'Of course I will. I miss all my children and their mummies and daddies when they leave. But I shall especially miss you, Izzy, you're a very special little girl.' Tears in her eyes most definitely now.

'Thank you for being such a good teacher and for looking after Izzy so well these past two years.'

Did she really just say those words?

'It has been my pleasure – and I really mean that. I'm sorry you and I have had our differences occasionally.'

'Me too.'

158

What was happening here? They'll be inviting each other round for coffee next!

'If you ever …'

No!

Once again, when Grace got home, it was as though a miracle had occurred – the house appeared to be an oasis of tranquillity.

'What's your secret?' Grace asked, mystified. 'Because whatever it is you're using – I need some of it!'

'Don't be daft,' laughed Kate. 'It's just that it always seems to be a quiet moment when you walk in.'

'Quiet moment? What are they?' Grace chuckled. 'Cuppa?'

'Don't mind if I do,' said Gran, predictably, as she sat at the kitchen table colouring pictures with Jessica.

'We could take ours through to the lounge if these two are alright here for a while.'

'Okay, Jess?' asked Kate, by way of permission.

'Yes, Mummy, I like being with Gran,' she said, tongue sticking out in concentration as she worked.

Gran looked up from her picture, crayon poised, as she smiled a gummy smile. Hmmm, someone who appreciated her at last.

'Oh my God, I can't believe tonight is happening!' said Kate, as they carried their tea through to the lounge. 'You're sure you don't mind having Jess?'

'And what if I say I do?' teased Grace.

'Ha ha. I'd leave her anyway! Oooh, I'm so excited, I didn't expect to feel like this. I feel like … oh, I dunno, like some virgin bride about to lose her virginity.'

'Hardly. But far too much information anyway! Have you heard from Tom today?'

'Yeah, he's going to pick me up on his way home. Reckons it'll probably be about seven-ish.'

'What are you wearing?'

'As little as possible.'

'Kate!'

'Okay, change the subject. I'm going to be in a state of total desperation by the time I see him at this rate. Talk about something else.'

'What shall we talk about then?

'You.'

'Me?'

'Yes.'

'But I'm not that interesting.'

'Ha ha. Tell me about your older two kids, Zak and Cleo. You must really miss not having them around.'

Weirdly and inexplicably, Grace's eyes threatened to overflow.

'Sorry, I didn't mean to upset you.'

'And I didn't mean to look like a soppy cow – too emotional for my own good, that's me. I do miss them though, the house is so quiet.'

'Quiet? Crikey – I wouldn't like to have seen it before!'

Grace blinked back her tears and forced a smile. 'It's strange when your kids grow up and move on, very strange.'

'It must be. I've got all that to come yet. Tell me about Cleo and that gorgeous little granddaughter of yours.'

'Cleo and Daisy,' Grace glowed with both motherly and grandmotherly pride. 'Amazingly enough things seem to be working out really well for them. I never thought the day would come when I'd be able to say that.'

'She must be a tough little cookie. It's not easy coping with a baby at the best of times, but moving to London as a single teenage mum – that takes some guts.'

'I know, I kept expecting her on the next train home but she stuck it out – she's been terrific. She's braver than me, that's for sure.'

'Her cousin gave her a lot of help you said. What's his name again?'

'Hugo, yes, he's been a tower of strength to her. She couldn't have done it without him. And now, of course, she's got Pete.'

'Daisy's father.'

'Yep. I never, in a million years, thought they would end up together but they proved me wrong. He moved down there about six months ago now and they seem really happy.'

Kate smiled. 'Weird the way things work out sometimes, isn't it.'

'Well that certainly is. Cleo did nothing but complain about him when she was living at home and he did seem like a bit of a plonker, to be fair. I could never understand why she slept with him in the first place. But then, Cleo was a bit of a wild child at the time, she went through a really rebellious stage.'

'But she's settled down now though,' said Kate.

Grace smiled, thinking of her little extended family. 'Yes, fortunately, and so has Pete. They seem really happy together and are certainly doing a good job of bringing up Daisy – they're both besotted with her.'

'I bet she's gorgeous,' said Kate, enviously.

'Sure is. I just wish I saw more of her, and of Cleo too, but that's the way it goes, families grow up and move on. Richard gets to see them more than I do – it's easier for him, being on his own. When I want to go it's like planning a military exercise, sorting out what to do with my mother and with the dog, to say nothing of Charlie and Izzy.'

'Couldn't you just leave Charlie to look after them all and have a lift down when Richard goes?'

Grace shook her head sadly. 'Sounds straightforward, I know, but I've tried it in the past and it just doesn't work. Charlie can get very jealous of Richard sometimes.'

'Well that's understandable. He's your ex. After all, you must have had feelings for him at one time – he's the father of two of your kids, for God's sake.'

'But precisely that! Richard's my *ex*-husband, Charlie's my husband now, he should have no reason to feel jealous.'

'Unless you've given him some.'

'Hmm, I suppose … well maybe, but that's all in the past. He is much, much better, but I still don't think he could handle the thought of me having a trip to London with Richard. I do manage to go down for a weekend by train occasionally though, or very occasionally Richard will come and look after things here and I go down with Charlie and Izzy.'

'That's good of him!'

'Richard? Yes, I know. He's a good man.'

'You said that with a wistful look in your eye, you realise that?'

'Rubbish! You can quash that thought before it goes any further – I got over Richard a long time ago. He does need someone though, he's very lonely.'

'Hmm,' said Kate, thoughtfully. 'Anyway,' she said, suddenly changing the subject, 'tell me about Zak, your lovely son.'

'Ooh,' said Grace, with feeling. 'He's another one I don't see enough of. He's part way through his English degree now – time goes so quickly. Then he's got to do his teacher training, of course. He's always wanted to be a teacher, never wavered from the idea at all. I suppose he's lucky in that respect, he's had something to work towards, goals he's wanted to achieve.'

'What made him choose Brighton? Seems an odd choice, he couldn't have gone much further away.'

'Originally that was his third choice, but with Cleo being in London it's worked out really well. It means he can hop on a train easily to go and see her at weekends – and he quite often does. What really swung it for him though was Genevieve. She got a place there too and they wanted to be together.'

'Is that working out okay now?'

'They've had their ups and downs but, well, they're still together, put it like that, although …'

'Grace!' Gran's sudden appearance at the door took them both by surprise. They'd been so engrossed in their conversation that they hadn't heard the tip-tapping of her walking stick on the floor of the hallway.

'Have you forgotten something?' she asked, amazing even herself with the fact that she was the one who'd remembered.

'Mother, you're the one who forgets things, not me.' Grace could be a trifle sarcastic at times.

'Not this time.'

'What are you talking about?'

'I'm talking about Izzy, your daughter. You've forgotten her again!'

'No I haven't, I … Oh my God! Is that the time? Why didn't you tell me?'

'I just did, didn't I?'

'I'll come with you,' said Kate, jumping to her feet. 'Bring Jess.'

'I haven't really got time to …'

'We can run,' insisted Kate.

That fleeting moment of friendliness Grace had shared with Mrs Clarke earlier in the day was gone. Predictably, with the exception of Izzy and her teacher, the nursery was empty, everyone had gone for lunch.

'I am so sorry,' said Grace, apologetically. And she really did mean it this time. She had been so determined that she would not be late today.

Mrs Clarke remained unmoving, unsmiling, un-anything

163

really, just white-faced, like a statue made of alabaster. Izzy, meanwhile, sat snuggled up on her knee, playing out some tragic orphan sort of scenario whereby she was about to be snatched away from the only person who cared.

No greeting of 'Mummy!' rang from her lips, just, 'I don't want to leave you, Mrs Clarke. Can I come to your house and stay with you?'

The alabaster statue seemed to have puddles forming where its eyes should be. This poor child – if only she could rescue her from such obviously disturbing family circumstances. For who would be left to take care of her now?

Tension mounted. Izzy remained unmovable.

'Come on, Izzy, say goodbye to Mrs Clarke and get your coat.'

Nothing. Grace felt an outburst coming on.

Sensibly, she attempted the power of persuasion first. 'If you're really good we can call at the chip shop on the way home. You can have a bag of chips for lunch as a special treat.'

'Chips?' Izzy was easily swayed sometimes. 'Not bread and jam like I had yesterday?'

The alabaster seemed to take on a rosy hue. Chips? Bread and jam? What sort of rubbish was that to feed a growing child? Such a sweet little thing too. There would be no hope for her now, none at all.

'Bread and jam? I didn't give you bread and jam for lunch!' said Grace, suddenly in defence mode, feeling a little bit hot under the collar at being falsely depicted as a bad mother in front of the ever-watchful Mrs Clarke.

'No, you didn't give me anything,' said Izzy, hamming it up for all she was worth. 'I was really hungry 'cos I'd been at nursery, but you said I would have to wait 'cos you were too busy. You were whispering things to Auntie Kate, so I climbed up onto the worktop and got the jam out of the cupboard. You didn't notice me 'cos you were *still* whispering things to Auntie Kate.'

The alabaster had started to crack, sort of like the ground's surface at the start of an earthquake, but on a much smaller scale, obviously. Whispering sweet nothings probably, nothing would come as a shock as far as this family was concerned. This poor child! Perhaps they should be reported to social services; she'd considered doing so before.

But it was Jessica to the rescue, or sort of, as she flew in where angels fear to tread. Strange that, she was often called angel, but that's by the by.

'Come on,' she said, walking up to Izzy and taking her by the hand. 'Come home with your sister.'

It was a game they played where they pretended. As an only child Jessica had always wanted a sister, and in Izzy she'd found a make-believe one.

'Okay sis,' Izzy replied, taking her hand and walking towards Grace.

Mrs Clarke was more than a little confused. The alabaster was now a shade of … I suppose you could call it puce.

'But I thought …'

'Let's go home with our two mummies.'

Oh good gracious me! Mrs Clarke clutched at her throat nervously, suspicions confirmed. Well, in her mind anyway. Sister? Two mummies? It was obvious, there was a lesbian relationship going on in that family now, in addition to everything else!

17

Tom declined the offer to come in for a coffee and see everyone when he rang from the motorway service station to say he'd be there to pick up Kate in about half an hour. It wouldn't have seemed right, not tonight. Apart from anything else he'd had a really hectic couple of days and was feeling absolutely exhausted. Nothing that couldn't be overcome once he got back home and relaxed, of course, just that socialising was definitely not high on his list of priorities tonight: he had other things on his mind, and one thing in particular. This was going to be their night, his and Kate's alone. It had a lot riding on it.

He drove slowly as he turned into the road where they lived, trying to see the house numbers. But then he saw her, his Kate, her face at the window, looking out for him, her golden curls cascading around her shoulders. His heart flipped like a tossed coin. Heads or tails? Both, it had to be, whichever. He had to win her back now, almost had, and couldn't believe his luck. He must never gamble with love, not ever again. The odds had been stacked against him, and now here she was.

'You look incredible,' he said, as she stepped into the car, her perfume filling the air. She kissed him in welcome, fleetingly, on the lips.

He felt work-worn and smelly and scruffy, and would have given anything to have at least been able to brush his teeth before they'd met.

'So do you,' she smiled, her teeth whitened to perfection.

'I think not,' he said, his vivid blue eyes twinkling in the way she remembered so well. 'I'm in desperate need of a shower, it's been a long day.'

'I'm sorry. Are you sure you ...?'

'Definitely sure.'

They drove along the road towards the place they'd used to call home, hoping they'd be able to do so again shortly. The pressure was on, and both felt it to a certain extent. Conversation was a little bit stilted at first, and understandably so. They talked about Jess, it seemed like a safe subject as well as being of equal importance to both of them. But wittering on about their daughter, no matter how wonderful they thought she was, was no substitute for talking about themselves and their relationship, for that was what tonight was all about: to judge whether they had a future together as man and wife once more.

There seemed little doubt, the way they were both feeling right now.

'She's so excited.'

'What?' asked Tom, trying to keep his mind on his driving.

'Jessica. She's so excited at the prospect of us getting back together again.'

'She knows?'

'Been discussing it with Izzy, apparently.'

Tom smiled. 'It really would make her happy, wouldn't it?'

'I think it would make us all happy Tom.'

He turned his head towards her briefly and twinkled a smile. 'It sure would,' he said, softly.

'I feel a bit like a bride, all pure and virginal, being driven off to my honeymoon in the wedding car, wondering what to expect.'

'There aren't many of those nowadays.'

'What?'

167

'Pure and virginal brides.'

'Tom! How do you know?'

'Well I wouldn't have thought so. And even if there are, you're certainly not one of them.'

'Don't spoil my fantasy,' she giggled.

They travelled in silence for a while, Kate deep in thought.

'What's wrong?' he asked eventually.

'I feel quite nervous; it's been a while. What if I've forgotten how? What if I'm all shrivelled up like a dried prune and can't do it any more?'

Tom couldn't help laughing despite the anxious look on her face. 'Oh Kate, what are you like? It's been equally as long for me you know, what if I can't? It's even worse for a man, so much more obvious.'

'You didn't seem to have much malfunctioning going on the other night, quite the opposite in fact. I don't think you'll be reaching out for the Viagra any time soon.'

'I'm so sorry about that, I just wanted you so desperately that things got a bit out of control. No excuse at all, though, I should never have behaved as I did, it was completely out of order. You'd said "no" and I should have accepted that.'

'Oh well, we can't change what happened. And anyway I do feel as though I led you on a little bit. Let's just draw a line under it and enjoy our time together now.'

'Suits me,' said Tom, his hand briefly caressing her knee before returning to the steering wheel.

Wow! Shrivelled up dried prune? One split second of hand-knee contact and she was gushing like a freshly squeezed orange.

'Tom?'

'Mm?'

She looked at him. He looked exhausted. Greasy-faced. Unshaven. It wouldn't be fair. He wanted to get home, have a shower.

'Nothing. It's okay.'

'What?' he asked, glancing at her briefly.

His twinkling eyes, the dimple in his cheek, that strong jawline ...

'Nothing. Honestly.'

'Obviously something. What were you going to say?'

God, even the stubble looked attractive. In fact, to be honest, he could have worn a Tesco carrier bag over his head and she would still have fancied the pants off him. For it was his body she was after. She'd waited long enough, this shrivelled prune was plumped up to bursting point.

'Could you stop the car?'

'Not feeling car sick, are you?' he asked, worriedly, checking his mirrors to make sure it was safe before grinding to a halt.

'What? No. I meant more private. A lay-by or something. Not right here at the side of a busy road.'

'I thought it was an emergency. I thought you felt sick. You do get car sick sometimes, I remember.'

'Well not this time,' she smiled. 'More like lovesick maybe.'

Tom looked a little bewildered. 'But the other day when ...'

Kate put her finger to her lips briefly, to silence him.

'And in any case, I haven't had a wash, brushed my teeth, anything.'

She looked into his eyes as her hand came to rest on his thigh in response, the warmth of it permeating through the fabric of his trousers to the all-yielding flesh beneath, and stimulating everything within a one metre radius of its palm.

'Okay,' he submitted, with a sudden intake of breath. 'Where?'

'Turn right just along here, there's a lay-by at the edge of the forest.' She sounded remarkably in control for one whose shrivelled prunes were now so plumped up they were on the boil and throbbing towards explosion.

It was over in a trice. On occasions gone by, tired after a long day, and simply wanting to go to sleep in their marital bed, she would have been glad of such speed, but not today. On this day, the idea of inventing a headache would have been a complete anathema to her psyche. On this day, at this moment, all that was on her mind was sex. Was that it?

'Sorry,' said Tom, breathing heavily as he withdrew. 'It's just that, well, it's been a long time. A very long time, in fact.'

It was understandable, she understood – she did! A year of enforced abstinence, what more could she expect? Understanding didn't help her though: just as her prunes had been about to boil over, someone had turned off the heat. Frustration, thy name is woman at times.

Another woman feeling frustrated, at that very same moment in time, was Grace. Not frustrated in the same way as Kate, but frustrated nevertheless. How come everyone else always seemed to be out enjoying themselves while she was left at home holding the fort? Because she was a woman? Surely not; not in this day and age.

She loved Charlie, of course she did, more and more each day in fact. She couldn't have chosen a better man to share her life with and she totally realised that now. Nevertheless he wasn't the sort of man who would ever dream of spontaneously whisking her away to do something exciting, he was a plodder, quite happy with his routine at home and he expected Grace to be so too. And she was, she enjoyed caring for everyone, most of the time. It was just that sometimes, well, a little frisson of excitement would be nice. Not tonight though, obviously.

'Mummy! Jessica can't find her toothbrush!' called Izzy

from the top of the stairs.

'Well help her look for it,' shouted Grace in reply.

'I have, but it's not there.'

'Okay, I'll be up in a minute.'

Meanwhile there was a scratch at the back door.

Alfie, legs crossed, desperate for a wee. She let him out into the garden and went upstairs to sort out the girls.

'Grace!' shouted Gran from downstairs. 'Are you making tea? I think everyone's forgotten about me.'

As if.

'Ask Charlie to make you some, Mother, I'm just getting the girls to bed.'

By the time Grace reached the bathroom, the missing toothbrush had mysteriously reappeared.

'Can you read us a story now?' asked Izzy, wide-eyed, defying refusal.

'I didn't hear a please,' smiled Grace.

'Please!' they chorused.

Who could refuse.

Finally, after having been cajoled into reading two stories, Grace made it back downstairs – to the chaos that called itself the kitchen. How could one little old lady be the cause of so much commotion in such a short space of time? Grace was almost rendered speechless.

'What on earth has been going on in here? I thought I told you to ask Charlie.'

'I suppose I'm going to get the blame for all this as usual, aren't I?' Gran glowered gummily.

'Well I can't see anyone else in the room, can you?' Sarcasm came quite naturally to Grace at moments like this. Understandably.

'Yes!'

'Who?'

'That dog! He's the cause of the most of it, not me.'

Poor Alfie. He slunk into his basket, tail between his legs.

Upsetting his mummy was the last thing he'd meant to do, she was his very favourite person in the world. He lay down with a sigh, head resting on his paws, dolefully looking up at them from beneath his furrowed brow. Perhaps if he was quiet she wouldn't shout. She didn't, not at him anyway, she sprang to his defence.

'You can't blame a poor defenceless animal.'

Yes, I'm a poor defenceless animal.

'He would have been perfectly alright in the garden until I came downstairs.'

'But he was scratching at the door to come in.'

'It's what dogs do, Mother, but he's patient.'

Yes, patient – she wasn't cross with him after all.

'He would have waited.'

'Why can I never do anything right around here? huffed Gran. 'I was only trying to help. He came in covered in mud, how was I meant to catch him? I tried mopping it up with the tea towel on the end of my walking stick but it just seemed to smear it everywhere.'

'And, incidentally, why does everything on the kitchen worktop seem to be swimming in milk?' asked Grace, her eyes scanning the rest of the room, almost afraid of what she might see next.

'Well he made me jump. He started racing around the kitchen like a mad thing and made me drop the bottle of milk.'

'And the bottle is where?' asked Grace, hesitantly.

'Well how am I meant to know? Honestly Grace, sometimes you ask the silliest of questions, you expect me to know everything.'

'Hmm,' said Grace, trying to remain calm. 'Just one more thing: what happened to your skirt?'

'What skirt?' asked Gran, puzzled, as she looked down at her bare legs.

'Precisely. You're not wearing one. You had one on

earlier, what happened to it?'

'Well I do know the answer to that one Grace. See, I bet that's shocked you, hasn't it? I remembered something!' said Gran, triumphantly.

'So where is it?'

'What?'

'Oh Mother!' Mostly Grace had the patience of a saint, but just sometimes … 'Your skirt!'

'What about my skirt?'

Grrr. 'Where is it?' Grace gritted her teeth so tightly they almost retreated back into her gums. Well maybe not quite, that could have turned her into a carbon copy of her mother – saints preserve us, and patient ones at that!

'It's in the bin. I do know some things you know. Even you didn't know the answer to that one, did you Miss Clever Clogs?'

'If it's not a silly question, what is your skirt doing in the bin?'

'Well it is a silly question actually – because it's just sitting in there, isn't it? What did you expect it to be doing, a tap dance or something? For goodness sake, Grace, even I know better than that!'

Through clenched teeth Grace rephrased her question. 'Mother, why did you put your skirt in the bin?'

'Don't you take that tone with me young lady, remember who it is you're speaking to and have a bit of respect. I put my skirt in the bin because the milk spilt all over it. I told you that already Grace. Keep up, I haven't got the time to have to keep repeating myself. I'm not like you, you know, a lady of leisure.'

'Thank you, that's all I wanted to know,' said Grace, mustering every ounce of patience she could find, as she moved towards the bin to retrieve the much discussed garment.

'I wouldn't if I were you.'

'Wouldn't what?'

'Get it out of the bin.'

'Oh for goodness sake, Mother! If it's only a bit of spilt milk …' snapped Grace, her hand reaching for the bin lid.

'Stop!' shouted Gran, gesticulating wildly with her walking stick and knocking over her cup of tea in the process.

'Mother! What? I can't cope with any more. Look what you've done now!'

'I'm only trying to tell you to leave it in the bin because there's not just milk on it there's …'

'What? There's what?'

'Wee,' said Gran, hanging her head shamefacedly.

'You mean you …?'

'No, Grace, not me. It must have been Alfie when he came in from the garden. I must have got him in too soon. He must have cocked …'

'Oh Mother,' said Grace, finding herself reduced to tears for no apparent reason. She'd had worse days but suddenly it felt all too much.

Gran stared at her in shock. Grace never crumpled. 'Sit down,' she said, caringly for once, 'I'll make you a nice cup of tea.'

'No-o-o,' sobbed Grace. 'Please n-n-o-o.'

'Mummy! Can I have a glass of water, please?' shouted Izzy, from the top of the stairs.

'Charlie-e-e!' shrieked Grace, feeling as though her whole world was caving in.

And Charlie appeared – like magic. 'Wassup?' he mumbled, bog-eyed, rubbing his scalp with the fingers of both hands trying to wake himself up. The house had been quiet, he'd must have fallen asleep in front of the telly, watching football and suddenly he'd been disturbed by this pandemonium.

'Whatever's the matter?' he asked his beloved Gracie, as

she fell gratefully into his strong comforting arms, in floods of tears.

'Oh Charlie, I don't think I can cope any more,' she sobbed.

'Gracie, Gracie, Gracie,' he said, stroking her hair soothingly. 'What happened?'

'Mother … Alfie … mud …' her words were punctuated by sobs.

'And then what happened?' asked Charlie patiently, wiping away her tears, trying to cheer her up.

'Milk. Spilt it everywhere.'

'Well, you know what they say, don't you?' he was determined to get a smile.

'What?'

'It's no good crying over split milk!'

It may have been a watery one, but he succeeded, nevertheless.

Later that night as they lay snuggled up in bed Grace started to relax at last. 'Sorry Charlie, I didn't mean to create such a fuss.'

'Hardly that, Gracie, I don't know how you cope with it all, I really don't.'

'That was the trouble tonight, I felt as though I was cracking up. It's so hard sometimes, I don't know how much longer I *can* cope with it all, if I'm honest.'

'You need a break, anybody would. How long is it since we managed to get away?'

'Ages. And that was only for a weekend.'

'Hmm. If you could choose, where would you go?'

'What do you mean? How could I go anywhere?'

'I mean, if you could go away on holiday, you, me and Izzy for two whole weeks and not have your mother, or the dog, or anybody else to worry about, where would you want to go?'

'But that's impossible, so there's no point in even thinking.'

'Gracie, humour me! Just choose – anywhere in the world.'

She closed her eyes.

'What are you doing?'

'Thinking.'

'That's more like it,' he smiled.

'London,' she said, decisively.

'London? But I said anywhere in the world. You could choose anything from a hot sunny beach in the Caribbean, to a sleigh ride in the Arctic, to shopping in New York, to romantic Paris, to Morocco, to Italy, to …'

'Stop!' Grace covered her ears, smiling, overwhelmed by choice in this fantasy. I would still want to go to London!'

'Crazy woman' he grinned, 'Why on earth would you do that?'

'Because there is nowhere in the world I would rather be, and nothing in the world I would rather do, than spend two whole weeks with my amazing daughter, Cleo, and my beautiful little granddaughter, Daisy. I miss them sooo much and any time I do get to see them is so precious, and always over far too quickly.' If she wasn't careful the tears would start to overflow again – they were welling, certainly.

Charlie hugged her tightly. 'I'm sorry, it must be hard for you, and yet you never complain.'

'I think I've done my fair share of it tonight,' she said, with a wobbly smile.

'Rubbish, you don't complain enough and that's the problem: people take you for granted – even I'm guilty of that, I know I am.'

'You're not, you're my rock – I don't know what I'd do without you, Charlie.'

'Well, hopefully, you'll never have to find out.'

'It's never going to happen, is it?'

'What?'

'Two weeks in London with Cleo and Daisy – it's just a dream. A nice one though.'

'Hmm, we'll see.'

18

'This feels weird,' said Kate, feeling strangely nervous as the car turned into the drive of what had been, and still was really, their house.

'I suppose it must do, it does to me too, in a way. A year ago it would have been the normal sort of everyday occurrence we wouldn't have thought twice about. It just goes to show how life changes.'

'Hmm,' said Kate, thoughtfully.

'Well, come on,' said Tom. 'We can't sit here all day. Unless you're waiting for me to carry you over the threshold or something.'

'No, definitely not that!' Kate sprang into action and exited the car quickly, before he had any silly ideas.

'Are you quite sure?' he teased.

'Absolutely positive.'

It was strange being in the house again, even though she'd been in there, albeit briefly, only a few days ago. This time the visit had more serious undertones. It was, more or less, a trial run before taking the decision to move back in permanently, although in reality that decision had probably already been reached.

There was, though, just a little niggle that kept running through her head. 'Never go back over old ground.' It was an old adage she'd heard her mother use scores of times, although she herself had never recalled it until now. Just an old wives' tale, probably. Surely going back over old ground could be beneficial. You'd know the pitfalls, all the little things that could go wrong. You'd know what to look out for the second time around. She would, that was for sure.

He put down their overnight bags in the hallway and followed her through to where she was standing lost in thought.

'Are you okay?' he asked.

'I will be. It just seems a bit surreal, that's all.'

'I know. Would you like to come up to the bedroom?' he asked, mysteriously.

'God, you don't hang about, do you?'

Tom smiled. 'I wanted you to see what I'd done, that's all.'

'What? You've not decorated, have you?'

'You're joking!' he laughed. He was not known for doing anything around the house without a considerable amount of persuasion. It had always been a bit of a bone of contention between them.

'Of course I am,' she giggled.

She climbed the stairs, a trifle hesitantly, unable to help but think of the last time she'd been in the bedroom they'd once shared: the anger, the mistrust, the overpowering need to escape.

'I know this must be difficult for you,' said Tom, seeing the look on her face. 'That's why I wanted to make it special.'

She peered nervously around the bedroom door, unsure what to expect.

'Oh Tom, it's beautiful!' she exclaimed in surprise. Fresh new bed linen covered the bed, chocolates and champagne were on the bedside table next to it, and the room was filled almost to overflowing with red roses.

'When did you manage to do all of this? You've just driven straight here from London!'

'Well, let's just say I had to get very organised the day I left!'

'I bet you did, as well. Thank you for doing all of that just for me, that was really sweet of you.'

'Who says it's for you?' he teased.

'Don't joke about it, Tom, I'm really touched – thank you.'

'I just wanted everything to be perfect, that's all. Now, before I do anything else, I really must have a quick shower. Make yourself comfortable and enjoy the chocolates while you wait if you like, but save the champagne for me.'

'I'll try my best,' she smiled, her eyes following him as he disappeared into the bathroom.

She kicked off her shoes and lay back on the bed, remembering times past. It seemed so odd to be back here again, almost as though she'd never left in a way. Same furniture, same peeling wallpaper. But with the addition of a few cobwebs, and those curtains could certainly do with a wash. What was she doing, thinking about the state of the house's cleanliness when she was here for a romantic encounter? For goodness sake!

Propping herself up on one elbow she tore the cellophane from the chocolate box and lifted the lid. She studied the selection, chose one carefully, and popped it into her mouth. Mmm. The taste filled her with delight, sheer ecstasy. Hang on a minute! What was she doing having near-orgasmic moments with a box of chocolates when she had her very own stud-muffin standing naked in the shower in the very next room?

She could still hear the cascading sound of running water, and was out of her clothes like greased lightning, discarding them on the floor as she rushed to the bathroom like some sex-starved nymphomaniac.

He was singing – tunelessly – he hadn't improved and wouldn't be making it onto *X Factor* anytime soon, although X-rated could be a different thing. He was unaware of her presence in the room, washing his hair with his back to the cubicle door – but not unaware of her for long as she stepped in behind him, cupping him in her hand. Her other arm encircled his waist as she pressed her naked breasts up against his back, intoxicated by his presence, the water, her nipples on red alert.

He turned to face her, slippery with soap, drawing her to him, his mouth probing hers. He was trying to take things more slowly this time, his hands massaging her body with the soapy gel, sliding, reacquainting themselves with the familiar contours, playing with her nipples so staunchly erect. But her hands were exploring his body also, seductively stroking, stimulating, tantalising, and slowly as he was trying to take this, it was hard not to be swept along on the sea of overwhelming need that threatened to engulf him. His hands homed in on her special place, sending tremors of desire quivering through her like firecrackers.

She gasped and shuddered as he teased her playfully, the water showering around them somehow seeming to stimulate her even more, if that were possible. Panting, desirous, she somewhat reluctantly pushed away his magical fingers of pleasure, overpowered by the urgency for more. And as he lifted her up into his arms, she wrapped her legs around his waist and held on, leaning her head back as he entered her deeply, pounding, pushing her back against the cubicle wall as the water cascaded upon them. Riding along on the crest of a wave, pounding, building until they finally climaxed as one.

'Wow!' she gasped, as her feet slid back down to the ground, and she ran her hands down over her face and body, an awestruck look upon her face.

'Are you okay?' he asked, in a half-whisper of exhaustion as he exhaled. 'Well, you're more than okay,' he said, getting his breath back. 'That was bloody fantastic!'

'It was, wasn't it?'

They leant against each other, for support almost,

drowning in love, and in the water gushing down upon them.

'Of all the times we've made love, that had to be the best ever,' said Kate dreamily. 'Tom?'

'Mm?'

'If absence makes the heart grow fonder, then maybe abstinence makes the sex grow stronger.'

'Nutter,' he said. 'You're not going to make me abstain for another year, are you?'

'Not a chance. I've missed you,' she said, looking up at him.

'I've missed you too. Tell you one thing though,' he glanced down at her, tenderness beaming from his eyes, looking as though he were about to impart a statement of love. 'That mascara isn't very waterproof.'

'Tom! I wondered what you were going to say then, you looked so serious.'

'Well, it's a serious matter when your wife turns into a zebra!'

'Tom!'

'Sorry, it's not that bad – just winding you up that's all. I wouldn't care whether you wore make-up, no make-up, streaky make-up, whatever. I love you 'cos you're you, the rest is not important.'

'Aw Tom, what a lovely thing to say.'

'Well, it's true. Now, are we going to stay in this shower all night or do you think we should move.'

'It's certainly getting very steamy.'

'The steamiest time I've had in the bathroom for ages!'

'Ha-ha.'

Champagne, chocolates, flowers, a sex god of her very own – how easy it would have been for this all just to have slipped away. Kate really did feel as though she was the luckiest girl in the world, right at this moment, as she lay back, stretching out on the comfortable bed, the familiarity of the whole situation finally beginning to return. She was starting to feel at home again. What she had forgotten though, was how much time this man of hers liked to spend in the bathroom.

'Tom! How much longer are you going to be? I'm getting impatient, what on earth are you doing in there?'

'Just making myself gorgeous for you, my sweet, I'll only be a minute.'

'God, it's meant to be "vanity, thy name is woman," not "vanity, thy name is man". Hurry up, I need you.'

'Again? Surely not that quickly, we've only just ...'

'Tom! I mean, to open the champagne. I'm waiting for you, but I might be forced to drink it all myself in a minute.'

That made him move. Finally out of the bathroom – a vision of naked masculine perfection to Kate's eyes. He leapt on top of her and pinned her to the bed, his hands linking with hers. Worth waiting for? He did smell rather lush. He kissed her long and hard, his mouth tasting like a mixture of toothpaste and mouthwash, chemical perfection; she liked a man who took care of himself.

'Stop!' she said, pushing him away after a while. 'I need some breathing space – we're getting carried away again. Champagne, conversation, it's not all about sex, you know.'

'Isn't it?' he grinned, raising himself above her, giving a couple of playful thrusts towards her groin.

'You couldn't anyway,' she teased, 'limp as ... as lettuce.'

'Lettuce?' laughed Tom. 'Lettuce? That makes absolutely no sense at all.'

'Oh, shut up. I know it doesn't. Get off me and open the champagne, I've been waiting for ages. You're probably hoping I'll forget about it so you can return it to the shop and get your money back.'

'The cheek of the woman!' he exclaimed, sitting up and reaching out for the bottle.

He twisted the wire to remove the cork, concentrating, not wanting it to spurt everywhere, he'd paid good money for this. Nevertheless, with a sudden pop and a swoosh it went, landing more on Kate than on the bedclothes, at least.

'Tom! I've just had a shower, I really don't want another one.'

'Sorry,' he laughed, putting the bottle down on the bedside cabinet for the moment.

'Waste not, want not, though,' he said licking the spilt bubbly from her legs. 'Yum.'

She squirmed on the bed with a sudden tingle of titillation. Oh my God – she was insatiable. This could not be, and besides, there'd be no bubbles left in the champagne.

'If your tongue travels any further up my leg, I shall …'

'You'll what? What will you do?' he teased, pausing briefly.

'I don't know exactly. But the champagne will go flat,' she said, somewhat breathlessly and a little distracted.

'Okay, you win,' he said, raising his head away from mission impossible. 'You'll keep, it won't.'

'Tom!'

'What? I thought that's what you wanted.'

'It is, but … ooofft.'

'What?'

'Nothing. Just pour.'

'Do you know what? I shall never understand women for as long as I live.'

They chinked their glasses together.

'To us.'

Tom looked her directly in the eye as he asked the question that was uppermost in his mind. 'Does this mean that we are definitely back together again?'

Her gaze never wavered. 'It's what I want more than anything.'

'Me too. And you can trust me totally. I would never ever do anything to put our relationship in jeopardy again. I have learned my lesson, this has been the worst and the toughest year of my entire life.'

'I love you.' she whispered, emotion welling.

'Love you too.'

There was a lot to discuss that night, but discuss they did, in between bouts of love-making: they could hardly keep their hands off each other. Initially, Kate had thought that they would leave things as they were for a few weeks to see how it went, but with the intensity of their new-found passion came the realisation that they couldn't bear to be parted ever again, not even for a few days.

'So when are you moving back in?' asked Tom, hoping that he already knew the answer to his question.

'Hah! My move was so slick you didn't notice – I already have! I'll have to collect our things from Grace's tomorrow though. Oh, and our daughter too – we mustn't forget her!'

'As if! She's going to be so excited!'

Kate simply could not sleep that night. So many things were running through her head. Was she doing the right thing? She really had meant to take things slowly. Had it been the champagne talking, relaxing her, giving her a false sense of security? Had she just felt sorry for him, seeing him here alone, away from his family, working hard, no one to come home to? Or had she just been celibate for too long, desperate, lusting after him, and had been more than favourably reminded what it was like to be in a state of wedded bliss? Because what she must remember was that it wasn't like that all the time. And hadn't been, if he had felt the need to go off with someone else.

Okay, maybe that was putting it a little too strongly. He hadn't exactly gone off with her, had he? No, but he had slept with her, been intimate, right here in this bed. This very bed. Ugghh, the thought made her shudder.

She glanced at the clock. Twenty past seven already. Hmm … there was definitely not going to be any more sleep tonight. Apart from anything else, Tom's rhythmical snores were driving her bonkers, she had forgotten quite how bad his snoring could be at times. Unable to lie still for another minute, she quietly slipped out of bed, into her clothes and down the stairs.

Panic had set in. Undoubtedly. And it wasn't a good place to be. Her heart was racing. She needed to get out. Needed to. *Had* to …

19

Grace heard what seemed the interminable sound of a car engine running outside, briefly interrupted eventually by the slamming of a car door. But then silence, at last. Should be a law against that kind of thing on a Saturday morning just as people were trying to have a lie-in. Even the girls and Gran had refrained from disturbing them so far this morning. But then the doorbell rang loud and clear. Blimey, the postman now, on top of everything else.

'Charlie!' she hissed, nudging him with her knee.

'Wassup?' he spluttered, through a sleep-filled haze.

'Doorbell.'

'But …' he rubbed at his eyes with his fists, still entrenched in the dream he'd been having. It had been so good he was reluctant to leave it.

The doorbell rang again, echoing through the stillness of the house. Well, that would certainly wake everyone now. Thanks a bunch, Mr Postman.

Wake everyone but Charlie, that is. He'd slid effortlessly back into his slumbers, intent on recapturing the elusive dream. Alfie gave a tentative yap from the kitchen below, in an attempt to perform his guard dog duties without incurring the wrath of his mum.

Grace huffed somewhat and dragged on her dressing gown. 'Tell you what,' she muttered crossly to herself, 'Why don't I just answer it myself?'

A somewhat bedraggled figure stood forlornly on the doorstep looking as though it had just rolled out of bed. It had.

187

'Sorry,' it said, eyes lowered, defeat oozing.

'Kate! But ...?'

'I know.'

Kettle on. Tea made. Kitchen table. The scene for all soul-baring.

'Mother, would you mind going back to your room for a little while, please? I just need to talk to Kate,' said Grace, barring her entrance as Gran was just about to hobble in through the door.

'Well I would, as a matter of fact. The day's half over and nobody's even bothered to come and see me yet, never mind bring me a cup of tea. I could be dead and buried for all you know but then, what would you care?'

'Mother, please. You know I care, but Kate has only just come back in and she needs to talk to me. In private, if you don't mind. We won't be long.'

'She's only just come back in? Has she been out all night with that man?'

'"That man" as you call him, is her husband.'

'Yes I know, the husband who slept with her best friend, she ...'

'Mother! Go and watch your television for a little while and I'll bring you a cup of tea. And don't say things like that, it's not very nice.'

'No, it's not very nice, and I should know,' said Gran, in a defeated sort of way, for once, as she did what was requested.

'She's right though, isn't she? People will just point a finger at me and say, "That's her whose husband slept with her best friend", and even if they don't say it, that's what they'll be thinking.'

'And do you care?' asked Grace, pouring the tea.

'Well of course I care,' snapped Kate, I don't want to be viewed as someone to be pitied, I've done nothing wrong!'

'That's not what I meant,' said Grace, picking up one of

the cups. 'What I meant was, do you really care what other people think? Is it important? Surely all that matters is you and Tom and how you feel about each other. Excuse me just for a minute while I take this through to Mother.'

Kate reached over for her cup and sipped at it gratefully. It had been a long twelve hours, most of them filled with joy and longed-for pleasure, but then in the cold light of day, the angst had started to creep back in. Inexplicably so. Why did that always have to happen to her? Why did she always have to spoil everything for herself by dissecting things too deeply? Why could she not just accept this second chance of happiness with the love of her life without expecting everything to go wrong?

'So?' asked Grace, returning, flustered by her mother, and finding it difficult to comprehend the behaviour of her friend sometimes, love her though she did. She had seemed so positive when she'd left yesterday.

Kate glanced up from her misery as Grace sat herself opposite, waiting for an answer.

'Panicked and ran, didn't I? Story of my life really.'

'And Tom?'

'Doesn't know yet. Or didn't.'

'What? You just ran off and left him asleep?'

'Yup. Well, took a taxi, anyway.'

'That must have cost you.'

'It did.'

'I may be a bit dense at times,' said Grace, looking mystified, 'but I really don't understand this.'

'Me neither.'

'So why?'

'Grrr! I don't know!' exploded Kate, throwing back her head, her fingers brushing back through the roots of her hair, the nails scraping her scalp as if attempting to chisel all of this irrationality from her brain. 'I'm so angry with myself right now!'

'Calm down,' Grace soothed. 'Start at the beginning and tell me what happened. If you want to, that is. Not the saucy bits though, and I'm sure there were plenty of those judging by your general state of dishevelledness,' she teased.

'Ooft, I never thought! Just jumped into my clothes and did a runner.'

'Obviously! I pity the taxi driver.'

It lessened the tension anyway.

Poor Tom. He awoke initially with a feeling of utter contentment – it was a feeling he hadn't had for a very long time. That was the best night's sleep he'd had in ages and, after his hectic schedule in London and yesterday's long drive, he sure had needed it. Nothing like a night of passion for leaving you totally relaxed. He smiled to himself as he forced his eyes to open, he was the happiest man in the world, and the luckiest.

He turned to snuggle up to her, thinking her still there, surprised to find her gone. An empty space in the bed next to him. At least the bedclothes were all ruffled, the pillow indented where her head had lain, so at least he knew it hadn't all been a dream, a fantasy. As if! Even a fantasy could never have been that amazing. What a night! And, what's more she was back to stay.

He hadn't expected it all to happen so quickly, but happen it had. Kate had moved back in to live with him. His Kate. His life was complete once more. They would go and collect Jessica today, tell her the good news. She would be absolutely over the moon. He couldn't wait to see her little face when they told her.

He glanced lazily at the clock, still in a state of blissful ignorance. Ten past ten already – how had it got to that time? Well, silly question, he knew exactly how. It must have been at least 5 a.m. before they'd even made any attempt to go to sleep. He smiled at the memory, grinned like the proverbial Cheshire cat in fact. Oh well, no hurry, they'd got all day.

The memory of last night was prompting all sorts of stirrings below that he wouldn't have expected to have the energy for this morning. Where was she? He bet she'd sneaked downstairs to make breakfast for them. She'd be bringing it upstairs on a tray at any minute, a romantic breakfast for two in bed like they'd used to have in another lifetime. Better stay quiet and wait, he didn't want to spoil the surprise. Couldn't smell bacon. But then, no wonder, there wasn't any in the fridge. There were some eggs, though, if he remembered rightly.

Relaxed, warm, comfortable and lulled into this false sense of security, he fondled himself lazily as he drifted on that blissful cloud that lies somewhere between sleep and wakefulness and is probably related to cloud nine.

'Ring him,' said Grace, after Kate had imparted the whole story. Well, not the whole story obviously, certain parts had to be censored.

'You're so bossy. Did I ever tell you that?'

'Well somebody has to talk some sense into you – clearly! Just think of the poor man waking up to find you gone. He must wonder what on earth has happened.'

'And has he rung to find out? Have you heard my phone ring? He's obviously not *that* bothered.'

'Oh Kate, you know that's not true! You know he's head-over-heels with you, nobody more so.'

'You're a bit quick off the mark to spring to his defence, aren't you?' said Kate, with a sudden rush of suspicion and a moment of déjà-vu.

'Oy!' combatted Grace. 'Now you really are getting para-noid. As if …'

'Sorry. Once bitten, and all that.'

'I know, but you can't let it rule your life forever. You love the man, let it go.'

'Easier said than done. And you know me and my panics.'

'That's what happened this morning?'

'Yep. I just had to get away. It was all moving too fast.'

'Then tell him.'

Grace went up to see to the girls, leaving Kate with some privacy to make the call. He was going to think she was so stupid.

'Hi,' she said in a half-whisper which hovered on the brink of pressing the red button through sheer embarrassment.

'Hey gorgeous,' he answered, rolling over on his happy cloud and propping himself up on one elbow to give her his full attention, as far as was humanely possible at least, for his head seemed to have turned into mush today. 'Is it ready yet? I'm waiting for you. Ready and waiting actually, we could always skip breakfast.'

The other end of the line went silent.

'Kate?'

'I'm still here,' she whispered.

'I know you are, I can hardly believe it. I'm coming down to you if you're not coming back up,' he said, scrambling out of bed, 'I can't bear to be apart from you for another minute, even though we're in the same house.'

'We're not.'

'Ready or not, here I come,' he said, leaping down the stairs two at a time.

'Stop!' commanded Kate.

'Where are you?' he asked, thinking she was teasing him, diving from room to room, searching in vain.

'Tom! Will you listen to me? I'm back at Grace's, came back this morning, you were still asleep.'

'What the f…?' he said, his hand to his head, as his body slid down against the cupboard door until he landed, squatting on his haunches, on the cold kitchen floor.

'But I don't understand. How did you get there? Is it Jess? Is there something wrong with Jessica?'

'Jess is fine, Tom. I took a taxi. I should have woken you, I know. I just panicked, had to get away, it just felt like things were moving too fast and I needed space.'

'But Kate, correct me if I'm wrong but you were the one who said you didn't want to wait any longer, I didn't force you.'

'I know, I know. I'd had champagne, the romance of it all, but then …'

'You panicked and ran.'

'You know me so well. I'm sorry, I should have woken you, talked to you. Are you very cross with me?'

'Just disappointed more than anything. And worried, too.'

'Worried?'

'That you'll panic even more and run back down to Cornwall. I couldn't bear it if that happened again.'

'I promise I won't.'

'And do I believe you?'

'Tom! Remember trust? I think we both need to take a refresher course on that one.'

'So when do I see you again? How does this work?'

'I'll ring you.'

'No, Kate, no, please! Please don't leave it like that!'

'Sorry, Tom, you have to trust me.'

A sudden shift of power there, to Kate. But not for long. For other factors came into play. Like Jessica for instance.

'Where's my daddy?' she demanded, storming into the kitchen smarting with the fear that the day she had so been looking forward to was about to be ruined.

'He's at his house. Nice to see you too. Come and give me a hug, I haven't seen you since yesterday.'

'But why isn't he here with you?' Jess persisted, hands on hips, taking a firm stance.

193

'Come here,' said Kate, holding out her arms to her little daughter, feeling guilt wash over her in waves.

'No! Not until you tell me!' Jessica was adamant.

'I had to leave, Jess, it's hard to explain. You'll understand one day when you're older.'

'I'm not a baby!' yelled Jess, tears springing to her eyes. 'Why do you always have to spoil everything! I *hate* you!' she screamed, as she ran up to the bedroom.

Somewhat taken aback at such an uncharacteristic outburst from her usually placid daughter, Kate felt stunned, tears welling in her own eyes also. She followed her up the stairs, finding a somewhat subdued Izzy sitting next to her on the bed attempting, in her own Izzy way, to give comfort.

'She's crying now,' she said, accusingly, glaring hostility at Kate.

'Yes, I know she is,' said Kate, pleading guilty to this mini judge and jury all rolled into one, but needing to appeal against her sentence – to the victim.

'Could you go downstairs to your mummy please, Izzy? I need to talk to Jessica on her own.'

Izzy glanced anxiously at her little friend, unsure of what to do.

'It's okay,' said Jess to her, between sobs, 'I'll be down in a minute.

'My mummy never breaks promises,' said Izzy, pointedly, determined to have a last say.

'Izzy! Come here now!' shouted Grace from the doorway after having overheard that final statement. 'Or you'll be on the receiving end of a promise you won't like in a minute!'

Left alone in the room, Kate sat down on the bed next to Jess and put her arm around her shoulders. Jessica shrugged it off and moved further away.

'I'm sorry,' said Kate hoarsely, 'I don't know what more I can say, except to say you know both Daddy and I love you very much. All of this is just a grown-up thing between him

194

and me, it's nothing to do with you. None of it is your fault and neither of us want to do anything that is going to hurt you.'

'Well it doesn't sound very grown-up and … and you do things to hurt me all the time.'

'Oh Jess, I'm so, so sorry. It can be very difficult being grown up sometimes, and sometimes it's better when mummies and daddies live apart, rather than together and arguing in front of their children all the time.'

'So … so does that mean … I thought we were all going to live back together again like we used to?'

'We probably are, darling, it's just … well, it takes a lot of sorting out, that's all.'

'Probably? What does that mean? I thought …'

'It means, young lady, that you have to be patient,' said Kate, giving her a squeeze.

Jessica brightened, just a little, and looked up at her mother wide-eyed and with the first grain of trust she'd shown that morning.

'So what about today, then?'

'Today?'

'Mummy! You said we would all be going out today, all three of us together. You said it was going to be special.' Her eyes, so big, so blue, and so like Tom's, looked questioningly at Kate, waiting for an answer.

Kate cleared her throat and swallowed. 'I'm sooo sorry, but I don't think that's going to be possible darling. Not today, anyway, maybe another day.'

'But you promised!' stormed Jess, leaping to her feet before throwing herself, face down and full length upon the bed, distraught at the unfairness of it all. 'You promised!' she repeated, in muffled tones.

Kate sat in silence for a second or two, almost drowning in the guilt of what they were doing to their poor little daughter who had done no wrong.

195

'I'm sorry,' she said. 'Wait there, I'll see what I can do.'
She had to phone Tom. Had to.

Izzy was waiting on the landing as Kate came out through
the bedroom door. She'd obviously been listening in. Kate
had to almost shield herself from the steely glare of this
feisty little missy. For one so small she sure could pack a
punch – even with just her eyes. If looks could kill Kate
would certainly be dead by now, several times over in fact.

Kate headed for the lounge. Great, it was empty, as she'd
expected it would be, for all activity centred around the
kitchen in this household. She took out her phone and
held it to her lips thoughtfully. How did she always manage
to land herself in these situations? More to the point, how
was he going to react? But Jessica's disappointed face kept
reappearing before her. She knew it had to be done.

'Tom?' He picked up straight away. She'd half expected
him not to answer when he saw her name register on his
screen.

'Don't tell me, you're going to Cornwall, your train leaves
in half an hour. 'Bye then. Have a nice life.'

'What?'

'Well, that's what you're ringing to tell me, isn't it?'

'Tom, don't be like that.'

'Well, how do you expect me to be?' He was decidedly
hostile, and understandably so.

'It's about Jess.'

That statement had an instantaneous effect, lifting him
from his pit of doom, his father-senses heightened in a
flash.

'What's wrong with her? Is she okay? I was so looking
forward to …'

'I know, and that's what made me ring. She was really
looking forward to today too, as you can imagine. She's
so upset, thinks we've let her down, broken a promise.
Well, it's me who has let her down, obviously, not your fault

196

at all and I tried to explain, as far as I could, how difficult it is for grown-ups sometimes. But she's distraught, Tom, absolutely distraught, she'd been looking forward to having a day spent with the three of us together, like I'd promised.'

The line was silent.

'Tom?'

'What?'

'Are you still there?'

'Of course I am. Where else would I be? I'm always here, here for you both, waiting. Maybe that's part of the problem.'

'What do you mean?'

'Well, maybe if I went off somewhere, made a new life for myself, had a life instead of just sitting here at your beck and call, waiting, then maybe you'd start to see things in a different way, realise things won't wait forever – not even me.'

Another power shift? It did shock her.

'Tom. I do love you, you know. It's just, I don't know what it is, I always seem to panic about everything and it makes me want to run. I try not to but something inside me takes over, it happens all the time.'

'Tell me about it,' he said sarcastically.

'I've got to get over it, I know, I love you and I want us all to be together. I thought last night that finally we could be, but then this morning, off I went again. What is wrong with me?'

'You're a nutter!' said Tom, lightening the mood, he could never stay mad at her for long. 'A loveable one though. So, where do we go from here?'

'Can we just take it more slowly?' she asked, with some relief.

'On one condition.'

'Name it.'

'That you promise not to go running back down to Corn-wall again!'

'Promise.'

'Hand on heart?'

'Hand on heart. It's too far to run all the way there anyway!'

'Kate!'

'Sorry, I promise, truly. I love you.'

'Love you too.'

'This doesn't solve the problem of our daughter, though, which is why I rang you in the first place.'

'Well, personally,' said Tom, cheering up more and more, 'I think a day out today for the three of us is just what is called for. Provided that you don't decide to do a runner half way through.'

'That would be great, she'd love it – the day out I mean, obviously.'

'And you?'

'And I would too.'

'I can be there in about an hour, that okay?'

'Absolutely perfect, Tom. Thank you so much.'

20

Chloe was simply loving having all of her family under the same roof, temporary though the situation was. After all of the stress she'd gone through recently it was exactly what she needed – to be at the centre of her family and know how much she was loved. She hadn't felt so happy for a long time, and then she felt a little twinge of guilt: should she be feeling so much joy when her husband had just died? That was the reason for this family gathering, of course: they were gathered here in readiness for John's funeral next week.

The only person to have shed a tear, however, had been Olivia. Much as she hated what he had become and the things he had done, he was still her father and she could not help but be saddened by his passing. Nevertheless, she totally understood why her mum and her brother felt the way they did: his behaviour had been despicable, had had them living in fear. They were glad he was gone.

Olivia was also the only one amongst them who had wanted to have any involvement with the funeral arrangements. She had been round to see Jackie and they had sorted it out between them. Not that there was much to sort out; John had not been a popular man, the mourners were likely to be few.

'What's up, sis?' asked Ben, as he flicked a sweet wrapper at her to rouse her from her sombre mood. Ben really couldn't cope with silence or sadness, and when the two were linked together it completely freaked him out.

'Well, what d'you think's up?' snapped Olivia, not at all impressed by his intrusion into her grief.

'Errr, the sky?' he shrugged, putting on the best clown face he could muster.

'Derrr!' sneered Olivia. 'You are an idiot, Ben, won't you ever grow up? I'm sad, can't you see?'

'Well of course I can see, derrr brain, that's why I'm trying to cheer you up.'

'I'll tell you what would cheer me up more than anything, Ben: you going away and leaving me in peace!'

'Oooh – temper, temper! You know you love it really, it's just like old times.'

'Yeah, right! We did have some good times didn't we, growing up?' said Olivia, thinking back to how it had been.

'Yeah, you were a right bossy little mare though, never gave me a minute's peace. You were worse than Mum!'

'That's 'cos she always gave in to you. You were a spoilt little brat, always whingeing to Mum and telling tales, and she believed you!' said Olivia smiling again now. 'I could never understand why she always took your side.'

'Hah, well,' said Ben, raising his eyebrows, a smug look on his face. 'Some of us just have it. What more can I say?'

'Pffft,' shrugged Olivia. 'Have what, may I ask?'

'We-e-ll, you know, a certain *je ne sais quoi*, that special indefinable charm that makes everyone love us. We can't help it, we're just born that way.'

'Oh Ben!' laughed Olivia. 'You're so full of yourself.'

'But you still love me, don't you? Case in point.'

'Of course I love you, you oaf, you're my bro', I'm stuck with you.'

'Cheered you up too, didn't I?'

'Yep. You may frustrate the hell out of me, but you always cheer me up.'

'I miss it sometimes,' said Ben, serious for once in his life.

200

'Miss what?'

'How it was, growing up, our family.'

'Me too. Good, wasn't it?'

'Sure was, we had some great times.'

'Where did it all go horribly wrong?' asked Olivia, close to tears again.

'Well it didn't, did it? It was only the Dad bit that went wrong. Mum's always been there for us, always will be.'

'I know, but … but I can't help but think that one day she'll be gone too and then it'll be just me and you, and J-J and … oh, Ben, I can't bear it!'

'For God's sake, sis, you're getting maudlin! It'll be us and our partners and our kids, if we have any.' A sudden wave of fear grabbed at him on that last thought. 'It's what happens, life goes in cycles, different generations. But hopefully that's not going to happen for ages yet. I couldn't cope without Mum.'

'Me neither,' said Olivia, choking back a sob.

'I mean I have to have someone to torment and Mum's perfect – she's so easy to wind up!'

'Ben Russell! Did I just hear you say I'm perfect?' asked Chloe, only half hearing the conversation as she moved towards them. 'You? Giving compliments? What's all this about?'

'I'm just saying, Mother dearest, what a perfect person you are to wind up. I suppose that is a compliment – in my eyes anyway.'

Chloe put her arm around his shoulders. 'Hmm, not the sort I had in mind but it's a start, and probably the best I can hope for coming from you,' she said, looking at him with pride. This mother–son thing, she always did have a special bond with Ben.

'You know I love you really, Mother.'

'I know you do,' she said, giving him a hug.

'Oy! Watch my hair!' said Ben, flinching to freedom.

'I could hardly do any other,' grinned Chloe. 'Talk about in yer face!'

'Ha ha. It's on my head actually,' said Ben, stepping briefly to one side in order to check the state of it in the mirror above the fireplace. 'Perfect, just like you, Mother – ha ha. Actually we *were* talking about you when you interrupted our conversation. Not about you being perfect, more about you being dead.'

'Ben!' stormed Olivia.

'Dead? What on earth were you saying. Not thinking of having me stuffed are you? Or sitting my ashes in a box on the mantelpiece?'

'Mu-um! That's not even funny!' Olivia burst in.

'Sorry darling, I know, bad timing. I shouldn't be joking about things like that when you've just lost your father.'

'That's why we were talking about you,' said Olivia, tears welling.

'About me dying? Because I'm not in any hurry to do that, believe me.'

'No, but you never know, do you?' said Ben, in all seriousness.

'Ben!' they both rounded on him, simultaneously.

'Actually, what we were saying was how neither of us could cope without you. You're the best mum ever. We love you loads.'

'Aw, thank you, that is such a lovely thing to say,' said Chloe, hugging them both to her, suddenly overwhelmed by emotion. 'I love you both too, I couldn't have asked for two nicer children. We've gone through a lot together, the three of us, good times and bad, and we've had a lot of fun along the way – and laughter too, thanks to Ben.'

'Glad to be appreciated, Ma.'

'Seriously, I love you both to bits and I'm so proud of the people you've grown up to be.'

'Even me?'

'Ben!'

'But most of all I just want to thank you for all the support.'

'God! This is starting to sound like an Oscar speech.'

'Ben!'

'For all the support you've given me over the past few years. I have been a bit of a nightmare, I must admit.'

Even Olivia grinned at that unexpected admission.

'It did seem a bit like we were the parents and you were the troubled teen at times.'

'Olivia!' Ben enjoyed getting his own back on that one.

'Well, I am grateful, and I couldn't have got through it all without you.'

'What? Even me?' grinned Ben, cheekily.

'Most certainly you. Who was the one who had to get me to the hospital when I went into labour with J-J?'

'God! Don't remind me! All that mopping I'd done for you and then you stood there and … errghh … all gushing all over my clean kitchen floor.'

'Well, that's what happens when your waters break, it's not something you have control over.'

'Jesus! Don't remind me! And then we had to rush to the hospital in the car with you screaming all over the place and Tom … Oops!'

'It's okay. You can say his name. It is allowed.'

'It's maybe best not to though,' said Olivia. 'Not seen any more of him, have you?'

'Nothing,' said Chloe, a look of sadness flittering across her face. 'Neither sight nor sound. And I wouldn't expect to now, not ever, he's getting back with Kate and that's the place he wants to be.'

'And you?' asked Olivia. 'Still missing him?'

'He was never mine to miss. I did wrong, but I'm a survivor.'

'That's the spirit, Ma.'

'One of these days someone will come along and snap you up, Mum. You deserve another chance of happiness.'

'Well, as long as I've got you two, and J-J, and my friends, then I'll be happy.'

'Friends? How's it going with Kate?' asked Olivia, wondering for a moment if she might be overstepping the mark.

'Hmm. Better than it could have done, but she's busy. She and Tom are trying to work things out and get back on track. And then, well, she's got a new friend now, Grace, and I feel as though I've been cast aside somewhat.'

'Surely you can have more than one friend.'

'I suppose. It's probably just me being paranoid. Whatever, I don't expect things can ever get back to how they were. We were really close at one time, but after what I did to her ...'

'Don't let it get to you, Ma.'

'Anyway,' said Olivia, trying to soothe her mother's obvious pain, 'if she moves back here to Little Smetherwick you'll see a lot more of each other, it's almost inevitable in a place of this size. You probably will get closer again then, given time.'

'I won't hold my breath, but you never know. Anyway, in the meantime I've still got Sandra, Caroline's mum. She's been like a rock to me just lately – I couldn't have managed without her.'

'And at least she doesn't have the type of husband you could run off with.'

'Ben!' burst forth Olivia, astounded.

Chloe, open-mouthed, just looked stunned by the fact that he could have said such a thing.

'It was a joke,' said Ben, hands up, in defence.

'Well not a very funny one.'

'Sorry, Ma – didn't mean anything by it. Point taken.'

He was rescued by his beloved Caroline, who came over to join them. She sensed his feelings of discomfort and stared at him with adoration. He could never do anything wrong in her eyes.

'Okay babe?' she asked. 'What's happening?'

'Uh-huh, only me putting my big feet in it as usual.'

'Nothing fresh there then.'

'Exactly.'

'We were just talking about your mum and dad,' said Chloe, making Ben's face turn into a shade that practically matched his hair.

It didn't go unnoticed. Caroline stared at him inquisitively. 'Mm?'

'Yes, Ben was telling us ...'

'Mu-um!'

'See how easily he gets embarrassed?' said Chloe, enjoying this for all she was worth. 'Ben was telling us how much he loves your mum and dad and I was saying what a fantastic friend your mum has been to me recently – I love her to bits.'

'Aw, me too. Both of them. They're brilliant.'

'Bet they can't wait to be grandparents.' Chloe was really enjoying herself now, she knew how Ben was not too keen on the idea of fatherhood and would put it off for ever if he had a choice.

But he didn't have a choice, for women were ganging up on him everywhere.

'They are looking forward to it, particularly Mum – she loves babies. I'm sure my Dad will make a brilliant grand-dad too, I can remember how great he was with me before he ... before he had to leave us.'

'When he came out, you mean?'

'Mum!' Ben couldn't believe what she'd just said. He squeezed Caroline's hand, worried she might take offence, although she seemed okay, amazingly.

'Sorry, I'm not saying that judgementally, not at all. I think David's a great guy, I really like him. I really admire him too, it must have taken a great deal of courage for him to do what he did – just imagine!'

'Mum – stop!'

'Sorry Caroline, I didn't mean to upset you.'

'No, truly you haven't. I'd much rather that it's all out in the open, that people talk about it – as long as it's not in a tittle-tattle sort of way, which this obviously is not. I love my dad and I'm proud of who he is.'

'And I love you, babe,' said Ben, kissing her softly on the lips, inspired by the inner strength of this beautiful wife of his.

'It was a different world when your dad was younger. In those days being gay was viewed as something to be ashamed of, something that a person was afraid to admit for fear of being viewed as an outcast. It must have been absolute torture, having to pretend to be something you weren't just so you'd fit in with the rest of society. Nightmare.'

'Yeah,' said Caroline, a faraway look in her eyes. 'That's how it was for Dad. He always knew he was gay but his parents were so strict and homophobic. In fact his own father actually beat him up once because of it.'

'How dreadful! You'd hardly believe it now, would you? Not in this day and age.'

'Oh, I don't know,' said Olivia, 'I bet there's still a lot of stuff goes on we never hear about – especially within families.'

'Far worse then, though.'

'Oh yes, I agree. It must have been dreadful. All that inner torment and not something that would ever go away.'

Caroline's eyes welled with unshed tears of emotion that she too had kept hidden and locked away. Although she totally accepted her dad's sexuality and remained staunchly proud of him at all times, it wasn't always easy being the daughter of a gay man. Certainly growing up without having him around, and not even knowing where he was, had not been a choice she would have taken. There'd always been an emptiness inside her just quietly gnawing away – hardly noticeable really, but there nevertheless.

She'd been a daddy's girl, heartbroken when he'd left, full of feelings of guilt that she must have done something to drive him away. Despite endless reassurances to the contrary from her mum, the guilt had persisted right through to that amazing day when she'd traced her dad and they'd gone to meet him. That moment of absolute ecstasy when he'd held her in his arms and called her his 'little munchkin' just like he'd used to. Twenty-nine Cedric Street. In her head she was back there right now, reliving that poignant moment, almost feeling his breath on her face as she stepped in through the front door.

'You okay babe?' Ben hugged her to him.

'Sorry,' said Chloe, seeing her distress. 'We should change the subject – talk about something else.'

'No, honestly, I'm happy to talk about it.'

'Well you don't look it,' said Ben, concerned, anxious that she should not be upset.

'Truly. I'm okay. It does me good to talk about it. Gets it all out instead of keeping it bottled up inside.'

'Your mum must have had it really tough too. All the gossip that must have gone on, and her left to pick up the pieces, bring you up all on her own.'

'And she still loved him too. Although she knew things weren't quite right, they really loved each other in their own special way – still do in fact. They're always at their happiest when they're together, they've got a really special bond.'

'And they've got you,' smiled Chloe.

'True,' grinned Caroline. 'It's great having him living so close to us again and Mum and Dad … well, they see each other every day.'

'Do you know what? I think I might ask them round tomorrow, while we're all here. We're just like one big happy family now.'

'Mum! Haven't you forgotten something?' Olivia butted in. 'My dad just died and you're here celebrating us being one big happy family!'

'Sorry, Liv, although I have to say it does feel like something of a celebration to me – that man put me through hell. I'm sorry though, he was your dad, I understand. Would you rather I didn't invite them?'

'No, it's okay. Just as long as we don't forget him altogether. He was my dad, after all.'

Caroline gave Olivia's hand a sympathetic squeeze. She knew exactly where Olivia was coming from on that one.

21

It would have been difficult to judge which one of the three of them was the most excited – although in all probability, it was probably Jessica. She'd been distraught, thinking the day had been ruined and convinced that she would never again have her mummy and daddy both spending time together with her. As for the thought of them all being a family and living together again, there just hadn't seemed to be a chance. But things had changed – just a little bit anyway. Her daddy was on his way to collect them, they were going to have a day out together after all! She was so excited, she could hardly stop bouncing up and down.

As for Tom, he was beside himself with joy – for the moment anyway. And living in the moment was all he could do for now, apparently. He'd been so convinced last night that everything was back on track. After all those months of waiting and longing and heartache, she'd finally come back home and was there to stay. Or so she'd said, and he'd believed her. He found her so hard to understand sometimes.

She'd been through a lot, he understood that, and it had had a profound effect on her. But he'd been through a lot too, and although things affect people in different ways, his own suffering had been equally severe, just dealt with differently. And that was where their relationship had gone wrong.

If only they'd pulled together and supported each other when Jake had gone, they wouldn't be in the mess they were in now. It could have brought them closer instead of forcing them apart. Why hadn't they comforted each other instead of turning their backs and seeking solace elsewhere? It was what he had wanted. He had been so desperately in need of her love at that point, but she had spurned him, changed into someone he didn't know, almost. And when she'd felt the need to escape, to run out on their marriage, albeit temporarily, he'd simply wanted to please her and so had let her go.

Mistake. Easy to say in hindsight, but he should have been stronger. Why had he just let her go? Why hadn't he made some attempt to stop her? Or gone with her to be there for her, been there with her in her time of need? Because he'd loved her, and if you love someone you let them go and hope they come back in their own time. You can't imprison someone, not even a partner. Give them freedom to fly and they come back to you. Or so he'd thought.

But she hadn't come back, not for a long time. Oh God! 'Lead us not into temptation and deliver us from evil ... for ever and ever. Amen.' He really should start listening to the Good Lord more often. When had he last gone to church? He'd go the very next Sunday he promised, if this all worked out, in fact they'd all go. It could be their salvation.

For lo and behold, he had been led into temptation while she was gone, twice actually, although he was trying to block the second one from his mind. He hadn't gone all the way with Caroline so that didn't really count, did it? Bad enough.

When she'd returned and then eventually discovered the worst of his misdemeanours, off she'd gone again – no wonder she was feeling insecure. He had to prove himself totally this time, had to stick around at all costs, had to persist, couldn't give up, not at any hurdle. They were halfway there now; this had got to work.

So excitement was the flavour of his day now, most certainly, despite its shaky start. He was on his way to collect his girls – both of them! It would be the first time they had spent a day together, all three of them, in a very long time. The Darrington family. The words rolled off his tongue like warm custard – comfort food, homely. But then, as if washed down with whisky, they hit the spot. Ping! Excitement all the way.

Excitement too for Kate. Her emotions were up and down like a yo-yo, but at the moment her yo-yo was most definitely up. Indeed, if she kept yanking the string hard enough then that's where it would stay. For this was where her happiness lay, in the bosom of her wonderful family and a mere short car ride away from her loveliest friend ever, the amazing Grace. What more could she ask? All she needed to do now was to learn to trust and stop running away from this paradisiacal place. Worry, fear, panic – they were destroying her life. Relax and enjoy, is what she should do: she could have it all. It sounded so simple, when she stopped to think about it in a calm and rational way.

The problem was that being calm and rational was not generally within the confines of Kate's psyche. Certainly not since the death of Jake, at any rate; the trauma of that unforgettable day had changed all that. Even just thinking about it now was tying her in knots. But she knew she couldn't let it destroy her. It almost had and she'd had to claw her way back – no sliding backwards now.

So, excited she most definitely was. She was! With reservations … Stop! This was exactly what she mustn't do. She must forget about the 'what ifs' and live for the here and now. She had the world at her feet and a man who loved her. If she could only stop worrying and move on, then she would be living the dream. Excited? Yes, she was. On a scale of one to ten? Um … maybe eight … Kate!

'He's here! He's here!' screeched Jessica, bouncing in

through the door, eyes alight, and the biggest beam on her face that Kate had seen there for a very long time. 'Hurry up, let's go!' she hissed, grabbing Kate by the hand and dragging her towards the door, not wanting to waste another second.

Excitement breeds excitement and seeing her precious girl in such a state of euphoria made her own level slide up the scale.

'Hang on! Let me get my bag,' said Kate, giggling almost like a teenager. 'What's the hurry?'

Jessica jumped up and down with impatience. 'It's Daddy, he's waiting! Hurry! Hurry!' Even her curls were quivering.

How could she fail to be influenced by that? So Kate, on a scale of one to ten now? A hundred, maybe?

'Let's go!' she said, grabbing the small proffered hand within her own.

It seemed to be family time all round, in fact. To his delight, Charlie returned home after a couple of hours finishing off a decorating job, to find a peaceful house for once.

'Blimey! Where is everybody?' he asked of himself, coming in through the back door and being met by a deserted kitchen. Deserted apart from Alfie, of course, who wagged his tail lazily but couldn't even be bothered to get out of his basket; he too was enjoying the tranquillity.

'That you, Charlie?' shouted a voice from above.

'No,' he groaned, happy as always to hear the sound of his beloved Gracie. 'Why, were you expecting someone else? I can always go back out again if you want me to.'

'Ha ha!' she said, coming down the stairs to greet him with a kiss. 'Had a good day?'

'With a bit of luck it might be about to get better,' he said, enfolding her in his arms, enjoying the warmth of her body next to his. 'You're hot,' he said.

'I know,' she said, somewhat exhausted, 'I took the

opportunity to do a bit of cleaning while everyone was out.'

'That wasn't what I meant,' he said, his eyes penetrating hers.

The penny dropped. 'Charlie!' That was absolutely the last thing on her mind – and what's more, it required energy.

'Bet you're going to say you've got a headache in a minute,' he grinned.

'Possibility. One might be on its way! Anyway, I've got a mother in the next room who is likely to walk in at any minute, and a daughter upstairs who will most definitely do the same, so any ideas you may have on that score ...'

'Score? Chance would be a fine thing.'

'Ha ha! Anyway, I'm far too exhausted.'

'Spoilsport!'

'Seriously, Charlie, I truly am.'

'You need a break.'

'Huh. Pigs might fly.'

The Darrington family. Tom had to keep pinching himself and saying those words to convince himself that it wasn't all just a dream. They were together again, the three of them, precariously so or not. They were having such a fantastic day, he didn't want it to end. But take it slowly a day at a time – that's what he'd promised her, and that's what he'd do.

'Don't walk on eggshells,' she'd said, but how could he not? He wanted everything to be perfect today. He wanted her to realise just how much she loved him and for her to think she could never bear to be apart from him ever again.

'I love you Mrs Darrington,' he said, turning to kiss the tip of her nose as they walked along.

Jessica looked up at them. 'Yuk – sloppy, sloppy,' she was about to say, but then managed to stop herself. She wanted her mummy and daddy to kiss because that would mean they liked each other again, and then maybe, just maybe, they could all be together for ever and ever, a proper family like before. She ran on ahead out of the way, glancing back over her shoulder at them to see if her plan had worked.

'Love you too,' said Kate, checking on Jessica's whereabouts before succumbing to his embrace.

'Yes-s-s!' said Jess, performing a little pirouette of excitement.

They caught up with her, holding hands, both radiating happiness. Jess was bouncing.

'What's the matter with you?' asked Kate, impervious to her daughter's plan.

'Nothing,' beamed Jessica, eyes screwed up by the force of her smile. She ran on ahead, hugging herself with delight.

'Hmm, we all know what she's thinking,' said Tom in a half whisper.

'I know, but I don't want her jumping to any conclusions, not yet.'

'Bit late for that.'

'I know. I'll talk to her.'

They walked along in silence for a while.

'Can I ask you something?'

'Well, you're obviously not going to ask me to marry you,' quipped Kate, 'We've already been down that route, still there actually.'

'On paper.' The words came out in a disdainful kind of way, although Tom hadn't meant them to at all, he was just being truthful.

'Tom!'

'Sorry.'

'Okay, so what were you going to ask?'

Tom turned to look at her as he spoke. 'Are you sure you still want to take this one step at a time? We love each other, we're happy spending time together, we make a great

214

family – we've got it all, what is there to wait for?'

'I know it doesn't make any sense, but don't rush me, Tom. I don't want to jump into it and do something I'll regret.'

'But …' Frustration was starting to get to him.

'Sshh!' she said, holding her forefinger to his lips. 'Let's just enjoy the day.' Her face was suddenly wreathed in smiles as she looked ahead to her still pirouetting daughter. 'Last one to reach Jess buys the coffee when we find a Costa. Deal?'

'Madwoman! You're on!'

Tchh – parents! Could there be anything more embarrassing in the world than having two of them, at their age, hurtling towards you, behaving like nine-year-olds? Jessica rolled her eyes heavenward in shame, but then had second thoughts. If they were acting like that then they must be in love again, she was sure of it – she'd seen it in films on TV. Better look like she was enjoying it, cheer them on. She could be moving back home again, into her very own bedroom with all the things she'd left behind, sooner than she'd thought. Maybe, even tonight if she was lucky. 'Come on, Mum!'

Charlie had an idea. It wasn't often he had an idea, not as good as this one anyway, and he was feeling quite proud of himself. Gracie was his world, but the problem was that her world was full of other people – too many of them by far, most of the time. She cared too much for everyone else and not enough for herself, that was the trouble. It wasn't that people took advantage necessarily, it was more because she was such a warm-hearted and caring person that it made people gravitate towards her in times of trouble or when they just needed a friend. She was a great 'Earth Mother' sort of person – in fact that was probably what had drawn him to her in the first place.

She was also soft-hearted – too much so in his opinion, particularly when it came to her mother. He knew for certain that he would not have put up with all the flak she took, had he been in the same situation. And particularly so now, having learned the sordid truth about Gran's behaviour in the past. Grace and Disgrace she'd called her daughters. Poor Anna, she must have gone through hell.

Obviously Grace had been astounded when her sister Anna had reappeared in her life out of the blue. Astounded, but also horrified when the family secret had been revealed. But then on top of all that, to lose Anna in such tragic circumstances so soon after she had come back into their lives – how had Grace coped?

But she had coped, stalwartly so, even having the strength to support Richard, who had become Anna's lover, and of course Hugo, Anna's son. She was a miracle woman, his Gracie, he knew it. She'd crumbled in his arms some nights when they were alone, but in the daytime she'd been strong for them all, always. Someone had to hold the family together and that was her job, she patched them up and stuck them all back together with that magic glue which calls itself love. Grace had oodles of it, she fixed everything – even her mother.

Nevertheless, try as he might, Charlie still could not get his head around that one. How could Grace manage to care for her mother, even bear to have her living in this house with them, knowing the things that had happened in the past? This wasn't all about the past either. Grace shouldn't have to suffer all the abuse she got from Gran on a daily basis. It must be so draining; he really didn't know how she coped with it. The constant complaining, being awkward for the sake of it – even lashing out at her sometimes. As for the arguments and all the muddles, they were never-ending.

But, big-hearted person that she was, Grace was of the opinion that she was still her mother and it was, therefore, her job to look after her. 'She has dementia, Charlie,' Grace would say when he confronted her about the situation. 'People with dementia are like that – muddled, argumentative, violent sometimes. It's to be expected, it's the way it is. I just have to get on with it – she's old, she's my mother, she gets confused easily and she needs looking after. Who is there to do that but me?'

Two little words sprang into Charlie's mind on occasions like this, they being 'social services'. However, having thrown them into the mix some time ago, to a rather raucous reception which resulted in he himself almost being hurled out through the front door by his ever-loving wife, he mostly found it best to bite his tongue.

'She's just a frail old lady, Charlie. I'm horrified by what happened in the past, of course I am, but I can't take that out on her now. She's got her own punishment, locked in the world of dementia, no escape at all and knowing that things can only get worse. How can I add to her troubles, throw her out, away from all that's familiar to her? How could I live with myself if I put her into a care home to live out the rest of her life with complete strangers? She'd have to go into a dementia unit, locked away with other poor souls who are in an even worse condition than she is. Just imagine, she'd go downhill so quickly, deteriorate and become like the rest, at least here she has some semblance of family life to keep her relatively sane.

Just imagine. Yes, Charlie could imagine. He could imagine a peaceful life, just himself with his Gracie and Izzy. Bliss. Family time for the three of them, their own choice of TV programmes in the evenings without having the volume turned to max, no arguments, no stress, days out like a proper family, holidays even. Yes, he could imagine, although he thought it best not to say. Tongue-biting was becoming a habit.

But he did have an idea, and surely she would agree to it.

217

Nothing he could do today, but tomorrow he'd get the ball rolling. If he could get it sorted she'd have to agree. He'd be insistent – not in his character normally, but she liked it when he was, he'd noticed that before. Anyway she'd hardly refuse, for the prize on offer would be too great. Yes indeed, tomorrow he would sort it out then come home and tell her what was happening. Be a man. Now, what was that he'd said about getting the ball rolling? Wasn't there some football on TV, just about to kick off now in fact?

Gran was sitting watching some cookery programme or other with Grace, the volume deafening. Being the man he was trying to be, he took control of the remote and flicked over the channel.

'Don't mind if I watch the footie do you? Just kicking off now,' he stated, reducing the volume from its ear-shattering level.

'Charlie, we were watching that!'

'Actually Charlie, could you sort Izzy out ready for bed? Oh, and Alfie needs letting out too, he's not been for ages.'

Be a man Charlie. Did you mean it?

He handed back the remote along with his formerly burgeoning masculinity.

'Okay, I'll do it now,' he said, drooping back out through the door.

Let's hope you do better than this tomorrow, Charlie.

22

Chloe was in a fluster. Cleanliness must be just around the corner somewhere but she hadn't seen it in a very long time. Domestic goddess she was not – how could she be? J-J was her priority and she was a single mum, no one to help, just herself. As for J-J, he should have been called J-M-J, for his middle name could have been selected at random from a seemingly never-ending list of words beginning with 'M', all of which depicted his character. Messy, muddled, maniac, monster, muddy – wherever he went, it would appear, chaos ensued. Having said that, he was also marvellous, miraculous, magnificent and his mummy's boy – how could she ever complain? He could never do anything wrong in her eyes, and now she had him back she would never complain again. Who cared about a dusty and untidy house anyway? No one. Well, maybe she did, today, anyway.

For today was the day she'd invited Sandra and David, Caroline's parents, to come round for the afternoon. It had seemed like such a good idea at the time and the words had just fallen out of her mouth. 'It would be lovely,' she'd said. 'Everybody's here.' And indeed they were, she had a houseful already, why on earth had she invited two more? Why? Because she loved having people around her, being needed. It was when she was at her happiest.

Anyway it would be good for Sandra and David to be included in family get-together – they were family, after all. Sandra had in fact become a really good friend, had been an absolute tower of strength to her during this recent crisis, but they hadn't seen much of David and she would hate him to feel excluded. In fact, even worse, what if he'd thought she was homophobic? Oh my God! That would be so bad, the thought had never crossed her mind before.

Okay Chloe – enough, you're really scraping the barrel now for excuses as to why you invited them. Nothing wrong with having guests apart from all the extra work. No trouble at all though, you said it yourself.

In fact, panic aside, she'd organised things rather well, she thought. Delegation, that was the key. And there lies the beauty of having lots of people around. You could hardly delegate when you lived alone with one small boy. However today, joy of joys, she had Olivia and Caroline banished to the kitchen to sort out the buffet, whilst Ben and Stelios had been only too eager to escape the flurry of flustered females in order to take the aforementioned small boy for a walk.

Cries of 'And make it a long walk if you don't mind please' followed them. Why would they mind? It was certainly better than housework – memories of mopping the floor in that particular kitchen had been enough to traumatise Ben for life. Ewww … never again!

'There's a pub just down the road, mate,' said Ben suddenly warming to the task in hand. 'Might as well walk to somewhere – don't just want to walk randomly, do we? And besides, it might rain.'

'But your mother, she would not like this,' said Stelios, pretty much stating the obvious really.

Ben walked and tapped the side of his nose, 'What she doesn't know won't harm her, eh?'

But Stelios was still not convinced. He did not want to get on the wrong side of what could be his future mother-in-law. And besides, Olivia would most probably kill him.

'We have J-J with us. He is just a child. We cannot take him in.'

'J-J likes pubs, don't you J-J?'

J-J smiled knowledgeably. 'Pubs,' he said, grinning ador-ation at his big bro'.

'Clever boy. Pubs. Yes. See?' said Ben turning to Stelios in triumph, 'He wants to go too. You're outnumbered, mate, come on.'

Two o'clock she'd told them to be back by – no later. Chloe checked the time again. Half past, and still no sign of them. Grrr, he'd be the death of her, that boy, so laid back it wasn't true. She could never understand from whence he'd acquired that character trait. It certainly wasn't from her, she was wound up as tightly as a coiled spring. Why she stressed about everything so much she could not explain, there wasn't the slightest thing to worry about when she stopped and thought about it logically. Sandra was her friend, she'd witnessed all sides of Chloe these past few weeks and would never sit in judgement. As for David, he was Caroline's dad and a lovely man, none nicer.

Somebody had once said to Chloe that fifty per cent of all her stress was self-inflicted – and it was, it's true. She hadn't had to invite them round, had she? Simply thought it was a good idea. And it was. They were all a part of the same big happy family now, and a close-knit one was how she wanted it to be. So somebody had to put in the effort to make sure that family gelled. And that somebody was her. Chloe still missed the special friendship she'd had with Kate and, although she yearned for it, she had almost come to accept that it could never be the same again. But at least with family around her she wouldn't be isolated, left totally alone. Thinking that could happen was probably her biggest fear in life.

'Have you heard from Ben, Caroline?' she asked, as she went through to the kitchen to check where the girls were up to. They would surely be finished by now, and indeed they were, just in the throes of tidying up after themselves.

'Not since they went out, no. Unusual for Ben, he's usually never off the phone when he's away from me.'

Alarm bells were starting to ring in Chloe's head. Ever since J-J's disappearance she worried it could happen again. Nonsense, she knew, but nevertheless. 'I've tried his mobile but it's going straight through to voicemail,' she said, an edge of anxiety creeping into her voice.

'Chill, Mum, they'll be back. Probably forgot the time.'

'Have you rung Stelios?'

'I tried a couple of times,' said Olivia, 'but he's just not picking up.'

'Probably in a pub somewhere, can't hear the phone,' said Caroline in an attempt to soothe.

'Pub? You must be joking! They wouldn't dare! And anyway, they've got J-J with them,' responded Chloe, almost affronted by the suggestion.

'Mum, this is our Ben we're talking about.'

'Oh, he wouldn't. Surely. Would he?'

'Hmm.'

Sandra and David arrived mid-debate, the boys still neither having returned, nor rung by way of explanation. Their absence remained a mystery and increased Chloe's stress-levels tenfold. It also made the house seem remark-ably quiet and the welcoming committee decidedly sparse.

'Sorry about the missing menfolk,' Chloe wittered worriedly, 'I can't think where they've got to, but hopefully they'll be back soon. Poor David, you'll have to submit to being surrounded by women for the moment – although I'm sure there are many men who would quite happily like to submit to that,' she giggled nervously, before the sudden horrified realisation of what she'd just said hit her.

Her foot was well and truly in her mouth. Jammed. Good introductory speech there Chloe – well done.

'Oh, I'm sorry. I didn't mean ...'

David laughed, he was not one to take offence, never had been. 'Yes, I have to say, I'd be much happier submitting to a group of men,' he said, pursing his lips and rolling his eyes heavenwards.

'David!' said Sandra, used to hearing him talk this way but unsure how Chloe and Olivia would take it.

Chloe sighed with relief as she quipped, 'A group? I'd be lucky to find one these days.'

Hearing their voices, Caroline flew in from the kitchen to welcome her parents. It was as if she hadn't seen them all year, whereas in reality hardly a day went by without her seeing one or the other of them, if not both.

'Munchkin!' David greeted her with open arms.

'Ew, put her down, David, you don't know where she's been!' joked Sandra.

'Oy!' laughed Chloe, 'I hope you're not referring to the state of my kitchen by that remark, madam.'

'Your kitchen? Whatever gave you that idea?' giggled Sandra.

It was good to see such an easy friendship developing between the two of them. Chloe had missed the friendship she'd had with Kate so very much – had felt lost in fact, no longer having a kindred spirit to exchange confidences with, to be there for, to help and advise. For that was what friendship was all about and she had felt totally isolated without it. In Sandra she now had a new ally, one who had been there with a never-ending supply of tea and tissues, one whose ears had been patiently receptive to all of her outpourings of woe. For Sandra had been there for her like a rock almost, solid and reliable, not only more recently during J-J's disappearance, but also at other times over the last twelve months when Chloe could quite easily have ended up having a breakdown had she not been there to lend her support.

Sandra equally appreciated the friendship. She had really

never had a close friend, not since childhood anyway. Her family had always been enough for her, first David and then Caroline. But now with Caroline no longer at home it was good to have another woman to talk to. David could be a bit like one at times but he certainly wasn't *all* woman!

Olivia played the perfect hostess with drinks and nibbles whilst Chloe entertained. David sat back and relaxed in their company. It felt so good to be accepted now for being who he was. For there had been a time where he'd thought his only option was to live his life behind a shadow of pretence. He'd spent years just feigning happiness, trying to face the world with a smile on his face while battling his demons within. He'd loved Sandra with all his heart, still did, but when it came to worshipping her with his body, that was a whole different ball game altogether.

Everybody's life goes through different phases, it's true, but for David, growing up as the only child of parents who totally abhorred homosexuality had made for an extremely difficult and traumatic adolescence. In a way, life had got even worse for him when he'd tried to conform to his parent's ideas of 'the perfect son' by finding himself a 'nice girl'. For that's what he'd done. He'd found Sandra, made her believe he was a genuine straight guy and they'd married. What's more, they'd had kids – well, one anyway. Caroline: she was the best thing that could ever have happened to him.

But then he'd gone. Left them. How could he? Those feelings he'd tried to hide for so long had exploded to the surface with a bang. A resounding bang, in fact. For into his life had walked Brian and he'd fallen heart-lurchingly in love. Once more he'd tried to repress his feelings, but this time it was different; on this occasion it had been an impossible task and he'd had to surrender, disgracefully.

For that was how he'd felt. Bad enough the pain he was causing by leaving behind his loving wife and innocent daughter, but times had been different then, and the thought of all the pain and scandal he was heaping upon them was almost more than he could bear. Consequently, to save them suffering at the tongues of gossip-mongers, David had moved away to start a new life with Brian and painfully cut himself off from Sandra and Caroline completely. It had been a traumatic time for all of them, but David had reached the stage where he could no longer carry on living a lie.

So despite the obvious sadness of being estranged from his much-loved daughter, David had, for the first time in his life, become true to himself. His life with Brian had been idyllic and they'd cocooned themselves in a bubble of happiness that they'd thought would never burst. But nothing lasts for ever. Brian had been diagnosed with cancer and David, distraught and loving him more than ever, had nursed him through his long illness. Understandably David had been overwhelmed by grief at his passing, and had sunk deeper and deeper into a state of depression.

Coincidentally, it was about this time that Caroline, just prior to her wedding, had decided to search for her father. Their reunion really had been David's saving grace, for he'd been at such a low point at that time that he really could not have sunk any further.

David would never forget that day, that moment when, utterly depressed, he'd reluctantly answered the door still in his pyjamas, to be greeted by the most wondrous sight he could ever have imagined. For there on his doorstep had been his lovely Sandra with his wonderful daughter Caroline, by now all gorgeously grown up. They'd fallen into each other's arms and hugged and hugged. It had been more than he could ever have wished for.

From that day forth, his life had changed once more. He'd sold the house where he'd been living with Brian, and bought a cottage in Little Smetherwick at the heart of his family, where he wanted to be. Both he and Sandra knew they could never live together as man and wife again, but now lived close enough to see each other almost every day. They delighted in each other's company and never again wanted to be apart. Their happiness when together was plain for all to see; in fact Caroline had been heard to lovingly describe them as being like two mischievous children.

'… wasn't it, Dad?' his daughter's voice cut through his thoughts; he'd been lost in the world of his memories.

'Sorry munchkin. What did you say?'

'You never listen to me, do you?' Caroline said, punching at him playfully.

'Of course I do – I just didn't hear you then, that's all.'

'You were asleep, more like,' she teased.

'I swear I wasn't,' he said, reaching for her hand and pulling her down onto the sofa next to him. 'I was just thinking.'

'About?' she asked, at his hesitation.

David glanced from one to the other, his two favourite ladies sitting either side of him. He put an arm around each and hugged them to him.

'Life,' he said.

'Sounds a bit deep,' said Sandra, jokingly as always.

'About how glad I am that the two of you came and found me and persuaded me to move back here. I hardly dare to think what might have happened to me otherwise,' said David, somewhat emotionally.

'David! Don't start getting maudlin, I was having a good time. You'll be starting me off in a minute.'

'You know what I mean, San, I just feel so lucky to have been given a second chance. I love you both so much and I couldn't be happier.'

Sandra blew her nose noisily.

'Mum!' said Caroline, embarrassed.

'Yes, look what you've done to me now, you daft lump,'

said Sandra, drying her eyes.

'I mean it,' said David.

'We know you do, Dad, and we love you too. Couldn't bear the thought of not having you around again now,' Caroline snuggled up against him, feeling so grateful to have him back in their lives.

Overhearing the remark, Olivia winced. For her own dad would never be back in her life again. He may have done some bad things but he had still been her dad, and she would never be able to see him again. A silent tear slid down her cheek.

The doorbell rang, continuously, someone's finger pressed permanently on the button. It was either an emergency, or it was …

'Ben Russell!' scolded Chloe, opening the door to her ever-loving son. 'What time do you call this?' I told you to be back by two o'clock at the latest. Everybody's here, we thought something had happened to you.'

'Sorry, Mrs Russell,' said Stelios, feeling he should take full responsibility for his future brother-in-law's misdemeanours. Sometimes it was hard to believe Ben and Olivia were brother and sister, Olivia was so sensible.

'I'm sure none of this is your fault, Stelios, I know exactly what my son can be like.'

'Hic.'

'Ben! Have you been drinking?'

'Well, just a very … not much.'

'I can smell it on your breath.'

'Pub!' said J-J, proudly holding on to his big brother's hand.

'Ben!' Chloe was almost rendered speechless as she glared from one of her sons to the other in the realisation that, at this point in time, the smaller son had far more sense than the larger one. For it was J-J who was leading Ben by the hand, not the other way round.

'Ben!' repeated Chloe. 'How could you take him to the pub? I trusted you! You know I was trying to make this a nice afternoon for everyone.'

'Sorry, Mrs Russell,' said Stelios, again.

'No, Stelios,' said Chloe, holding up a hand to stop him from apologising any more. 'I'm not blaming you at all, Ben can be very persuasive when he sets his mind to it.'

'Hic.'

'Coke,' grinned J-J.

'You gave him coke as well?' admonished Chloe. 'You know he's not meant to have that. All those Es, he'll be running round like a lunatic all afternoon now.'

'N-tic, n-tic, n-tic!' J-J chanted loudly and he ran into the lounge full of excitement at seeing so many people.

'See what I mean?' said Chloe. 'Case in point.'

'Sorry, Ma,' said Ben, shamefaced.

'Well sorry's just not good enough, Ben. Sometimes I despair, I really do.'

'I love you, Ma,' he said, throwing his arms around her and draping himself, unsteadily, upon her.

'I love you too,' she said, her space invaded by alcohol fumes. 'But I do wish you'd stop and think about what you're doing a bit more sometimes. Actions have consequences, you know, and the consequences are not always good.'

'You worry too much, Ma.'

'But you don't worry enough, Ben. Now go in there and entertain our guests and let's hope they don't die of alcohol poisoning from that heady aroma you brought back with you.'

'Ben!' exclaimed David, rising to greet him. He loved this rakish young son-in-law of his, even though he obviously swung the other way and was completely straight. He certainly provided some good eye candy and there was little enough of that in this village.

'Hey, how are you doing, you old poofter?'

Caroline raised her eyes heavenwards. She was used to their behaviour and was just glad they got on so well – things could easily have been so different.

'Okay, Mum?' she asked Sandra, who was sipping her tea and looked miles away.

'Yes, ta love. Come and sit next to me,' she said, patting the vacated seat. 'I was just thinking how lovely it is, us all being together like this – just how a real family should be. I love Chloe, we get on so well. I never really had a friend before, not a proper one.'

'I know, it's just great, isn't it? And I know Chloe really likes you too. She's had to move on after all that trouble with Kate and I think you came along for her just at the right time.'

'Funny old world, isn't it? Talking about Kate, what's happening with her and Tom now?'

'Think they're getting back together – well, trying to give it a go anyway, as far as I know.'

'Don't think I'd ever be able to trust him again after what he did. Got an eye for the ladies, that one. Did she ever find out about what went on between you and Tom?'

'Ssh – Mum! Keep your voice down! There was no "me and Tom", as you put it, it was just a bit of a … a bit of a fumble, that's all.'

'Well, I don't think Kate would be too happy if she ever found out, that's all I'm saying.'

'And hopefully she never will. Can we change the subject now, please?'

'Okay, babies! When are you going to make me a grandma? I'll be getting too old if you wait much longer.'

Tears welled in Caroline's eyes and didn't go unnoticed. Sandra covered her hand with her own work-worn one.

'Sorry love, I didn't mean to upset you. I didn't realise there was a problem, you've never said.'

'No problem – other than Ben, anyway. He really doesn't want kids, his face blanches at the thought of it.'

'Did you not discuss it before you got married?'

'Well no, it was such a whirlwind. I just presumed … He loves J-J.'

'Not quite the same though, is it? He's probably terrified at the thought of all that responsibility. After all, he's really still just a big kid himself – look at him now!'

J-J, now totally hyper from all the E numbers in the coke, and Ben, equally hyperactive from the alcohol, were rolling about together on the floor in a somewhat boisterous and rather noisy game of monsters.

'Ben! Get up! You're making yourself look ridiculous,' said Caroline, crossly.

Ben looked stunned. Even through his alcoholic haze.

'You okay, babe?' he asked, coming over to where she sat next to Sandra. He couldn't fail to notice her teary eyes. He reached out his hand to hers and pulled her to her feet, enfolding her in his arms. 'Love you,' he said, breathing heavily into her neck.

'Love you too,' she sniffed, sadly.

His hands wandered lovingly down her back to fondle her bum cheeks as he pushed himself up against her. His appendage was certainly stiffening, beer or no beer.

'I know what'll cheer you up,' he said, feeling hornier by the minute.

'Ben! Stop it! You're making a complete exhibition of yourself now. You think that's the answer to everything. Well, I've got news for you, it isn't,' she cried, running out of the room in tears.

Ben glanced around the stunned faces still remaining. 'Time of the month,' he grinned knowingly, trying to lighten the mood.

No one believed him. Neither had they heard a cross word exchanged between the two of them ever before.

23

Charlie was really rather proud of himself, was beaming like a Cheshire cat in fact. He'd won the heart of his lady and he'd secured it even more now. For totally off his own bat, and without Grace knowing anything about it, he'd managed to sort everything out so that the three of them, Izzy included of course, could go down to London to stay with Cleo and Daisy, for two whole weeks. A holiday – eureka!

Grace was overjoyed. Charlie – her hero. He had organised everything, even Gran. Grace loved it when he was masterful. He was usually a big softie, but when he took control of a situation in this kind of way he went up tenfold in her opinion of him. She loved him, she loved him: she did, she did, she did!

Okay, so Gran was not too chuffed, but hey, it had to be done. They needed a break, no one could deny that. So the social workers had been and assessed Gran, and assessed the situation. They were astounded that Grace had managed to care for her mother for so long without taking a break. That's what respite care was there for, to give carers a chance to get some normality back into their lives, albeit briefly. But Grace had been afraid to get social services involved after the horror stories she'd heard; she'd thought it easier just to carry on and cope as she had been doing.

However, the situation taken out of her hands, she felt some relief – and excitement! A holiday! And the social workers hadn't seemed like monsters after all, quite human actually! Whether she'd still be thinking that in a few weeks' time may be a different story, but for now at least she was intent on enjoying herself, without worry and stress, for two whole weeks.

And so she'd been assessed and, amazingly enough, there was just one room vacant in a dementia unit – it must be fate. They'd been to see it and it wasn't great but it was the only one currently available. Gran would just have to make do. She could cope for two weeks, surely. She'd got no choice, she'd simply have to. Even Grace was feeling determined now.

'You can say it all you like,' said Gran, dunking furiously into her cup of tea with an increasingly soggy biscuit, 'But I am just not going and you can't make me.'

'No I can't make you, Mother, but neither can I leave you here all on your own, you wouldn't be safe – anything could happen.'

'I've lived on my own before and survived and I can do it again. I'm not totally useless, you know.'

'I know you're not, Mother, but you need looking after. They'll be nice to you in the home, make you lots of tea, you'll make new friends.'

'Friends? With those old codgers? You must be joking! Did you see them? They're as old as Methuselah! Wandering about talking to themselves and shouting at everybody. Places like that are meant for old people, not for the likes of me.'

'But you are old, Mother, you-'

'*I am not old!*' shrieked Gran, dentures flying out onto the table in protest, and the soggy end of the biscuit plopping into the teacup with a splash. 'Look what you've made me do now!'

What an appropriate moment that was for Charlie to walk into the kitchen. Even Alfie had retreated to his basket, body a-quiver. Biscuits or no biscuits, it wasn't worth the risk.

'What's going on in here?' asked Charlie, in a tough and masterful sort of way.

Hastily Gran grabbed her dentures and replaced them in her mouth. Without them she was unable to clamp her teeth together to strike a stubborn pose – gums were not half as effective.

'I'm just saying that I don't want to be packed off to a house full of old people. If I'm going on my holidays it might as well be to somewhere nice. I want to go somewhere with people my own age – might even find myself a nice toyboy. You'd like that, wouldn't you, if some young man came and whisked me away?'

Charlie tried hard to keep a straight face.

'But Mother, you've got to go.'

'I have not got to go anywhere, Grace. Don't you tell me what I can and can't do,' Gran's teeth clamped together more firmly than a freshly sprung mousetrap. She was adamant, she was going nowhere, her face said it all.

When Charlie winked a warning to Grace to leave it to him, she was more than happy to do so.

'Remember how we talked about this before, Gran?' he said. 'How I told you it's only for two weeks to give Grace a break? We'll be back before you know it. And remember that carer we saw when we went to look around? I saw you giving him the glad eye, and I saw him looking at you too. I reckon he quite fancied you, actually.'

It's hard to think that the words 'coy' and 'Gran' could ever appear together in the same sentence, but on this occasion they did. Gran suddenly came over all coy.

'Oh Charlie, don't be silly – why would a handsome man like that ever fancy me?' she said, just a trifle bashfully and in a giggly sort of way.

'Now you're being silly, Gran, you're a beautiful woman, you turn men's heads wherever you go.'

Gran's rheumy eyes almost lit up as she preened herself

and adjusted her pink hairnet to a much more jaunty angle.

As for Grace, laughter bubbled up inside her so much she almost wet herself. A flirty Gran? Practically doubled over, she excused herself hastily and ran from the room.

'Where are you going, Grace?' asked the wannabe concubine of a Gran.

'Bathroom,' spluttered Grace, the laughter almost exploding from her.

But Gran was in her own fantasy world of young studs and fast cars. She would polish her dentures in readiness.

'Okay,' she said to Charlie, 'I'll go. But only for two weeks, remember. Don't think you can dump me in that place for ever.'

'Thank you,' said Charlie. 'That's fantastic. We'll come and collect you as soon as we get back from London, I promise.'

'Okay. That's unless I get a better offer of course,' she replied, a knowing look in her eye.

It was Charlie's turn to suppress a bubble of laughter now. 'Would you like a cup of tea?'

'Indeed I would. Put the kettle on, this calls for a celebration.'

Grace was in the middle of a wardrobe fluster when Kate arrived back with the girls. They'd been into town for a treat and both Izzy and Jessica were full of themselves and anxious to show off their mini purchases. They'd had pennies that had been burning a hole in their pockets for such a long time, it had been great to actually be allowed to spend them at last.

For Kate, however, the experience could hardly be described as a treat. She usually quite enjoyed shopping, but with two small girls in tow it had been quite draining; she felt totally exhausted, in fact. However, Izzy and Jess had enjoyed themselves, which had been the whole point of the exercise; she could go shopping for herself another time.

Grace made suitable approving and delighted noises as she perused the purchases. Bangles and beads, predominantly pink and sparkly, plus numerous things for Barbie. Amazing how far pennies went when you were that age. But then, look at the size of Barbie's hips in comparison to her own, no wonder Barbie's clothes were so much cheaper. Huh, Barbie.

'Why can't I look like that?' asked Grace, of all and sundry.

'Would you want to?' responded Kate, bemused.

'Well look at her, nice face, fab hair, big boobs, tiny waist, pert bum. Who wouldn't?'

'Me for a start,' said Kate, dismissing the idea as preposterous. 'She's all plastic, fake everything.'

'And you wouldn't be my mummy if you looked like that,' said Izzy, cuddling up to her.

Grace bent down and hugged her, kissing the top of her head. 'Aw, thanks, Iz. I'd rather be your mummy than a plastic Barbie any day.'

Kate hustled the girls downstairs to play with their purchases.

'Okay, shoot – what's wrong? Incidentally, you don't mind if I take my shoes off and lie down on your bed while I'm listening, do you? My feet are killing, and I'm absolutely whacked. That child of yours can talk for England!'

'Go for it. I know, she is a bit of a motormouth.'

'A bit?' chortled Kate, flopping down on the bed with a sigh of relief. 'Okay, now, tell me.'

'Nothing's wrong – quite the opposite in fact. Charlie's sorted it all out – he's managed to get Gran to go into respite for two whole weeks while the three of us have a holiday. We're going to London to stay with Cleo. I can hardly believe it, two whole weeks!'

'Wow, that's fantastic, Grace! If anyone deserves a break it's you. When are you going?'

'On Saturday, hence the panic: haven't got a thing to wear.'

'Looks like it.'

'Ha-ha, nothing suitable I mean. They're all too tight, or too short, or too falling to bits.'

'Then buy some new when you get there. You're going to London, for God's sake, all those shops,' said Kate, wincing suddenly in remembrance of the pain her poor feet had suffered that very day.

'To be truthful it's not the clothes, it's me. I'm too short and too fat. Too old, too wrinkled, too everything. Or every wrong thing, anyway. D'you think I need a boob job, or lipo-suction, or a facelift maybe?' she asked, in all seriousness, as she scrutinised herself in the mirror on the wardrobe door.

'Pfft – don't we all!' replied Kate, rolling her eyes.

'I'm serious,' said Grace, peering at herself even more closely. 'Look at this,' she said, pulling at the flesh that was meant to be her chin but which looked more like a turkey's gizzard.

'You do talk rubbish at times,' laughed Kate. 'You've got a gorgeous face, a great personality and a husband who thinks the sun shines out of you. What more do you want?'

'I notice you don't mention anything about my body.'

'Oh shut up!' laughed Kate. 'Listen though, on a more serious note, I'd better move out if you're going away at the weekend, you won't want a squatter living in the house. Perhaps it's a sign. Perhaps that's the push I need to move back in with Tom.'

'Only if you want to,' said Grace, turning, worriedly. She'd been so 'me, me, me' about the situation, she hadn't really given Kate a thought. 'To be honest, I'd be quite happy for you to stay here while we're away – it would save me having to put Alfie in the kennels, which I'm dreading,

236

and you could keep an eye on Richard for me too.'

'Are you sure? It would be better. I know I'm going to move back in with Tom at some point, but I'm still appreciating being able to take things slowly at the moment. As for Richard, I'd love to keep an eye on him,' she winked, a smile on her face.

'Kate! You've got back your lovely Tom, let's not add any more complications.'

'I'm joking. Just a bit of eye candy, that's all.'

'You're insatiable,' chuckled Grace.

And so the day dawned. Not the exciting one, the one they were all looking forward to; no, this was the day Gran was to be put into the home. It was only going to be for two weeks, Grace had to keep reminding herself. Nevertheless, she felt interminable guilt. Putting her mother into a care home – it was something she had vowed she would never do.

Gran, in contrast, seemed quite excited. 'Did you pack my best nightdress, Grace?'

'Yes, Mother.'

'The pink one with the little blue flowers on?'

'Yes, Mother.'

'What about my twinset, the one that I wear with my pearls?'

'Yes, Mother.'

'And all my new lingerie?'

Lingerie? Since when had she called it that? 'All there, Mother.'

She arrived at the home in style, somewhat reminiscent of the Queen Mother, even wearing a hat: she'd insisted. 'You never know who you might see,' she said. The Zimmer frame had never been known to move so fast, like greased-lightning in fact, as she shot in through the door like a bat out of hell. We've all heard of horse power, but this was gran power on speed, by the look of things.

Things couldn't have worked out better for her, actually. For the aforementioned carer, the man of Gran's fantasy land, was there at the reception desk to greet her. Which he did, with a hug, making her as pink and as flustered as an adolescent with her first teenage crush. Oh my God, they could hardly bear to watch. When he said, 'Let's go to your room,' she thought her luck was in. Grace's breakfast was in serious danger of being regurgitated.

They went through to help her unpack, Grace feeling saddened by the sights she saw on the way. An elderly lady sat on a bed rocking back and forth, a doll in her arms; a man wandering around blindly, shouting 'Help me! Help me!' and a lady muttering agitatedly, eyes wide with terror, as she constantly packed and repacked the meagre contents of her handbag.

'Toilet!' shouted a timid-looking lady, as the carpet around her feet suddenly changed to a darker shade of green.

'Oh Mabel – you've done it again! What have I told you about that?' admonished another carer, thus reducing the timid lady to tears.

'I want to go home,' she wailed.

'Well you can't, I told you.'

Others sat hunched around tables, barely able to move, or not remembering how. Food sat on plates in front of them untouched. 'Had enough?' asked a carer, taking it away. No response. They didn't even know it had been there in the first place.

Grace's heart lurched with anxiety. Could she really leave her mother in a place like this? Entrust her to the care of others? She had to, she knew she did. She so needed a break and it was her only option. But her mother … But Cleo and Daisy, how long was it since she'd seen them? She felt torn, absolutely, right down the middle between the generations of her family. Who needed her most? She looked at Charlie for guidance, her face in anxiety mode.

'Alright Gracie?' he asked softly, squeezing her hand in support. 'It's only for two weeks, remember – two weeks. You need a break. You need to see Cleo. It's not forever.'

Grace squeezed his hand gratefully in acknowledgement of his words and followed, with as much determination as she was able to muster, the staunch little procession which made its way to what was to be Gran's room.

'Is she coming to live here?' shouted a half-crazed voice from the open door next to it. A wild-eyed lady closely followed, body hunched over a Zimmer frame, one shoe on and one shoe off, her clothes somewhat askew.

'Only for a little while, Edith,' shouted Gran's carer.

'Huh, that's what they said about me but I'm still here. I want to go home, I told you. Where's my coat?'

'You go back in your room, Edith, I'll be in to see to you in a minute.'

'No! I'm coming in here.'

'Bugger off!' said Gran, standing her ground. This was her man and she wasn't sharing him with anyone.

'Mother!' Grace was shocked, she'd never heard her mother speak like that before, not ever.

'Oh, don't worry,' said the carer. 'They say plenty of things worse than that to each other, believe me.' The carer giggled reassuringly.

But Grace was not reassured. She had a bad feeling about this.

'She'll be fine. Just two weeks, Gracie, that's all, and then we'll all be back home with her driving you mad again. Let's enjoy a little break while we can. She'll survive, she's as tough as old boots.'

Grace was in guilt overdrive. 'But just look at this place, Charlie. How can we just leave her? She's my mother, my responsibility. I couldn't live with myself if anything was to happen to her while I was gone.'

'Gracie, look at her. Does she look as though she doesn't want to be here to you?'

Indeed. Gran seemed to have transformed herself, developing a trait that had never been seen before. Sex seemed to be uppermost in her mind, unusual for one who had always been such a prude. 'Tart' was now the word that sprang to mind, and not of the jammy variety.

The carer was obviously gay, which made it a little less seedy somehow. He just winked at Grace about Gran's behaviour, he'd seen it all before. If it helped them settle in by having a little crush on him, then all was well and good. It was never going anywhere obviously, and as for telling them he was gay, there didn't seem much point. After all, 'being gay' had simply meant 'having a good time' when the people of this generation had been younger, and they were confused enough already.

'Would you like me to help you off with your coat?' the carer asked Gran.

'Coat! Coat! Get me my coat! I want to go home!' came the half-crazed voice again. She was back.

'I thought I told you to bugger off!' shouted Gran, fiercely blocking the entrance to her room.

'Out of my way!' yelled Edith.

'Make me!' challenged Gran.

This could be Zimmer frames at dawn. They both raised them to attack.

'Ladies, ladies, ladies!' intervened the carer. 'Come along, Edith, back to your room,' he said, leading her away.

'Well find me my coat then! I want to go home!'

'Come on, you'd better have your cup of tea first, they'll be round with it in a minute.'

'And biscuits?'

'Yes, you can have biscuits.'

Gran followed them with beady eyes. 'Where's he going?' she asked jealously.

'He's only gone to take that old lady to her room, he'll be back in a minute.'

'Well he'd better hurry up, I haven't got all day, you know.'

By the time the carer returned they'd unpacked Gran's case, hung her clothes in the tiny wardrobe, put her 'lingerie' in a drawer and her toiletries in the cupboard.

'Ah, my lavender water,' said Gran, as she sprinkled it liberally upon herself.

'However much are you using?' asked Grace in surprise.

Gran, absolutely drenched in the stuff, simply glared at Grace as though she'd asked the most stupid question in the world.

'A lady has to smell her best at all times, I've told you that before. You go around smelling like a pan of chips half of the time. It's time you learned to have a bit of class, young lady, no wonder you can never find yourself a man.'

'Mother! I've got a man – I've got my Charlie,' she responded, gazing up at him with adoration.

'I said a man, Grace, not a Charlie.'

'Mother!' Grace could not believe what she'd just heard.

'Don't rise to it Gracie,' said Charlie, he certainly wouldn't.

'But …'

'She doesn't mean it.'

'Who's she? The cat's mother? Don't talk about me as though I'm not here.'

'Then don't talk about my Charlie like that.'

'You think you can say what you like to me, don't you, just because I'm a poor defenceless old lady.'

'Mother!' warned Grace.

'Gracie!' warned Charlie.

But battle ensued.

'Yes, but I'm going to tell everyone what you're like now.

241

How you lock me away in my room for days on end, I never see a soul.'

'Mother, of course I...'

'Yes, you see, embarrassed now aren't you? Now everybody's going to know just how cruel you are to me.'

'Mother!'

'Locked in my room day after day I am, it's just like a prison cell.'

'Mother,' hissed Grace, 'Could you stop?'

'Stop? Yes that's what you'd like, isn't it? You'd like me to stop telling everyone the truth about the way you treat me. Cruelty, that's what it is.'

'Mother, I have never been cruel to you. I do everything for you.' Grace had never been so embarrassed in her life. It was bad enough having these heated dementia-fuelled discussions in the privacy of their own home, but played out in public it was a nightmare.

'Everything? You don't even give me any food to eat, never mind the occasional cup of tea. I'd have died of starvation if I'd stayed in that house for much longer.'

It was all too much for Grace. She felt as though a million pairs of ears were listening in to this conversation and believing every word her mother said. Try as she might, she could hold back the tears no longer.

'Well, doesn't that just prove it,' Gran's eyes didn't miss a thing when they chose not to. 'Tears of guilt, aren't they?'

'Mother, I...' sobbed Grace.

'Pah! Always were a cry-baby, weren't you? Not like that disgrace of a sister of yours, hard as nails she was.'

'Gran,' said Charlie, quietly touching her on the arm, trying to calm her.

'Get your hands off me!' she bellowed. 'You men are all the same. Help! I'm being attacked! Rape!'

The carer to the rescue. He ran into the room at such speed and with such a look of panic on his face that just for a moment, it would appear that he actually believed it too.

'Okay?' he asked of Gran.

'No! Tell them to go away! They've been wanting to get rid of me for all of these years, now is their opportunity.'

'But Mother,' said Grace, through her tears, 'you know that isn't true. You're only coming here for two weeks while we go and visit Cleo, we'll be back here to take you home before you know it.'

'Pah! Calling me a liar now, are you?'

'No, all I'm saying is that we'll be back again in two weeks and then you can come home.'

'Go on then, go. Don't let me keep you.'

'I think it might be as well if you leave her now, let her settle down. She'll be fine, you'll see,' said the carer, sounding a lot more positive than Grace felt.

'You go home and enjoy your rest, you've earned it,' he said, winking acknowledgement of the situation to Grace.

'Yes, that's right, you go home and leave me here,' said Gran, suddenly sitting down on the edge of the bed as if defeated.

Guilt heaped on Grace in bucket-loads.

'Come on Gracie, let's go home,' said Charlie, putting a comforting arm around her.

'Home? Home? Am I going home? Where's my coat?' Edith was back.

'And you can bugger off as well, I've already told you once.'

'Okay, Mother,' said Grace, feeling like the worst daughter in the world, 'We've got to go now. But we'll be back to take you home in two weeks, okay?'

Grace bent to kiss her, but instead received a resounding slap across the face.

'Oy, don't start pretending to be all lovey-dovey just because you're trying to impress people. You don't usually give me a kiss, so stop showing off,' Gran growled.

243

Grace clutched the side of her face, in shock rather than pain. She hated leaving her like this, hated leaving her full stop – the guilt was insurmountable. Charlie, his arm around her, guided her towards the door.

''Bye Mum, see you soon,' she called, to the little old lady they were leaving behind. She'd marched in so positively earlier in the day, standing so tall and in control. Now the same little old lady seemed to have aged twenty years in a matter of hours, shrunken and stooped, confused and sad.

'Oh Charlie, I can hardly bear to leave her.'

'She'll be fine when we've gone – be strong.'

'Graaaace!' came her mother's plaintive cry as it echoed down the corridor.

'Oh Charlie!' Grace winced.

'Come on, you have a daughter to visit.'

24

Phew! They'd gone at last. After waving them off, Kate closed the door with a sigh. She thought she'd never be able to convince Grace to go, she'd been so worried about leaving her mother, especially after the fiasco they'd had to endure at the care home this morning. Poor Grace, if anyone ever needed a break it was her. It would do her good, if only she could stop worrying for long enough to enjoy it.

Alfie sat behind her in the hallway, emitting the occasional whimper, his eyes pools of anxiety, glistening at her pleadingly. Where had his mummy gone?

Jessica knelt beside him on the floor and threw her arms around his neck. 'They'll be back soon, Alfie, I promise.'

A little reassurance is better than none. His tail swished slowly from side to side on the floor a few times, before he licked her on the nose in thanks. Then he jumped up and gave himself a shake – time he pulled himself together. Was that sausages he could smell? Yes, leftover ones in his bowl! Yum! This was going to be okay after all.

'Will we be seeing Daddy today?' asked Jessica, ever hopeful.

'Later, darling,' replied Kate, clearing away the general kitchen clutter that had been created in the whirlwind departure of Grace, Charlie, Izzy – and Gran, of course. Kate could almost feel sorry for her if she hadn't been so nasty to Grace. For it was Grace, after all, who was Kate's main concern. She was in need of a break so desperately

245

and now everything was tinged with guilt, even more so than it needed to have been. Poor Grace. But hopefully, once she'd got away from the situation and put some distance between them, she'd be able to relax and spend some quality time with her family. If anybody deserved that, Grace did.

Kate marvelled at their friendship. She would do absolutely anything to help Grace and to ensure her happiness. In fact she'd even offered to go and visit Gran in the home, and that was saying something. She couldn't deny the relief she'd felt, though, when Grace had declined the offer, thinking that Gran might have found it too unsettling. Phew. Grace had laughed at the expression on her face.

They'd certainly helped each other through some traumas; their friendship had become a huge part of both of their lives. Grace often joked that Kate had been her saving grace, and vice versa. 'With a name like Grace I'm always needing saving,' she giggled.

'Well, with a name like Grace, you need to save me,' Kate would quip.

They were like sisters, in a way, but more so. Although Kate had never had a sister to compare. Grace had, however: she'd had Anna. Her untimely death had left Richard so distraught that one of Grace's many worries was that he could try and take his own life. Which is why she'd specifically asked Kate to keep an eye on him while she was away.

'When?'

'Pardon?'

'When? You said Daddy would be coming round later. When?'

'Oh, not until this evening, probably, he's got some work to do today.'

'But I'm bored.'

'Missing Izzy?'

'Yep.'

'Okay, tell you what, we'll go into town on the bus and have tea and cake in a café. How about that? I feel like spoiling us today.'

'Yum. Cake with sticky icing on top?'

'Okay, whatever you like.'

'What about Alfie?'

'I don't think he likes cake,' said Kate, smiling at Jess and taking her hands in her own.

I do, I do. Alfie's tail wagged in anticipation, but then drooped in the realisation that he was to be left behind.

'You can have a chewstick, we'll be back soon,' said Kate, as she gave one to him.

He settled down to chew it with a sigh of gratitude. Life with these two wasn't so bad after all.

In a coffee shop in Chester sat Sandra and Caroline. It wasn't often that the two of them managed to spend an entire day together recently, as Caroline and Ben seemed to be joined at the hip and Sandra was not one who would wish to intrude into their state of newly wedded bliss. But, unexpectedly, Caroline had rung this morning to ask whether she fancied a trip into town. And who was she to argue? There was nothing she'd like better than to spend a whole day with her beloved daughter. She missed the trips out that they used to have together.

They'd bounced along in Caroline's battered old Mini and it had felt quite like old times as they'd raised the roof with their loud and tuneless singing. When it came to 'It's Raining Men', one of their all-time favourites, it was, in fact, amazing that the glass in the car windows remained intact.

'Okay,' said Sandra, as the song came to an end, 'is there a purpose to today?'

'Purpose? What do you mean? Shopping – I thought that was why people went to shops.'

'Ha-ha, cheeky madam, don't be sarcastic. I meant are you looking for anything in particular?'

'No, just a bit of retail therapy, that's all.'

'What's up?'

'The sky, Mother.'

'Oy! Behave yourself! There's something wrong, isn't there?'

Her mother was far too intuitive. Caroline shook her head vehemently in denial. 'Of course there isn't, I just want to go shopping with my old mum, that's all. Do you have a problem with that?'

'Yes.'

'What?'

'I'm not old!'

The giggling started again, although underneath it all Sandra knew that something was troubling Caroline. She'd get to the bottom of it before the day was out, she was sure of it.

After trying on what seemed like the entire stock of the first four shops, the pair were exhausted. Coffee was definitely called for, the stronger the better. Having decided that clothes sizing must definitely have gone smaller recently, neither wanted anything to eat.

Stuffing the bags containing their purchases beneath the café table, they sat back and sipped at their black coffees. Simply imagining the cream and sugar and the added sprinkling of chocolate they could have had, made them feel deprived and aggrieved, but somewhat virtuous. When they were skinny with sylph-like figures they'd remember this moment with gratitude and ... well, they'd be able to have all the cream and sugar and chocolate they liked then.

'Okay, so what's wrong?'

'My coffee's too strong.'

'It's because it's just black. It's not half as nice without all the accoutrements, is it?'

'Be nice with a choccy biccy dipped in.'

'Mmm. Or even sipping it while eating a chocolate bar.'

'Mmm.'

'Flippin' awful, isn't it?'

'And I fancy a sandwich now, or a cake.'

'Oh, sod the diet! We'll start tomorrow.'

Back at the table with a selection of goodies of the fat-producing yummy variety, Sandra was determined to get her daughter to spill the beans.

'So ...' she said, licking the cream from her fingers with a look of 'died and gone to heaven' upon her face.

'So what?' asked Caroline, eyes closed, sugar-rush all-consuming.

'Why do you look so miserable?'

'Do I look miserable, at this precise moment?'

'No, you look as though you're just about to have an orgasm, actually.'

'Mother!'

'Well you do. But you know what I mean, you've got a sad aura about you, and I don't like it. You've been so happy since you've been with Ben.'

'I am. I am happy, it's just ... well, all this baby stuff. I want one, he doesn't, basically.'

'Oh love, there's no hurry is there? He'll come round to the idea, I'm sure of it. Give him time. You're young, there's plenty of time yet.'

'Not for me there isn't. I feel really broody, Mum. I just can't stop thinking about babies – they seem to be every-where,' she said, her teary eyes scanning the room and alighting on one at the table across the other side, as if to prove a point. 'Ben's really good with children, I don't understand why he's so adamant that he doesn't want one of his own. I think he's just not grown up himself yet, that's the problem.'

'That's exactly it, love. He still wants his freedom. A

baby's all-consuming, you know. It's different when it belongs to someone else and you can hand it back, but when it's your own you never have a minute to yourselves. Babies are hard work and I don't think Ben is ready for that sort of commitment yet. He wants you all to himself, he dotes on you, Caroline.'

'Yes, I know he does, and I love him too but …'

'Caroline!' shouted a vaguely familiar little voice, as Jessica ran towards her, stopped in front of her and suddenly became strangely tongue-tied.

'Hello!' said Caroline, surprised to see her. 'My! How you've grown! You'll soon be as tall as me!'

Jessica gave a smile and welcomed the hugs both from Caroline and her mum.

'Hi! I thought it was you two when we first came in, but you looked so serious.'

'Unusual for the two of us, I know,' said Sandra, brushing away tears she hadn't even realised were there. 'Why don't you join us?'

'Well, are you sure?'

'Quite sure,' nodded Caroline in the affirmative. She loved Jess and hadn't seen her in such a long time. It was good to have a little person to cuddle right at this moment; actually, it might cheer her up a bit.

Jessica loved Caroline too and it didn't take her long to get her tongue back again.

'Do you remember when I was your bridesmaid, Caroline?'

'How could I forget? You were the best bridesmaid ever.'

Having listened to the adults gossiping for a while, Jessica started to get fidgety, but then she had an idea. The café they were in was called The Crypt and it was in a shop called Browns. She was sure they sold toys there, lots of them. Barbies too, probably. And she had her purse, with pennies in.

Okay, Caroline was easily convinced. They would leave their mothers to talk and they would visit the toy department. What's more, there would probably be a baby department close by with cute little clothes, maybe even cots and prams. 'Let's go,' she said, taking Jessica firmly by the hand.

Left to their own devices, the conversation between two women invariably turns to the topic of men, and this was no exception.

'So, how's David?' asked Kate.

'Oh, he's fine – never looked better, in fact. It's great having him close by, I see him virtually every day, we're such good friends. It was awful for me losing contact with him for all those years – I really missed him.'

'It must have been difficult for you.'

'Oh, it was, love. I really love him, you see, despite everything. He had to be true to himself, though, and I understand that, but I'm so glad to have him back in my life again even though we can never be more than just the very best of friends. I felt as though a part of me was missing before, it's only now that he's back and part of my life that I feel whole again.'

'Oh Sandra, that's so sweet. Is that enough for you, though, that you can never be together in that way?'

'It is for me, love, it is for me.'

'David is a very special person, I can see that.'

'He is indeed. But enough of my wafflings, how are things going with you and Tom?'

'Fine, yes. Well, sort of.' The doubt crept into her response, even though she hadn't meant it to.

Sandra looked at her with wise eyes, but said nothing. Kate really appreciated this reaction. Had Sandra become inquisitive and started to pry, Kate would have been disinclined to confide in her, for if there was one thing she disliked it was people who poked their noses into other people's affairs – quite literally.

'Oh I don't know,' she burst out, almost like a bottle being uncorked. 'How can I ever trust him again?'

She stared directly into Sandra's eyes, as though hoping to find an answer written there. But they were hooded as they looked back at her, a secret hidden beneath their lids.

'It's all so stupid,' Kate continued, 'Tom is the absolute love of my life, I could never imagine myself with anyone else, and yet now I feel as though he's broken something that was so precious. How can things ever be the same again?'

'Only you can decide that, my love.'

'I know, and that's where I'm struggling. I want it to work out both for myself and for Jess, it would be the best thing for all three of us to be back together as a family. And when we first met up again properly I wanted to move back in with him straightaway, my feelings were so strong I couldn't bear for us to be parted. But then I panicked; it happens all the time. I started thinking about all the "buts" and "what ifs" and I fled. What is wrong with me? Sometimes I think I'm going mad.'

'You're definitely not going mad, love, you've had your confidence shaken, that's all.'

'I love him with all my heart, truly I do, but he betrayed me, and with my best friend, of all people. How can I just put that behind me? I trusted them, both of them.'

'She hates herself for what she did to you. You know that, don't you?'

'I know she does, but it doesn't make it any better.' Kate took a sip of the dregs of her coffee in an attempt to take the bitter taste from her mouth. It didn't work. 'How will I ever learn to trust again, Sandra?'

'Maybe you won't, maybe it's something you'll just have to learn to live with. Or not, as the case may be.'

'I've told him I just want to take things slowly, but then there's the added pressure of Jess. She wants us to go back

and live with her daddy *now*. Obviously, she can't understand what we're messing about at.'

'I understand how difficult that must be for you, it's all
extra pressure. But at the end of the day it's about what
you feel comfortable with yourself. You should never do
anything you don't want to do just for the sake of children.
Time will come when they fly the nest and then you're left
to pick up the pieces.'

'That's so true. Like I said, I just want to take things
slowly. I've got to learn to trust him again.'

'Then do that, do what's best for you.'

There was a comfortable silence for a moment or two,
as Kate mulled over her thoughts. But then it came. The
loaded question.

'Do *you* think I can trust him?'

Sandra was caught completely off-guard. Her eyes darted
uncomfortably down to the table and back up again. She
was known for her honesty, but honesty is not always the
best policy. Caroline would be really cross, kill her, most
probably, if she betrayed her confidence. And it was a long
time ago, and it really was none of her business anyway, and
it would only …

'Sandra? Did you hear me?' For some reason, something
had started to prick at the suspicious nature that Kate had
recently acquired. Whatever it was had probably rebounded
from the pricking of Sandra's conscience.

'You're a sensible woman, a very wise woman actually,
and I'd really value your opinion. Do *you* think I can trust
him?'

'Oh love, I really don't think I'm the right person to ask.
What do I know? I've hardly had much experience of men,
have I? And anyway, I hardly know Tom, not really, I only
know what I've heard, and…'

'Heard?' Kate's ears picked out the word from the waffle
instantaneously. 'Have you heard something about Tom?

Do you know something I don't know?' Her eyes homed in on Sandra's, screaming suspicion.

'No, no, it's nothing – really it isn't. It was a long time ago anyway now, and if I say anything it's just going to make matters worse. Oh, me and my big mouth! Just leave it, Kate. It's nothing, believe me.'

'Tell me.' Kate was resolute. Understandably so.

Sandra wanted the ground to open up and swallow her whole. She'd done some stupid things in her time, but …

'Tell me,' repeated Kate.

'Okay, I'm going to have to now, but remember this was ages ago, before Tom slept with Chloe, before Caroline met Ben.'

'Caroline? What's she got to do with it? Oh my God! Caroline? Not Caroline! but she was Tom's secreta… Oh! Isn't it always the secretary?'

'Stop! Look, it's not as bad as its sounding, truly it's not. Caroline had a crush on Tom for ages, she was young and single, and a bit naive if I'm honest. Anyway, you were in Cornwall, she was moving into her new flat and she asked him to give her a hand. Well Tom, being the nice man that he is, agreed and went along there in all innocence, only to be pounced upon by my scheming daughter.'

'Oh my God,' Kate felt decidedly sick.

'It's really not as bad as it sounds. I believe quite a lot of fumbling went on but apparently Tom put a stop to it before it got out of hand.'

'I really don't want to ask this, but I've got to know,' said Kate, looking as though she was about to throw up her coffee at any minute. 'How would you define "quite a lot of fumbling"?'

Sandra was embarrassed to the extreme and ashamed beyond measure. 'You know, being intimate with each other without going the whole way. Oh God, I wish I'd never

254

opened my mouth, I should never have said anything, this was all so long ago.'

'But he was married to me!'

'And he loved you, still does. That's why he stopped himself with Caroline. He loved you, it was you he wanted. That's what he said to Caroline.'

'Jeez, I don't believe this!' said Kate, slumping forward in her seat, elbows on the table, head in her hands. 'I never even suspected.'

'Eh love, I really wish I hadn't opened my big mouth. I shouldn't have said anything, I've only made matters worse. It was nothing, truly it wasn't. Just a silly crush Caroline had. Tom loved you. He put a stop to it.'

'Didn't stop himself with Chloe, though, did he? How d'you justify that?'

'I don't, love. All I know is that he was lonely, he needed you, she was there and, well, I don't have to spell it out to you do I?'

'Oh God, men are bastards. And what makes it worse is … I love him.'

'Then forget I said anything, love, that's the best advice I can give. He loves you, of that I'm sure. You could drive yourself mad going over and over it and never getting anywhere. I don't condone his behaviour, far from it, but a man has his needs, that's all I'm saying.'

'So you're saying it's my fault that all this happened, my fault for going away and leaving him. My baby had just died but instead of falling apart as I did, I should have been at home, laid in the marital bed, waiting to give comfort to my oversexed stud of a husband. Is that it?'

'Kate, love, don't be like that, you know that's not what I meant at all. It must have been a terrible thing for you to have to go through, I can't begin to imagine what it must have felt like and I don't blame you at all for needing to get away and spend some time on your own. Everyone has to learn to cope in their own way in times of tragedy, and for Tom, as far as I can see, his was …'

'Sex.'

'Well, I wouldn't have put it quite like that but, yes, in a way, he needed to feel loved.'

Kate remained silent for a moment or two, her hands holding onto her coffee cup like some kind of lifebelt. She truly felt as though she was drowning, her head was all over the place. She stayed there for a while, but then surfaced with a sudden gasp.

'I don't understand why, when he was confessing all about Chloe … why didn't he tell me what had happened with Caroline? I asked him whether there was anything else I should know about and he said, point-blank, that there was not. We were meant to be clearing the air ready for a fresh start and yet he lied deliberately. How could he do that to me? This is meant to be about learning to trust – how can I trust him now?'

'Look, I don't approve of what he's done, not in any way at all, but I can understand why he did it. He loves you, he's trying to win you back, he probably already feels that he's treading on thin ice. You know about Chloe and are trying to move on from that, why would he want to throw a spanner in the works now by raising the subject of Caroline? To Tom, it happened a long time ago, it was not something he had instigated, and it hadn't meant anything to him anyway. After all, it's you he wants to be with. Why would he jeopardise that now, just as things are starting to fall back into place?'

Kate looked confused, felt it in fact. 'And so you think I should do what exactly?'

'Knowledge is power, that's for sure, but again, it's not up to me to tell you what to do. I think if it was me, I'd just keep quiet about it – not want to upset the apple cart, so to speak. But you're different, you'd be dwelling on it, churning it around inside. Oh, I so wish I'd never said anything!'

'No, I'm so glad you did. If there's one thing I don't like it's secrets, especially about stuff like this. I needed to know.'

'What are you going to do?'

'That remains to be seen,' said Kate, feeling totally confused now, as she stared into the distance, her future unknown.

25

'What time is Daddy coming?' asked Jessica, as they rode home from Chester on the bus.

'I don't know exactly,' replied Kate, her voice sounding brittle, as if it came from another world.

'But he is still coming?' Jess persisted, feeling decidedly insecure. Ever since she'd come back from seeing the Barbies with Caroline, her mummy had been acting very strangely.

'I expect so.'

'Expect? You mean he might not be coming now?'

Tears were welling in her big blue eyes, it did indeed seem to be a possibility.

Kate noticed, and felt a twinge of guilt. 'He will come, I promise,' she said, even though her spirit was feeling somewhat less generous.

He actually arrived shortly after they got back to the house, which was good in a way, as it meant Jess was around to take off the pressure for a while, giving Kate time to gather her thoughts. Her greeting of him on his arrival had seemed just a little on the cool side, but he'd put it down to tiredness and thought little more of it, never realising for a moment what was on her mind.

They ate together, listening to Jessica's chatter, and Tom was the one to take their little daughter upstairs to bed that night.

'I'm sleeping in Izzy's room while she's away,' said Jess. 'Mummy said so. She said I snore too much and she wants a bit of peace,' she giggled.

Tom smiled. He could think of a very good reason why Kate would want Jess out of the room, and it was nothing to do with her snoring. He read the obligatory bedtime story, although he had difficulty mustering much enthusiasm for princesses in ivory towers this evening. But finally the prince fell in love with his beautiful princess and the two of them lived happily ever after. If only life were that simple, thought Tom, as he made his way back down the stairs.

Kate was waiting for him. After an entire afternoon of deliberation, soul-searching, and whatever else, she had come to the conclusion that maybe Sandra was right. She loved him and that was the most important thing, maybe now was not the right time to start upsetting apple-carts all over again.

The television was on. Her attention briefly left the screen as he came into the lounge. 'Okay?' she asked.

'Her eyes were closing even before the end of the story. She'll be fast asleep by now,' he said, settling down next to her on the sofa and taking her hand in his own. 'I've missed you,' he said, turning towards her and kissing her cheek.

'Missed you too,' she said, flinching ever so slightly. 'D'you mind if I just see the end of this programme? I was watching it.'

'Oh, sorry.'

Was there something a bit different about her tonight? She seemed very tense, although he could soon remedy that. Their thighs were almost welded into one with the amount of heat that was radiating from his alone, although she hadn't seemed to notice.

Okay, she had noticed. But she was just wondering how, and whether, she was going to be able to react, knowing what she knew now. It was easy to pretend, but her body had a mind of its own. 'Knowledge is power,' Sandra had said, she hadn't said that knowledge can also make you frigid.

Something she hadn't actually noticed was that his hand

was now creeping up the inside of her thigh. This would normally create a flush of excitement but, on this occasion, there was decidedly a drought. She pushed his hand away, gently but determinedly.

'What's wrong?' he asked, his own bits a-fluster.

'Bit of a headache.'

Hmm. He had a bit of a something else.

'Would you like me to get you a couple of paracetamols?' They work quite quickly.

'No thanks, I'm fine.'

'Fine? But I thought …'

'Well, you know.'

'Well, I don't actually.'

They watched the television for a while longer. Tom started to yawn. He stretched. 'Phew, ready for bed, I think.'

She stared studiously at the screen.

Okay, hints were getting him nowhere.

'Am I staying over?'

'Well, um …'

'Jessica said you asked her to sleep in Izzy's room, so I thought …'

She could hardly throw him out. She'd just have to think erotic thoughts. Maybe Johnny Depp would do it. It worked when she was on her own.

'Okay.' It was now or never. She loved him and she just had to put Caroline and whatever else that had gone before, right out of her mind.

She went up to the bathroom to psych herself up, Captain Jack Sparrow playing heavily on her mind. No, actually, *Chocolat* … she could eat him whole in that! Those beautiful brown eyes piercing deep inside her soul … ohh!

By the time she emerged, Tom was already in bed. Not quite the same as Johnny, but close enough. He was a hunk, and what's more he was *her* hunk. She slipped under the duvet, giving an involuntary shiver as her naked flesh came into contact with the cool cotton of the sheet. She snuggled up to him, glad of the heat from his body. 'You're freezing,' he said.

'I know, sorry.' She felt really nervous somehow, which was probably what had made her feel cold and shivery. This was her Tom, her man, the love of her life, what had she got to feel nervous about? Cold or not, his hand seemed to be making its way to the frozen north; hopefully it wouldn't encounter an ice-cap. His fingers teased, pleasurably at first, certainly there didn't seem to be a drought – not a deluge, but certainly not a drought. Johnny, remember me … she was away.

He rolled on top of her, she parted her legs, wrapped them around his back, and … 'Oww!'

'What? Sorry. Did I hurt you?'

'No it's … aghh!'

It would appear that Johnny had flown out of the window, only to be replaced by a vision of Caroline with Tom. How could he possibly say there had been nobody else, when he knew full well that there had been. Her legs fell back down onto the bed with a thud, almost injuring her no-longer-flexible friend in the process.

'D'you have any KY Jelly, that might help?' panted Tom in a state of desperation.

'You lying scumbag!' spat Kate, somewhat venomously.

He scrambled back up onto his knees, understandably taken aback. He'd been a man on a mission in the mission-ary, but it seemed his performance was now defunct.

'What?' He stared at her, dumbfounded. 'Where did that come from?'

'It came from right there, between your legs,' she said, her accusatory stare causing more droop and shrivel than had ever been know to man before. Well, to this man anyway.

'What are you talking about?'

'I'm talking about you, husband dear. I got a confession out of you about sleeping with my best friend, I asked you point-blank whether there was anything else I should know about and you said …'

'No-o-o!' A groan escaped his throat as his head fell down towards his chest.

She had expected at least a half-hearted attempt at denial, but none was forthcoming. With a certain amount of loathing she glared towards his man-bits, shrunken and shrivelled. A walnut, more like. How could a tiny little walnut like that cause so much trouble? Easily. It was attached to a hunk, a handsome hunk, a kind and generous hunk, a hunk who also happened to be … her husband!

'Tom! How could you?'

'Caroline.'

'Yes, Caroline. Why didn't you tell me when you had the chance? "Wipe the slate clean … learn to trust again", that's what I said. "Only happened once", you said, "only one time". You were lying through your teeth, you scumbag. How am I ever meant to trust you again now?'

'But I didn't sleep with Caroline, we didn't have full sex, I stopped it before …'

'Tom! Any kind of intimacy with another person is a betrayal as far as I'm concerned. We're married, for God's sake.'

'I know but … How did you find out anyway?'

'None of your bloody business. Just get out, Tom, I've had enough! I can't take any more of this deceit, how can I possibly have a relationship with someone I can't trust?'

'But I can't just leave like that, not after all we've gone through.'

'It's precisely because of all that we've gone through that I'm asking you to go.'

'We can work it out.'

'We *cannot* work it out! We've tried that already and look

where it's got us. You're still just a lying, cheating scumbag and I can't take it any more.'

'Look, can you just hear me out? I've lived like a monk while you've been gone. You were the one I wanted, and no one else. I've jumped through hoops almost, to try and win you back, and couldn't believe my luck when we started to see each other again. But I always knew I was treading on thin ice and could fall through and drown at any moment if I didn't tread carefully. So what was I meant to do? That brief moment of madness with Caroline had been ages ago and was something I'd been trying to forget. It was of little or no importance to either of us, and especially to me.'

'Huh! If it was of so little importance, then why the hell did you do it?'

'Pathetic … I know it sounds pathetic, but I had needs. I needed you, she was there, she wanted me. I was like putty in her hands, basically.'

'Tom!'

'Just saying.'

'But you could have stopped her. Why didn't you stop her?'

'I did stop her. We didn't have sex, not the full thing.'

'But close enough,' she said, bile rising to her throat at the thought.

'I'm so sorry,' he said, for he truly was. 'How can I ever make it up to you?'

'You can't, that's the thing. For not only were you being unfaithful, yet again, but you lied about it too. Where is the trust in that? Tell me, because I'd like to know.'

Tom sighed, feeling everything just slipping away. 'But can you understand why I didn't tell you? After Chloe, and all that we went through because of it. We were just starting to get our relationship back on track, things were beginning to go right for us again. When you asked me whether there was anything else I had to confess to, well, how could I possibly have told you about Caroline then? It had been a long time ago, it had seemed trivial, it wasn't even as if we'd gone the whole way, and it was certainly never going to go anywhere, just a stupid mistake. And I knew, that was the thing, I knew that if I had confessed then that would have been the end of us, and I couldn't bear for that to happen.'

'Like now, you mean.'

'No Kate, no. Please. We can't let it destroy us.'

'It just did, Tom, it just did,' she said, defeated, tears spilling down her face in quick succession.

'But Kate, I love you.'

'Then you have a funny way of showing it.'

'Can we not put this behind us?'

'You just don't get it do you?' Anger was taking over now. 'You lied to me, Tom! On top of everything else you've done, you lied. Cheated and lied. How could I ever trust you again?'

'Of course you can trust me. I love you. It was only …'

'Of course? There's no "of course" about it! And as for love, I'm actually starting to hate you now for what you've done to me!'

'Oh Kate, don't …' his hand reached out to her.

'Don't touch me!' she screamed, rolling off the bed and onto her feet. 'Just get out! I n…'

'Mummy?' The bedroom door slowly opened. 'Why are you shouting? I don't like it when you shout.'

'Oh angel, it's okay. I'm sorry. I promise I won't shout any more. You go back to bed.'

'Daddy, why is your face all wet?'

Seeing Tom rendered incapable of speech, Kate answered for him. 'Daddy's just been washing his face, he mustn't have dried it properly. You go to bed now, I'll see you in the morning.'

But Jessica was not to be fobbed off so easily, and was a lot more astute than they gave her credit for.

'Will Daddy see me in the morning?'

'Um, no, Jess. Daddy's got to go home now, but I expect you'll see him very soon.'

'When? When will I see him?' She had a bad feeling about this.

'I told you, Jess, very soon. Now do as you're told please and go to bed!' Kate's heart was breaking, she needed space to feel it shatter, an empty room in which her tears could flow.

'I want Daddy to tuck me in,' persisted Jess, knowing full well she was treading on dangerous ground.

'Jessica! I will not tell you again. Now go to bed!' yelled Kate. She glared at Tom, defying him almost to undermine her.

But Tom's heart was breaking also. He got up from the bed where he still sat, and dragged on his clothes.

Jessica stood in silence watching for a moment, taking it all in. But then, without warning, she hurled herself across the room in sudden realisation.

'I hate you!' she screamed at Kate, kicking and punching at her in fury. 'You spoil everything! I want to be with Daddy – I love Daddy!'

'Hey, hey,' said Tom, pulling her away from Kate and lifting her up into his arms. 'You know you don't mean that, you love Mummy too.'

He cuddled her, reassuringly, and waited for her to calm down.

'Okay angel?' he asked, lifting his hand to tilt her face up towards his once her sobbing had ceased.

'S'pose,' she said sadly.

Undermining or not, he wasn't even going to consult Kate on this one, Jess was his daughter too and his love for her was paramount.

'Would you like me to take you back to bed now?'

'Okay, Daddy. Love you, Daddy,' she said, a slight edge of triumph in her voice as she gazed into his eyes.

He hugged her tightly as he carried her through to her room, his whole body shaking with emotion, not knowing when he would see her again, not knowing when he would see either of them.

'Daddy?' she asked, gazing up at him as he lowered her gently onto her bed.

'Yes, angel?' he replied, trying to still the tremor in his voice.

'Your face is still all wet. It's taking ages to dry.'

Alone in the bedroom Kate's head felt numb, although her heart … that was a different story. For her heart felt as though it had been blown up with a bicycle pump, up and up and up. Inflated by sadness, and by anger too, bigger and bigger. There had to be a safety valve somewhere, to release the pressure, otherwise she may explode.

With a groan of despair she fell down upon the bed, curling herself into a ball, foetal-style. She was angry with him, certainly, but she was angry with herself too. It wasn't meant to have happened like that. She'd meant to try and keep it to herself, put all the bad things behind her and start again. That's what she wanted. She loved him, for God's sake! And so what had she done? She'd thrown him out. It was the end for them this time, truly it was, she could feel it.

How had everything ended up in such a mess again? They loved each other, needed each other, how could she bear to let him go? She couldn't, she couldn't. This was absolute madness, but it was the only sensible thing to do. For how could she ever trust him again?

She half expected him to come back into the bedroom when he'd finished seeing Jess, really expected him to have another go at persuasion. And what would she say when he did? She loved him – could she move on from this, give him another chance, try to trust him all over again? Was that not preferable to never seeing him again, losing him forever?

The decision was taken out of her hands. The front door slammed. He was gone.

26

To Kate, the days that followed seemed interminable. Her whole body felt heavy and oppressed, almost as if she was trying to walk through a swamp in thick fog. As for Jessica, her storm clouds rarely lifted. She had been that much younger when they'd split up originally, more malleable and willing to fit in. But circumstances had forced her to grow up more quickly than she probably would have done, in many ways, leaving her judgemental and more than keen to voice her opinion.

Obviously, therefore, during this time Kate and Jess just did not gel, making it even more difficult for each of them, not having the support of the other. Even more difficult also because each was the only support the other had at the moment. With Grace and her family away and Tom keeping his distance, who else was there to turn to? Chloe maybe? Or maybe not. Kate certainly didn't want her getting any ideas about Tom being free and single again – he certainly wasn't that, hadn't been the first time around either.

'Fancy a walk, Jess?' Not that Kate did herself, but she thought it might pass a couple of hours. They couldn't just sit here and vegetate for ever.

Walk? Alfie was out of his basket like a rocket, his eyes like two flying saucers. Did somebody say 'walk'?

'No,' said Jess, her whole body rigid with hostility.

'No thank you,' corrected Kate. Manners were important, even in times of conflict.

The correction was received with a thunderous glare.

No? Alfie padded slowly back to his basket, his tail between his legs, hangdog expression personified.

'We could take Alfie,' Kate blackmailed, in a nice persuasive sort of way. The need to get out of this house was paramount.

Alfie did a u-turn and was back, sitting like a good dog, alert, eyes wide, tail a-quiver.

Jessica looked at him, she couldn't let him down, he was all she had at the moment, or it felt that way.

'Walkies.'

Well I'll be doggone – as a temporary measure substitute for his mummy, she would most definitely do.

The whole week was pretty fraught. Kate heard nothing from Tom, but neither did she contact him. Both were stewing in their own juices with Jess caught in between – not a happy place for any child to be.

Kate was getting more and more down. She truly believed that it was over for her and Tom now, and felt that in the end, it was she who had brought about the final downfall of their marriage. She felt lost, and had no one to turn to.

She was still having some fun times with Jess, it wasn't all hostility, but several times this week, in moments of frustration, Jess had turned on her with 'I hate you!' knocking what little bit of self-esteem Kate had left, right back down to the ground. It made her feel overwhelmingly guilty too – what had she done to this child? Jess had been such a happy and placid little girl, now she seemed to get volcanic eruptions of burning rage. Woe was Kate.

The misery was, in fact, beginning to become all-consuming, and was dragging her down to a place she didn't want to be, a place where she could not possibly go. She'd been there before and did not want it to happen again. And so Kate made a new friend. A friend who made her happy sometimes. And that friend's name was gin.

It wasn't as though she was drinking all the time. It wasn't as though she was drinking too much; in fact if anyone had had the audacity to suggest this she would have been deeply offended. No, it was just a little tipple, or maybe two or three sometimes, when she needed cheering up.

It was Saturday night. Virtually a whole week had passed without any contact with Tom whatsoever. She had survived, was about all she could say. After a somewhat fraught day, Jess was now sound asleep upstairs in bed. And Kate? Sat alone staring mindlessly at the television, which had absolutely nothing worth watching anyway. She felt so lonely, that had Tom rung at precisely that minute, she would have forgiven him completely and begged him to come over. But he didn't ring. She could have rung him of course, but maybe that was a step too far. She didn't. Okay, what next?

She'd just pour herself a G&T while she was thinking. Hmm, rather nice this Hendrick's gin, somebody had recommended it once before. With cucumber, not lemon, they'd said, and they were right. Winning combination. Another? Don't mind if I do.

The second one slipped down all too easily. These glasses must be very small, perhaps a tumbler would be better. As she moved to the kitchen in search of one, the cucumber leered at her from the worktop where it lay, the splendour of its shape seeming to mock her frustration. She wrapped her fingers around its form, massaging it almost. It was long and firm and as she lay it back down she chopped off the end with a very sharp knife! Tom Darrington, let that be a warning to you.

Quite therapeutic that moment had been; well, just a little bit anyway. For as she returned to the sofa and lay back to sip at drink number three, a glimmer of a smile appeared on her face, the first to have been seen there all week. Men? Who needed them anyway?

The ring of the doorbell, she presumed, was on the television. She hadn't been watching – Saturday night television was always a load of old codswallop, she didn't even know why she'd bothered to put it on, other than for company. That was it actually, the house was far too quiet without it. Silence is golden. Golden Balls – wasn't that what Victoria called David Beckham? God, her mind was jumping about all over the place now, but with all thoughts leading to sex. It must be the gin, better stop after this one.

There it went again. The doorbell. And it wasn't on the television, it was here, it was the front door. But who could that be? She didn't know anyone, except, except … Tom. Tom! It must be Tom, he'd come to persuade her. And she'd say yes, she'd forgive him, for she wanted him so badly it hurt. Hurt a lot actually, in her hand. In her hand? Why did wanting Tom so badly make her hand hurt? She looked at it. Blood. Dripping. Shit!

How stupid was she? She must have been so excited thinking it was Tom that she'd squeezed the glass and … ow! She didn't dare to look. The doorbell rang again. Tom! He'd rescue her, he'd sort her out. She rushed to the door, glass, blood and all.

'Tom?'

It was not him.

Kate squinted at the man in front of her, half-recognising him but too woozy to think straight. She did not like blood.

'Richard,' he said, by way of introduction, sussing the situation and feeling he should take matters in hand, so to speak.

'Come and sit down, let me look at it,' he said firmly, leading her back to the sofa.

'Ow,' she said, almost like a child, and feeling unable to be anything other than compliant as he lowered her down.

'Now, hold your hand up above your head while I look at it.'

'Feel like I'm in school, putting my hand up,' she joked,

feeling somewhat hysterical, willing herself not to faint.

'Oh my God!' he exclaimed, prising her fingers apart and away from the glass.

'What?' she screamed, feeling the blood rushing from her head downwards, like it was on an express train.

'It's okay, it's okay. It wasn't the glass at all. You had a little knife in your hand too. That has cut into you, not the glass.'

'Isn't that a bad thing?' she asked, faintly.

'No, of course not. It means it's a clean wound instead of one full of glass. We might have had to get you to A&E otherwise.'

'But it's still bleeding,' she said, timorously, venturing to look up at it but then wishing she hadn't.

'Well of course it is, you cut it. There should be some of those butterfly plasters in the first aid kit, they'll hold it together and stop the bleeding. Wait there, I'll go and get them.'

'Be quick,' she said, head whirring, room tilting.

'Keep your hand up, you'll be fine.'

He was such a kind man. Why had Grace ever got rid of him? Well, she'd still got a kind man, she'd got Charlie. It was just her who got the cheating, lying love-rats, not Grace.

Richard was back, applying the dressings as if he'd been doing it all his life.

'Just one question,' he said.

'What?' She even managed a smile now the blood was no longer dripping.

'Why was there a knife in your hand? Were you planning to commit a murder?'

'Ha-ha,' she responded to his teasing. 'I'd just had a very satisfying moment chopping the end off a cucumber, if you must know.'

Don't ask, Richard.

They settled down now that the drama was over, and sat in

front of the television like an old married couple. It had remained on through the crisis, droning on to no one in particular, but now it became the focal point of the room once more. *Take Me Out* was just coming to an end.

'Saturday night froth,' commented Richard.

'What do you usually do on a Saturday night?' she asked.

'Watch *Take Me Out*,' he grinned.

'Me too,' she said, with a giggle, 'it's about all the excitement I get on a Saturday unless there's a babysitter going spare.'

'And what then?'

'I'd probably still stay in, to be honest, I'm a bit of a homebird really.'

'You didn't mind me coming round did you? Only Grace said …'

'To keep an eye on me. She told me to keep an eye on you too! What's she like? Still making sure we're alright, even when she's on holiday!'

'That's Grace for you!'

'Actually it was a good job that you did come round. I might have bled to death, or fainted in a heap, or anything.'

Richard smiled and looked at Kate's hand. 'How's it feeling?'

'Much better, thanks to you. It seems to have stopped bleeding altogether now, thank goodness.'

'You'll have to be careful with it for a few days. Keep it dry and keep the butterfly thing on, give it a chance to heal.'

'Thanks, Dr Richard.'

'My pleasure,' he grinned.

'Hmm, *Take Me Out: The Gossip* – would you like to watch this or should we resort to a G&T?'

'The latter sounds good to me.'

'I've had two and a bit already, but I'm sure another one won't hurt. I'll make it weak.'

'Is this the offending cucumber?' he asked, following her

273

through to the kitchen and viewing it with some disdain. 'I don't even like to touch it.'

'But you'd like a slice in your gin?' she asked, smiling.

'Only if it's to be recommended.'

'Oh it is – truly.'

They carried their drinks through to the lounge.

'This is for medicinal purposes only, you realise that?'

'Of course,' he said. 'As your doctor I prescribe it,' he grinned.

'Here,' she said, as he hovered hesitantly. 'Sit on the sofa with me.' She patted the vast empty space. 'It's a big sofa and I promise not to leap on you like some sex-starved kitten.'

Again their eyes were drawn to the television, which was still on in the background.

'Actually, I quite like this part.'

'Me too.'

'Shall I turn it up a bit?'

'Go for it.'

Eventually the programme came to an end, and so did the gin.

'Like another?' she asked, to be polite, although she knew that she shouldn't herself, she was feeling ever so slightly squiffy.

'Actually, I won't if you don't mind, I'm driving. I should be going soon anyway, I've taken up enough of your evening.'

'Not at all, I'm really glad you came round, I was in need of some company.'

'Me too. Grace always knows best, even from a distance.'

'Have you heard from her?' asked Kate.

'Not a thing.'

'Me neither. Wouldn't expect to really though. She needs a complete break without having to worry about what's going on back home.'

'I'm sure Cleo and Daisy will be keeping her well entertained.'

Kate smiled. 'Do you get to see much of them?'

'A lot more than Grace does, that's for sure. I don't have the responsibilities that she has, I can just whiz off down there any time I like – weekends, anyway.'

'Responsibilities. Gran, you mean.' Annoying though she could be, Kate couldn't help but smile whenever she thought about her.

Richard likewise. 'Yes, Gran. I wonder how she's getting on.'

Gran. She really wasn't having the best of times. For one thing, the other people who were here with her were senile – totally. Not only did they look strange and act strange, they actually *were* strange. There wasn't one of them she could hold a decent conversation with, in fact most of them only seemed to know one word – 'Nurse!' They shouted it constantly. What a stupid word to say, anyway, they weren't in hospital, they were in a residential home – it was meant to be a kind of hotel really. Or so she'd thought.

The food was okay, she'd say that much. In fact, in a way, she supposed it was even better than at home. At least here the service was good and it always came on time. What was even better was the fact that she often managed to have two meals rather than just her own, as the other guests seemed to ignore the plates of food that were put in front of them. She hated to see waste. She couldn't just leave it there, could she?

Anyway, nobody seemed to mind, nobody seemed to notice even. As long as her clothes didn't start to get tight; that would be the only problem, if she was to put weight on. But then she could always go and have a rummage through someone else's wardrobe, pretend she was Gok Wan and give herself a makeover. It would have to be the wardrobe of someone with taste and style and expensive clothes, though, and there weren't many of them around here. No point in rummaging through the wardrobe of someone who wore cheap tat, she'd rather be bursting at the seams of her own than do that. Some of them actually had clothes which smelled as though Alfie had sneaked in and cocked his leg up on them. Perhaps he had, although she hadn't seen him. He was a naughty dog. Even naughtier if he'd been in here and not come to say hello to her. She'd have given him a whole Jammie Dodger, if she'd had any.

Thinking of Jammie Dodgers, of biscuit barrels, of Alfie, of home, her sight was getting quite blurred. What was wrong with these glasses? Were they hers? Had somebody mixed them up? She reached up to her face to wipe away some water that seemed to have splashed there.

'Alright Gertie?' asked one of the staff, noticing that she was upset.

'My name is *not* Gertie, as I've told you before. It's Gertrude, but I would much prefer to be referred to as Gran. That's what everyone calls me and that's what I'm used to.'

'Okay then, I'm sorry. Would you like a cup of tea, Gran?'

'Yes please!' chorused virtually all twenty residents. There were a lot of Grans about.

Gran looked around in astonishment, feeling even more distressed. They were all making fun of her now. Well, she was not going to put up with it for another minute, she'd had enough. Jaw jutting with firm intent, she grabbed her Zimmer frame with both hands and pulled herself up from the whiffiest and most uncomfortable chair in the house. Pah! This wasn't even her Zimmer frame, this one had wheels! No matter, it might go faster.

'Nurse! Nurse! She's stolen my Zimmer frame!' screamed Edith.

276

'Bugger off!' Gran yelled over her shoulder, in no uncertain terms.

'It's okay, Edith, she'll be back with it in a minute. She's only having a little walk around, giving herself a bit of exercise, aren't you, Gertie?'

Volcanoes erupt, fireworks explode, but Grans, what do they do?

Well, this one initially turned crimson, but then progressed to a shade which could only be described as puce, before venting forth from her fully inflated and excessively powerful lungs the most ear-shattering cry ever heard. Hearing aids squealed in fright. An agitated Mabel wet herself.

'*My name is not Gertie!*' yelled Gran. All eyes were upon her.

'Why don't you come and sit down, Ger… Gran, and have a nice cup of tea.'

'Thank you,' said all the other Grans, or ninety-nine percent of the … um, inmates, for that is what it would appear they were.

Yes, Gran had reached the door. The locked door.

'Where are you going, Ger… Gran?' asked the keeper of the key.

'Into the garden,' Gran replied, quite proud of her quick thinking. She could always do a runner once she got out there.

'Not today, it's raining.'

'No it's not, I'm not stupid.'

'Well, the grass is too wet.'

'I want to go outside now! Open this door!' commanded Gran.

'Come and sit down and have a nice cup of tea.'

'Open this door now!' yelled Gran.

'Not today. Come back over here with the others.'

'I want to go home!'

'Your daughter will be back for you soon.'

'Gra-a-a-ce!' came Gran's piteous cry, as she attacked the door with the Zimmer frame.

'Gran?' Kate responded to Richard's question. 'Oh I'm sure she'll be fine. She's a tough old bird and I think she was quite looking forward to going in the end. Somehow, Charlie managed to convince her.'

'He's a good man.'

'One of the best. And they seem really happy.'

'I'm glad,' said Richard, and he genuinely meant it. He wanted nothing but the best for Grace.

'Would you like a coffee before you go? Not that I'm throwing you out or anything, I'm enjoying your company.'

'Love one, if I'm not keeping you up that is.'

'Me?' laughed Kate, 'I'm the world's greatest insomniac, didn't you know?'

He followed her through to the kitchen again when she went to make the coffee. She filled the kettle and plugged it in. Her eyes alighted on the remains of the cucumber which languished on the kitchen worktop.

'Looks a bit shrivelled,' commented Richard.

'So would you if I'd chopped your end off,' she giggled. 'Oops, does that sound a bit rude?'

Her back was towards him as she poured the coffee. His eyes, involuntarily, travelled down the length of her. She had a good figure, that was for sure.

They returned to the lounge and to the sofa, each, for some inexplicable reason, slightly more aware of the other's sexuality now. Prickles of something resembling mutual attraction were starting to set off alarm bells. This really was a no-go area.

'Perhaps I should go,' he said, reason unspoken but understood by both.

'Finish your coffee first,' she said, unwisely perhaps.

The room was suddenly quiet. Even the volume on the television seemed to have gone lower.

Richard spoke first, to fill the silence. 'So, how've you been?' It seemed like a pretty dumb question but it was the best he could muster.

'Um … now, let me see,' said Kate with a half smile, rolling her eyes heavenward in pretence of deep thought. 'Daughter hates me, on–off husband probably now off for good, best friend on holiday just when I need someone to talk to. Will that do for starters?'

'Hmm, sounds about as good as my life.'

'Okay, tell me yours and I'll judge.'

'Ready for this? Kids both moved down south and I hardly ever see them, ex-wife now married to Mr Perfect. The love of my life, my beautiful Anna, murdered, dead before …'

'Oh Richard, nothing could be worse than that,' she said, putting down her cup and holding out her arms to him, feeling his distress.

'I'm sorry,' he said, unable to hold back his tears. 'I don't know what you must think of me. People look at me as though I should be over it by now but I just can't seem to move on.'

'It's still early days, you had so little time together. So tragic that she was snatched away from you so soon. My problems are trivial in comparison.'

'Sorry,' he said, trying to pull himself together. 'You must think I'm such an idiot.'

'Nothing of the sort,' she said, feeling emotional herself seeing him so distressed. 'And please don't be sorry, it's good to let it all out sometimes.'

'I seem to do nothing else these days,' he said, sitting back to look at her, noting her tear-filled eyes. 'Thank you for caring.'

Something seemed to happen in that moment,

something totally unexpected which took them both by surprise. For, without either being aware of moving towards the other, their mouths suddenly became interlocked. The worst thing was that neither felt they wanted to prise them apart.

In Richard's case the moment of impact came with such an outpouring of pent-up emotion he could barely breathe. A year and a half had gone by since Anna's death and, missing her so much, sex had been taboo. The only release from his sexual tension during that time had been played out by his own hand – a solitary occupation. Now, to feel someone else's lips on his was more than he could bear.

For Kate it was different. She knew she should stop, but something was preventing her. Was it lust? Probably. Was it tit for tat? Probably. Was it the gin? Even more probably. But what she knew more than anything at this moment in time, as they indulged each others' bodies with the delights of sensual pleasures, was that her own sexuality felt on an all-time high, and she needed him inside her right now.

'Upstairs,' she requested, managing to extract her mouth briefly and with some difficulty for the length of time it took to say the one word.

She attempted to back towards the door, her lips still locked to his, her body still bent into a sitting position. He pulled her back down with a grunt.

'Wha...?' she managed.

His eyes looked sort of panicked. Lustful but unsure. He came up for air with a 'schmwack'.

'Shouldn't,' he gasped.

'Shouldn't?' she asked, through the most kissable lips he'd seen in a very long time. 'But we can't do it here, Jessica might walk in on us. There's a lock on the bedroom door.'

'Shouldn't because you'll regret it tomorrow, wish you

hadn't,' he said, stumbling over his words, his breath coming in short sharp bursts. He would burst out of his jeans in a minute.

'You don't want me? Think it's all in the heat of the moment?' Well heat of something, she was on fire, might have to dial 999 in a minute unless he came to the rescue.

'Maybe. Of course I want you but …'

'Then come upstairs,' she said, grabbing him by the hand and leaving him with no option.

27

Things usually happen for a reason and it certainly seemed so in this case. For at that point who would have thought that anything could have stood in their way? But fate intervened. For as they scuttled up the stairs, decision made, sex an overwhelming need, they opened the bedroom door, only to find what is commonly known as the best contraceptive in the world, the best contra-sex-ive, actually. A child. Jessica must have woken up and got into her mother's bed.

Seeing her lying there looking so peaceful, so innocent, provided them both with a guilt trip and a half. How could they even have considered it? It's amazing, actually, how quickly things can shrivel up in situations like this, in fact they both felt they'd just stepped into a cold shower.

He beckoned her from the room. 'I should go,' he said.

'Must you?' she asked, knowing the answer full well, feeling embarrassment now at what had happened between them.

'Let's just have a little chat before I go,' he said, understanding exactly how she was feeling as he felt the same way.

They returned to the sofa which, only moments before, had been such a hotbed of passion. This time there was a considerable space between them.

'I'm sorry, I shouldn't have done that,' he said, head in his hands.

She reached out to touch his shoulder reassuringly, but then withdrew her outstretched hand, almost afraid of reigniting the sexual tension.

'My fault more than yours, I think,' she said, somewhat ashamed. 'At least you suggested we shouldn't let it go any further. I was like a cat on heat.'

He lifted his head, a half-smile at her description. 'It was the gin.'

'In that case I'm sworn off it for life!' she said.

'You're missing Tom, too,' he said, pointedly.

'I know I am – desperately.'

'Then tell him. Life's too short – I should know.'

'Oh Richard, I am sorry.'

'It's okay. I suppose it did me a favour in a way. Proved that maybe I will be able to move on, given time.'

'That's good. I'm glad. As for me … do you realise that Tom is the only man I've ever slept with? Incredible, isn't it, in this day and age?'

Richard was wide-eyed. 'You mean if we'd have gone all the way … oh my God!'

'I know, I'm so glad we didn't now. I do love Tom, you know.'

'Then tell him. Remember what I said. Life's too short. Ring him tomorrow and sort it out.'

Kate went upstairs when Richard had left. She looked down at her sleeping daughter who lay spread-eagled on the bed. The face of innocence. I wish you could stay like that forever, Kate thought to herself, life gets far too complicated when you get older.

She moved her over gently, trying not to disturb her sleep, and climbed in next to her. Her head was reeling. Would life ever settle down for them and get back to normal? Since Jake had died, nothing seemed to have gone right for them at all. Admittedly, a lot of that was down to her, the angst within herself. If only she didn't have to churn everything around in her head and worry so much, life would be a whole lot easier.

And now she had something else to worry about. She couldn't believe she'd been on the verge of having sex with another man – was she completely insane? Tom was the love of her life, the one and only. What had she been thinking about? Was it the drink that had done it? Had it made her more relaxed and released her inhibitions? She'd never touch another drop if that was the case, anything could happen, tonight had proved that.

It did make her realise, though, how easy it was for anyone to slip into this sort of situation. Not that she was condoning her own behaviour, which tonight had been totally out of character. What had Tom done that was any worse than the way she had behaved tonight? Okay, he'd actually slept with her best friend – a bad one, that. But she herself had been on the verge of sleeping with her best friend's ex-but-still-very-much-around husband, and would totally have done so, without a trace of recrimination at the time, had she not received the short sharp shock of a timely wake-up call from her innocent sleeping daughter. As for Tom's little dalliance with Caroline, it probably equalled her own with Richard. What a hypocrite she was.

From this whole sordid mess one fact rose up and stood clear and bold above the rest – she loved Tom. The question was, what was she to do about it? And unfortunately it was no longer the only question. She knew about Chloe and she knew about Caroline too, now. Did that mean she should confess about Richard? She knew how bad it had been, having to find out all these things for herself. Would it be better just to tell him the truth straightaway? Sort of, 'Oh, by the way, I nearly had sex with Richard, Grace's ex.'

Well, maybe not quite that bluntly, but things needed to be out in the open if they were to stand any kind of chance of success in a fresh start. Fresh start? She was maybe getting a little bit ahead of herself here. He wasn't even

284

speaking to her now, as she recalled. But he would do. He had to. She loved him. He loved her.

With immense feelings of guilt and the agonising over what she should say to Tom, Kate unsurprisingly had very little sleep that night. But despite the consequential rather woozy head, she was up early the next morning – even before Jessica, which had to be a first.

This mess had to be sorted out once and for all, it couldn't possibly be allowed to drag on any longer. Time was passing them by and life was too short. Richard had been right on that one. It wasn't even eight o'clock yet but Kate decided to ring him there and then. If she waited any later Jess would be up, ears wide open and flapping, and there would be no privacy to make the call. It wasn't fair to keep involving her all the time, she was just a child. Any discussions or heated debates about their future should be kept private, just between the two of them.

She pressed his number. Voicemail. She panicked and pressed 'End'. Not the sort of thing you could leave a message about exactly. Hmm. What to do? The decision was taken out of her hands. Within seconds he rang back.

'Did you just call?' he asked sleepily.

'Sorry, did I wake you?'

'Well it *is* Sunday morning,' he said, somewhat grumpily.

'Sorry.'

'What's wrong?'

'Wrong? Nothing, I just wanted to talk to you, that's all.'

'At eight o'clock in the morning?'

'Well, yes.'

This wasn't going well.

'Tom?'

The line had gone silent. Was he still there?

'What?'

'Oh … I thought you'd hung up.'

Silence.

'Listen,' said Kate, jumping in with both feet, no time to test the water first. 'Can we meet and talk?'

'Kate, how many times have we done this? We've got such an on–off relationship I don't think I can take it any more. It's making me ill, I can't sleep, I can't eat, nothing. Painful as it is, I think we should call it a day. Now.'

Kate's eyes and mouth all rounded in shock, as the air flew out from her lungs in a sudden whoosh. She'd always been the one calling the shots, but at this precise moment she felt as though someone had shot her.

'No, Tom, no! Please no. That's why I rang. I wanted to say I'm sorry and I love you and I want us to be together always. Time's passing us by. I just want us to put everything behind us and make a fresh start.'

'How many times, Kate, how many times have we said this? What's so different about now?'

'Something happened. I want to tell you about it. It's made me realise a few things about myself … and about life.'

Whether she was doing the right thing in confessing, Kate was unsure. Panic fluttered inside her like butterflies' wings, but she was tired of secrets and lies. Everything had to be out in the open now if this was ever going to work. Why, oh why had she done it? But then, if she hadn't, she would never have been able to reach an inkling of understanding of Tom's past behaviour.

As for Tom, he was still silent. What could possibly have happened? Just another ruse to get him to go back over there, most probably. Then he'd see Jess and be drawn in all over again. Well he wouldn't be, because he wasn't going. He'd made his decision and he'd stick with it. Only one problem: he loved her.

'Tom?'

'What?'

286

'Please can I see you today?' She'd beg if she had to.

Silence.

'Tom?'

'I'll be there at two.'

Kate tried to keep her distance during the afternoon when he'd arrived. She'd thought he might appreciate some time alone with Jess, and anyway it would be easier to talk to him later when Jess had gone to bed. But Jessica had other ideas. She sensed the tension and wanted them to spend the afternoon all together as a family. She had such happy memories of what it used to be like to have a mummy and a daddy and she wanted it to be like that again. Nothing would stand in the way – not if she had anything to do with it.

'So what did you want to talk about?' asked Tom, as Jessica skipped on ahead.

It was a lovely sunny day for their walk in the park. Jessica was pleased, she wanted everything to be perfect for them. They'd been a bit frosty at first but they seemed to be talking now – not much, but just occasionally. That was a good sign. She'd keep out of their way as much as she could, just keep glancing back to make sure they were okay. If they got back together would they have to get married again? Would she be a bridesmaid like she was for Caroline and Ben?

'Nothing,' said Kate, in response to his question.

'Don't say that!' snapped Tom. 'You specifically said something had happened and you wanted to tell me about it. Don't play games with me, Kate, I really can't take it any more.'

He seemed sort of brittle, not his usual self at all. This was the wrong day to be telling him something so major, but yet she knew she had to. She just hoped it didn't all go horribly wrong.

'I will tell you, honestly, but after Jessica's gone to bed. It's not something I can talk about while she's around.'

Alarm bells were starting to ring in his head, for some reason. He looked at her quizzically.

'I will tell you, I promise.'

'So you keep saying.'

'She loves it when we're all together,' smiled Tom as he came back down into the lounge after taking Jessica up to bed.

Well, that was a good start, at least he was smiling … for the moment, anyway. She knew she would wipe the smile right off his face with what she was about to tell him. But it had to be done. And she hoped it would be just a temporary thing that he would get over, as she had now done. After all, her misdemeanour of last evening had been nothing in comparison to his. Her thing with Richard had just been an impetuous flirtation, not a falling in love. She could only hope that she would be able to convince him to see it that way too.

She was sitting on the sofa in readiness, wine poured. After last night she'd sworn off alcohol for good. But hey, that was last night, tonight she needed it. Just not gin and tonic, that's all.

'So, what is this earth-shattering thing that's happened? What dark and mysterious revelations have been uncovered?' he asked, as he sat down next to her, picked up his glass, and chinked it to hers. 'Cheers.'

He seemed quite amenable really.

'Don't make light of it, Tom, it's no laughing matter. But it has helped me to see things a bit more clearly and put things into perspective.'

'What are these "things" you keep talking about?' he asked casually, still completely oblivious.

'Affairs, casual sex, dalliances, call them what you will.'

'Oh Kate, we've been through it all so many times. What more can I say? I'm sorry, I wish it had never happened.

288

And that's what it was, something that just happened. I love you so much and if I could only turn back the clock. I don't know what else I can say. How I can ever explain and make you understand why I did what I did when I love you so much? I don't understand myself, except I had this need for you and you weren't there. And that's no excuse I know but …'

'Stop,' she said, holding a finger over his lips to silence him. 'I do understand now.'

'What?' he asked, puzzled. 'What do you mean?'

'When I just said "dalliances", you thought I was talking about you, but I wasn't.'

'I don't understand.'

'I was talking about me,' she said, hanging her head, shamefaced.

'I'm confused,' he said, nervously running his fingers through his hair, a puzzled frown on his face, suddenly afraid that he was going to hear something he wasn't going to like.

'I'm so, so sorry, Tom. I know I shouldn't have … well I didn't, but I almost did. But after all that I've said I shouldn't even have been tempted. But I was, and I nearly did and … oh, Tom, I'm so sorry!'

'About what?' The hairs on the back of his neck were on full alert. He was beginning to get the picture but was praying it was the wrong one. Surely not. Surely she wouldn't, not after all she'd said.

'Last night I had a … oh, it sounds so seedy when I say it now, and it wasn't like that at all!'

'Say it, Kate!'

'Okay. I know it was wrong, but last night I had a bit of a fling with someone and we almost ended up having sex. But it was just "almost". We didn't actually …'

Tom slumped forward in his seat, his head in his hands.

'Tom?'

Silence.

'Tom, say something.'

'What do you expect me to say? "Well done"? "Congratulations"?'

'Don't be like that, Tom.'

'So how do you expect me to be? Over the moon? Delighted?'

'It wasn't anything serious. He was upset, I was a shoulder to cry on, I'd had a lot to drink. I thought we, you and I, might be over. We were consoling each other and it just sort of happened.'

The silence seemed interminable. Tension hovered, but then swooped in for the kill.

'*What* happened exactly Kate? And where was my daughter while all this unburdening of souls was going on?' spat Tom. 'She was here with you, I can't believe you would …'

'She was upstairs in bed, Tom, asleep. We were downstairs, we kissed, we…'

'Don't!' interjected Tom, holding up both of his hands, a look of utter disgust on his face. 'I don't want to hear any more!'

'But you asked.'

'I know I did but … so what stopped you?' he asked tentatively, hoping he already knew the answer to this one, hoping it was because she loved him.

But that was not to be.

'Because, when we went upstairs, Jessica had moved into my bed and was asleep in there and…'

'Oh my God! And that's the only thing that stopped you?'

'Well it brought me to my senses, made me realise what I was doing.'

Again Tom slumped forward in his seat, his fingers brushed backwards through his hair until his forehead came to rest in the palm of his hands. He uttered not a word, just a long, low groan of defeat.

290

'Tom?'

'What?'

'Say something.'

'What do you expect me to say?'

'Well, yell at me. Scream, shout, throw something. Anything.'

'You know what this is, don't you?' he asked, after several minutes of intense silence.

'What d'you mean?'

'Tit for tat, isn't it? You've just done this to get back at me, to make me see what it feels like.'

'Don't be ridiculous.'

'Don't call me ridiculous,' he spat venomously, sitting back up and glaring into her eyes with a terrifying coldness she'd never ever seen there before.

'Tom, it was nothing like that at all! No. It was the gin, the heat of the moment, missing you. It was all just one big mistake.'

'Well one big mistake too many,' he said, getting to his feet. 'I'm off. We're finished, Kate. It's over. Final this time.'

'But Tom!' she said, grabbing at him in desperation as he walked towards the door. 'It can't be over, I love you!'

''Bye Kate,' he said, walking away, tears streaming down his face. 'I love you too,' he said, so softly that it was audible to no one but himself.

28

Life has its ups and downs, it's the same for everyone – even Caroline and Ben. For while Kate and Tom were in mid-crisis, Grace and Charlie were holidaying in London, and Chloe had joyously resigned herself to simply being a mum and enjoying her friendship with Sandra, for Caroline and Ben things had started to go wrong.

Their problem really stemmed from the fact that, in his own head, Ben still thought of himself as a teenager. Many people do, this is very true, but the difference is that in Ben's case he continued to act like one too. Even his vanity about his appearance had started to grate on Caroline somewhat, which was weird as she'd always found it an endearing quality before.

Caroline was far more mature than Ben, but their differences of character had always complemented each other well. As the more sensible of the two, Caroline was the one who could be relied upon to keep their lives on track, whereas Ben was the one who always put the fun into their relationship. They thought that theirs was a match made in heaven and that nothing could ever go wrong. Indeed, many couples feel this way as they set out along the path of life together; it's only when life starts to throw things at them that sometimes cracks can start to develop. With Ben and Caroline it wasn't a crack in their relationship exactly, more a little chink in their perfect bubble of togetherness.

Caroline's problem though, was that Ben still lived in a teenage world of fun and frivolity; responsibility didn't enter his psyche or even go remotely close. He wouldn't ever notice a little chink in their perfect bubble unless it grew so big that he could fall through it. He loved his beautiful wife and not only did she look after him and cater to his every need, but they had fun together. Why would they want to change all that by having a … a …

Baby. Yes, Caroline's maternal clock was ticking, a loud, echoing tick which chimed a reminder at hourly intervals. And alarm bells were ringing when it came to Ben, for would he ever make the decision to settle down and bring up children of his own? Children? The thought of having one sprog was bad enough. In fact he'd never forget the day his mother had gone into labour with J-J and he'd had to accompany her to the hospital. It had been enough to leave him traumatised for life – had done so, actually. No, sprogs were not for him.

'But you're good with babies,' Caroline persisted.

'Other people's, yeah, just for a couple of hours now and again. Having your own is like a life sentence.'

'Ben! How could you say that?'

'Well it is.'

'Just think of having a little person exactly like you, a mini Ben.'

'Got one. My little bro, J-J. And I don't have to look after him – Mum does, ha ha!'

'Ben, this is serious. I've been so broody now for such a long time and I can't wait any longer.' She was trying so hard not to cry, but the floodgates just opened. 'I want us to have a baby,' she sobbed.

'Oh babe,' he said, his arms around her, he hated it when she started blubbing. 'We will one day,' he promised.

'Soon?' she asked through her tears.

'Soon as,' he said, breathing somewhat heavily. For some reason her tearful vulnerability was making him feel decidedly horny.

As for Caroline, having been made a promise like that, she wanted to make love to him for ever more. Trouble in the Russell household? Not any more. Ben's only regret at this moment was that he hadn't said 'yes' earlier if this was her reaction. The *Kama Sutra*? She must have written it!

At the complete opposite end of the spectrum of happiness and peace and harmony were Kate and Tom. It seemed almost as though they were fated never to be together again – karma, as opposed to Kama of the Sutra kind. They were both heartbroken and utterly devastated, and completely incommunicado. Obviously, remaining as such, the future together which they both wanted and hoped for was slipping irretrievably from their grasp. And yet they loved each other. They needed an intermediary, but the only one currently available was Jessica, and she was far too small. Nevertheless, her mummy and daddy or not, she felt like banging their heads together.

Jessica was livid, and totally distraught. They'd been so close to all being back together as a family and it had all gone wrong – again. She blamed Kate totally for sending her daddy away. It was always her fault.

'I hate you!' she screamed, for the umpteenth time.

As for Kate, she was at the end of her tether. For this time it really had been her fault. What a stupid thing to have done! It made matters worse that she had absolutely no one to talk to about it, no one to unburden herself to. Against her better judgement she'd even tried ringing Grace, but there was no reply from her mobile. It would have been unfair to burden her anyway.

She considered trying to talk to Chloe, but dismissed that as a bad idea. Okay, Richard. She talked herself into it. At least he was a good listener and he knew all about her situation, and if the conversation was on the end of a phone at least there wouldn't be any temptation to leap upon each other for sympathy and consolation.

Richard was, in fact, pleased to hear from her. He offered to come over for a chat but she politely declined, feeling it safer to keep him at arm's length. It was good to be able to unburden herself, although the only advice he could give was to give Tom a bit of space to think things over for a few days and then try to contact him again. Richard himself felt really bad that he was the cause of the problem this time, but as Kate pointed out, she had no one to blame but herself, she'd known what she was doing, gin or no gin.

Kate asked whether he'd heard anything from Grace, and Richard sounded just a little concerned when he said he hadn't. He usually spoke to her every two or three days and had never gone this long before. He joked that not many men had such a good relationship with their ex-wife and Kate agreed – no wonder Charlie got jealous sometimes. However both Kate and Richard were in complete agreement – Grace was a very special person, they were missing her and couldn't wait for her return.

Another person missing Grace was Gran. She had known this would happen. Grace had stuck her in this nuthouse with a load of senile delinquents and told her it was just for two weeks. Well, what a pack of lies that had been. She'd abandoned her completely, never come near. She'd been here for months, years in fact, and where was Grace? Forgotten all about her poor old mother – living it up at home, spending all her money more than likely.

'A cup of tea, Gertie?'

'Gran!' bellowed Gran.

'What? What? I'm sorry, I'm sorry,' jumped the nervous little old lady sitting next to her, spilling her own tea in the process.

'You see why we can't call you Gran, Gertie? Almost everyone's a Gran in here.'

'There's only one Gran,' growled Gran.

'Thank goodness,' hissed the carer, under his breath.

'So do *not* call me Gertie!'

'Right. Gotcha. How about Gert then, instead?'

Gran lashed out at him with her right hand, frustrated beyond measure.

'Now now Gert, that's not very nice, is it?'

'Well you're not very nice,' she said, kicking her foot towards him. 'Now bugger off and leave me in peace.'

'With pleasure,' said the carer, audibly this time, as he made his way towards the tea bar to join the others for their staff tea break,

'Has anyone else noticed Gertie's displaying a lot of aggressive behaviour? We must make sure it gets put into her report.'

There was nothing wrong with Gran's hearing on occasions such as this and she heard every word loud and clear. She was sick of it, sick of them all – young whipper-snappers like that telling her what to do. Well, she'd had enough and she was getting out of here, Grace or no Grace.

She looked at the staff, all sat together in a huddle enjoying their tea break. There weren't many of them, actually, to be responsible for all this lot of insaniacs. There, she'd made up a new word, she wasn't as stupid as they all thought she was. Then she looked at the insaniacs, studied them one by one. No-hopers, the lot of them. And yet they all wanted to go home, it was all they ever said, 'I want to go home,' they wailed. 'I want to go home.' It was enough to drive even her demented. So what she didn't understand was why didn't they do something about it instead of sitting there like stuffed ducks waiting for the tea trolley? It was their only excitement of the day, no wonder they were insane, they'd probably been perfectly normal when they'd first arrived.

It was a bit like being in jail, she supposed, although

she'd never actually been there herself, obviously. But they had locked doors and prison warders just the same, even if they did call themselves carers. There weren't any bars on the windows here, but that was the only difference as far as she could see. That was an idea: she could charge at the window with her Zimmer frame like some spear-carrying Amazon. She could almost hear the war-cry now. Hmm, but the warders would notice and soon drag her back, especially when the glass broke. She'd be locked in her cell, solitary confinement for evermore. Clang, chink, and that would be her.

But no, a better idea was hobbling into her mind. Ideas usually creep but, because of her arthritis, this one had to hobble. It was a good one though, and well worth the wait. A riot. Yes. She'd seen them on the telly. The prisoners are unhappy so they start a riot and break out of jail. It's a bit like Monopoly where you have a 'Get out of jail free' card, only in this game you don't even need a card and it's much more exciting. Monopoly can get a bit boring if it goes on too long.

Yes, a riot. She'd seen them on the news. In fact that could happen to them – she'd be the hero, interviewed on *News at Ten* by Alastair Stewart. She liked him, he was a lovely young man. She could wear her hat like the Queen. So how do you start a riot? She sat and thought for a while. She'd have to go round everyone and tell them her plan. All they'd have to do was shout a lot, and they'd be good at that, they shouted 'Nurse!' all the time. She'd have to think of a better word than that though, obviously. How about 'Riot!', surely they could manage that.

So what happened next when she'd seen them on the telly? Yes – she remembered! They just punched the prison warders, stole all the keys, then let themselves out. Simple. If anyone was good at punching it was her, she'd soon teach the insaniacs what to do. They'd be better than that

Muhammad Ali by the time she'd done with them. And then, the best bit of all in her opinion, they climbed up onto the roof and did a little dance of triumph, waving sticks in the air. Well most of them had sticks already so that wouldn't be a problem.

Oh, and she'd almost forgotten this bit. The paparazzi would come, loads of them, flashing lights, desperate for photos of them to put on the front of the next day's newspapers. Headline news, that's what they'd be, before she was whisked away in a limousine to *News at Ten* and Alastair. Hang on, where was her hat? She'd have to make sure she was wearing it before she started the riot.

In fact that could be the sign – yes! Oh, she was so clever when she put her mind to it. Right. The warders were still in their huddle discussing last night's activities with their boyfriends. Yes, even the man one, she'd never known anything like it … well, she had actually, there'd been a policeman/woman once … But enough of this, she had work to do. While the warders were otherwise engaged, she'd talk to the insaniacs, incite this riot. Wasn't there a song once: 'I Predict a Riot'?

The first one Gran approached was the timid lady. She wasn't expecting much resistance from her, she always did as she was told, even if she didn't always quite make it to the toilet in time.

'So,' said Gran, hopefully. 'When you see me put on my hat I want you to shout "Riot!"'

'Quiet,' whispered the lady, 'Yes, I'm quiet.'

A rather large elderly gentleman was munching on a biscuit as he listened to what was said.

'Diet, yes, I should be on a diet.'

The third one she spoke to was silent, staring back at her with an expressionless face, the fourth simply burst into tears, the whole idea too much to comprehend. Did Gran feel defeated in her plot to overthrow all? Not at all. It was her only hope. She'd do it herself if she had to, she could see the headlines now: 'Lone Rioter Wins Freedom for All'.

Okay, Edith. She was her last hope. She was always wanting to go home and this was the only way she'd achieve it. Gran sat down next to her.

'Bugger off,' said Edith, automatically.

'Bugger off yourself,' said Gran.

'What d'you want?' growled Edith.

'Do you want to go home?' asked Gran.

'Home? Yes,' said Edith, brightening up.

'And me,' piped up the man next to her.

'Me too,' said another. 'I only ...'

'Well shut up and listen then, we're going to start a riot.' Oh, Gran loved the power of being in charge!

They looked at her in amazement. A riot? Who heard of such a thing – apart from on the telly. She seemed to know what she was doing, that Gertie. They'd led such quiet lives.

'Now, remember what I told you,' said Gran. 'I'll go and get my hat and when I come back and put it on you all shout "Riot!" and wave these sticks and punch the warder. er ... nurses. Okay?' she said, collecting random walking sticks and handing them to her little gang. This really was quite fun.

'Aaagghh!' screamed the timid lady, overhearing, a puddle forming around her feet.

'Riot!' shouted Edith, heading towards the carers brandishing her stick.

'Not yet!' scolded Gran, but too late, the others were on their way, arms flailing.

Nothing for it but to lash out at the nearest one then.

'Gertie!' admonished the carer, totally unfazed.

They'd seen it all before. 'I think we have a granny riot going on,' he said, smiling as he separated the unruly bunch with a promise of chocolate biscuits.

Chocolate digestives and they were putty in his hands. But Gran? She refused all. Just hobbled into a corner to lick her wounds, and dream of home and Grace …

29

Grace's head was pounding. She had to force herself to open her eyes, rather gingerly at first, wondering whether it would make her headache worse. The light seemed so bright, the room full of strange sounds. Beeping and clicking and whirring. What was that? She opened them fully now, panicked to see, through a haze, that she was in a different room, a strange room … and where was Charlie?

She blinked a few times, and closed her eyes. Perhaps she was still asleep and having a dream. She waited a few seconds, then opened them again. The haziness had cleared but it had definitely not been a dream. White and clinical. A hospital bed. She was in hospital? She tried to move, tried to sit up, but everything was hurting, not just her head.

'Ah, you're awake at last, sleepyhead. How are you feeling?' asked a young nurse, wreathed in smiles as she appeared, as if by magic, from nowhere.

'Where am I?' Grace asked, totally disoriented.

'You're in hospital. There was an accident.'

'Accident? Where's Charlie? What about Izzy?'

Grace was suddenly plunged into panic, the bleeping of the heart monitor increasing to an unhealthy rate.

'It's okay, don't worry, everyone's fine, but you'll make yourself worse if you don't stay calm.'

'But where are they? What happened?'

'There were only the two of you in the car, no one else. Who's Izzy? Is she your daughter?'

'Yes, the youngest.' Gradually it was starting to come back to her.

They'd been going to have a day out together, just the two of them for a treat. Izzy had wanted to stay with Cleo and play with little Daisy – so Charlie had suggested that they ...

'Charlie?' she said, trying to get out of bed to find him. 'Ow!' she winced, giving in to the pain.

'Charlie?' He was dead, he was dead, she knew it. She'd killed him, she'd been driving, she'd ...

'Grace! You really do need to stay calm, you're going to make yourself worse otherwise.'

'But Charlie...'

'Charlie's absolutely fine, I promise you, he's in safe hands.'

'Safe hands? You mean with God in heaven – he's dead, isn't he? I killed him, I killed my Charlie,' she sobbed, sending the bleeps into overdrive.

'Stop it, Grace, you'll be killing yourself in a minute,' said the young nurse firmly as she pushed her gently back down on to the pillows and held Grace's hand in her own to give comfort. 'Charlie is not dead, do you hear me? He's been down to surgery this morning.'

'Surgery? Can I see him? Where is he?'

'Grace, really, I mean it, you need to stay calm for your own health, you'll have that poor machine taking off in a minute. He's had surgery for a broken arm, that's all. It had to be pinned because it was such a bad break, but apart from that he's just got general cuts and bruises, nothing serious, he's a lucky man.'

'So can I see him?' mumbled Grace, a little incoherently.

'He's in recovery, but ...' the nurse's voice seemed to be slipping further and further away. The pain ...

The crash team were there within seconds. They could not have acted any faster. As Charlie struggled to fight his

302

way out of the anaesthetic, further down the corridor his beloved Gracie fought a battle of her own.

For the heart he'd won, and loved, and cherished, had ceased to beat. Grace, that much loved person upon whom so many depended, that central pivot in so many people's lives, was slipping away.

Back in Grace's house, Kate felt a sudden cold shiver, as though someone had walked over her grave. Alfie must have felt a similar sensation as he left his basket with a sudden whimper and came and sat beside her, offering her his paw.

'Good dog,' said Kate, taking the proffered paw in one hand and stroking him with the other.

Poor boy, he must wonder what had happened to everyone, especially Grace, he usually followed her everywhere. She'd take him for a walk later, although she needed to feel a bit better first. She was feeling decidedly panicky, for some strange reason. Gasping for breath and sweating profusely, she pushed past Alfie and opened the back door to get some air. She gulped at it in mouthfuls, seemingly unable to get enough. Alfie stood beside her looking up at the sky in total concentration until he suddenly tilted back his head, nose in the air, and let out the most haunting and eerie wolf-like howl imaginable.

A sudden calm descended. A white feather fluttered to the ground. All was at peace.

'Mummy?' shouted Jessica as she ran out through the open door to join them. She felt as though something was happening but was on the periphery, not really understanding. 'What was that funny noise? It sounded really scary.'

'It was just Alfie, darling, nothing to worry about.'

'I've never heard him make a noise like that before, I was really frightened.'

303

'Dogs do that sometimes. He sounded like a wolf, didn't he?' said Kate, holding out her arms to her.

Jessica cuddled into the warmth of her mummy, reassured. 'Look at the rainbow,' said Jess suddenly, pointing up at the sky.'

'Oh,' said Kate, feeling calmer herself now. 'Funny, I'm sure that wasn't there a minute ago.'

'I know a song about rainbows,' said Jess, smiling as she remembered her little friend. 'Would you like me to sing it for you?'

Kate nodded, unable to speak, feeling suddenly tearful for no apparent reason.

'Red and yellow and pink and green,
'Orange and purple and blue,
'I can sing a rainbow, sing a rainbow,
'Sing a rainbow too.'

'That's lovely Jess. Where did you learn that?'

'From Izzy. She said her Auntie Anna had taught it to her.'

Unexpectedly the tears overflowed. Stupid really, she'd never even met Anna but she remembered that poignant moment at her funeral when she'd gone there to support Grace. 'Somewhere Over the Rainbow.'

'Why are you crying, Mummy?'

'I really don't know, Jess. I think it must just have been one of those days.'

But deep down Kate knew it was more than that. It was a power that had come from beyond the earth, overwhelming – an inexplicable force. Something had happened, she didn't know what, an other-worldly experience that had taken her breath away and left her emotionally drained. Suddenly, she felt at peace.

At the same time that Kate was experiencing a force from beyond, Grace was experiencing a different kind of force, a force of the electrical variety, as the hospital crash team attempted to jolt her heart back into life.

She was travelling down a long dark tunnel and she didn't want to go. She couldn't just go and leave everyone, they couldn't manage without her, but at the same time a bright light was drawing her towards it, faster and faster. And she wanted to go, it was getting brighter and warmer and would be her salvation, eternal happiness lay within. What was more, she could hear Anna calling her, reaching out, telling her it was easy, just to come in.

But the road wasn't smooth, wasn't easy. Something kept getting in the way, jolting her, trying to make her turn back. She was shocked the first time and tried to ignore it because the bright light looked such a welcoming place. She carried on. There was Anna, she could see her … but then, ouch, it happened again. Who was doing this? Who was stopping her? Didn't they understand? This was a beautiful place of peace and joy and light. She had to go, go, go …

Pahhh! It felt like an explosion. The light went out, the tunnel was gone. There was noise, strange noises, and voices, people.

'We've got her! Well done, guys.'

What? Who was …?

'Grace, Grace? Can you hear me?'

Grace opened one eye. She was alive.

Kate couldn't sleep. She'd been tossing and turning all night. After her surreal experience earlier that day she couldn't help but think that something was wrong. She also couldn't help but think, for some inexplicable reason, that it was something to do with Grace. Kate had been trying her utmost not to ring Grace's mobile: she was on the first holiday she'd had in years and it seemed a bit mean to interrupt. Nevertheless, she was worried. If she still felt like this in the morning she would ring. Grace had the patience

of a saint, but even she wouldn't appreciate a phone call at
4 a.m.

But she knew a man who might. And she knew whose
arms she wanted to feel around her as she lay alone in the
big empty bed worrying about her friend, worrying about
the future, worrying about everything. She loved him. He
was the love of her life. They had something so precious,
why did they have to keep breaking it all the time?

Should she or shouldn't she? What had she got to lose?
He already wasn't speaking to her.

'Tom?'

'Jeez! Don't you know what time it is?'

'Sorry, did I wake you?'

'Well no, actually, I was awake anyway.'

'At 4 a.m?'

'I don't sleep well. Not since … well, you know.'

'Oh Tom, I'm sorry.'

There was silence for a moment or two. 'What did you
want?'

'I just wanted to say I love you.'

'"I Just Called To Say I Love You" – that was our song,'
said Tom, poignantly.

'You remembered.'

'Well of course I remembered.'

Silence again. Thought processes whirring, words needing to be chosen carefully.

'I love you, Tom.'

'I heard you.'

'And I'm sorry.'

'But …'

'But what?'

'But we've done this so many times. One minute we're
back together, the next we're not. It's messing with my
head, Kate, it really is. I simply can't take it any more.'

'We can't just end it, Tom. What we had was so special

and it got broken but we can't let this be the end of it, it was too good for that. We tried gluing it back together and it kept falling apart again. But we've got to work harder at it – use Superglue or something. Whatever it takes we've got to mend it.'

'Broken like my heart, you mean,' he said, sadly.

'Exactly. Whatever it takes, Tom, we belong together.'

Silence once more.

'Tom.'

'I don't think so. You were right when you said it was what we had. Goodbye Kate, have a nice life.'

She stared at her mobile through a haze of tears. This could not be. She could not live the rest of her life alone. He was her soulmate, without him she was nothing. She sobbed into her pillow for what seemed like hours.

In reality it was just seven minutes.

'Okay,' he said, quietly as she answered her phone.

'Oh Tom,' she wailed, in an outpouring of emotion. 'I love you so very much.'

'I love you too,' he said, pain spilling from his voice also.

The next morning saw a very different Kate. She was dancing around the kitchen as she scrubbed away at the worktops, making even them sparkle with joy. Tom had business meetings all day today but he was going to come over this evening and hopefully, after Grace got back at the weekend, they would never have to be parted again.

Grace! How could she have forgotten! She'd spent half of the night worrying that something might be wrong and then, because of all the pontificating and then the excitement about Tom, she'd forgotten all about it. Great friend she'd turned out to be! Actually, in the cold light of day, it really didn't seem to be quite so important. It probably had been just one of those things. A string of coincidences that had, once again, made her add two and two together and make fifteen. She had a habit of doing that, even Grace would tell you.

Should she ring and intrude on their holiday? Maybe not, after all they'd be home at the weekend. To say that Alfie had howled, she'd had a panic attack, and then she saw a rainbow, so there must be something wrong, sounded a bit silly now – even to herself. She shouted Jessica and Alfie in from the garden. They'd go for a walk, catch a bit of this glorious sunshine, it would do them all good. Alfie thought it was the best idea he'd heard all day, and spun around in circles to register his approval.

By the time they got back there was a car parked on the drive. Kate's heart gave a little back-flip of excitement thinking, for a moment, that it was Tom, That he'd got away early. The car was the same colour, for sure, but it actually belonged to Richard. Kate's heart flipped in a nervous sort of squelch-mode now. She hadn't really wanted to come face to face with him again, especially so soon after the other night.

He stepped out of the car, looking fairly embarrassed himself too.

'Sorry, I had to come and see you,' he said, leaving her to take it completely the wrong way.

'Richard! I don't think that's a very good idea. Particularly…'

'No!' he said, holding up his hand to silence her. 'I don't mean that, I mean … Can we go inside for a minute? There are far too many twitching curtains around here.'

'Tea?' she asked, as they went into the kitchen and she took off Alfie's lead.

He looked at his watch. 'I really shouldn't, I've got to get off.'

'Off? Where are you going?'

'London.'

Kate looked up, startled.

'I had a call from my Cleo this morning. I'm sorry to be the bearer of bad news, but Grace and Charlie have been involved in an accident. It's not as...'

'Grace?' Kate clutched at her throat in alarm. That feeling she'd had, a premonition. 'Is she okay?' She hardly dared to ask.

'They're both going to be alright now although it was apparently touch and go with Grace for a while.'

'Oh my God! Grace! What happened?'

'They'd gone out, just the two of them. Izzy had opted to stay with Cleo, fortunately. Grace was driving. She's not long since passed her test as you know. Anyway, somehow the car spun completely out of control – hit another car coming from the opposite direction at quite a speed. They're lucky to be alive, the car's an absolute write-off.'

'Oh my God!' repeated Kate.

'There was a young lad on his own in the other car. He's in the hospital too, but not badly injured. Are you okay?' asked Richard. He knew how close she was to Grace.

'Just shocked.' Wide-eyed, Kate held her face in her hands, in shock. 'I sort of had a funny feeling that something was wrong. Are you sure Grace is going to be alright? Should I go to her? What's happening?'

'I think you could be more use staying here, to be honest, and I'll explain why in a minute. As I said before they are both going to be okay but it will take a little while, particularly for Grace, she got the worst of it. Her head took a bit of a battering and she lost quite a lot of blood. They thought there might be some internal bleeding as well but they've given her a scan and, fortunately, it seems to be all clear. She was unconscious for quite a while they said, but the worst thing was that when she eventually came round she was in such a panic that her heart stopped.'

'Her heart *stopped*! Oh my God – Grace!' Kate could hardly take in what she was hearing. 'I should go to her. I should ...'

'No, honestly Kate. You can't do any good there at the moment. Anyway, thank God, they did eventually manage to resuscitate her, although her life really was hanging in the balance for several minutes. Oh, Kate, I don't know what I would have done if anything has happened to her – she's my rock.'

'I know, it's the same for me. Life would be unbearable without her.' Kate's face was ashen with the shock of it all. 'So what's happening now? How is she?'

'She seems to be fairly stable at the moment. They've got her sedated of course but hopefully things will now start to improve. She's not had any visitors so far other than Charlie. They're just trying to keep her as quiet as possible.'

'So I wouldn't be able to see her even if I went down?' said Kate resignedly.

'Probably not, not yet anyway.'

'And Charlie – how's he?'

'A lot of cuts and bruises but he broke his arm quite badly – had to have it operated on. Then, on top of it all, he had a bad reaction to the anaesthetic.'

'Is he alright now?'

'He's still under observation, but they were able to wheel him through to sit with Grace for a while today.'

'He must have been so worried about her, poor man. He's besotted with his Gracie.'

'Absolutely.'

'Pffft,' sighed Kate, 'I can't believe all this has happened. Poor Grace. I wish there was something I could do to help.'

'Oh, but there is, although you may not like it.'

30

As Richard explained, the main reason he was going down to London was to help his daughter. He wanted to see Grace, of course he did, when she was eventually allowed visitors, but meanwhile Cleo had been left with a lot of responsibility and she was still barely more than a child herself. Richard's intention was to use Cleo's home as a base from which to work for a couple of weeks – or until things got a little bit easier down there. As a sales rep he travelled all over the country on appointments, a lot of his business being in London anyway, so it really was immaterial where he was based.

Just one major problem then, really.

'What's that?' asked Kate, in all innocence. 'Anything I can help with?'

'Possibly, but I'm not sure how you'll feel about it.'

'Try me,' said Kate, curious indeed.

'Gran,' said Richard, in a word.

'How do you mean?' asked Kate, not comprehending.

'Look, don't feel you have to do this. It is a pretty big ask.'

'I'll do anything that will help Grace after all she's done for me.'

'Well, as you know, Gran was only supposed to be having respite care for two weeks and she was due to come back here at the weekend.'

The penny started to drop. 'But can't they keep her for a bit longer?'

'Well, that's what you'd have presumed but it's more complicated than that.'

'Isn't it always.' Kate was really not liking the sound of this, but a friend in need … hmmm. 'In what way is it complicated?'

'Well the room she's in was only available for these two weeks, it's booked for someone else from Monday onwards, and they don't have any more beds available.'

'What about a different care home?' Kate knew what was coming, and she was trying to wriggle out of it faster than a worm on speed.

'There's just one vacant bed, but it's in a care home about twenty miles away which has a really bad reputation. It was Charlie who rang from the hospital to tell me all of this. He said he heard a lot of bad reports about it when he was asking around to decide where to send her in the first place. What he doesn't want to do is to give Grace any stress. At the moment she's so well sedated that she's not worrying about anything, but in a few more days … well, you know what she's like.'

What else could Kate say other than 'yes', reservations or not.

'But won't Gran get a bit distressed, coming home and finding me here instead of Grace?' she asked, in trepidation overload.

'From what I've heard, she'll be so glad to get out of that place, she won't care who's here with her. She hasn't settled down the whole time she's been in there, they said – been causing havoc. I think the staff will be glad to be rid of her.'

'How do you mean, exactly?' ventured Kate, unsure. Did she really want to know?

'I think she really didn't like the thought of being locked in. She's been trying to break out the whole time – even tried to incite a riot, at one point apparently,' grinned Richard.

'Oh my God that's so funny,' laughed Kate. 'But actually,

though, you can understand. I don't think I'd like locking in either. Poor Gran, it must have felt like being in jail after the freedom of living here.'

'I know. It is sad really.'

'Okay, I'll do it,' said Kate, resignedly. 'But is it that straightforward? Do I just go and get her?'

'Charlie will have to ring the social worker first, and they'll probably want to check you out. But I can't see there being a problem. After all it's the same house she's coming back to, and you haven't got a criminal record for bumping off old ladies, have you?'

'Ha ha! No, but I'll probably be certified insane for agreeing to this!'

After Richard had left Kate kept going through everything he'd said in her mind. Poor Grace, how dreadful. And how weird that she herself had sensed something happening to her. Very strange. That really did prove what a strong connection there was between them. What a relief it was to know that she was going to be okay. She couldn't bear to think what her life would be like now without Grace being a huge part of it. In fact tears welled and overflowed at the mere thought. She really wanted to go down and see her, give her a hug, make sure she was okay – but she understood what Richard meant and was sure he'd let her have a full report once he'd seen Grace for himself. Anyway, hopefully, maybe in a couple of days Grace would be able to speak to her on the phone from the hospital, once she was well enough.

Kate dried her eyes and tried to pull herself together. Crying into the washing-up would do no one any good. The best way she could be of use to Grace right now was to stay strong. Take care of Gran for her for the moment, and help Grace as much as she possibly could when she eventually came home.

Gran. That was going to be an absolute nightmare, she just knew it. However, before that happened, Kate had something else on her mind, something that would hopefully put a smile on her face. She did feel quite guilty, nevertheless, that she could even be having these thoughts when her best friend lay – had in fact almost died – in a hospital bed. The good thing was, though, that Grace would have approved, wholeheartedly in fact. Actually, if they were as attuned to each other as it would appear, she probably already knew, and if so, it would be doing her good … as long as she didn't get too excited of course.

So Kate allowed herself to think of Tom and his impending arrival. They hadn't discussed whether he'd be staying over but … ooft, she was desperate. It had been a while, in fact even just the thought of it was practically orgasmic. Undulating undies – they were, she was sure of it. Could be a new invention. They were certainly hitting the spot, and powered only by the imagination – no batteries needed.

'What's happening, Mummy?'

Who said that?

'Jess!' said Kate, with a sudden sharp intake of breath. 'Sorry, I was just. Um, I was just …'

'Staring at the ceiling. What were you looking at?'

'Um … spider. Yes, I thought I saw a spider, but it must have gone.'

Her mummy could be very weird sometimes.

As for Mummy herself, was she turning into some sort of desperado? No, she was far too self-composed for that. Actually, that was not true, for if Tom had walked in through the door at that precise moment, Jess would have been banished to the garden with Alfie while she dragged him upstairs by the short and curlies to give him five minutes of action that he'd never forget for the rest of his life.

Kate decided upon a plan of action. She would keep Jessica so active all day that, by the time Tom arrived in the evening, she would be so exhausted that she'd be unable to stay up late. Once Jess was in bed, Kate would have her man all to herself. Devious and cunning maybe, but this time she was determined. This time it was for keeps. Tom was right, they couldn't keep messing up their relationship all the time, it was not doing either of them any good. They needed stability to function properly, decisions had to be made. She couldn't just keep squatting at Grace's house forever. It was nearing the end of the summer holidays for one thing, and a new school year for Jess was approaching. Decisions had to be made – and soon.

But it wasn't just about the practicalities of home and school. After all, they could have returned to Cornwall and carried on as before. Kate's mother would have liked nothing better, obviously. But even she realised Kate had a life in Cheshire and that was where her heart lay.

And so the day passed in a flurry of activity. They walked Alfie to the point of exhaustion almost – even his! They gardened, baked, painted, played board games and even did French knitting. By the time Tom actually arrived, even Kate was starting to wilt.

'Daddy!' Jessica flew into his arms, overjoyed to see him again.

'Angel! I've missed you so, so much.' That was an understatement. He'd really thought that this time the split had been final and it would just have been back to having occasional access all over again.

Kate stood aside, enamoured by the bond shared by father and child. Despite the fact that she hadn't initially been the cause of it all, she felt a lot of guilt for what she'd put them both through. Overwhelmed with love for their little family unit, she vowed this could never be allowed to happen again. From now on, any problems they had must be worked through rather than run away from. In fact, from henceforth, that was the way she must learn to live her life, she'd wasted far too much time running away from situations she couldn't cope with.

'Kate,' said Tom, breaking through her thoughts and holding an outstretched arm towards her, Jessica perched happily on his other one.

She leaned in against him, hugging him tightly around his waist.

'I love you,' he said. 'We've got to stop doing this to each other. I love you both so very much. Can we draw a line and start again?'

'It's what I want more that anything,' breathed Kate, 'I love you too.'

As for Jessica, her little face was wreathed in smiles, this was the moment she'd been waiting for. She threw her arms around their necks, hugging their heads both together and to her own. Mummy and Daddy – they were back.

After a celebratory meal, of Jessica's choosing, at that upper class establishment otherwise known as McDonald's, the family returned, the evening having been an undoubted success.

'Tummy ache now,' smiled Jessica, so full up she couldn't have eaten another thing.

'I'm not surprised, Miss Greedy. How many chicken nuggets did you eat?' teased Tom.

'You're Mr Greedy,' said Jess, cheekily prodding at his slight paunch with her finger. 'You ate loads more than me.'

'That's because I'm a daddy and daddies eat everything. They even eat little girls sometimes,' said Tom, grabbing her suddenly, as she squealed with delight at his teasing.

Kate looked at the scene with an overwhelming sense of happiness and contentment. Things were really coming together for them at last. Whatever else may get thrown at them, even Gran, it must not be allowed to get in the way of this wonderful rekindling of their marriage.

As for Jessica, despite the excitement of the evening, she

was struggling to keep her eyes open. Tom winked at Kate.
'I'll take her up, shall I?'

'No, no,' wailed Jess, crabbily exhausted now. 'I want to
stay downstairs with you.'

'But Mummy wants to watch this really boring programme on the television now, you'd hate it. If we go
upstairs, I could read to you instead. Your very favourite
book – you choose.'

Kate smiled as Jessica's face brightened. He was so good
with her.

'Okay with you?' he asked, turning as if seeking Kate's
approval, his eyes so blue they almost took her breath
away.

'I'm more than okay,' she said, hoarsely.

'I know you are,' he said.

He was gone for ages. In fact, by the time he returned Kate
had almost nodded off. Only almost though, for how could
she possibly fall asleep when the man she'd lusted after for
almost all her adult life was right here within these four walls?
She felt his presence in the room before she even opened her
eyes. A sense of inner peace somehow and yet intermingled
with excitement. How could that be? Shivers ran down her
spine and yet she felt an overwhelming warmth within. She
opened her eyes as well as her arms and her heart to him and
he fell down into her warm embrace.

'This is for keeps this time, isn't it?' he asked, pausing to
draw breath after a long and passionate embrace.

'It has to be, I can't live without you Tom, you are my life,
I've proved that to myself over and over again.'

'No more running away?'

'No more. And I'm so, so sorry for what I did, or nearly
did, the other night. I wasn't thinking straight, I don't know
what came over me.'

'I can hardly judge after what I've put you through,
though, can I?' He kissed the tip of her nose as he looked

longingly into her eyes.

Her eyes suddenly welled, seemingly inexplicably sad.

'Hey, what's wrong?' he asked, unsure what had caused the sudden change in her.

'Grace – I keep thinking about her.'

'Poor Grace. I couldn't believe it when you told me.'

'Such a shock. And on the first holiday she'd managed to have in ages, too. She was so excited when they left.'

'At least they've both survived and are going to be okay, that's the main thing.'

'Just shows though, doesn't it? You can't ever take life for granted, you never know what's around the next corner – quite literally in this case,' she grimaced, that wasn't even funny. 'And that's another reason, Tom, why we should draw a line under what's happened and make a fresh start. None of us know how long we've got on this earth, but what I do know is, that whatever length of time I've got left, I want to spend it with you.'

'Oh Kate, Kate, Kate,' he said, kissing away her tears. 'You know how I feel about you. There is nowhere in the world I would want to be other than with you. We were made to be together, undoubtedly so, and I promise I will never ever do anything to hurt you ever again. I love you, Mrs Darrington, you are my life as well as my wife. This is the first day of the rest of our lives, do you realise? Let's make happy times ahead for both of us.'

'Oh Tom, I love you. Could you hold me?'

'I am,' he said, loving her so much, tears were pricking in his own eyes now.

'Tighter,' she said. 'I want to block out all the bad things that have happened. Just the two of us together.'

'You are staying tonight, aren't you?' she asked softly, after a while.

'But this is Grace and Charlie's house, it feels a bit uncomfortable somehow.'

318

'Tom, I promise you,' said Kate, 'It's what Grace would want. She'd love the thought of us being back together.'

And, to be honest, he was really not in a fit state to argue. Passion in his position didn't need much persuasion, and uncomfortable he really was by now. So up the stairs they stumbled, frantically desirous, not really conscious of 'where' any longer just the 'what' and 'with whom'.

They almost fell in through the bedroom door, locking it behind them. Even the bed was too far as, mouths joined together with deep probing kisses, he pinned her against the wall. She loved his strong masculinity as he leant into her, writhing against her, wrestling off her clothes and throwing them haphazardly to the ground. She loved his smell, everything about him, his taste, his touch. She almost ripped the shirt from his back in her haste to feel more of his hot burning flesh pressing up against her now naked breasts. Her nipples were on full alert and suddenly in sensitive overdrive as he teased them with his tongue. She raised her head, eyes closed, enraptured. Tom's hands moved swiftly, releasing himself from the restriction of his clothing before running desirously over the seductive flesh of her curvaceous form. Their breathing was rapid, rasping almost, as excitement mounted, a rediscovery of the familiar, the one each had longed for – the one.

A sudden gasp, a whimper of rising passion as hand, fingers, started to play. Tentatively at first, teasing, tantalising, tormenting … tremors of delight transcending all thought. Stimulating senses, suddenly not needed. Need, need, urgency … Tom almost dragged her to the bed; unwilling victim she was not.

'Oh Tom!' she gasped, as he entered her. So familiar and yet almost unbearable, excruciatingly … ooft! This was ecstasy she was in the land of … of … Burning, passions rising, pounding, climbing, soaring, explo-o-ding with a sudden rush.

Pffft. They fell back down beside each other upon the bed, perspiring, hearts pounding, all tension gone.

'Oh my God, that was so good,' gasped Tom.

'Like coming home, so to speak,' giggled Kate, feeling intoxicated, almost.

'I love you,' he said, turning his face towards her, his body spent.

'Do you?' she teased, safe in his love now.

'Idiot,' he grinned. 'You know I do.'

'Love you too,' she whispered, feeling whole again, once more.

There was certainly not much in the way of sleep that night for Kate and Tom. Alternating between making love and making plans, the hours quite simply disappeared. They never wanted to be parted again after waiting so long for this moment, but obviously it was going to be impossible to live together properly for the time being. Kate was going to be having the responsibility of Gran from the coming weekend until Grace was better, for a start. Gran would hardly condone having Tom coming to stay here with her – Kate could just picture her reaction. She already thought that all men were only after one thing.

'Hmm … not a bad thing to be after though, is it?' Tom said, blue eyes twinkling that old magic that never failed to give her butterflies.

It was a bit of a dilemma really, because not only was there a responsibility for Gran in the immediate future, there was also the fact that none of them knew exactly how long it would take Grace to recover from the accident. She'd almost died, she could hardly be expected to make a speedy recovery and come rushing back here fighting fit and ready to take care of everyone as she had before. Tom or no Tom, Grace was her best friend in the entire world. There was no way she could possibly abandon her as soon as she came back from London. She would need help and a bit of TLC and Kate would be there to give that, in the same way that Grace had been there for her.

'But …?' questioned Tom, plaintively.

'I know,' said Kate.

She knew how much he wanted her to move back to the house with him, but her loyalty lay with her friend – it had to, and she hoped he understood.

'You know there's absolutely nothing I want more than to move back in with you, but Grace needs me.'

'I need you.' Divided loyalties, or what? 'And then there's Jessica's schooling – the new term will be starting soon, we have to decide where she's going to go, and do something about it.' As a form of blackmail, he was pulling out all the stops.

'Don't think I haven't thought about it.'

'I know. Just saying.'

'Tom, don't think I'm dipping out of this. I love you, I'm with you and I'm never going to disappear again. It's just that I can't move back in with you for the moment because …'

'Grace needs you.'

'Got it in one. I hope you understand.'

He looked at her, the little frown of worry on her brow tugging at his heart-strings.

'I understand one thing.'

'What's that?' she asked, reciprocating the love that beamed from his eyes towards her.

'You're one very special lady, Mrs Darrington. Grace is as lucky to have you as her friend as I am to have you as my wife.'

'No, I'm the lucky one,' she said, as her hand reached for him.

'You're also insatiable,' he breathed, his voice attaining a new pitch altogether on the last syllable of that final word.

31

Surprisingly, and yet not so, after a night where sleep had been the last thing on their minds, both were feeling amazingly invigorated the next day. Tom was somewhat reluctant to leave for work but unfortunately did not have a choice. However, he was going to return that evening. Until the arrival of Gran at the weekend, they wanted to spend as much time together as possible, realising just how much their activities, both sexual and otherwise, would be curtailed afterwards. What had Kate let herself in for?

Thoughts about their future together were uppermost in her mind today. She could hardly bear the thought of being parted from Tom now, and yet Grace obviously would have to take priority for the moment at least. She just hoped that Tom really did understand about this. She hoped he didn't think she was using it as an excuse to be non-committal, and that at some point she'd take both fright and flight yet again. And, to be fair, that worried her too. She really needed to be with him all the time to feel secure in their relationship.

Another little niggle she had … well, it wasn't so little actually, was the thought of going back to live in Little Smetherwick. It wasn't about the house, she loved the house and it couldn't have been more perfect. It was about the memories that came with it. Jake, her beautiful baby boy, had died there. Chloe, who had been her supposed best friend, had slept with her husband there. So many secrets, so many lies. What would it be like living back there again? Chloe living just down the road, popping in and out to see them, worming her way back into their lives again, into Tom's affection. Caroline, even, Tom's ex-secretary, the one he ...

Stop it! She was starting to get panicky again and she had promised herself she wouldn't do that. Not ever again. Stop. She gave herself a shake in an attempt to pull herself together. This was ridiculous behaviour. Tom loved her, and she loved him. End of.

But in actual fact, if Kate had happened to have X-ray vision, she would have been panicking even more. Tom was on his lunch break and had nipped out to the supermarket to get a sandwich. There had been a time when he'd had a secretary who would have done that for him, he thought, thinking wistfully of Caroline; but not any more. The secretary he had now worked to the letter when it came to job description. Oh well, no matter, Kate would probably be delighted when she met her – she was fifty-plus, with a plus-plus figure and about as much sex appeal as a slab of stone.

A smile played on his face as he thought about Kate. Together forever now ... so long as she didn't do a runner again. The thought terrified him. He, more than anyone, knew what she was like, although she had promised she would never, ever do that to him again, as he had promised equally that he would never ... Oh my God!

Tom lunged forward into the chiller cabinet, attempting to conceal his face amongst the BLT and chicken avocado selection. It couldn't be, surely, not today, he hadn't seen her since ... He glanced around, she was across the other side of the shop, staring intently at the loo rolls, obviously in desperate need to compare the number of quilts on each sheet. He grabbed an egg mayo and ran for the checkout. Egg mayo? He didn't even like egg mayo. What the hell.

'How's Kate?'

What? Who said that? In his haste he hadn't even noticed. The person on the checkout was Sandra – Caroline's mum, Chloe's friend. Jeez, his world was closing in. But of course, Sandra worked in the supermarket – font of all gossip, he should have remembered.

He looked up as he handed her the cash for his sandwich.

'Oh hi, I'd forgotten you worked in here. Don't come in much.'

'Thought I hadn't seen you,' she smiled, her eyes warm. There wasn't a bad bone in her body.

'How's Kate?' she repeated, and genuinely seemed to care.

'Oh she's fine, thank you. She's staying up here now, not going back to Cornwall.' He actually felt like shouting it to the world, when he thought about it.

Sandra sensed his delight. 'You must be so pleased to have your family back again. Little one okay?'

'Just great, thanks,' he replied, glancing nervously over his shoulder. Still by the loo rolls – a lot of comparing to do when it came to quilted tissue and aloe vera, obviously.

'Chloe,' said Sandra, following his gaze as she held out his change. 'Maybe you should speak to her, clear the air.'

Words of wisdom from a wise woman – but rejected.

'Maybe another time,' said Tom. 'I don't think she's noticed me.'

'Oh, I wouldn't be sure of that.'

Tom took his money and ran. That was the trouble with this place, everybody knew everybody, and everyone's business was public knowledge. He usually shopped elsewhere but he'd only needed a sandwich. At least he'd got away without …

'Tom Darrington! Are you ignoring me?'

'Excuse me!'

'Stop!'

324

Three voices.

He turned around. Chloe – clutching a pack of Andrex Quilts, being accosted by a security guard, and Sandra puffing along behind to sort out the incident.

Jeez – all this for an egg mayo.

The greatest temptation of all was to do a runner. How easy that would have been. But no, he guessed he just wasn't that kind of guy. So what kind of guy was he? He was a family man, an upstanding citizen – and the guy who had messed up Chloe's life. Well, that was exaggerating some-what, but he felt guilt about her nevertheless. Time to stop pontificating and face the music.

'Chloe! Of course I wasn't ignoring you. I didn't even see you.'

'Liar,' she said, aware that her cheeks had suddenly taken on a hue which gave the appearance of wearing make-up made from a raspberry smoothie rather than Max Factor Second Skin foundation.

'She wasn't going to steal them,' said Sandra, trying to persuade the security guard to let Chloe go. 'She's my friend, she was distracted, that's all.'

'Just doing my job.'

'Well if she wanted to steal something, she wouldn't have chosen toilet rolls, would she? Use your common sense,' said Sandra.

'And you say she's a friend of yours?'

'The best,' said Sandra, feeling nothing but pity for poor Chloe at this moment. She stood there looking absolutely mortified.

'Well, go on then,' he said, retrieving the quilts, 'but if it ever happens again …'

'It won't,' said Chloe, humiliated way beyond the bounds of humiliation.

Sandra hovered. Should she stay, or should she go? Some-one had taken over her till. Somehow she didn't like leaving the two of them alone together. Somewhat worryingly there was a feeling of *je ne sais quoi* in the air. Imagination? Maybe.

'Can we go somewhere?' Chloe asked of Tom.

His heart sank. He didn't need this. Not now. Not when … 'I really don't think that's a very good idea.'

'Please?' Her face, even after all this time looked ravaged by the pain he had caused her.

Who could resist? Not Tom obviously.

'Okay. The Ring O'Bells?'

'Thank you.'

'Chloe!' warned Sandra.

'It's okay. I'll ring you later. And thanks,' she said, as the two women hugged.

Meanwhile Kate was obviously completely oblivious to the clandestine conversation which was about to commence. Which was probably just as well. Had she the slightest inkling, she would have flown to the Ring O'Bells and knocked seven bells out of both of them faster than you could say aloe vera or aloe Chloe or even aloe Tom. Yes indeed, it was probably just as well.

Instead, Kate immersed herself in a mission of her own. It wasn't going to be the easiest and most straightforward of missions, she realised that, but it had to be done. The fact that she was taking a seven-year-old child with her for protection didn't mean she was a wimp – not at all.

Holding tightly on to Jessica with one hand, Kate pressed the doorbell with the other, and waited for the lady on the front desk to let them in. She did so, somewhat grudgingly it has to be said, looking as though her paperwork was of far more importance, displeased at being disturbed.

The air was a little bit whiffy as they stepped in through the door, although amazingly their noses seemed to adjust to the smell after a few moments of being inside.

'Who are you here to see?' A smile might have been nice.

Would have been welcoming, at least.

'Gran. Er, Gertrude. Er …' What *was* Grace's maiden name? How could she not know that?

'You do *know* who you've come to see, do you?' Cheeky mare.

'Well of course I do. She's my friend's mother. I'm just not sure of her surname, that's all.'

'Lucky for you we've only got one Gertrude then, eh? She'll be in the main lounge. Go through.'

Obviously didn't graduate from charm school. 'And where is that exactly?'

'Down the corridor, turn right,' she said vaguely, not even glancing up, her mind once more on the job in hand.

Jessica was the one clutching tightly now, although she was the first to spot her. 'Look! There she is!'

True enough, there she was, surrounded by her little band of buddies and wearing the most ridiculous hat Kate had ever seen. What was that about not settling in? She looked to be absolutely in her element.

Gran turned at the sound of someone coming into the room. 'Hello?'

'Hi Gran, it's only us. We thought we'd come and visit you.'

'Who are you?'

'Kate, remember. And Jessica.'

'*Who?*'

'Remember, we came to stay with you at Grace and Charlie's house?'

'Oh, I do remember,' said Gran, narrowing her beady eyes at Kate, who moved in a little closer so she would be able to see her more clearly. 'You're the one whose husband went off with her best friend, aren't you?'

'Well I …'

If ever there was a good test of Kate's panic attacks, this was it.

'Come in and sit down, so we can all have a better look at you.'

'Well, um, is there somewhere we could go that's a little bit more private? Your room, maybe?'

'Oh, no, no, no – it's much better out here. And besides, these are my friends, they all want to meet you too, don't you?'

'Bugger off!' said Edith.

Kate looked startled. Jessica, petrified.

'Oh take no notice of her, she says that to everybody. Don't you, you silly old bat?'

'Bugger off!' repeated Edith

There was nothing Kate wanted to do more. Why had she come here? What was she letting herself in for?

'So what do you want? asked Gran.

'We came to see you,' said Kate

Jess simply curled up against her looking traumatised.

'Well you've seen me,' said Gran, stating the obvious.

'And we wanted to talk to you.'

'Well you can talk. What do you want to talk about?'

'About … um … about whether you'd like to come home at the weekend. Grace isn't back yet but …'

'Home? I am home, you silly woman – what are you talking about? Hah! People think *I'm* stupid!'

'This isn't your home,' said Kate, rather bravely. Or maybe just lacking in forethought.

Never argue with Gran, it is an important lesson to learn. 'Of course it's my home you stupid woman!' bellowed Gran. 'These are my friends, we all live together. You can't take one without taking all of us. One for all and all for one!' she said, raising her clenched fist in triumph. Yes! She'd remembered it!

Jessica's eyes were as wide as saucers, and Kate's not far short.

'But I thought you didn't like it here,' ventured Kate.

'Like it? It's the best place I've ever been! That place where I was before, they used to lock me away in a tiny little room and starve me, never gave me anything to eat. Went on for years, that did, absolute cruelty. I wouldn't go back there now, not even if they paid me.'

'So you want to stay here forever?'

'Well of course I do. What would this lot do without me – eh? Now bugger off and leave us in peace, would you? We've got things to do.'

'Bugger off,' echoed Edith.

So they did, somewhat bewildered.

'A half of bitter and a G&T please,' Tom said to the barman.

This was so wrong. What was he doing here? Risking everything, and for what? For Chloe. To appease his conscience. He could feel her eyes boring into the back of him and, when the drinks came, could hardly bring himself to turn around and face her again. The pain in her eyes, knowing he'd been the cause of it.

'Don't look so worried, Tom, I'm not going to cause a scene,' she said, as he joined her at the table.

He smiled. That same lop-sided grin she remembered so well, and loved so much.

'How have you been?' he asked.

'Well, you know, busy. J-J keeps me going, he can be quite a handful at times.'

'That sort of age.'

'And that sort of character, I'm afraid,' she said, with a rueful grin.

'Chloe – I'm sorry.'

'For what? For ever getting involved with me in the first place?'

'You know that's not what I meant.'

'But you are though, aren't you? Obviously you are, all

the trouble it caused.'

'For you too,' he said, looking her directly in the eyes for the first time since … since …'

'Oh Tom, I'll always love you, you know that.'

He looked away, hurriedly. Reaching for his drink. Silence.

'Sorry,' she said. 'I didn't mean to say that.'

Silence.

'Tom? Did you ever have feelings for me, or was I just a temporary substitute for Kate, a bit of comfort?'

He turned to face her again. 'How could you ask that? You know how much you meant to me.'

'Just not enough – obviously.'

'That's unfair. You know how much I love Kate. But I also loved you too.'

'Loved? As in past tense?'

'It has to be, Chloe.'

Silence.

'I loved you both,' he said, after a while. 'I was torn. I didn't ever think it possible to love two people at the same time but it is … it was. I did.'

'So how did you choose? In the end, why did you just ignore me? I was there, Kate was gone.'

'Because Kate and I had history, we had marriage, we'd had children, a shared life. I couldn't just let that go.'

Silence.

'Can I ask you something?' said Chloe, tentatively.

Tom looked at her, his eyes speaking volumes.

'If it had turned out … if you had been J-J's father, would it have made a difference?'

'Let's not even go there,' said Tom, reaching for his glass.

'But I need to know.'

'Honestly, Chloe, I don't know the answer to that, but it was one hell of a mess we got ourselves into, wasn't it?'

'So you were relieved when things turned out the way

they did, that John turned out to be J-J's father and not you?'

'Well, of course I was. Weren't you?'

'That says it all, Tom,' she said sadly, taking a gulp of her drink, trying not to let her emotions get the better of her.

He turned to her as she spluttered. 'There's gin in there you know,' he teased, smiling at her. It was the smile she remembered. Easy and natural with her, the way it had used to be. It tipped her over the edge, her lips quivered against the ice cold glass, her teeth chattering on the rim.

'Hey,' he said, covering her hand with his own. 'I'm sorry, I didn't mean to upset you.'

She fought to regain control. Of her emotions, of her voice, of her longing for him at the feel of his hand on her own.

'Chloe, I really am so sorry,' he said, knowing he should move his hand from hers, knowing something was happening, feelings were intensifying.

But he didn't. He couldn't.

Tom, of course you could, this is danger – red alert. Stop.

She put down her glass and, drying her eyes, she turned to him. She was amazed by what she saw in his face, a longing for her that she'd never, ever expected to see there again. She knew she should stop it right there and then, she knew it was wrong, she knew she'd be hurt all over again. But he was the love of her life. This was probably the last time they would ever … ever.

Her lips parted and she moistened them with her tongue, leaning tentatively towards him, expecting rejection.

No Tom, no Tom, no Tom, no!

Too late.

With about as much resistance as a bee has to a pot of honey, and despite knowing of the sting he was about to inflict, Tom's lips tentatively met hers, oblivious to their surroundings, oblivious to anything but each other. It was a

331

gentle, probing kiss at first, tender, unsure, but stoking up fire, passion.

Stop! Tom broke away, heeding the alarm bells which suddenly started to ring warning signals in his head. Chloe gasped, was left wanting more – so, so much more. She hadn't expected any of this when she'd got out of bed this morning; feelings of longing for Tom had been locked away, long ago, in the deepest recesses of her mind. A simple trip to the supermarket and now all this had happened, unlocking passions she'd tried so hard to dampen down.

'I'm sorry,' said Tom. 'We can't, we mustn't, that was wrong. I don't know what happened, it was a mistake.'

'A mistake?' That brought her to her senses. 'A mistake? Is that all I am to you Tom – a mistake?'

'Chloe, you know full well that it isn't. You know how I feel about you, and nothing's changed – try as I might to pretend otherwise. But I'm getting back together with Kate now, and it's taken us a long time to reach this point after all that went on before. I can't risk losing her again, really I can't.'

'I love you Tom. I wish I didn't, but I do. You can't help who you fall in love with.'

It was with regret that they parted, but part they knew they must: Chloe back to her world empty of the man she loved, and Tom back to work. It had been an exceptional lunchbreak, one that would be remembered for a very long time. And nothing to do with the egg mayo.

Someone else would remember that lunchbreak too – someone there for a quiet pint, standing at the far end of the bar. Someone concerned to see the closeness of the couple, but concerned in a sympathetic kind of way. Someone who had also had secrets of the heart themselves, a long time ago. Someone who knew how tough life could be.

32

Kate's instant reaction upon receiving a phone call from Richard was to panic. It was her usual reaction to everything, fight it though she may.

'It's not Grace, is it? Is she okay?'

'Yes. Good news all round, really, that's why I'm ringing.'

'So tell me.'

'Give me a chance! I was allowed in to see Grace for the first time today and they say she's doing really well.'

'Wow – that's such a relief! How did she seem?'

'Well, to be honest, to me she looked pretty rough, but that's only to be expected after what she's been through. She says herself she's feeling much better and can't wait to get home. Oh, and she said to tell you to hurry up and get things sorted out with that man of yours, she wants you properly back together again by the time she's home. You're wasting precious time and life's too short. In fact both she and I are in full agreement on that one.'

'Well, tell her to stop being so bossy! Anyway, you may both be pleased to hear that we *are* sorted out – we're back together and nothing can come between us ever again. In it for the long haul now. In for keeps.'

'Well, thank God for that!' The warmth in his voice registered his genuine delight and he hoped he'd gone a little way, at least, towards making her realise what she wanted.

'How about Charlie?'

'Charlie's doing great. I think for once in his life he was genuinely pleased to see me! Think they'll probably be letting him out tomorrow, which would be great, especially for Izzy.'

'How's she doing?'

'Missing her mummy and daddy, obviously, but she's been really good. It's nice she's been able to spend time with her big sister – although I think she's probably talked Cleo's head off, you know what's she's like.'

'I know, a right little chatterbox, isn't she? And such an old head on her shoulders too. It's so quiet around here without her.'

'Anyway, one of the main reasons I rang you, apart from to let you know I've seen Grace of course, was to tell you the good news about Gran. You're let off the hook, apparently.'

'I've been to see her today.'

'That was brave of you! Well apparently she suddenly seems to have settled in really well. Since trying to incite that riot the other day, which I have to laugh at every time I think about it, everybody seems to want to be her best friend – and she's loving it!'

'It certainly seemed that way today. Quite incredible!'

'Well, social services got in touch with Charlie today to let him know that she can stay there for as long as we want her to now.'

'But I thought there was someone else going to be needing the room after this coming weekend?'

'There was, but sadly the person died yesterday so, as a consequence, it's obviously vacant.'

'That's good news. Not for the person who died, obviously, but definitely good news for me.'

'That's what I thought. Gran's happy enough there and she can stay for as long as we want her to now ... forever even, maybe, We'll see how Grace feels about it when she gets home, but for now, problem solved.'

'Yay! Thanks Richard.'

*

Tom got absolutely no work done at all that afternoon. He was so annoyed with himself. He glanced at the sandwich lurking forlornly on his desk – he wasn't even hungry now. He picked it up and hurled it into the waste paper bin with a growl. But you can't go taking your frustrations out on a sandwich, it was hardly the egg mayo's fault. And he hadn't even liked egg mayo in the first place.

Shit! What a stupid thing to have done! He slumped forward at his desk, his head in his hands. Why had he agreed to go with her? And then to kiss her in public – was he insane? The village pub – it was a small village and always rife with gossip, it would be all over the place by now. Oh God, if only he could turn back the clock. How many times had he said that this past couple of years? If there was a medal for stupidity, he would have most certainly won the gold.

The thing was now, should he tell Kate what had happened, or not? Should he trust to luck that she would never find out or, should he be honest with her and tell the truth? What she didn't know would obviously never hurt her, but if she found out from someone else, which was quite likely to happen in the situation in which he had put himself, then … well, he could hardly bear to think of the consequences. No more secrets, no more lies, was what they'd said, but the thought of her reaction … And would that be the end of them forever? What an idiot he'd been – again. You would have thought he'd have learned his lesson by now.

Both Kate and Jessica were overjoyed to see him when he drove over after work that night, making him feel an even bigger heel than he already did. They were at the window, looking out for him, their faces wreathed in smiles. They ran to the door to greet him, Kate throwing herself into his arms.

'Hey, what's all this?' he asked, somewhat perplexed.

'Just that I love you,' said Kate.

'And I love you too,' said Jess, hugging into both, not wanting to be excluded.

'What a greeting from my two favourite ladies. I've missed you.'

'It feels sort of special tonight, now we're back together properly,' said Kate. 'Jess was worried that one of us would go off again, like before, but I've told her – this time it's for keeps, isn't it Tom? We're a family, no more secrets and we're together forever now. Tell her Tom – that's true, isn't it?'

So what could he say?

'It's true. We're a family, and we're together forever now. Nothing can change that – nothing can be allowed to come between us.' Oh Tom.

Sandra walked home from her job at the supermarket with a heavy heart that evening. Apart from the usual stresses and strains of a busy day on the checkout, she'd been fretting about Chloe and Tom and what might have happened between them. It was none of her business, she realised that, but she felt as though she'd been complicit in their meeting and held herself responsible, in a strange sort of way, for its consequence – whatever that might be.

She knew, from the in-depth conversations she'd had with her friend, that Tom was the love of Chloe's life. The likelihood was that dangerous ground would have been trodden on that afternoon. Whether it had been trampled underfoot or tentatively explored, Sandra was concerned for the outcome. Raking up the past is not always a good thing, even though at times it can be quite beneficial, but whatever the afternoon had resulted in, she would be there for her friend to help her pick up the pieces.

Sandra did as she always did, or more often than not, on her way home from work: she called in to see her beloved David.

'Kettle on?' she asked, giving him a hug as he let her in.

'Of course, there'd be hell to pay if it wasn't, wouldn't there?' he said, laughingly. 'And I've told you before – let yourself in, you don't have to ring the doorbell, that's why I gave you a key.'

'I don't like to do that, David, you know I don't. What if you were with some hunky man, and I just walked in on you!'

'Chance would be a fine thing – my love life's about as good as yours!'

'Good job we've got each other, eh?'

'Aye, it sure is. That strong enough for you?' he asked, indicating the tea.

'Looks like dishwater. Here, out of the way,' she said, bustling in to take over.

They had a wonderful relationship, these two, filled with mutual support and humour, and love, it has to be said, despite the obvious differences in their sexuality, and despite all that had gone before.

'How's that lovely daughter of ours? I haven't seen her for a few days.'

'Me neither, actually,' said Sandra, pouring. 'There, that's more like it.'

'What?'

'The tea. You'd think you'd have learned to make a good cuppa at your age – I don't know how you managed for all those years without me to look after you.'

'Me neither,' he said, wistfully, thinking of the past. Leaving his family, loving Brian …

He looked at her, suddenly filled with emotion. 'I do love you, you know San. Not that I'm about to chase you up to the bedroom anytime soon,' he said, with a watery smile.

'Well thank God for that, you daft lump, these legs aren't capable of running up the stairs two at a time these days.'

Her eyes transformed themselves into salty waterfalls in an instant. 'David?'

'What, my love?'

'I love you too.'

'I know you do. Now can we please drink this tea before any more saltwater drips into it?'

'David?'

'Drink!'

'I am,' she said, sipping. 'But David, I saw Tom and Chloe today.'

'Did you?' he asked, tension suddenly creeping in.

'Together,' she added.

'Together where?' he asked, casually.

'In the shop. They came in separately but then ... well, it's a long story, but they left together. To go to the Ring O'Bells. To talk.'

'Hmm.'

For David had been the one at the bar. The one who had seen the looks pass between them, the kiss.

'Is that all you can say: "Hmm"? I'm worried about Chloe, about what might have happened.'

Should he tell Sandra what he had seen or should he keep it to himself? He didn't like to keep anything secret from his San, but in this case ... He knew what harm village tittle-tattle could do, that's what he'd moved away to avoid all those years ago.

'David? What are you thinking? Should I call in and see Chloe before I go home – make sure she's alright?'

'I think it's always best to keep out of other people's business,' he said wisely. 'Let them sort it out between themselves. She'll come to you when she's good and ready but, for now, I think we should try and forget what we've seen.'

'What we've seen? What I've seen, you mean. And that's strange advice David – how can I forget? They were in the shop ...'

'Just drink your tea, San, and stop your sticky-beaking. When she wants your advice she'll ask for it.'

Kate was just bouncing with happiness. Ignorance is bliss, or so they say, and that is very true. Tom was hers forever now, Jessica was happy again, her best friend was on the road to recovery, and she no longer had to face the prospect of looking after Gran. Nothing in the world could mar her joy now ... or not as far as she knew at least.

She almost leapt upon Tom as he got into bed beside her that night but, unusually, he seemed unresponsive and tense.

'Not gone off me already have you?' she asked, teasing him with her tongue.

'Just had a really stressful day at work, that's all,' he said, hating himself for having to lie to her again after all that he'd promised. But how could he do any other?

Kate continued on her mission. This was not like him at all. 'You really are stressed, aren't you. Just lie back and enjoy.'

Still not having the desired effect, she persuaded him to roll over onto his front, so she could give him a massage, that always brought success. She straddled his back and worked the tense muscles of his neck and shoulders with her fingers, digging in hard with the heels of her hand.

'Wow, you really are tense tonight. What on earth have you been up to today?'

If he was small and soft before, he was suddenly minis-cule. 'Nothing, nothing at all, just work.' How had he got himself back here? Secrets and lies all over again and they'd only been back together five minutes.

'Tom Darrington, if I didn't know you better I'd think you'd been off with another woman. But you wouldn't, would you? Not ever again. You promised and I believe you. I believe you and I trust you, Tom, ooft ... I love you so much.'

339

How bad did he feel?

'I love you too, you know I do. I think we may have to resort to other means tonight though.'

'Yeah, please now,' she said, rolling back down onto the bed next to him, legs apart, 'I can't wait any longer.'

And as his fingers teased and brought pleasure and gasps of delight, his mind wandered, inescapably, to the events of that day. To how he'd put everything at risk once more.

As for Chloe, she was home alone. She should be used to that by now. J-J, the only little man she had, was asleep upstairs in bed. She could have phoned Sandra; had promised to, in fact. But she didn't want to speak to anyone other than the one person she could never speak to again, the one person who would now be at home making love to his wife … his wife who used to be her best friend.

Chloe ran to the bathroom, and threw up. It had all been too much today. Feelings and longings and secret thoughts had all been locked away and now they'd been revived. Life could be so cruel. She'd only ever had two men in her entire life and both, in different ways, had treated her like shit. Tom loved her at least, she knew that now, she'd seen it in his eyes. But it was going nowhere; how could it? He had a wife, he had a child, and he'd chosen Kate above her. If only …

Chloe: don't even go there.

33

Time was passing, the new school year was starting, decisions were having to be made. But, most importantly of all, the good news was that Grace, Charlie and Izzy were coming home – they'd be back the day after tomorrow! Jessica was beside herself with joy when she heard the news but, strangely enough, it seemed to have caused a bit of tension between Kate and Tom. In fact, it triggered the first argument they'd had since getting back together.

'But I thought you loved our house – I don't understand why you keep putting off moving back there.'

'I do love it, and I'm not putting it off.'

'You are so! You've been making excuses ever since we got back together.'

'Well I like it here.'

'But it isn't our house.'

'I know, but …'

'Ours is handy for shops, the school, everything.'

'And has Chloe just down the road.'

'Aha! So that's the real reason.'

If she did but know it, that was what was putting him off too. They'd be bound to run into her, as he had the other day. It was a small village, gossip was rife, it really would be tempting fate.

'Well of course it's the reason. I can't just put it out of my mind, can I? She'd be there on the doorstep, I know she would, if I moved back there again.'

A fleeting vision of Chloe, the pain in her eyes when he'd

left her … his heart lurched. And then he looked at Kate, his beautiful wife, standing there before him, knowing how much she loved him, how much he loved her. It couldn't be his fault that he'd fallen in love with two women, could it? And yet it was. But Kate was his wife and he was the luckiest man on earth to have won her back again. He had to do everything within his power to keep her this time. If Kate wanted to move away from Little Smetherwick, then move they would – it would be better for all concerned. Lead us not into temptation. Temptation would certainly be far less elsewhere.

Once the decision about moving was made, Kate wanted to rush over to Little Smetherwick straight away and make a start on getting the house sorted out. But, for some reason, Tom was loath to let her go.

'You really don't need to, Kate,' he said. 'There's nothing particularly for you to do. It's reasonably clean and tidy and you took most of your stuff when you moved out. Besides, you've got nowhere else to put things at the moment.'

'You sound as though you don't want me to go,' she said. 'You've not got some young floozie hidden away over there, have you?'

Don't even joke about it, Kate. 'As if.' Hah!

'So, are you going to ring the estate agent, or shall I?'

'I'll do it from the office. Must go – I'm so late!'

'Well, it's not every morning you decide to move house. They'll simply have to understand.'

'Don't think it works that way, Kate,' he said, kissing her as he left.

She followed him with her eyes. That was remarkably easy. Tom loved the house and he loved Little Smetherwick. It just proved how much he loved her if he was willing to give all that up for her. Kate turned back towards the kitchen and the ever-faithful Alfie, who wagged his tail gingerly from side to side, his eyes full of questions and full of trust.

'Good boy,' she said, tickling his ears with her fingers as she cupped his head in her hands. 'Guess what? Your mummy's coming home tomorrow.'

Alfie gave a little 'woof' and a spin of delight, his waggliness increasing tenfold.

Chloe, on the other hand, was decidedly miserable. A black hole had opened up and she'd fallen right into it with a plop. J-J was her only saviour.

'Park?' he asked expectantly, staring beseechingly into her eyes.

Who could resist? She had nothing better to do and being trapped within four walls of misery was enough to drive anyone insane.

'Okay. Go and find your shoes then. A bit of fresh air will do us both good.'

The park was just a short walk away, although Chloe took them on a slight detour, passing Tom and Kate's house on the way. Why she did that, even she didn't understand. Perhaps it was to feel closer to Tom, or perhaps it was just to visit happy memories of the times they'd all shared together there. The close friendship she'd had with Kate, putting the world and each other's worlds to rights over endless cups of tea and coffee. They'd shared Christmases there, Bonfire Nights, lots of special occasions – memories to treasure.

Then the turning point for everyone – Jake's death. Chloe would never forget it. She'd been there. His tiny crumpled body, burnt and lifeless. Tears cascaded down her face now as she thought about that day – how, in an instant, happiness had turned into tragedy and had affected all of their lives. Kate had rejected everyone, understandably, even Jessica. She'd had a breakdown, gone away, and left Tom alone to cope.

And what had she herself done, good caring friend that she was? That's right. She'd slept with Kate's husband. How was that meant to make things better for anyone? Too right. It was not. In fact she had merely succeeded in making things a whole lot worse for everyone. So, however miserable she was feeling right now, well, she deserved it. Judgement, karma … she deserved the lot.

'Park?' interrupted a little voice from by her side.

'Sorry, darling,' she hadn't even realised she'd stopped walking, was just standing still, staring at the house, tears streaming down her face. 'Yes, park,' she said, clutching his tiny hand tightly, a lifeline in a drowning world. 'Come on. You show Mummy the way.'

The trouble with Little Smetherwick was that wherever you went or whatever you did, you always bumped into someone you knew. Today was no exception. For walking towards them as they strolled through the park was none other than David: Sandra's David.

'Chloe! How are you?' he asked, although he regretted asking as soon as he'd done so. It was obvious from the look on her face.

'Fine thanks,' she said, in automatic response mode. But then saw his expression. 'Okay, so I'm obviously not fine,' she grimaced, 'it's just been one of those days.'

'Anything I can do to help?' he asked.

It was half on his mind to tell her he'd seen, he knew, he understood but, despite the sympathy he felt for her, he knew it would only cause embarrassment. His heart went out to her nevertheless, he was a sensitive man. He took her hand within his two.

'Ring Sandra, Chloe. It's good to have someone to talk to at times like this and my San, well, she's a very caring woman.'

'I know she is, and I will. Thanks David,' she said, grateful for the fact that he didn't pry, she could see in his eyes that he knew something. He had merely extended the hand of sympathy, and for that she was glad.

Tom carried on through the park, deciding to drop in at the pub for a lunchtime sandwich before making his way back to the office. What made him do that? He never went for a drink at lunchtime. Was he trying to recapture that moment yesterday, the one he'd shared with Chloe? As he was ordering at the bar, someone tapped him on the shoulder.

'David!'

'Tom.'

'Been a while since I've seen you.'

Pity David couldn't say the same. 'Thought I saw you yesterday, actually.'

'Where?' Tom's guard was up.

'In here,' said David, looking over his glass at Tom as he took a sip from his pint.

Nothing further was said on the subject but Tom knew his card had been marked.

'Just been to see the estate agent,' he said. 'We're putting the house up for sale. There's a board going up later today.'

'Probably a wise move,' said David, meaningfully.

Further down his pint, David became more relaxed, feeling a little less anger towards Tom. After all, no one more than himself knew how difficult love could be, or how many complications could arise because of it. His attitude softened.

'I saw her earlier,' he said.

'Who?' said Tom, flustered, caught off guard yet again.

'Chloe,' David answered, watching Tom flinch.

He hadn't said it to be cruel, he just cared about both of them. About all three of them, actually. David was a very caring person, he didn't like to see anybody hurt. He'd caused enough hurt himself in the past, for which he felt eternal guilt, he didn't like to see others going down that route.

'How did she seem?'

'Upset.'

Tom looked glum. What else did he expect? 'Where was she?' he asked.

'In the park with J-J.'

'When was that?'

'Just before I came in here.'

Tom downed the rest of his pint in one. 'Better be getting back to the office.'

An obvious lie. Predictably he turned left, rather than right, as he came out of the pub door. Rushing along – but to what avail? He knew he was playing with fire but couldn't seem to stop himself.

Chloe was the first to see it, as she came back from the park. She didn't have to pass the house, tried not to in fact, but her legs took her there anyway. A truck outside the house – what was that all about? She could see it from a distance down the road. Two men jumped out with a board, a sign. Surely not. But it was. She got closer and it was: a 'For Sale' sign, bold and clear. The men hammered it into the ground. Hammered it into her heart more like – more pain with every blow.

Well, if anything was final, that was it. How could it have come to this? Her love for Tom, her friendship with Kate … no hope for either of them now. How could the house which symbolised so much for her have been put up for sale without her even knowing? But it had. The end. Finito.

She hurried past this time, hardly bearing to look. Eyes down, collar up, her heart exploding with sadness.

By the time he reached the park she had obviously left. It was probably just as well, for what exactly had he hoped to achieve? Some kind of romantic joining together of souls in the English countryside? And what of Kate in all of this, Tom? Remember her – the love of your life? The one you've agonised about being reunited with for over a year. The one with whom it's now all coming together. Your beautiful wife, mother of your child.

Oohh. He sank down onto a park bench, his head in his hands. This was madness. He had to put Chloe right out of his mind. There could be no more moments like yesterday, no thoughts of her ever again. He loved Kate. He loved Kate more than anything, anyone. He had to stop this, concentrate on what he'd got, be thankful; it was what he'd wanted and he'd won her back.

Perfect timing. Almost as though she could sense what was happening. His mobile rang: Kate.

'Hi. What are you up to?' she asked. Her voice tinkled with happiness, sparkled with every word.

'What? What do you mean?' he asked, guilt oozing.

'You're sounding incredibly guilty, Tom. Is there something you're not telling me?' She said it in a teasing kind of way but, understandably, suspicion was always uppermost in her mind.

He pulled himself together and managed to turn the conversation around. He could be quite adept at this when the need arose. 'Okay, you've caught me out,' he said.

'Huh?' she asked, although hardly daring to do so.

'I'm just on my way back to the office from the pub. Thought I might as well call in there for a quick sandwich after I'd been with the estate agent. Bumped into David in there actually, so got a bit delayed. Anyway, good news about the house. The valuer's been round already this morning and the sign's going up later today.'

'Blimey, I didn't think things moved that fast!'

'Me neither, and I don't think they do normally, but it's a good house, in a good position. They don't get houses like that coming on the market very often – he seemed really keen to get his hands on it.'

'Wow! Tom?'

'Mm?'

'We are doing the right thing, aren't we? It is what you want too … I haven't just bullied you into it, have I?'

'Stop worrying, Kate. It is a lovely house and in many ways I shall be sorry to leave it, but it's the sensible thing to do. We'll be making a fresh start – away from all the bad things that have happened there, all the things that went wrong.'

'Like Jake …' she said, struggling to hold back the tears.

'Yes,' he said softly, 'like Jake, but like other things too.'

'Chloe,' she whispered.

'Yes,' he said, in shame. 'Her too.' It would have to be. He had no other choice. He loved Kate. End of.

34

Chloe felt as though the end of the world had come. She was trying to be strong for J-J's sake, but it was hard, so hard. That black hole she'd fallen into was swallowing her whole. For her child she had to fight back, scramble up the side, battle her way out. If she had simply had herself to think of, she could have allowed herself to drown in this sea of gloom, disappear into oblivion. But no, she had J-J, she couldn't abandon him, she had to claw her way back.

She needed friends and only had one left, Sandra. And Sandra was there, on her doorstep, within minutes of her call.

'Eh love,' she said, sympathy overflowing together with the tears they shared. 'As soon as I saw you both in the shop together yesterday, I knew it would all end in tears again. And look at me now! Meant to come round here as a good listener and a shoulder to cry on, not to be in floods alongside you.'

'Sandra, you've been such a good friend to me recently,' sobbed Chloe, 'I couldn't have asked for anyone better. I'm so sorry, I seem to do nothing but pile all my troubles onto you. And I'm so stupid, I create half of them myself.'

'Just glad to be here for you love. I enjoy our friendship, even if it doesn't look that way at this precise moment,' she said, attempting a feeble smile. 'Anyway, I'm sure I'll get my own back one of these days when I have a problem and need someone to talk to.'

'I'll always be here for you, Sandra, just as you have been

for me. What I like about you is that you don't judge. You just listen to my problems and sympathise, you don't take the moral high ground.'

'To be honest love, I don't think it's fair to judge, nothing's ever that straightforward. It's very rare in life for something to be clearly black and white, grey areas tend to have a habit of creeping in.'

'You're right, I know. And I seem to be in the middle of one right now.'

'You have to let him go, Chloe.'

'I know. I am … I did … But then …'

'I know. But you have to again.'

In complete contrast to the way Chloe was feeling right now, was Kate. They used to be best friends, so close, and now they were miles apart, both literally and figuratively speaking. The gap could never be bridged and this latest episode had made Chloe realise that at last. Kate on the other hand had moved on a long time ago.

In fact Kate, oblivious to any misdemeanours or disreputable thoughts, could not have been happier. At last everything seemed to be going right. The love she shared with Tom seemed even stronger now, if that were possible. They could move away from Little Smetherwick and all the bad memories it held and – this was at the forefront of her mind right now – Grace was coming home tomorrow!

She couldn't wait to see her, she'd missed her so much. But also, Kate needed to reassure herself that her very lovely friend really was okay. Kate had spoken to Grace on the phone earlier and she really had sounded like a shadow of her former self. But she supposed that was to be expected after all that she'd gone through. Kate said that Tom and Jess and herself would move back to Little Smetherwick tomorrow, until the house was sold, to give them some space, but Grace had been insistent. She wanted them to stay there with them, there was plenty of room and she was going to need some help – certainly until she felt stronger, at least.

Tom, when Kate told him, felt a little uncomfortable about this. With Grace and Charlie back in residence, he really felt they should leave. However, with the thought of moving back to the house now with Kate and Jess, having Chloe down the road, and any gossip that could possibly ensue, he really did feel safer to agree. It was understandable as well that Grace would appreciate having Kate around, particularly when Charlie was at work. And back to work Charlie would have to go, broken arm or not. It was his own business, he couldn't afford to take any more time off.

After a restless night of intermittent sleep, Chloe had finally managed to doze off, but her slumbers were abruptly interrupted by the sound of J-J moving about in his bedroom. Twenty past eight already? How could that be? For a moment, just for a moment, still lost in the world of sleep, she thought it was an ordinary day. But then – whoosh! It hit her. For most people it was an ordinary day, but for her this was the first day of the rest of her life knowing that Tom was moving away. He had made his choice, and there was now no possibility whatsoever that he could ever be part of her life again. Sledgehammer to her head – bang! That was how it felt.

'Mummy!'

'Coming, darling.'

For what choice did she have? Silly really, when she stopped and tried to think about it logically. It had only been a relatively brief encounter, and she had managed without him for all of J-J's life, but there had always been that thought that one day, maybe one day … And he'd lived just down the road, within touching distance almost. She'd felt comforted just knowing he was there.

'Mummy-y-y!'

'Okay, darling, I'm coming now.'

And indeed she was. No time for 'if onlys'. She had a little son who needed her and she was a person who needed to be needed. What more could she possibly ask for? Apart from a man, that is. And not just any man, just one specific man. Stop it!

Maybe fate was lending a helping hand in trying to lessen Chloe's sadness. Whatever. But suddenly she found herself in huge demand and being descended upon by all and sundry. The central figure in a loving family, everything she would wish for. Almost.

The first was Olivia.

'Mum! Sorry I've not been in touch for a while but, well, you know how it is, hectic as usual. Anyway, I'm just ringing to ask if it's okay if we pop over later – I need a hug from my mum.'

'Of course it is, darling. Why, what's wrong?'

'Nothing. Absolutely nothing. I'll tell you later. We'll be over in a couple of hours then, okay?'

'Look forward to it.'

Chloe glanced around. The place looked a bit of a pigsty, but it would have to do. She used to be so houseproud, but these days ... Catching sight of her reflection in the mirror she saw something in much more urgent need of attention. Herself. Time, most definitely, to pull herself together, try to resurrect this remnant of womanhood that was Chloe Russell and attempt to restore it to its former glory. Otherwise, there was nothing like a daughter for sussing out that something was very badly wrong.

However, before she'd even made it to the bathroom, small child in tow, the phone rang for a second time. Bet they've changed their minds, thought Chloe to herself. Such negativity. It wasn't that at all.

'Ben!' she exclaimed in surprise.

'Sorry to ring so early, Ma. Hope I didn't disturb any goings-on, a fluster of frenzied ... eww! Stop. I need to delete that bit from my mind. You're my ma, I couldn't even begin to...'

'Ben, what is it you want?' she interrupted, his frivolity a little too close to the mark on this occasion.

'Ooh, hang on! Do I sense a tad of secrecy here? Have I stumbled across...?'

'Ben! You *will* be stumbling in a minute if you don't shut up.'

'Ooh ma! I remember this happening once before, there's definitely...'

'Ben!' Firmness itself.

'Okay, your secret's safe with me, Ma.'

Did he ever know when to stop? 'Ben!'

'Okay, I give in. Anyway, just been speaking to my beautiful sister, ha ha, and she says they're coming over to yours today. Is it okay if we come too? You'll only talk about me if I'm not there.'

'Of course it is. I'm surprised you even bothered to ask.'

A houseful, then. No time for brooding today. Not quite full, though, as the phone rang again. Sandra.

'Just ringing to check you're okay, and see if you'd like company.'

'Actually, Sandra, I've suddenly found myself about to be inundated with family today. They're all coming round. Why don't you come over and bring David? You're family too, after all, apart from being my very much appreciated best friend.'

Sandra glowed at the reference to their friendship. No one had said ever said that to her before. Apart from David, obviously.

'Are you sure? Do you feel up to it? Have you not got enough on?'

'I'm quite sure. I think having company will be good for me today. And I'd love you to come, nobody more so.'

And so they gathered in Chloe's little house, one big happy family. Despite the ache that still gnawed away inside her for the loss of the love she'd hoped for with Tom, when she glanced around the room she realised how blessed she was in life to have such a loyal and loving family. She may be alone in many ways, but she knew they'd always be there for her, no matter what. They would see her through, all of them.

Her eyes moved around from one to another as they chatted amongst themselves. Olivia, the daughter she loved so much, to whom she felt so very close, seemingly had eyes for no one but Stelios today. It was lovely to see, he was a good man and he seemed to idolise her. Chloe had no worries at all on that score, they would make the perfect partnership.

Then there was Ben, her rogue of a son. She never ceased to smile when she looked at him, even though he did frustrate the hell out of her at times! But his heart was in the right place and he always meant well – you could certainly never be miserable when he was around. She did worry sometimes that he was the perpetual Peter Pan, but then, it was a mother's job to worry. Preserving the inner child was meant to be a good thing, the fact that he did it to an extreme was just … well, that was just Ben.

Actually, Caroline had done wonders for him. She'd been a really steadying influence. Married and settled and with a responsible job – who would have thought it? Chloe loved Caroline like a second daughter. She'd been unsure at first, when Ben had suddenly sprung the marriage thing upon her, but she was indeed a lovely girl and Chloe couldn't have wished for a nicer daughter-in-law. She felt very blessed.

Sandra. What a wonderful friend she'd turned out to be. Chloe still missed Kate and the friendship they used to share, obviously, but she realised now, more than ever, that they could never have that back again. Circumstances had forced them apart and they really were better that way now, sad though it was. And so Sandra was the one who'd been there for her when J-J had been missing. Sandra was the one she confided in and looked upon as her friend. And Sandra had become her rock. She was kind, she was loyal, she was patient, and Chloe felt privileged now to be able to class her as her friend.

As for David, he was just an amazing man. Chloe could understand why Sandra loved him so much and had stood by him through all. They certainly seemed to get on well together, like two sides of a coin, almost. He seemed to have a deep understanding of people, an unusual trait in a man. When he'd arrived today he'd looked at Chloe with such warmth and … sympathy almost. It had made her feel quite emotional, and he'd hugged her, noticing.

Finally there was J-J. The little man of the house, who she loved to distraction. He was the centre of her universe – had to be. He was tearing around like a mad thing and yet encapsulating the innocence of childhood, all at the same time. The focus of everyone's attention, seven adults, their eyes all upon him – and he loved it. He scrambled up onto Olivia's knee, a place of safety after being chased by his big brother Ben.

Olivia helped him up and gave him a hug.

'Hey, shrimpy, you're going to have to get used to sharing all this attention shortly.'

Eyes rounded upon her.

'What do you mean,' asked Chloe, expectantly.

'Oops, sorry. I didn't mean to blurt it out like that, I meant to tell you properly.'

'You always were a blabbermouth, sis.'

'Ssh!' said Chloe. This was no time for interruptions.

'I'm pregnant,' beamed Olivia. 'Stelios and I, we're expecting our first baby in the spring.'

'Wow!' said Chloe, it was absolutely the best news she'd had in ages. 'Congratulations!' she said, coming over to her. I can see why you said you wanted to come over for a hug from your mum now. Come here,' she said as they fell into each other's arms.

'I know we maybe should have waited and got married first, done everything the right way round … but, hey, it happened and we're absolutely over the moon. The wedding can wait until afterwards.'

'So pleased for you. You too, Stelios. I'm going to be a grandma – wow!'

And so it was congratulations all round. Both Sandra and Ben were a little bit sensitive as to how Caroline was feeling on hearing the news; they knew how desperately she was longing to have a baby and both noticed the look of envy that briefly flickered across her face. It had been almost a reflex action, she hadn't wanted it to show – she was happy for them, truly she was. She just wished that it could have been her too.

Ben squeezed her hand and leaned over to whisper in her ear.

'I love you. It'll be our turn next.'

'Love you too,' she said, quietly.

Ben, not one to sit back quietly, stood up. 'Congratulations, sis. Can't believe it, the golden child having a golden child of her own – blimey! Another little sprog in the family, and I shall be its uncle. Uncle Ben – sounds like some sort of rice! And actually it won't be long until it gets a little cousin because Caroline and me, well, we're at it like rabbits, aren't we?'

'Ben!' interrupted Caroline, blushing to the very roots of her hair.

'Blimey, you've gone red!' he said, stating the obvious.

'Not surprising.'

'Sorry, just saying ... just wanted them to know we're trying for a baby too.'

'I know, but it's not the sort of thing you ... oh, never mind.'

He sat back down next to her. 'Love you,' he said.

'Love you too.'

'Perhaps we should be going home now,' he said, looking at her with his puppy-dog eyes.

'But we only just got here.'

'I know but we've got a lot to do – if you know what I mean.'

'Ben!' grinned Caroline, smiling at this loveable rogue of hers.

His reaction to the news had been so typical: sibling rivalry never ceased. Ben was always in competition with his sister – even over something like this. No doubt he'd be hoping for twins.

35

They were home! They were home! They were home! And it was hard to tell who was the most excited, Grace? Izzy? Kate? Jess? Or even Alfie. The men were much more calm, doing the basic essentials like bringing in the luggage and checking football scores.

'Three-one? That's unbelievable!' exclaimed Charlie, furrows of frustration in his brow.

'Charlie! How can you even think about football at a time like this?' scolded Grace.

'But they're up for relegation and ...'

'Stop! If I hear another word about it I'll ... I'll turn around and go right back to London.'

'Don't you dare,' said Kate. 'I'm not letting you out of my sight. You're going to rest and get well, and I'm going to look after you.'

'Did anybody ever tell you, you're very bossy?'

'Yes. You did. Frequently. But I don't care.'

It was so good to be back together again. Kate was somewhat alarmed by Grace's appearance, though: it was obvious to anyone what a harrowing time she must have had.

Alfie was absolutely overjoyed to have his mummy back, although even he seemed to sense how gentle he must be with her. As she sat down on the sofa he appeared to stick himself to her leg with Superglue. He had absolutely no intention of letting her out of his sight ever again, if she was going to disappear for that long. Others tried to get him to go into his basket out of the way, but although he was

358

usually such an obedient dog, he was having none of it. Grace was appreciative of the comfort his warm furry body brought to her anyway. It was true what people say about pets bringing stress relief – she could have done with having him with her in hospital, he certainly made her feel much more relaxed.

'Richard, thank you so much – I don't know how we would have managed without you,' said Grace.

'Oh I'm sure you'd have coped.' Richard had actually been glad to be of assistance. It had been good to feel wanted for a change and now, he thought, smiling to himself, he was wanted in a way that he'd thought would never be possible ever again.

'What are you smiling at?' she asked. 'I know I must look like a freak but ...'

'No, it's not that.'

'What? So I do look like a freak?'

'No, don't be silly, of course you don't,' he said, still grinning like a Cheshire cat. 'Just something I'll tell you later.'

He shrugged off the question, mysteriously. Grace was even more intrigued.

Charlie came into the room just at that moment. A sudden silence descended. He wished he didn't have this overwhelming sense of jealousy as far as these two were concerned, but he always got the feeling that he'd just interrupted something whenever he walked into a room where they were alone together.

'Wassup?' he asked, in his usual way.

'Nothing,' came the reply, as always.

He sat down next to Grace on the sofa as if staking his claim. With a groan Alfie shuffled up a bit to let him in. One way or another, between dog and men, there seemed to be a lot of testosterone jostling for position. Grace smiled. It was good to feel so loved, even though it could be infuriating at times.

'I was just thanking Richard for all he's done for us – driving us home and everything. I don't know how we'd have managed, my one-armed husband wouldn't have been able to drive us, that's for sure, and we haven't even got a car now until the insurance gets sorted out.'

'Oh, I'm sure we'd have coped,' responded Charlie, chip on shoulder transforming into mega boulder.

The kick on the shin that Grace gave him hopefully went unnoticed by Richard.

'Er … but thanks anyway, mate, it saved us a lot of hassle.' Mate indeed.

Izzy had never been known as a shy and retiring wall-flower type at any stage of her short life, and today was no exception. Loud, boisterous, rumbustious even, today she was all of those things and more – excitement overload. Children in general would have been suspected of con-suming sweets and fizzy pop in vast quantities in order to reach that energy level, but for her it was simply normal behaviour, coupled with the fact that she was very pleased to be home.

Jessica actually didn't think she liked her very much today, which was a bit disappointing, as she'd been looking forward to having her little playmate back again. But Izzy was decidedly being a show-off, like she had been when they'd first met her. Jess hoped she'd settle down again – and soon.

'Have you ever been to London?' asked Izzy.

'No,' said Jess, reverting to the shy little voice she'd had when she'd first arrived.

'The Queen lives there – in a palace. It's just like the palace in my fairytale book.'

'Is it pink?' ventured Jess, somewhat bravely.

'Hahaha, it's not pink. You're silly,' said Izzy, laughing, implying that her friend was the most stupid person in the world. 'My sister lives in a palace too. I stayed there with her,' said Izzy, her nose in the air, amazingly not growing.

Jess retreated into her shell.

'I think someone here's telling fairytales,' said Kate, over-hearing and not liking to see her daughter get crushed. 'Would you like a drink, girls?'

'Erm, could I have a mango tea with lemon, please?' asked Izzy, trying to sound frightfully refined.

'It's ordinary tea or squash for you, young lady,' said Kate, cutting her down to size.

Grace wandered into the kitchen to see what was going on, Alfie seemingly attached to her by an invisible thread.

'Hey, I thought you were meant to be resting,' said Kate, quietly concerned about her friend's pallor.

'Not much rest in there when you get caught in the crossfire between two men – believe me,' she grinned.

'Well sit down there instead, then,' said Kate intimating the kitchen table. 'I don't want you lifting a finger today.'

'I'll lift two in a minute,' combated Grace, enjoying her first bit of banter in what seemed like ages.

'What does that mean?' asked never-miss-a-trick Izzy.

'Nothing,' said Grace, realising the error of her ways.

'How can two be nothing? Two is two. One, two… '

'Okay Izzy, you're right. I'm silly. Now take Jess and Alfie and go and play in the garden for a bit, would you? I want to talk to Auntie Kate.'

And what Jessica really liked about that moment was that, try as she might, Izzy could not get Alfie to leave Grace's side but one word from her, and off he trotted. Balance redressed. Best friends again. It didn't take much.

'Okay you, now spill the beans,' said Grace when they'd gone.

Kate poured them both a drink and sat down. 'Never mind me – what about you? You're the one who nearly died.'

'Don't remind me. God, Kate, it was so bad. I keep having

nightmares about it, seeing the other car looming towards us, thinking it was the end. I shall never forget it as long as I live. Your life really does flash in front of your eyes.'

Kate reached across the table and covered Grace's hands with her own, eyes welling. 'I don't know what I would have done if I'd lost you.'

'I can hardly bear to think about it. And then there was that moment in the hospital too. I really thought I was going, I could hear Anna's voice calling me … everything.' Tears were streaming down Grace's face as she spoke, the memory of that moment still so fresh in her mind.

'I had a sort of sensation … premonition … something, about it,' said Kate as she explained what had happened and how eerie it had seemed.

'Well I think that just proves the closeness of our friendship,' said Grace, moved to even more tears by the story. 'As if we needed proof. I'm so glad to have you in my life, you've made it sort of complete somehow. I don't think I could cope without you being part of it now.'

'Well, me too. And likewise,' said Kate, hardly able to speak. 'So don't go pulling any more stunts like that again, do you hear me?'

Charlie wandered into the kitchen with Richard. Conversation between them was always a bit stilted, it was hard to stay alone in a room together for long.

'Women!' said Charlie, tutting. 'Any tea in that pot, Gracie?'

'Sorry,' said Kate, 'I meant to bring you a cup through, but we got sort of distracted. I'll bring it now. Go and sit down.' A dismissal if ever there was one.

'Are you staying to eat with us, Richard?' asked Grace.

'If that's okay,' said Richard. 'I've a bit of an announcement to make.'

'Hmm, the mystery deepens,' said Grace.

'No mystery. I'll tell you after the meal. Celebrations all

round, I believe,' he said, looking pointedly towards Kate.

'Yes, you dark horse, I haven't had your update yet. It's been all me, me, me, so far,' said Grace.

'Grace, my love, there is absolutely nothing worth celebrating more than your life – that you've been spared and that you have been safely returned to us,' said Kate with such depth of feeling that they all shed a tear – even the men.

Richard was the first to recover himself. 'Hear hear!' he said, brushing his face with the back of his hand.

'I don't know how I could have coped without my Gracie,' Charlie's voice wobbled.

'Me neither,' said Kate tremulously.

All this love in the room. Grace was overwhelmed. 'D'you know what? I think I need something stronger than tea. There's some Cava in that cupboard – it's not every day that someone wants to celebrate my life.'

By the time Tom had finished work and driven over to join them, they were a little on the tipsy side. His head had been full of sobering thoughts all day; it hadn't been the best. Faced suddenly with all this merriment and jollity, he felt decidedly intrusive, remarkably straight-laced and undeniably stone-cold sober. Fortunately they welcomed him with open arms.

'Get the man a drink,' said Charlie, and there was a glass in his hand almost before he knew it.

'I feel a bit bad to be staying here now you're back home again,' he said, after pleasantries had been exchanged and Grace's remarkable recovery acknowledged.

'Tom, you're more than welcome to stay for as long as you like. I'm really glad to have you both here anyway, at the moment. I've still got some recuperating to do, as you can see, and there's no one I'd rather have here to help me than Kate – bossy as she is! And, can I just say how pleased we all are that the two of you are back together at last!'

'I'll drink to that,' said Charlie, raising his glass.

Kate's arm was around Tom, and she looked up into his eyes with a smile.

'Me too,' she said. 'Together forever.' She raised her glass and chinked it to his.

He looked into her eyes, so trusting and brimming with love. He loved her so much at that moment, so very much that it hurt. His Kate. Together. It was what he'd dreamed of. Chloe? She was gone. Had to be. Forever? That was a very big word.

'Love you,' he said, and meant every word.

They sat around the kitchen table together, four adults somewhat squiffy, one adult much less so, two rather excitable and giggly children and one very happy dog. Only one adult missing then. Gran.

'I do miss her not being here, you know.'

'Who, Gracie?'

'My mum, Charlie. It doesn't feel the same somehow.'

'No, it's a lot more peaceful,' said Charlie, his opinion much more boldly stated after two glasses of red on top of the Cava.

'Sshh!' giggled Kate, by way of reprimand, not wanting her friend upset.

'Charlie! That's not a very nice thing to say about my mother.'

'Well she wasn't very nice to you sometimes.'

'She couldn't help it. And she gave us some laughs, didn't she?'

'Especially with her teeth,' giggled Izzy.

'That was funny,' said Jess.

'Well she can come back whenever you feel ready, but you need to get properly better yourself first. At least she's happy where she is at the moment. We can make the decision later – no rush.'

'Suppose,' said Grace, somewhat glum.

Thoughts of Gran seemed to sober them up somewhat. Silence descended all around. Now seemed as good a time as any.

'Would anyone like to hear my news?' asked Richard, his voice breaking through the silent moment of sobriety and providing them all with a more cheery thought to hang on to.

'Of course we would,' said Grace, feeling almost guilty that she'd forgotten to ask.

'I'm moving to London.'

'What?' said Grace, almost stunned by the news. He couldn't. He'd always been there for her. Just down the road. 'Oh Richard,' she said, clasping her hands together almost prayer-like.

'It's for the best, I think. A fresh start. There's nothing much here for me any more, other than memories. I always stuck around while Zak and Cleo were growing up so I could be there for them, but now they're both down south anyway. I travel about with my job so I can be based anywhere – London's more convenient actually. Cleo would love me to be down there too, just to help out occasionally. I was having a long chat to her about it.'

'Oh Richard,' repeated Grace, still striking the same pose.

Charlie was not blind to his wife's reaction. 'Well, I think it's a great idea, mate. You go for it,' he said, smiling.

And Tom wasn't far behind him in encouragement either. 'You should, Richard, a change will do you good.'

Both men were in full agreement on this one. A little less testosterone around here could only be a good thing. Game, set and match.

Richard looked from Grace to Kate, and back again. He hadn't meant to inflict pain on Grace, particularly at this moment in time. He still had a special place in his heart for her and it would always be there, no matter what. But now was his time to move on, to start a new life. And Grace had the support of others now, she was not alone.

'There's another reason as well,' he said, as they looked at him questioningly. 'A lady. We met on the first day I was down there to see Grace. It may come to nothing, I don't know, and I'm not just moving down there because of her, that would be stupid – obviously. But I've seen her a few times and there's an attraction and … well, I'd just like to see how it goes.'

'Well! You kept that quiet,' teased Grace, unsure what else she was feeling other than how much she was going to miss him.

'Grace, I could hardly have talked to you about it – you were unconscious at the time,' he said, lightening the mood.

'Ha ha!'

'Well, good for you mate,' said Charlie, 'I hope it works out.'

'Me too,' said Kate. 'And don't worry about Grace, we'll all still be here to make sure she keeps out of mischief.'

'Huh! Chance would be a fine thing with you around, my bossy friend,' laughed Grace, covering her insecurities well. She knew Richard would have to move on at some point in his life, he couldn't be expected to hang around here at her beck and call forever. It had just come as a shock, that was all.

'So will you be selling up? Everything?' asked Grace, feeling last ties, and a big part of her life, slipping away.

'You're selling your house?' asked Kate, taking a sudden interest, purely from a selfish point of view. It would be a bit small for them, but for a temporary measure … it couldn't be more convenient, it was practically on Grace's doorstep.

'Actually no, I thought I might rent it out for a while. Just so that if the London thing doesn't work out, I'll have somewhere to come back to.'

Kate looked at Tom. 'Are you thinking what I'm thinking?'

Tom grimaced ever so slightly. 'If we could afford it. We've still got the mortgage on the other place, remember?'

'I know, but they said we shouldn't have any trouble finding a buyer, and I could look for a part-time job and … and I might even sell a painting or two!'

'Sounds like your mind's made up,' said Tom.

'Well it does seem like a good solution – like fate almost,' she said looking at him with puppy-dog eyes even more appealing than Alfie's.

'Well, we'll look into it, do a few calculations, see what we can come up with. We don't even know how much he wants for it yet, but it would be good for a temporary measure, I agree.'

'Ideal solution. We'll have a chat about it, Tom, see if we can come to some sort of agreement,' said Richard.

Bonhomie overload around the table.

Charlie was grinning from ear to ear. 'Great idea, mate,' he said, as Richard and Tom shook hands. Could this be the termination of all this testosterone-fuelled tetchiness, at last?

'Love you,' said Kate, turning to give Tom a hug.

'Love you too,' he said. And he truly did.

Jessica was simply beaming. She loved having her mummy and daddy back together and being happy again. She loved having a sparky little friend like Izzy with whom life was never dull. And she loved the fact that, after his mummy, Alfie loved her best – not Izzy – as he shuffled around to lean against her and nuzzle her with his cold, wet nose.

Grace glanced around the table, feeling such warmth from all the love that was in this room. She raised her glass towards them, tapping the side of it with the wedding ring on her finger in an attempt to get some hush.

'Can I just say something?' she asked, putting her glass back down before she started.

'What? You're asking permission to speak? Well, there's a first time for everything I suppose, Gracie.'

'Shush, Charlie. I want to say this quickly, before I start to get too emotional. You guys, all of you, in this room mean the world to me, each and every one of you, and I absolutely love you all to bits. But there's one special person here today who has become a huge part of my life even though I've not known her for all that long. I never really believed in true friendship before because I never actually had such a close friend, but now I do, and I couldn't be happier. Kate, we've been through a lot together in such a short time and I'm so, so glad to have you in my life, our friendship means everything. So, before I dissolve into floods completely, here's to you my so beautiful friend – love you lots,' she said, raising her glass.

Kate dabbed at her own eyes to stem the flow, but was too overcome with emotion for her tears to cease. She wanted to give a more wordy response but 'Likewise', was about all she could manage. Although, through lips a-quiver, 'Love you too', and 'Friends forever' did follow suit.

'Huh – women!' said Charlie, rolling his eyes heavenward, as though they were the most inexplicable creatures in the world.

Jessica sucked her thumb, before burying her face in Alfie, feeling just a little bit weepy herself. Alfie gave a sigh, he'd thought everyone was meant to be happy. Humans were very strange creatures.

Izzy? Well, she was never one to be ignored. Attention had a centre and her place always had to be in it. However, a motormouth and a loose cannon are not a good combination – and Izzy was both.

'Uncle T-o-o-o-m,' she said, rolling her eyes, smiling up adoringly, ensuring that he was completely within his

368

comfort zone.

He was growing to love this little minx, despite himself, she certainly was a feisty character for one so young and tiny.

'Yes Izzy?' he said, trustingly.

He was used to Jessica, meek and mild. But this was Izzy.

'Have you still got your bit of fluff on the side?'

Eyes rounded upon her – horrified. Not least of all Kate's and Tom's.

Izzy looked around puzzled. Why were they staring? Adults could be so strange at times.

'*What* did you just say?' asked Grace, almost too afraid of the answer.

'I just asked Uncle Tom if he'd still got his bit of fluff on the side – what's wrong with that? Gran said he'd like a bit, so I made him a fluffball and he put it on his kitchen side – didn't you Uncle Tom?'

Uncle Tom had turned a very strange colour and seemed to have been rendered speechless.

He pulled himself together. 'Yes, Izzy, you did make one for me and yes, thank you, it's still on my kitchen side. I don't think I could ever throw it away.'

Kate glared at him. The eyes said it all. Hidden meanings all round. Never had a fluffball held more significance.